THE MOVING FINGER writes

jock alexander

Verse 51

The Moving Finger writes; and, having writ,
Moves on: nor all thy Piety nor Wit
Shall lure it back to cancel half a Line,
Nor all thy Tears wash out a Word of it.

Rubaiyat of Omar Khayyam, Astronomer
Poet of Persia, Done into English
by Edward Fitz Gerald

Murder, mayhem, drug smuggling and high stakes gambling give Alexander's readers an insight into the life of a London gangster.

Spanning two continents, characters come alive as we follow them down the murky road of intrigue, murder and hostage-taking enticed by easy money.

A rising star in the world of crime, Jimmy Sedgewick, muscled his way to the top of the heap. Jimmy's own life is threatened by a Russian Mafia boss who tries to extract money owed him, making Jimmy desperate enough to devise a plan to kidnap a billionaire's son.

A decorated hero, Alister MacKinnon unwittingly becomes embroiled in the plot after the plane carrying the mark crashes near his cabin in the Canadian wilderness. Drawing on prowess earned as a soldier in the French Foreign Legion, he orchestrates a daring rescue, ending up critically injured in the attempt.

With fight scenes vividly portrayed, this page turner takes the reader on an action-packed journey fraught with intrigue and suspense.

Elizabeth Radmore, author of ALMOST MAGIC, the sequel to CUSHLA, Memories of a Gypsy Girl.

This is a work of fiction. All incidents, characters, actions and related dialogue are the invention of the author. Any resemblance to persons living or dead is purely coincidental.

While I danced with my protégés, Nancy my wife was left without a partner. In appreciation of the hours she spent alone and of her unhesitating support through thick and thin, I dedicate The Moving Finger writes to Bonnie Nancy.

Thanks and a bear hug to Soheir Girgis, Elaine Barre, Sheila Curry, and Don Taylor, who, in your own inimitable way, gave freely of your expertise. A salute to Adjudant Emilio Condado Madera, Conservateur du Musee de la Legion etrangere, for his advice on the awarding of medals. Thanks to Angeles Devesa, Fabiola Arias, Stacie Madelung and Robin Wark, of Trafford Publishing, always ready to help.

Photo credit: Glen Kletke.
Cover design: Sheila Curry.

Beware of the following, not all of them play by your rules. Shake hands with:

Jimmy (the Baker) Sedgewick, no longer kneads dough, but now he needs dough and lots of it, dough spelt c-a-s-h.

Michael Braithwaite, media baron began his working life as a day labourer.

Alister (Ally) MacKinnon, quiet and unassuming, is familiar with death and violence; don't arouse him.

Fiona Grant-James, the wilful daughter of wealth and position.

Margaret (Jonesy) Jonescu, rises to the occasion and takes charge, in the face of danger.

Leonid Gerchinka, formerly of the KGB, is now a crime czar in the new Russia.

Robert Halthorpe, a compulsive gambler, loses when the Grim Reaper throws the dice.

Simon Braithwaite, comes to manhood overnight as death scowls over his shoulder.

Alexei Stataspovich, and Peter Mallory, enforce the law—of the jungle – in the city, they enjoy their work.

PROLOGUE

There was no one in the office. I wandered to the end of the corridor off the main hallway, and opened the door marked Private. The body, naked, lay on a shiny metal table, the eyes were closed. The incisions of the autopsy conducted in Canada stood out against the white skin. A small wound below the heart — could it be a stab wound?— had been stitched carelessly. Where the hell was Bert? I had to get the obituary info for today's paper. As the cub on the local paper I get to write the obits, big deal.

Noises behind a door and there he was all spiffed up in his black pants and white shirt. "Hi Trevor." Drying his hands he said, "I'll get you the info, they left me in charge. We have two funerals today and wouldn't you know the secretary is sick."

"Poor Bertie, all alone. Just gimme the info and I'll leave you to it."

Hanging up the towel, Bert leaned against the sink; he wanted to talk. "Old man Halthorpe is one cold fish." Nodding at the body, he went on, "His mum was in early this morning. The body arrived yesterday. We hadn't even taken the body out of the bag, but she had to see, 'my baby'".

"Is that what she said? Some baby, from what I hear he was quite the lad."

"Yeah, anyway she started to cry, just then she was joined by old man Halthorpe."

"And what did he say?"

"He gave her a handkerchief and said, 'Come dear. He is gone and we have to live with what happened.'"

"What did he mean by that Bert?"

"Don't ask me. They left and I got down to business."

Bert was no fool, he liked his job, and knew better than to repeat all that he heard while on the job. He didn't say a word to Trevor about the emotional exchange between the Halthorpes as they were leaving.

A sobbing Mrs. Halthorpe grabbed her husband's arm and shaking it said, "It was that man Sedgewick; he led Robert astray."

"Quiet, we will discuss this later, this isn't the time or place."

"And that awful Russian, poor Robert... ."

"That's enough, we have to go."

HALTHORPE Robert Charles Edward

As the result of a flying accident, Robert, 27, youngest son of Sydney Robert James Halthorpe and Jane Shirley Ann Halthorpe (nee Arbuthnot). He is survived by his parents, a brother John, and sisters Margaret, (Mrs. Adam Appleyard); and Joan, (Mrs. Herbert Morgan). A private funeral service will be held in St. Michael's Chapel, Saint Barnabas Church, Addlesbury, 10:00 a.m. Tuesday, 7 December. Interment will be in the family vault at Saint Barnabas Church. Educated at Cambridge, Mr. Halthorpe developed an early interest in flying, gaining his pilot's licence while at Cambridge. Upon graduation, he obtained a position with Charter Air of London, flying as co-pilot and pilot before leaving the firm to take up a position with AirWays of London. At the time of his death, Mr. Halthorpe held the position of chief pilot at Dilsworth Recovery.

In the quiet of the church, waiting for the coffin, the only voice was that of the organ. I went over the conversation I had with Bert two days earlier. When I quizzed him about the small wound, he shrugged. He told me that all questions about the accident would be dealt with by a Mr. MacKinnon. Old man Halthorpe insisted to Bert's boss that if anyone asked questions about the family or about Robert, they were to be referred to Mr. MacKinnon. Bert did mention that the people here for the funeral were staying at the Goodham Arms Hotel. Who is this Mr. know-it-all MacKinnon? My curiosity aroused, I decided I'd nose around, and maybe I'd have something that would get me out of here and up to London to work for one of the biggies.

The family sat straight-backed and silent. The mother kept dabbing at her eyes with a handkerchief. Old man Halthorpe, his face set in stone, made no noticeable effort to comfort his wife. The others weren't talking either; two men, a boy, and two women, not exactly a crowd to see him on his way. The younger of the women, Janice Scott, I figured her for Robert's girlfriend. The other one, Margaret Jonescu, was with Michael Braithwaite, owner of the plane that crashed. The other guy was Mr. know-it-all, Alister MacKinnon. The kid was

Braithwaite's son Simon, about fifteen I'd say. He limped to his seat at the front of the church. The kid got banged up in the crash when the plane went down. The crash never made headlines in the Canadian papers, I'm told, and was a brief item on the telly here in the U.K.

The service didn't take long, there was no eulogy. They were a subdued bunch, no chit chat while waiting for Bert and his buddies to carry the box from the hearse to the vault. Mind you, the weather didn't help any, one of those fine-misty days that chill to the bone. If I'd only had a camera, the group standing around the door of the vault, their dark suits and dresses, quite Gothic, would have made a great pic.

My editor told me before the funeral there was to be no pics of those attending the funeral. This was unusual, I never went anywhere without a camera and a spare roll of film. When I quizzed him he admitted the request came from Braithwaite. Old man Braithwaite was a big noise in newspapers, and other enterprises. I'd never heard of him. My boss said that was the way Braithwaite wanted it.

I should have twigged that Braithwaite was not one of your ordinary run-of-the-mill toffs. There was something about him, a presence that set him apart from the others. I know it sounds daft. He seemed a friendly sort. After the interment, he nodded my way and said hello, something the local gentry would never do. Chatting with the family members as they all walked from the vault, through the cemetery, to the hotel; all were paying close attention to his every word. Even old man Halthorpe deferred to him; which should have tipped me off; he is an arrogant old snot. Around here people defer to him. He's head of various committees and on the social scene he's the big cheese. If you don't write the story the way he wants it told then there is a phone call upstairs and I get a bollockin'. They do very well thank you in banking and in the lawyering business up in London.

Now the other guy, MacKinnon, he was easy going, friendly. After the funeral, he invited me to join him at the Maiden's Head. Things were looking up. The family sat around a couple of tables in a room off the saloon bar. We sat at a small table on the other side of the room. When he brought the drinks to the table he said with a nod over his shoulder, "Best to leave them alone at a time like this."

We shot the breeze. He asked me about the paper, the usual stuff, did I like my job, were the editors OK. He was familiar with the news business, asking me about the equipment, circulation and advertising. As if I would know anything about that sort of thing. I did give him an earful about the old farts and their old-fashioned ways. He laughed.

While we were all taking it easy in the pub, I thought I would ask a few questions. MacKinnon never batted an eye when I asked how Halthorpe died. Injured when the plane crashed; he succumbed to the cold before he could be taken to a hospital. Without being asked, he told me that the cause of the crash was faulty wiring. The authorities went over the plane with a fine toothcomb and it was agreed that faulty insulation caused shorting in the plane's control system. Was MacKinnon on the up and up with me? Was he lying? Why all the secrecy on the part of the Halthorpes? Was there something that MacKinnon wasn't telling me? The plane had landed on his doorstep so to speak.

My complaint about the no pics edict from on high had him chuckling. When I went on to say, "Who did old moneybags Braithwaite think he was, telling us we couldn't take his picture."

MacKinnon laughed and came back with "When you have a bank account that runs to more than the usual number of zeros, a request is often regarded as an order." He went on, "Michael's camera shy for good reason. If he is easily recognized then he loses the edge anonymity gives him in his business dealings.

I had to agree it made sense when put that way. Just then young Braithwaite joined us. MacKinnon knew my name. "Trevor, I'd like you to meet Simon Braithwaite; Simon, Trevor Caldicott from the local paper." We shook hands and that was it. The others were pushing back their chairs and it was back to work for me. In a low voice I heard Simon say that they were going back to The Grange, wherever that was, and later he would be going back to Seattle with his Dad. MacKinnon said he was going up North for a couple of weeks and then he too was heading to Seattle.

When I got back to the paper, I rattled off a few paras. The usual stuff: In a quiet dignified service attended by family and friends, Robert Charles Edward Halthorpe, 27, son of, and so on and so on. Free for the afternoon; I had a committee meeting to cover later. I went upstairs to the library and started going through back copies of the paper in search of some information on Braithwaite— nothing. I hit the bull's eye in Who's Who, there was the best part of a column listing his companies, the committees he was chairman of and the charities he favoured, the whole nine yards. It was obvious why the old farts would be quick to grant his request. His middle name was spelt p-o-w-e-r.

Sitting in the quiet of the library, questions came to mind. What caused the wound in the area of his heart? What happened out there in the frozen wastes of Canada? Did he really die of exposure? Was there a cover-up? Was old man Halthorpe just throwing his weight about, as usual? Why so secretive? Was there something about the accident that he wanted hidden? Wow, just think, it would be the story of the year with banner heads, "Murder in the Air, Crash Cover-Up Exposed," above my byline. Did he jump or was he pushed? I intend to find out. Where to begin? MacKinnon said he was going North; he may have left a forwarding address. I'll pop into the Goodham Arms Hotel and make a few discreet enquiries.

At the hotel, I was in luck. Molly was on the desk; she and her partner had won top prize in the regional ballroom dancing competition and I had been assigned to cover it. She said she liked my story on her win and asked for half-a-dozen pics of the two of them with their large trophy. This would be easy.

"Hello Trevor, hobnobbing with the Halthorpes. Must have been a shock for the family. His mum, she looked all in, poor dear."

"She was pretty upset, almost passed out at the vault. The old man didn't seem to be that upset about the death." I didn't want to rush things but I thought enough had been said about the funeral, time to get MacKinnon's address. "The people that were staying here, did they leave a forwarding address? MacKinnon wanted some pics and like a clown I forgot to get his address in Scotland.

Would you happen to know where he was going?"

"Can't help you, sorry; none of them left a forwarding address. Sorry Trevor."

Bloody hell. "Oh well I guess I won't be able to send him the pics he wanted." I figured better go all the way with my big act. My sad face set Molly to thinking.

"Just a minute, maybe I can help you. MacKinnon, you said. I heard him and the boy talking just before they all left. He said something about going home and then he said it would be good to visit with his Mum and see the sights of Burnsbrae. I remember because he joked with the boy that if they had pavements, only he called them sidewalks, they would be rolled up at night. Burnsbrae, I'm sure that's what he said."

"Thanks Molly, you're a pal." Never heard of the place. I'd check it out when I got back to the office. There would likely be an inquisition when the call came up on next month's telephone list. What the hell! From experience I knew that the place to start my search would be the local Post Office. On the second ring: "Number please."

"Is this Burnsbrae Post Office?"

My answer was, "Of course, what can I do for you?"

I had decided to play the somewhat flustered friend of MacKinnon who had lost his address. "I wonder if you could help me. I've lost my friend's address and I need to get in touch with him. We are supposed to get together later in London. I had his...."

"Who is this friend of yours? I need to know his name if I am to be of any help."

"Oh yes, excuse me. His name is MacKinnon." I held my breath, would it work?

It did, she came right back with, "That would be Alister, but he is in Canada, hasn't been home for quite a while. Last time it was for his father's funeral. His mother lives in the village but she doesn't have a telephone. I could send someone to bring her to the phone, that's what I do when he calls."

"Thank you, but I don't know the lady. Alister and I met a long time ago. I have never been to Burnsbrae; we met in Canada." I had to think fast what could I say that would keep gabby on the line. Canada was the magic word.

"Canada, he did quite well for himself out there. He left here to work in the gold mines, apparently made his fortune. He came home for a while after he finished his time in the French Army."

This was great stuff — Scots mercenary involved in mysterious death in Canada's frozen wasteland — I could see the headlines. The old dear was in high gear now, must be a slow day at the Post Office.

"His mother and father were worried sick when he didn't come back with the other boys. They'd gone to the football matches in France. Everybody thought that he had gone to America to be with that Fiona Grant-James." She continued, her voice laced with a dash of acid. "The laird shipped her off as soon as they found out about the two of them. Alister and Fiona that is."

I refrained from asking questions, concerned that if I stopped the flow to get details she would ring off.

"He didn't go to America to be with her, no, he up and joined some Foreign Legion in France. I think she broke his heart. Alister was a fine upstanding young man. The Grant-James girl led him down the garden path if you ask me. He never married. I liked Alister."

Gabby sounded as though she had had a crush on MacKinnon.

There was a brief pause and then a sigh. "I have a call coming in. I'm afraid I cannot help you, sorry." She hung up and that was the end of our little chat. MacKinnon served in the French Foreign Legion, those guys are professional hard cases. Whew, he must have been a hellion when he was my age. He certainly looks every inch the executive now with his expensive suit and quiet manner. It's hard to imagine him in one of those Beau Geste get ups.

1

Robert had, on more than one occasion, been threatened with "grievous bodily harm" if he didn't "pay up". The man behind the threats, James Sedgewick, was an overweight tub of a man, an entrepreneur in crime. Jimmy owned a nightclub, a restaurant, an escort service, a couple of rock bands, made book and on occasion dabbled in importing — drugs. Although his muscles had softened under the easy life he now led, his rise to power and dominance in London's underworld had been made with his fists. His hard features and bent nose had the roseate hue of someone who enjoyed rich food served with expensive wines. His five-foot-eight-inch frame was thick through the shoulders, but his easy life had turned what had been muscle to fat and now his gut ballooned over his belted narrow waist.

Jimmy first saw the light of day in the bedroom of a three-storey tenement in Newcastle. His father, who had lived through the war to end all wars, was on the dole. Clever with his hands, he earned a few extra pennies fixing furniture and other small carpentry jobs. Growing up in the hard times of the 1920's, Jimmy led a life no different from thousands of boys. As a toddler, his playground was the street and the alleys and stairwells of the tenements. At school, he and his pals lived with the strict, sometimes harsh treatment of the teachers. They accepted the quick open-handed smack on the head, the pummelling on the shoulders, as simply a continuance of their parents' discipline. With the opportunities for mischief ever present, Jimmy and his pals found life an adventure. Cash was not a necessity. A quick hand, and if spotted swift feet were all that were required to provide sweets and fags for the street-wise Jimmy and his pals.

Jimmy left school at fourteen and went to work as an apprentice baker. He, as did his contemporaries, lived at home, sharing a bed and a small room with his two younger brothers. Friday was pay day, the high point of his week. After handing over his "digs" money to his

Mum he would get "toshed up" and meet his pals for a few pints. As long as he had money to buy a pint, no barman questioned whether he was of legal age to drink.

In the raucous atmosphere that pervaded the local boozers, Jimmy and his pals were teased unmercifully by the older men they rubbed shoulders with. All of it ribald and much of it about, "getting your wick dipped." Saturdays at work, slightly hung over and with only a few hours' sleep, he would be the butt of his fellow workers' off-colour humour. He gave as good as he got; Jimmy was OK.

Jimmy lost his virginity to a tough street-smart whore. She saw him across the street from the alley she was standing in. When he staggered and almost fell, she quickly crossed to his side. Taking his arm she fell into step beside him and said, "Hello dearie, how about it? I'll give you a good time. Have you any money on you?" Steering him towards an alley, she kept up her chatter. Jimmy, befuddled by having sampled some cheap gin, allowed himself to be led to the alley entrance. "Now dearie, the money. Let's see what's in your pocket besides that big thing sticking out down below." His head abuzz, Jimmy thrust his hand into his pocket. A slack drunken smile came with the realization that he was finally about to get his wick dipped. Opening his hand he said, "Here take it, the lot." Satisfied with the amount she hauled Jimmy into the darkness of the alley and went about earning her fee.

Two weeks after war was declared, he and three of his pals joined up, the plan being that they would volunteer together and so would stay together during their service. Officialdom decided otherwise, two went to the Navy, one to the Air Force, and Jimmy, because of his flat feet and baking experience was sent to the Army Catering Corps. Posted to Europe, he served his country dishing out meals to infantrymen on guard during what became known as the "Phoney War". When the Nazi juggernaut began its charge through the Lowlands, and the Allies were headed for the French coast, Jimmy, now a sergeant, worked himself and his cooks hard to give "My boys, at least one square a day."

When this was no longer possible, Jimmy joined the scramble for the French coast. He arrived back in England, one of the thousands saved by the armada of small boats that went to rescue the British Expeditionary Force at a place called Dunkerque.

Master of his own kitchen again, he soon earned a reputation for working wonders with the wartime rations. Jimmy had flair, he was a natural. When his day ended in the kitchen and the "janker wallahs" had shined all the pots and "bashed" next day's spuds, a few of his chums from the sergeants' mess would join him in his office and play cards. In the give and take of the game usually, "catch the ten" the day's happenings in camp would be analysed and the latest rumours repeated and argued over. While all this was going on each player would take an occasional lip-smacking sip from his large issue tea mug. Sometimes the drinker would put his mug down and declare, usually after having had a few sips, "Damned fine stuff. Where do you get it, locally?" The answer was always a smile and a top-up.

The recipe for Jimmy's cocktail was simplicity itself: boiling water poured over whatever fruit he could scrounge and sugar. The natural yeast in the fruit and fermentation produced a pleasant-tasting but dangerous tipple. Those who allowed the taste to mislead them regretted their mistake when reveille sounded the beginning of another day.

Each day Jimmy was charged with feeding seven hundred men three meals. With all the food and supplies this required, it was easy for Jimmy to put aside (fiddle) items to be used in place of cash on the local black market. A half-pound of sugar bought two rabbits, a pound, a nice catch of fish. Such extras were usually served up as late night snacks after the card game was over. The first time rabbit was served questions were asked: "Nice chicken, how'd you get your hands on it Jimmy? What did you have to pay for it? Can you get me some of this, I'm going on leave next week?" He kept his questioners guessing for about a week before telling them the white meat they had thought was chicken was in fact rabbit. At first they refused to believe him, "Yeah, pull the other one Jimmy."

Having been born and raised in cities, they weren't aware that wild rabbit was a popular dish in many rural areas of the country. The proof that the meat was indeed rabbit was provided by one of the soldiers on jankers. Part of his punishment for not having his boots shined was to work in the kitchen. He happened to be gutting and skinning a rabbit as Jimmy's pals passed through the kitchen heading for their nightly card game. The discovery in no way dampened their enthusiasm for what became known as 'Cheecken a la Jeemie."

Army cooking was a dull routine of meat and potatoes with baking an exotic practice of civvy street. Proud of his skill in concocting highly edible cakes and pastries, he was frustrated at not being able to demonstrate his artistry. The ribbons on the wall of his former employer's shop attested to his light touch with flour, butter, eggs, and milk.

When one of his pals told him that he had been granted leave for his son's christening, Jimmy seized upon this as an opportunity to do some baking. The lip smacking comments about the cake led to Jimmy being called upon for a repeat performance when his pals had a birthday. The carefully decorated cake was smuggled to the home of the birthday boy's current girlfriend. And so "Jimmy The Baker" was born.

In time the news of his prowess with pot and skillet got back to the officers' mess. The duty officers in making their rounds came to realize, too late, the wonders being worked by Jimmy in the kitchen. Before he could be transferred he was promoted and posted overseas to a headquarters mess in Cairo.

Arriving in Egypt in 1941, a newly minted sergeant major he soon became known as an "operator". At first he fiddled mess supplies to provide variety in the mess meals and some cash on the side for himself. In drinking in the backstreet bars and eateries frequented by those on the fringe of the vast underworld that thrived in the alleyways and souks he saw the money, sometimes in large amounts, that changed hands in under-the-table deals. Determined to get his hands on some of that money he began to move deeper into the hidden life of the city. Some of his early forays into this alien land did not pay off.

One night while using the urinal in one of his favourite haunts the well- dressed man at the next stall took a shiny object out of his pocket and passed it to a surprised Jimmy. Looking at the dull yellow metal he asked, "Is this what I think it is?" His answer was a nod and a whispered, "yes." Handing the gold wafer back to the man, he buttoned up his trousers and waited. The other bod was selling, let him make the first move.

"I have plenty more effendi, you like? Good buy sir. Go back Blighty rich man." The seller spoke like an Arab street vendor hawking illicit goods, but his clothes said he was several rungs up the ladder from the cheats on the streets. It was early evening and the club was almost empty. They were alone in the toilet.

"Suppose, just suppose that I had a use for that stuff, how much would it cost me."

Looking furtive the seller came close and said, "For you effendi, only two hundred pounds."

Jeez, he thought, I could sell the stuff for five or six times that amount. Naw it was too good to be true. "That's two hundred for the lot, right?"

Showing his teeth in what passed for a friendly smile, the seller shook his head and said, "For you, six bars, solid gold, one thousand." After some hard and fast bargaining, with Jimmy expecting one of his three pals who were with him to come looking for him, the deal was clinched at seven hundred and fifty pounds for the bars. After a careful second look and hefting the gold bar the deal was on. Next day the exchange took place in an alley at the rear of the mess where Jimmy worked his culinary magic for the general.

Days later gloating over the bars he dropped one. It landed on the floor under his bed after striking the metal frame. When he bent to pick it up he saw the dull base metal that had given heft to the paper-thin layer of gold. Angry and preoccupied with thoughts of revenge Jimmy was lax in his kitchen duties which resulted in the General leaving the mess in a huff because the food was not up to "snuff." This was one of the few times that Jimmy didn't sort out a cheater.

No one double crossed "The Baker." When he couldn't persuade the cheater with a few well placed punches to pay up; the boots went in. Another early fiddle that went wrong was what decided him to carry a gun. A well-placed kick in the balls stopped a knife wielding attacker in his tracks. It happened at the close of a deal, the attacker had been paid, but changed his mind and pulled a knife, he wanted all the money. In a mad red rage Jimmy put the boots to the would-be robber. When Jimmy came to his senses his assailant lay moaning at his feet. His face was a bloody mess and he appeared to have broken ribs. One arm clutched his ribs, the other limp at his side was obviously broken.

Learning from his mistakes Jimmy moved on to bigger deals. He also learned from the mistakes of others. In their sweeps of the souks, bars and cafes the military police seemed to have a special antenna that directed them to the heavies who were flogging HM goods in a big way. A couple of times Jimmy was picked up in such a sweep. He was let go when a check of his pay book revealed that his name was not on their list.

A brief conversation between two policemen after the first raid convinced him that the smart money kept its head down.

"The stupid arse hole, if he had used his head instead of his prick he wouldn't be in this pickle. His bragging to the binte in Maxie's could be heard at least three rooms away. I couldn't believe it, here was this drunken clown telling this whore all about his fiddles."

No large bundles of cash in the hip pocket; boozing and brothel creeping to be done quietly. Wham, bam, thank you ma'm, and on your way Jimmy lad.

Flogging supplies was endemic in the Army. It was almost a tradition among the rank-and-file that you flogged what wasn't tied down and wasn't charged to you. In this atmosphere of thievery the MPs went after the big-time operators first and the small fry when they had nothing better to do.

Clothing, medical supplies, booze, home-made and prime bottled were all part of his dealings. Talk to Jimmy, he'll see you right, was the message on the bush telegraph for anyone who wanted a buyer for his fiddle or wanted cash for one. Although making a lot of money, his frugal ways and a strong intuitive sense kept him clear of the authorities. Twice he had to scamper over rooftops to the sound of heavy army boots charging upstairs after kicking in a door.

In his underhanded dealings money, a surfeit of the stuff, eventually became a problem. What to do with it. There was no way he could send his ill-gotten gains home, anyway his Mum and Dad were both earning "a bundle" working on the home front making aircraft parts. Banks were out. A visit to a bank would set bells to ringing. When the ringing stopped he would be on his way to the glasshouse and at least one year of harsh prison discipline. His dilemma was resolved when Captain David Jones, sat down at his table and introduced himself as David Jones. The upper-class accent and manners of the newcomer to the Pink Lady, one of Jimmy's favourite haunts, triggered alarm bells in Jimmy's lower-class sensibilities. He hadn't come this far to fall for the easy friendliness of some poncey military police officer in mufti. The same canny North Country instincts which had curbed his urges to go off on drunken spending sprees, now advised caution. Play along and in time he would show his hand.

On his second visit to the Pink Lady, Jones invited Jimmy to join him in sampling the delights offered upstairs. Afterwards, sitting in the plush comfort of the parlour sipping whisky, David casually mentioned that he had a few gem stones he would like to cash in. Could Jimmy help him? Since their first meeting Jimmy had found out that David was well known in the alleys and dark corners of the city. There had been a disagreement over mess funds and blows had been struck. The other officer had died on the way to hospital after hitting his head on the corner of a heavy wooden table. Jimmy agreed to buy the stones on condition that a jeweller he knew okayed them.

His pockets stuffed with cash Jimmy stepped into the blackness of the narrow alley, Jimmy put his hand on the gun at his waist. Standing still to peer into the narrow alley, he eased off the safety catch. A dim light in a doorway and he knew that all he had to do now was to climb the rickety stairs and make the exchange. For the sum of ten thousand pounds, a bulky package of notes, he became the owner of a handful of gem stones, most of them uncut diamonds.

Now the problem of getting his ill-gotten gains back to Blighty was solved. The gems could be carried in a pocket of his uniform without raising any eyebrows. A nod of approval from the cadaverous jeweller and Jimmy handed over the money. Jones left as soon as he was paid. A celebratory drink offered by the jeweller was refused with a lecherous leer. "I don't' want to keep the lady waiting, thanks awfully but no thanks."

Jimmy swaggered back down the dark alley, the buildings on either side no more than six feet apart, his eyes not yet fully attuned to his surroundings. Pleased with the transaction he smiled and ran his fingers lightly over the pocket that held the small bag of stones. A tiny scratching sound behind him wiped the smile off his face and brought immediate action. He turned to face the danger and backed against the nearest wall.

He had passed a deeper shadow, likely a doorway he realized, a few steps back. Someone stood in the middle of the street, a shadowy figure in the poor light. Fear clutched at him turning his mind to mush. What to do. Touching the pocket that held his fortune he decided that there was no way this thieving bastard was going to rob him.

The panic was put aside, to be replaced by anger. A movement by the shadow warned that he was getting ready to attack, likely with a knife held low to rip at his guts. A quick thrust followed by a slash to the throat. There were tales aplenty of drunks having their throats cut and left naked in an alley. Well this bugger had met his match. Jimmy swore and grabbed the nine milli Browning holstered under his loose fitting jacket.

Just then a shadow moved on his left. Damn, I should have brought along a couple of the lads. Bugger it, how stupid can you get. Determined his latest fiddle wouldn't become the stuff of gossip and eventually reach the ear of authority, he had kept it a secret. Enveloped in a mad rage, and his senses fine tuned, Jimmy could clearly hear the calm breathing of the attacker on the right: he waited confident of the outcome.

No bloody thieves were walking away with what was his. I'll kill the bastards. Unaware of the gun in Jimmy's hand the one on his right with a quick intake of breath telegraphed that he was about to charge. The one on the left, stepping out of the deep shadow, moved slowly towards him and stopped, a dark menacing figure, about fifteen feet away.

The madness took on a new dimension, one where time became fuzzy at the edges. The one on the right came at him with long floating strides. Detached from what was happening, Jimmy in one smooth easy movement calmly squeezed the trigger. The arm with the knife, held low to rip at his guts, dropped loosely to the assailant's side. Two steps and he collapsed in a heap four feet from his target. Turning to his left in an easy balletic movement, Jimmy saw blood appear below lefty's chin as he went down.

How long he leaned against the wall, the gun loose in his hand, he didn't know. When he finally focussed on the two bodies at his feet, he stepped away from the wall and started to walk away. Before he had gone more than a few steps he stopped. There was nothing to fear from the two lying in the dust and refuse of the alley. Walking back slowly, tight faced and eyes hard, he knelt down and pulled aside the burnoose of the first assailant. Defeated by the layers of material underneath he gave up and moved over to the other one. Pulling aside the hood of the burnoose, he swore. There was enough light for him to see that lefty was Jones. The double dealing bastard. The small amount of cash and the papers he found in Jones's suit he stuffed in a pocket. Where was the money?

Still kneeling over the body, he carefully looked up and down the alley. No one around, obviously Jones had arranged for the alley to be empty. Death, like any other commodity in the souk, was for sale, and came cheap. Afraid that the shots might have been heard by a police patrol he walked quickly to the street and headed for a bar, he needed a drink.

The next day, Jimmy mechanically went about overseeing the kitchen staff. The cookhouse gang razzed him about the state he was in and joked that she must have been one horny binte. The killings in no way upset him unduly, being resolved in his mind with the adage better them than me. The following day he was his old self and was quick to answer the obscene suggestions bandied about the kitchen on what had transpired between him and the binte with equally obscene remarks about the jokers' ancestry.

The killings added another layer of cynicism to the already calloused conscience that more and more was defining his personality. The change did not come about overnight. At first he had only scorn and contempt for the people he had to deal with. When he moved from wheeling and dealing on behalf of getting extras for the mess to dealing in illegal commodities was when his conscience lost out to cash in the pocket.

Jimmy's chums never questioned his absences from the mess. Unaware of how wide and varied his dealings were in the hidden commerce of the city, they shrugged and assumed he was having it off with a woman. After all he was always good for a piss-up followed by a slap-up feed. So what if he was a bit edgy and spent more time off alone than with them. When he did join them in the late night card games most of the time he was the Jimmy of gossip and outrageous yarns. The more astute of his pals, however, noticed that often he had other things on his mind besides the cards in his hand.

In the fluid conditions of an advancing army there were unlimited opportunities for the unscrupulous to make money, and Jimmy made sure he got in on the action. France and Italy, especially Italy, provided rich takings. Stationed in Germany at the end of the war, he was shipped back to England in early 1946 for demobilisation. He walked out of the "demob" centre with close to thirty-six thousand pounds in jewels, cash and a handful of gold sovereigns tucked away in his kitbag.

After a few days at home he headed for the bright lights of London. There was nothing to keep him at home having found out that his pal in the RAF was in the Far East and the two in the Navy had gone down with their ships in the Battle of the Atlantic. Now they would never get to swap war stories. London "the Big Smoke" was where the smart money gravitated at the close of the war. Rationing was still in effect and there were opportunities galore for easy money to be made in the shadowy world, fronted by brightly-lit restaurants.

One of Jimmy's cooks, whose family had a restaurant in the east end of the world's largest city, had told him at the demob centre that if he ever came to the Smoke to look him up. When Jimmy appeared on the family doorstep two weeks after demob, he was invited to stay. The offer of a job in the restaurant's kitchen met with a quick yes. This was what he needed, a base from which to check the action. Find out who was doing what and what the pecking order was. Within three months, most of his jewellery had been converted to cash and tucked away with his gold in a safety deposit box at the bank where he had a modest account.

Six months later with all his "goodies" converted, he quit working at the restaurant and went to work for one of the local hard boys. When Jimmy The Baker darkened a doorway, mayhem was sure to follow.

George Atkinson, a small-time bookie and sometime loan shark met his Maker in an alleyway. Few mourned his passing. Georgie, his throat slashed from ear to ear, was found by the police. Jimmy had regularly placed bets with Georgie, whose place of business, a corner booth in the local café, was just around the corner from Jimmy's digs. He got to know Georgie and usually joked with him about his daily forecasts. Several times he had seen Georgie's wife Sarah having a coffee in the café while waiting for her old man to finish for the day. Their son Tommy was killed in a road pile-up during the war in the desert.

The daughter, Patricia, owned a women's hairdressing shop. A tall slim girl, she had her mother's blonde hair and blue eyes. He had been smitten by Patricia the first time he saw her standing in the doorway of her shop talking to another woman. He saw her around the neighbourhood, usually in the company of other women. Alone, she walked with a confident step and had an aloof detached manner, she was some woman. When they passed on the street, she never gave him more than a cursory glance. Everyone in the neighbourhood knew who Jimmy was, but not even a nod from the haughty Patricia.

What sort of person was she behind that snooty attitude? Did she think she was better than her neighbours? Maybe she was shy. Maybe it was her protection against the whistles and lecherous innuendo she attracted. What to do?

Jimmy readily admitted to himself that he wasn't any Cary Grant, and yet there was something about him that women wanted. He never lacked for female company. He admitted that his longing in secret for the beautiful Patricia was becoming an obsession the day he saw her standing across the street laughing at something her companion had said, her male companion. A wild surge of jealousy took hold of him. She looked glorious, her head thrown back in laughter, obviously enjoying whatever it was that had been said. Jimmy swore, the little runt had better be careful. A wrong move and I'll fix him.

When he began day dreaming about the two of them dating and moved on to having her in bed, he swore, you daft bugger, stop acting like a kid. She's just another binte. But try as he might to forget her she remained a constant face in his mind's eye. No one could ever accuse him of being shy, but this woman was different. His feelings each time he saw her became more intense and confused. She was special, the usual glib approach wouldn't do.

The demise of Georgie awakened Jimmy to his civic duty. Making book was not the sort of job for a woman, it required a man to run the business. The other bookies would steal her business, using any sharp method they thought they could get away with. Better that he in all kindness offer to manage the business for the widow. A couple of days after Georgie's funeral a serious-faced Jimmy visited the grieving widow and proposed that he manage the business. Sarah agreed, knowing that she would be elbowed aside as soon as Jimmy became familiar with running the business. However she didn't surrender the business without first taking steps to ensure her financial future. Sarah insisted that if Jimmy met certain conditions all stipulated in writing, the bookie business was his.

Jimmy surprised the locals by readily agreeing to Sarah's proposal. Four months later the principal condition of the contract was met when Sarah's Bouquet opened for business. Sarah's dream, cherished since childhood, of owning her own flower shop was now a reality.

The opening was a splashy affair quite removed from the back streets of Jimmy's endeavours. In the time leading up to the gala opening Jimmy and Patricia became quite pally. She confided to her mother that when she was alone with Jimmy, he was not the hard man everybody said he was. Jimmy made her laugh with his pithy quips and observations directed at passers-by and at the people they knew. She found him interesting. He was ambitious, she too wanted to get ahead in business.

Shortly thereafter, he and Patricia became engaged. The inevitable happened and when they came down the aisle as man and wife some women commented that the high waistline of the wedding dress did wonders for the bride's figure. Some of the less charitable in the neighbourhood after a few drinks and a hasty glance over their shoulder, likened the union to that of Beauty and the Beast. Jimmy with his square jaw, the lines around his mouth, the hard grey eyes, and the scars on his close-cropped skull was more intimidating than imposing.

Their son, Adam, was a seven-month baby. Jimmy doted on his

son. Sarah insisted that they live with her. Sarah, wise in the ways of the street, wanted it known that she and Jimmy were connected. With the menacing figure of Jimmy, a rising star in the criminal firmament, on the sidelines, her life was free of such petty nuisances as small-time "wide boys" hitting her up for cash — or else.

By the mid 1950's, the ambitious Jimmy hadn't been idle. A little bit here a little bit there and in time he had intimidated his way to an ever-growing criminal fiefdom. His lust for power was abetted by the muscle of the "Baker's Dozen", the heavies who did his bidding.

Patricia, busy with her business and her responsibilities as a new mum, didn't pry into her husband's affairs.

When a row of tenements came on the market, Jimmy and an ambitious young contractor pooled their cash and became the owners of ten run-down houses. Jimmy saw the enterprise as a means of laundering some of his ill-gotten gains; also as the fulfilment of an ambition to own a club and fancy restaurant. During work on the site passers by were often entertained by Jimmy's and the contractor's on-site loud profane arguments.

Six months after the purchase Jimmy moved into the two end houses the interiors of which had been ripped apart to form a large house, one fit for a man on his way up. The contractor being the minor investor in the project had to wait until Jimmy's restaurant and club was open for business before he could get to work on his own house, the one at the other end of the row.

Word of the renovations, in such an unlikely neighbourhood, caught the attention of one of the Sunday papers and resulted in an initial front page story followed by weekly updates. The publicity brought the curious to see what all the fuss was about. The opening by the local member of the municipal council made the front page.

The menu for the day was highlighted in a box under the picture of the ribbon-cutting ceremony. Readers with pretensions of "knowing food" smiled when they read the menu. Planning on having fun with this jumped up restaurateur's menu they went "slumming in the East End" prepared to show him up. With great glee they joked about what they would complain of: poorly prepared, sauce too thin, overdone, underdone. Mind you, down the East End you couldn't better them for fish and chips or their bangers and mash, but food of superior quality?

Those who set out to embarrass the East Ender were unable to find fault with the menu and became the loudest in their praises of the Phoenix's kitchen. They were soon joined by others who had heard about this great place in the East End. The restaurant received its official seal of approval when it became the after hours eatery of Mike Marr and The Others. Mike's band, critiqued as being on the leading edge of the new sound, had a national audience.

Mike, no newcomer to the music scene, paid attention when it was suggested that he should sample the groceries at the Phoenix. The food lived up to its billing and the band was always assured of a table. Mike never did find out that the owner of the Phoenix was the major backer of the band. The owner sat at a table on a raised dais at the rear of the restaurant. Mike was introduced to him and afterwards confided to the band "A hard man, wouldn't want to meet him in a dark alley. A grip like a vice, I thought he was gonna break my hand, the bastard."

Jimmy's success gave Patricia the incentive to examine closely what, until then, had been a dream of opening a second shop. Financing was no longer a problem and encouraged by her old man she set up her second shop two doors down from her mother's flower shop. Her husband, always on the lookout for a big score, was already casting around for other sources of revenue. Both of them were ambitious and wanted to better their lot, but their means of attaining this end were vastly different. It could never be said that they were a handsome couple. With motherhood, she had bloomed if that was at all possible; she with her figure softer, not quite so angular, still caused heads to turn. Now Jimmy's once muscular frame was layered with softness. He was still a brawler at heart. But now, others dealt with the slow-paying punters.

2

It was an easy birth. Aided by a midwife, Jane Halthorpe was delivered at home of a seven-pound four-ounce boy. The fourth child, the second son, born to the couple was christened Robert, Charles Edward. The father Sydney Halthorpe was a senior partner in a London law firm. The family was also well known in City banking circles. He was a member of the right clubs and had recently taken up golf at the invitation of his increasing number of American clients.

Robert, growing up in a household where guests were always around, meant that he was accorded more attention than was good for a little boy. Guests seeking favours brought expensive toys, the more mercenary gave cash. The undue attention resulted in temper tantrums and a series of frustrated nannies who were not allowed to deal appropriately with the fractious child. The housekeeper, gardener and cook dreaded when his parents went off for a day or two and left him in the care of the current nanny. They clenched their teeth and kept their hands busy when "the brat" was on the loose.

Robert, in the eyes of his mother, could do no wrong. When nanny was seen swatting him on his trousered rear, she was immediately sent packing. When she tried to explain the punishment was warranted, Mrs. Halthorpe refused to believe her. Robert would not hold a cat by the tail and dip it, repeatedly, into the water barrel beside the garden shed.

Growing up in the company of adults gave him an astuteness beyond his years. When the current nanny, who was also his teacher, used his pocket-money to explain simple arithmetic to the seven-year-old, she was able to hold his attention. With no means of disciplining her charge, she had to stifle her frustration when teaching other subjects, and carry on as best she could.

Suddenly aware of money and the power it bestowed, (even in his limited concept of buying sweets and other goodies) he let it be known that toys didn't interest him anymore, hard cash was what he wanted. When this statement was made in front of a roomful of weekenders, it was greeted with laughter and pooh-poohed by his parents. Word got out the Halthorpe brat wants the readies, forget the toys, give him cash. With the extra cash the nanny found she could set a higher level of problem. When not under the jaundiced eye of nanny, he would sometimes sneak off and keep the gardener company. This crafty fellow would spin yarns about his time in the army. Before the tale ended, Robert would find himself helping with whatever it was the gardener was doing.

His world of indulgence and rebellion came abruptly to an end the day he left for boarding school. At the age of eight, he was sent to Saint Michael of the Mount School. His going was the cause of many tearful entreaties by his mother, but his father remained firm in his resolve, sure that the experience would do Robert good. He would be with boys his own age.

At school all attempts to get his way were dealt with immediately. His tactic of lying down and drumming his heels on the floor resulted in him being hurried to the infirmary by two prefects. There he had to stand up straight in a corner, no leaning allowed, under the watchful eye of matron. On his second trip to the infirmary he kicked over a flower pot on a tall stand outside the Headmaster's office. The Head ordered the sullen pouting boy into his office, the prefects were told to return to class, but lingered at the closed door. When a yelp came through the door they grinned, little snotty was getting three of the best.

The caning had a lasting effect on him. After the caning, the Head gave one of his standard lectures: "Halthorpe you were caned for good reason. You must follow instructions and respect the property of others. You are guilty on both counts, hence your punishment. I trust you will correct your ways and go about your work here at school cheerfully and with vigour. Stand up straight, a Saint Michael's boy doesn't slouch, and wipe that pout off your face."

Walking awkwardly back to his classroom he vowed, never again. Back in the classroom he was greeted by grins and sly smiles, his classmates knew what had happened. One of the prefects had been overheard in conversation with the class master. They paid close attention when he went to his desk and grinning looked on as Robert sat down— carefully.

The caning elevated him to the small group in his form who had made the fearsome trip to the Head's. The others who had yet to make the slow walk down the shiny-floored corridors to the Headmaster's study, now gave him their OK. His early behaviour had coloured him a mommy's boy, a sissy who couldn't play football or rugby. Sports were important at Saint Michael's. He settled into the cloistered life of the all-boys school, gaining a reputation as "a brain."

All the boys knew that he was flush and anyone who wanted a few bob for whatever reason talked to Robert. The source of his power was the cash he sneaked into the school when returning from holidays. His deep pockets also set him above the bullying and petty annoyances that were the bane of all but a few.

Saturdays the senior boys were allowed to stay in town until ten-o-clock in the evening. For most of the seniors, this allowed them to see a movie and if they were flush eat a fish and chip supper while waiting for the bus. The more randy and daring of the seniors gave the flicks a by and went after the local "skirts." The girls knew what the boys were after and went along for the lark as long as the money lasted.

Empty pockets brought about a dramatic change in the relationship. A fun-loving girl who, just minutes before, hadn't been averse to some orchestrated groping, came over all prim and proper. Dad would get nasty if she didn't leave for home right this minute. Such escapades required more than the weekly sum each boy was allowed as pocket money. Robert provided the extra lolly.

The skirt chasers had to pay up for their sinful ways. Short of cash for the time it took to pay the loan, they wandered about the school grounds lying about what had happened with the townies. In the evening they entertained themselves in the dorms playing cards or board games.

Robert did well at Saint Michael's. He was one of the top boys in his class. When he moved on to public school he continued to study hard, winning the top prize in Latin and History and a second in English Lit., all to the delight of the academics. In sports he was the despair of the keen young sports master. An indifferent rugby and hockey player, he was constantly being reminded to, "Follow up, the ball, the ball, go, go, go, tackle him, tackle. Oh God."

It was a foregone conclusion that he would go up to Cambridge and upon graduating would work in the City. Later he would marry, preferably someone with money, a titled parent would be nice, his mother thought, and have a family. That was the plan until his first flight. In his second year at university, a friend introduced him to flying. It was love at first sight. Using a gift from his doting grandmother he was able to finance flying lessons and solo time of 50 hours. Determined to make flying his career, he soon became known as a young man who would turn his hand to anything and in payment would accept free flying time in lieu of cash. If there was a chance, no matter how slim, that he could get some time in the air, classes were forgotten.

In time it became a standing joke in the clubhouse of the small aerodrome near the city, that if you didn't want to get your hands dirty or you wanted a plane flown between points A and B on the cheap, give Robert a call. He was the despair of his tutors, who knowing his potential, tried unsuccessfully to persuade him that flying was fine as a hobby but as a career, no. He got his degree but not with the accolades and honours that had been the promise of the first year.

At his graduation party his father asked him with a smile, "What are you planning on doing with your life now? Maybe a desk at the office?"

"Now that you mention that horrible word work there is something I would like to do, fly. Do you know, I have 300 hours solo on single-engine and almost a hundred hours on twin-engined, aircraft?"

"Well I am impressed. Did I pay for that many hours?"

"No sir, most were paid for with hard work."

"Digging ditches I suppose?"

"Of course. No! I sweated at the "drome," doing anything that needed to be done. Dad you have friends in the flying business."

"Yes, and you want me to have a chat with them. Get you a plum job."

"Something like that, yes. Would you?"

"No promises, but yes I'll talk to a couple of people at the club."

One year after graduation, Robert looked very grand in his uniform. He was co-pilot of a Brampton-Naismith, flying the wealthy and their cars to and from the continent. Life was grand, he had a small flat within a twenty minute drive of the aerodrome. His blonde good looks, bold blue eyes, confident demeanour and his commanding six foot two inch frame brought second looks from women in airports, restaurants and on the street.

Those who had the chutzpah to demonstrate that they wanted more than a look were never turned away. Life was as it should be; he was a popular figure around the aerodrome. Women enjoyed his company; always the gentleman, his easygoing ways and quick wit had them laughing all the way to bed. Occasionally, when he had nothing better to do, he would join his family for the monthly weekend get together.

Some of the flights were one way, and the company, ever mindful of profit, would make the crew wait at their destination while every effort was made to arrange a return flight. Robert and his pilot Sandy McEwen passed the time while waiting for their orders by playing poker. At first they kept score with matches. Robert suggested playing for pennies, "Just for fun, it will make the game more interesting."

"OK, but just for pennies."

Playing for money, if only for pennies, brought an added dimension to the games for Robert. There was an excitement in the games that was not there before. At first he went along with gambling for pennies. But, he reasoned, if the stakes were higher then surely the electric feeling that grabbed at his gut would be heightened too.

At first Sandy put Robert's enthusiasm for the card games down to boredom. In time he came to realize that it wasn't boredom that seemed to drive his co-pilot to shuffle the cards; neither was it winning. At odd moments, usually when airborne, he would briefly wonder what it was that his co-pilot found so attractive in gambling for pennies. As soon as they were free on a one-way flight he would get out the cards and insist that they play. All the while boasting to Sandy how, this time, he would "clean your clock, send you home to the missus broke." The threats were delivered with a friendly grin. All attempts by Robert to increase the stakes were turned down by Sandy, who remained firm in his resolve to keep the stakes at a penny a point.

"If you want to play for higher stakes you should try your luck at a gambling club. Me, I have a wife, kids and a mortgage; the stakes are high enough for me Robbie."

"You know, I might just do that— play with the big boys."

It wasn't until quite some time later that Robert got the opportunity to play with the "big boys". In between Sandy's refusal to be drawn into playing for higher stakes and his date with the big boys, Robert moved on to betting on the ponies. At first he based his betting system on whether or not the horse's name was to his liking. He told himself that he was above the level of the average punter he saw with a hungry look lining up at the tote wickets, or shiftily placing a bet in a pub. It was all a lark, it was fun. He got a perverse pleasure in mixing with the seedy characters he met in the bookie haunts he frequented in pursuit of his secret excitement.

Most of them were involved in some shady scheme in order to sustain their habitual gambling. When he occasionally thought about them, it was to marvel how they could allow themselves to become so shabby, so pathetic He discovered that his (embellished) tales of the rough types he met while placing a bet, bedazzled some of his lady friends, some of whom chivvied him into having them tag along on his visits to the bookie's. Soon he abandoned his hit-and-miss system and began studying form. The change didn't make any difference to his winnings.

Robert eventually got his chance to play for high stakes, higher than he could really afford. He and Sandy were over-nighting at a French aerodrome just across the border with Monaco, waiting to pick up the owner of a yacht who was returning on the morning tide from a voyage around the Greek islands. Knowing this, he had made plans to gamble at the Casino. In pursuit of his plan, he had packed a business suit and a thousand pounds, the money borrowed from his bank. Robert had exercised all his powers of persuasion in convincing his bank manager the money was to fix the plumbing in his flat.

Burns said it best: "The best-laid schemes o' mice and men gang aft agley." When Robert and Sandy entered the foyer of their hotel, they had to push their way through a large group of sailors to get their room key at the desk. They were informed that their usual room had been reserved for them. Grabbing the key, Robert turned and bumped hard into an earnest-faced sailor about his own age.

"Excuse me."

"That's OK."

Looking back at the group around the desk Robert grinned and said, "Looks like a rugby scrum, any second now I expect to see the ball come flying out."

"Yeah sure, gotcha, and I was hoping for some quiet time away from this bunch. Thought I was smart bookin' a room here, shit."

"It usually is quiet, we have stayed here before on overnighters."

"Who do you fly for? I see you have wings up."

"You too. Off the aircraft carrier?"

"Yeah, we have a week ashore while she takes on supplies and engineering does some work below decks. Hey my name's Jason Jackson, everybody calls me JJ."

"How do you do. I'm Robert and this is Sandy. Meet JJ, he's just off the big carrier we saw on the way in." While making introductions, the trio had moved a little apart from JJ's shipmates. Robert and Sandy were about to head up the stairs to their room, when loud voices at the hotel door caught their attention, turning they saw four flyers make an entrance.

"Now the shit has hit the fan," JJ said.

"Wild men JJ?" Sandy asked with a grin.

"Oh yes, muy macho. When these guys are on the loose, the shore patrol usually pays a visit. Stay up most of the night playing poker. And as we are here for a few days you can bet there will be booze and broads."

One of the four walked over and slapping JJ on the shoulder said, "We missed you, where did you take off to?"

"I got held up and took the next liberty boat."

"Pete's rented a suite on the third floor. Ain't it great to have an old man who's loaded? C'mon up, the action should start as soon as we get things squared away at the desk." Looking over at Robert and Sandy, he said, "Bring your buddies and lots of cash, I feel lucky tonight. I aim to even the score with Pete for that shellackin' last time out."

"Thanks, but no thanks," was Sandy's answer.

Robert gave Sandy a glance, shrugged and said, "Count me in."

When Sandy reached over to answer the early morning phone call he was confronted by Robert, fully clothed, dead to the world on his bed. He said to the phone, "Thank you, better send up a pot of strong coffee." Shaking his head he headed for the bathroom. The coffee arrived as he was putting on his trousers. "That's fine, just leave it beside the bed. That's OK, I'll take it from here." Shaking his head and muttering under his breath he grabbed his co-pilot by the shoulder and shook him. His answer was a groan and a mumbled, "Go away."

"Get on your feet you silly bugger, it's time to go." Grabbing Robert by the shoulders he pulled him upright, "Open your eyes, c'mon pull yourself together, it's after seven, time to go," and began shaking Robert.

"All right, I'm awake, let go!"

"Open your eyes. What time did you get to bed? Broke I'll bet. Let's go, breakfast's on me."

Robert rubbing at his face and blinking against the morning light filling the room, jumped to his feet, a wide grin on his face, said, "For your information old chap, old pal, I won, close to three thousand dollars."

"The Yanks let you walk away with that amount of cash and didn't say anything? Tell me another one."

"Well Mr. Gloom and Doom what the hell do you think this is?" Brandishing a large wad of paper, "Have a gander Sandy; its all cash. And I'll buy breakfast and pay for the taxi to the drome. What a night! I was ahead about five hundred around one o-clock and when I suggested that I needed my beauty sleep as I had to fly tomorrow, make that today, they got a tad excited.

"One of them, he'd been into the booze a bit much, called me a limey welcher. Well that did it, I made a grab for him, but one of the others pushed me back into my chair. Anyway, when things quieted down I insisted that the name caller and I play a game for the five hundred, he lost. So I thought what the hell, I'm on a winning streak here, why not stay with it, and the rest is history."

"Tell me then what time did it break up?"

"I think it was about five-o-clock when I fell on the bed and passed out."

"Well sunshine, pull your finger out and get cleaned up and into your working clothes. You look as though you've been dragged through a hedge backwards. Get a move on, we haven't got all day." After a hurried shave, Robert downed his second cup of coffee while changing into his uniform. Breakfast was just a whiff of bacon and eggs as they rushed through the foyer.

"I guess some of the Yanks are having breakfast," Sandy said as he hurried through the foyer.

They had just completed the pre-flight checks when their

passenger, a Mr. Nikolakakos, stepped out of the Rolls-Bentley which had pulled up at the plane's ramp. No time was spent on pleasantries. As soon as the car was tied down and the ramp secured, Sandy brought the engines to life and acting on instructions from the tower was airborne and calling for wheels up. Their passenger, a large briefcase open and papers strewn about him, was dictating to one of the two secretaries who accompanied him.

In the air a smiling Robert relived the previous night's games.

"You look like the cat that ate the canary; a penny for your thoughts."

"I was just thinking about my date with Janice," he lied.

The insidious lusting after the gut wrenching excitement of gambling had him in a vice grip. The "game" was secondary, the means to an end. Gambling was the ultimate thrill. Robert didn't follow the usual downward spiral of the habitual gambler; fate played a hand and, dealing from the bottom of the deck, left him out in the cold.

3

When Lady Luck frowned on Robert he knew that the heavies would call to demand he pay up or else.

"Robbie old son, how are you?"

"I need more time, a couple of days Pete. I'll get the money. Tell Jimmy, all I need is two or three days."

"Robbie if it was up to me, you know I'd give you the time, but I'm just the messenger," Pete said with a slight movement of his shoulders and an apologetic grin at the corners of his mouth.

The message was in the form of a fist hammered into his gut two or three times. If the amount owed was larger than usual a few well placed kicks to the ribs underlined the message. The delivery was made by the large man in the too small suit who always accompanied the well-dressed Pete on these occasions. The last time "Horse" (no one dared to use his given name of Horace) had delivered the message he had whispered to a retching Robert, "Next time y'know, it could be your knee." Pointing his forefinger and raising his thumb as representative of a gun, "Bang and your knee is gone. See yah Robbie."

Peter Mallory, Jimmy's collector, had hated school. When he quit school he didn't follow the usual route of his peers and get a job. While he liked having money in his pocket, he wasn't prepared to work for it. At least not at any of the jobs his schoolmates earned a living at. He had other ideas. While still at school, he was arrested for shoplifting and let off with a warning. To get even with the newsagent who had caught him stealing a carton of cigarettes, he planned and carried out a burglary of his shop. His partner in crime was the slow-witted Horse.

The money from the till was soon spent on visits to the local flicks. Getting rid of the two pillow cases filled with cartons of cigarettes took a little more time. At fifteen, Peter was learning the ways of the streets fast. Horse was the one who offered cheap cigarettes to workers having a brew in their local; Peter stayed in the background. Horse, surrounded by clamouring workmen, was selling off the last cartons from the robbery when Jimmy sat down beside Peter.

"Buy you a drink young fella?"

"Sure." Some poofter trying to pick me up. Horse'll have fun sorting the nance out.

"What'll it be?

Looking around the smoke-filled room, Peter, who had never been in a pub until the cigarette lark, looked at the smiling face opposite and said, "A pint."

"Right you are young un. A pint it is." Catching the eye of the barman, Jimmy shouted above the din, "A pint for my friend."

Although he had never seen the big guy before, Peter's street sense, and a second long look, told him that this was no poofter. He had a tough look about him and his eyes spoke of a man it wouldn't be smart to cross. Trying to copy the drinkers around him, Peter took a hearty pull at his pint. Horse, who had joined them at the table, slapped him on the back as he began coughing and spluttering over the drink.

"Take it easy young un, plenty more where that came from. How about your friend? A pint for him too?"

Horse, came upright in his chair, looking to Peter for guidance, a pleading light in his eyes.

Peter's nod brought a beatific smile to the heavy features of his accomplice. Jimmy sized up the heavy-set Horse. It was difficult to assess his age. His meaty hands, thick wrists and bullet head set on wide shoulders telegraphed his strength; dull listless eyes his less than average intelligence. Sitting around the small table the only sound was Horse downing his beer.

"Your pal's thirsty." Enough of this patter; let's get down to cases, looking directly at Peter, he continued, "I'm looking for a couple lads I can trust. You and your pal, I think are the right fit. How would...."

Getting to his feet, Peter said, "Nothing doing. I'm doing OK on my own."

"Hear me out. If you don't like my offer you can walk away." Grabbing a passing waiter by the arm as he wove his way to the bar through the crowd, he ordered, "The same again." Cheeky little gett. "How much do you make floggin' fags? A few bob? I can put you in the way of a fair bit o' cash. More than you...."

"I'm not interested. I'm doin' OK."

The two headed for the door, leaving Jimmy muttering uncomplimentary remarks as he paid for the three frothing pints the waiter set before him with a flourish. Little gett! Ten minutes alone with the two of them. I'd soon sort them out. Rankled by the audacity of the youngster, Jimmy decided to keep tabs on the comings and goings of the pair.

Several months after his unsuccessful recruiting bid, Jimmy saw them on the street. The kid had black eyes and a bruised face; the other one walked with a limp and favoured his left side. Making a few enquiries, he found out that they had stepped on the toes of a petty crook when they stole cigarettes from his Mum's shop. When Mum's boy found out who the villains were, he talked to a few pals who were happy to gang up on Peter and Horse.

Before Peter and Horse were finally recruited by Jimmy they served a full criminal apprenticeship. Both had been sent away for a series of B & E's. Peter was always good for cigarettes at a great price. Back on the street, Peter decided that cheap fags were too chancy. But what enterprise next? Talking to Horse, although Horse never replied; he only nodded and made noises in his throat, Peter was in fact thinking out loud:

"I'm skint. We've got to get something going. Some fiddle that's safe. Maybe take over a couple of tarts. Walk into a jewellery store and do a smash and grab. Hey, would you like that Horse, smashing all that glass? You'd have a great time." Horse gave a wolfish grin and nodded enthusiastically. Peter had his problem solved when he met one of the "boys" he had known in the nick. He spotted him, a Glaswegian hard case, stealing an apple from a market fruit stall. Peter sidled up beside the thief and said, "Hello Jock, keeping your hand in I see."

The hard-eyed stare changed to a grin. "Well look who it is. Peter! Aye why the hell pay for it when you can steal it. Hello Horse. What are you two up to?" After a brief pause, "Lookin' for some action?"

"Wouldn't mind havin' a go, if the money was good."

"Skint? C'mon I'm buying. I've got to meet a couple of guys down the street. C'mon."

Striding into the George and Dragon, Jock kept going, ignoring the few people in the bar, through a fancy glass swing door that opened into a cosy little bar. The lone occupant looked up from his newspaper as they barged through the door.

"Order up what you want. I have to talk to Bobby."

Standing at the bar, Peter and Horse watched as Jock carried on an animated whispered conversation with the loner at the table. Jock, known to those who had been on a job with him as Mad Jock, was doing time for armed robbery when Peter got to know him. Motioning for them to join him at the table, Jock said, "Bring me a pint."

"Mmh! I needed that," Jock said and put down his half-empty pint jug. "Bobby, this is Peter and Horse. They're OK." The man named Bobby examined them with a cool detached look and nodded. Jock looked across the table at Bobby a question in his eyes. His answer was a slight nod.

Grinning Jock turned to Peter and said, "Can you drive? We need a driver for our next job. Our driver is down at the local nick. He was supposed to be here with Bobby. He's been nicked for possession of stolen goods; the silly prick."

"Sure."

"Do you have a licence?"

What d'you know, Bobby talks, "No, but I can drive anything with wheels."

"OK, but I want a demonstration. I'm not buying a pig in a poke."

"OK by me."

Horse nudged Peter, "What about Horse?"

"What about him?"

"He wants to rock and roll too. Horse is handy...."

"He's in. We need him with us inside."

The smash and grab robbery of a prominent jeweller's went without a hitch. Bobby and Jock picked up after Horse. Dressed in dungarees and carrying a plumber's satchel, Horse marched into the shop and using a heavy hammer hidden in his toolkit smashed the glass show cases. Stunned by the suddenness of the raid and the noise of the glass tumbling in shards at their feet, the sales staff stood petrified while thousands of pounds' worth of jewellery and watches were thrown into the plumber's satchel. In just over a minute after the first hammer blow fell, the robbers were crowding into the getaway car. Peter burned rubber as he pulled away from the kerb. Two lefts, a right then another left and he parked behind a sleek black Rover.

Bobby took charge, "Let's go, into the Rover and we're off. Nothing's been left in the car? OK, get a move on then."

Before getting into the new car, Peter looked up and down the street. As he bent down to get in beside Horse, he saw a man leave a Mini and stride purposefully towards the car they had just left. As Bobby drove away, he looked out the rear window and saw the man get behind the wheel of the getaway car.

The next two jobs were repeats of the first. After the second haul, Bobby said there would be one more job and then they would lie low until contacted for the next round of robberies. When quizzed by Pete, Jock said that the robberies were planned by some bent toff. Bobby was the only one who had any dealings with the man in the shadows.

After each robbery the four of them holed up in an apartment, never the same one twice. When Peter objected, Bobby said, "The geezer who plans the jobs insists that this is the way things are done. He says that the twenty-four hours after a robbery is when we are most likely to be picked up by the Bill."

"What does he know? I didn't see him sticking his neck out on the job. We take the risks. All he does is sit on his arse and plan."

"That's right and that's the way we'll stay out of the nick."

"OK, OK, pass me the bottle."

After the first flush of excitement at pulling the job off passed, Bobby brought out the booze and ordered take-out. Their bellies full, the women were ordered up and it was party time. Horse didn't like it when the whores were around and teasing him because he wouldn't go into one of the bedrooms with one of them. Jock, not feeling any pain, started to tease Horse and jokingly accused him of being a poofter. This was too much, the beast escaped its hiding place. Making unintelligible noises, Horse grabbed Jock by the throat. Before Pete could convince Horse to loosen his grip, Jock was semi-conscious.

When Jock got up from the floor where Horse had dropped him, he said, "You silly bugger. What'd you do that for? I was only kiddin'."

"You shouldn't have called me the name you did. My Mum ses not to have anything to do with women. They're dirty. Get you in trouble."

"It's OK Horse. Take it easy," Pete said. "I'll look after you. Remember I promised your Mum. It's OK, big fella. Jock didn't mean anything."

"Awll right Peter, if you say so."

Just then Bobby came back from delivering the stuff to the toff and with enough of an advance on the current job to keep the boys happy. Bobby had never met the planner, a fact he kept from the others. Each time he left the stuff at a location named by the planner. Detailed instructions and plans for each job were delivered by messenger. With the door locked he walked into the large kitchen and sensing something was wrong, he wanted to know, "What's going on here?" When no one answered, a menacing edge to his voice, he said, "What happened?"

When one of the women told him, he kicked at a chair sending it flying into the wall. "This is the sort of shite we don't need. This is just the sort of thing that could get us all sent down."

"What about them?" Pete said with a nod at the women.

"That's all been sorted out. They know what'll happen if they grass us. Right girls?" His answer was four bobbing heads.

Leaving the apartment two days after the robbery, the headlines in the papers had shrunk to one-column width. As he handed Peter his and Horse's share of the cash, Bobby repeated his end of job mantra. "Don't go off on a mad tear and start throwing cash about. Lay low."

"Be sure and give us a call when the next job comes up."

"Right ye are."

They never found out who shopped them. They had time to ponder who it might be, but the name of the informant escaped them. Horse's Mum bragging about the grand well-paying job her son had, went on a furniture buying spree. An envious neighbour, gossiping about Horse's sudden wealth, while waiting for her order of fish and chips, alerted a police informant eating at one of the tables. The informant needed a few quid to place a bet on a greyhound that was a dead cert to win the first race at the local track. The overheard conversation, somewhat embellished, was repeated to his ambitious police contact and earned him a couple of quid. The young sergeant was fast tracked to inspector as a result of his nosing around in response to the tip.

4

Robert's attempts to hide his gambling from his associates and acquaintances became more and more difficult as his fixation took an ever stronger grip on his life. Ever increasing amounts of money were required to still, briefly, the rampant thing within him. Among the few people who called Robert "friend" none were aware of his double life. Some of them, in his absence, made comments about his "old banger" of a car. "Old Rob" usually changed "wheels" every two years. Others, more effete, saw that his shirts were getting a bit frayed where it showed. They shrugged, Robbie was loaded. He had a great job. So he was going through a rough patch, trust old Rob, he'd sort things out.

Living only to place a bet, Robert was able to dodge a reckoning for a time, but as in all things there came a time when he couldn't ante up. Knowing that Jimmy's thugs would be looking to settle accounts, he stayed away from his usual haunts. He knew his game of hide-and-seek with the "heavies" couldn't go on for long. If he could only get enough time to put a couple of winners together, he could sort things out.

When the hoarse voice said his name in the dim-lit hallway it was too late to do anything except cringe in expectation of the first blow. He knew who was behind the voice; at the same time he realized that in his haste to get off the street and into his apartment he had failed to notice that most of the lights in the hallway were out.

"Robbie old chum, you should talk to the landlord about the lights.

Not dodging us Robbie? Me and Horse are hurt, offended that you would sneak around behind our backs. Ain't that right Horse?"

"Straight up Pete. We missed yah Robbie."

"We only want to have a quiet friendly little chat, that's all Robbie. Maybe it's because we don't have the proper lah de dah way of talking, like Robbie's pals. Could that be it Horse?"

"Nah Robbie is a pal Pete."

"OK if he is such a pal why does he do the Artful Dodger on us?"

"Look Pete, a coupla days and I'll have the cash, no problem."

Robert, his gut in a knot, unsuccessfully tried to put on a bold front. He knew that this was the end of the line with Jimmy. Somewhere in a back alley in a seedy rundown part of town some drunk would find him passed out, his blood pooling in the dirt. As the picture flashed across his mind's eye, Robert, his stomach heaving, began to retch. Horse gave him a push that slammed him against the wall as vomit splattered on the floor.

"You arse hole, if my pants are dirty I'll belt you around the head. You dumb prick," Pete cursed as he hastily stepped away from Robbie.

"Aren't you a right proper dickhead. Jeez he stinks Pete, what are we gonna do?"

"Let's get him upstairs, he can sort himself out and get some clean gear."

Half-an-hour later, a subdued Robert sat in the back of a car with Horse beside him. Pete had said Jimmy just wanted to talk, have a little chat as he put it. Robert was scared. He owed Jimmy a bundle; he would make an example of him. It was all over, he was as good as dead. Jimmy would kill him and dump the body in some alley. He could see the puddle of blood from his slashed throat. Oh God! He shivered. Horse would do the job after beating him senseless. He sat, in a fever of fear, hunched in the corner of the car. Horse pulled him out of the car, and helped by Pete, hauled him down the alley between buildings to the back door of the club.

Jimmy was at his desk, a bottle and a glass at his elbow. When Robert and his escort entered the office he poured himself a large whisky. After a couple of sips, he looked over to where Robert, with head bowed, waited for the first blow. Pete, his hands in his pockets, and Horse with arms folded, nonchalant onlookers, waited for their orders. Horse, a disappointed look on his face, was ordered to wait outside in the bar.

Unknown to Robert, one of Jimmy's drug couriers had been picked up by Customs. It must have been a tip off as they knew exactly where the drugs were hidden on the long distance lorry. And now he needed a temporary replacement to ferry drugs while he organized a regular courier.

"Now Robbie, you are in a bit of a bind, aren't you old boy. You owe me five thousand smackers, a nice tidy sum you'll agree. The cat got your tongue?" said with a movement of his lips and show of teeth that might have been a smile.

"Gimme a couple of days Jimmy. I'll get the...."

"It's OK Robbie, now listen. You will pay what you owe me that's for sure and here is the way you will settle up."

"A couple of days, that's ... ."

"Shut up and listen you stupid bastard. I'll do the talking here. On your next trip to France, phone me at least a couple of days before you take off. Give me all the details of where you are going, how long you will be over there and who it is you will be flying. Got that, simple enough eh Robbie? The return trip will be the really interesting part. Oh yes Robbie, on the way back you will ferry a few kilos of a restricted substance and deliver it to me here at the club, bring a date, the drinks are on me."

"For God's sake do you know what you are asking me to do? I could go to prison, Jimmy I'll do anything but not dope."

"That's the deal, pay up or else," the threat brought Robert up short. "All you have to do is walk through with the stuff in your briefcase. The Customs blokes know you. It'll be a doddle. Trust me Robbie you can do it."

In the time between the threat and the flight to France, his imagination ran wild. Often he would wake up in the night with the clang of cell doors still ringing in his head. He became irritable and morose. When Lindsay, his current date, commented lightly about the change he snapped at her, "Nag, nag, mind your own business. We're not married."

Surprised, at this outburst, she gave him a long look and putting her hand over his asked, "What's the matter Robert? It's not like you to be," she paused searching for the right word, "to be like this, so abrupt."

He wanted to tell her, but couldn't. No one knew that his gambling had gone beyond, way beyond, having a flutter on the ponies. He knew that he would go through with the drug deal. The very real fear of Jimmy had an immediacy that outweighed any imagined fear of punishment.

The day of the deal he had a brief stopover in Paris before flying to Rouen. The pick-up at Rouen went smoothly. The transfer was made in a tiny cluttered office at the rear of a small café. The owner, in passable English, invited Robert to join him for a coffee. In a cold sweat, with his imagination conjuring up pictures of gendarmes rushing in to haul him off, he refused. But the owner was not to be put off. He insisted, grabbing Robert by the sleeve of his jacket. The owner's voice became louder each time the invitation was repeated. In between the invitations, he kept yelling in French to someone in the kitchen located behind the zinc-covered bar.

The coffee was brought to the table by a young woman. Robert who had been literally pushed into a seat by his smiling host was introduced to the waitress. The beaming face across the table proudly declared "My daughter Simone." He shook the small dainty hand offered shyly. A long loose blue dress couldn't hide her generous figure. Had he been more aware and had his wits about him, Robert would have seen through Dad's clumsy attempt at matchmaking. He gulped the coffee, thanked Simone and her father and hurried out the door.

Airborne he began to think about getting the dope out of the aerodrome on landing. His imagination, taken up with a series of wild scenarios of what would happen at Customs, was threatening to turn his brain to mush. Gripping the controls hard he mouthed "get a grip." If he didn't control his emotions and put on a bold front, he might as well hold out his hands for the cuffs.

His co-pilot, as soon as he completed his landing procedures, excused himself and hurried towards Customs. Robert dawdled across the tarmac. The people in Customs were sharp; he had seen them at work. They could spot a phoney a mile off. They were sure to notice that his briefcase was heavier than usual. They weren't dummies. The briefcase was heavier by three kilos. He was sure to be stopped and asked to open it. What'll I do? With each step towards the Customs shed the briefcase seemed to get heavier. God what if the locks on the briefcase gave way and the stuff fell out.

His footsteps echoing in the large shed, he realized that if he was to get the stuff through Customs he would have to put on a first-class performance. I sure as hell don't want to go to jail, get a grip Robert. The thought of jail stiffened his resolve. He smiled at the officer on duty, who waved him on. When one of the other officers called him as he was about to leave the Customs area, he came close to wetting his pants. Steeling himself, he waited. Do I run or just wait and talk myself out of this fix, he thought.

"What do you fancy at Newmarket this afternoon? I hear that 'Sunny Boy' in the second is a good bet."

Robert gasped. "Sure, try a couple of quid if you want to gamble, but my money is on 'Maple Jim Jam' in the same race. He's a cert. I've got fifty quid on him. He should romp in at least a couple of lengths ahead of the field."

"Well thank you Robert, but my money's on Sunny Boy."

Robert caught up in the rush, the excitement that only gambling gave him, forgot about what was in his briefcase. "If you are so sure of Sunny Boy, how about a little side bet. I have ten pounds that says he won't even place."

"You're on. It's like stealing candy from a kid. A tenner, right?"

It took three more trips ferrying coke before he was off the hook to Jimmy. The fear of discovery, the terror of the consequences if caught accompanied him on each trip. For weeks after bringing the dope through Customs he relived the fear, the terror, nightly waking up in a sweat after struggling to escape from some dark maze. On one such awakening it hit Robert like a blow to the gut; Jimmy now had the power to control his life. And at any time could order him to do another drug run. A phone call by one of Jimmy's thugs posing as a concerned citizen was all it would take to send him to prison. Even if the police had no proof of his drug smuggling they could ruin his flying career simply by questioning him about a drug case. He could imagine the talk:

"Have you heard the latest? Robbie Halthorpe had a chat with the heavies from the drug squad."

No, I knew he bet on the ponies, but drugs, never. I don't believe it."

"There's no smoke without fire."

"That was all though, he wasn't detained?"

"No, but maybe the next time we hear of Robbie it will be under big headlines in the papers, complete with picture."

Desperate to escape Jimmy's grip on his life, Robert began to look for another flying job. His search was successful much sooner than he had hoped for. And all as the result of his mother's nagging.

"Yes mother, of...."

"You always claim you are so busy. Daddy's having some people down this weekend for golf. Why don't you join us then?"

"I'm busy this weekend mother. I have to pay...."

"Don't be silly Robert. Have one of your friends take over for you."

"Mother it's not that simple. I have obligations. I can't just up and walk away from them."

"I agree, you have obligations to your family. I haven't seen you for months."

Another boring weekend and of course there will be the little darlings dashing about and making a nuisance of themselves. "I'm sorry mother I can't visit this weekend. I'll try next month, really, I will."

"You always say that Robert; anyone would think you don't want to see the family. Just this once for Mummy. I'd love to see you. I'll get cook to make your favourite dishes. Come down. Robert."

It has been some time. I suppose I could go down. It might be fun; last time Sybil was a surprise. Seconds would be nice. "Mother don't go on so. For you, I'll try and get away.

"Oh Robert it will be so nice to see you. Come early so I can have you all to myself for a bit. See you Friday."

"Now mother, slow down, I said I would try and get down this weekend."

"Yes dear, try hard. It will be so nice to see you."

I may as well go down, — I'll phone Sybil — if I don't she'll keep on with her nagging phone calls. People down for golf; Dad's playing the golf gambit, he's a crafty one.

Clients were invited down to Halthorpe House for a weekend in the country. Unless they insisted otherwise, they came down in the train with Halthorpe and walked the half mile to the house. After dinner the ritual was for all to walk down to the Maiden's Head in the village and take in some of the local colour and a couple of pints of the local brew.

Saturday morning was usually spent on a tour of the extensive grounds and garden. If the previous night's visit to the pub precluded the walk about, a slow saunter to the village for some hair of the dog was in order. The afternoon was given over to golf and when there were no golfers, a lazy afternoon in the house or perhaps a drive in the country.

A duffer on the golf course, Halthorpe gave up trying to improve his game when he made the discovery that his business success with Americans was in direct relation to his poor showing on the golf course; they loved to win. He always suggested that a "bob or two" be wagered on the outcome of the game. When paying up, he made a fuss, swearing that if he had known he was playing a professional he wouldn't have wagered a penny. The Americans feeling great and secretly pleased at having beat the crap out of the limey were now primed for the initial pitch, made in the clubhouse over drinks.

Sunday after church and lunch in the pub the walk back to the house was when Halthorpe with rueful glances would make mention of his drubbing on the links before deftly moving on to make his final pitch for whatever was the current deal. It could be real estate, investing in a new or old business, gold plated venture capital or a tax write-off, all grist for the Halthorpe legal mill.

Arriving early as requested Robert spent time with Mummy chatting about inconsequential things in the solarium. On the phone Sybil's mother told him she was spending the weekend with friends in Scotland; it was to be a dull two days. At dinner he met a Michael Braithwaite and Sir Robert Grant-James. Sir Robert was represented by his father's law firm. From the conversation at dinner, Robert gathered that his father was advising Sir Robert on the sale of his shares in a group of newspapers in America. Braithwaite, he guessed, was being wined and dined as a prospective client.

Saturday, while he and his father were having an early morning walk Robbie found out that Braithwaite was causing a stir in "the City". He was becoming a major figure in the manufacture of plastics, had bought a group of county weeklies and was making a bid for the Valley Group of newspapers in Canada. It was rumoured that Braithwaite was also interested in acquiring radio and television stations in the U.S. He already had a toehold in this area in Australia.

Talk at breakfast was about airports. Braithwaite said, "It's ridiculous the amount of time spent hanging around airports. It's so damned frustrating."

"Not to mention the time spent circling on hold. I agree Michael. I don't travel as much as you and Sir Robert but I hate to spend time looking down at the city I should be doing business in."

"Exactly, that is why I am being driven to conclude that it would be cheaper to have my own plane."

When Robert heard Braithwaite's mention of buying a jet he listened closely. Flying a private jet, just the job; could be my ticket to good times, away from Jimmy.

"Perhaps cheaper, but not likely," Robert said. "There are advantages though. One is, you would be able to set down at small airports without having to queue up in the air. Also you could get to wherever you wanted to go on the ground faster. Also you wouldn't have the bother at Customs."

"Surely you would have to deal with Customs no matter where you landed Robert."

"That's true Dad, but there wouldn't be the usual line-ups you find at the big airports. Another thing you would escape is the traffic tie-ups you find at every major airport. All of which means, when flying by a regular airline, when you get to your meeting you are in such a foul mood no one wants to talk business with you."

"Rather a depressing picture Robert."

"But fairly accurate Dad."

"Robert is a pilot. Flies mostly to the continent."

"I have done a few long hauls, some of them over water Dad. That flight to Africa with the tribal chieftain was the most memorable. He looked over at the other two and continued, "Had to put down on a dirt runway in some backwater in Ghana. The plane, a jet behaved beautifully, I shoe horned the B-N, Brampton-Naismith in with just feet to spare. It was quite an experience."

"What is your opinion of the Brampton-Naismith Robert? Have you a lot of time on them? I hear that the Lear is a very popular business jet."

"Speaking as a pilot, they fly beautifully. The cabin is a bit cramped, and providing you don't want to serve a banquet," said with a grin, "the Lear will get you there and back comfortably."

"Interesting. You favour the Lear then?"

"I have flown a Lear, but the B-N is the one I have time on. However there are other business jets on the market. The Lear as you no doubt know is an American product. There are several models available in Europe. If I was buying a jet I'd have a look at the Brampton-Naismith. Its range exceeds the Lear by quite a bit. A trip across the Atlantic would be no problem."

"Buy British, yes, I like that."

Nothing more was said about business jets until Braithwaite, Grant-James and Halthorpe senior returned from the golf course in the late afternoon. Robert, lounging in a big soft easy chair and trying to stay awake, heard laughter coming from the study and decided to investigate. His siblings and their children, their many children, were off adventuring at a neighbour's farm. He found his father and his guests relaxing with drinks and replaying the game. The other member of the foursome was absent on some sudden business emergency. Robert poured himself a drink and sat down. His presence was recognized by nods from the golfers. Judging from the air of good will and bonhomie alive in the room, Robert guessed that the business talk had gone well. Braithwaite leaning towards Robert over the arm of his chair said, "Your advice was appreciated. Would you consider giving me a hand if I decide to buy a business jet?"

"Of course, I'd be happy to help in any way I can." Things are looking up. On the Wednesday of the following week there was a note in his letter slot in the hangar office informing him that Braithwaite wanted to talk to him.

"Hello Mr. Braithwaite, Robert Halthorpe, I just got your message."

'Hello Robert. I'm looking for a pilot for my latest acquisition. Would you be interested in flying for me — a Brampton-Naismith business jet?"

"Certainly!"

"When can you start? I need you to get acquainted with the plane and fly it back to Dilsworth as soon as possible."

"Could you give me a couple of days to sort things out here? It is rather sudden, but I am sure I can sort things out in a couple of days," he said hastily.

"Fine. I'll expect to hear from you in forty-eight hours. I could be out of the office when you call, just leave a message with Jonesy, my right arm."

Surprised by the soft-spoken female voice, Robert, expecting Braithwaite's "right hand" to be male and with an ego, hesitated before saying, "Mr. Braithwaite, he's expecting my call."

"Mr. Braithwaite is out of the office. Your name please?"

"Halthorpe,Robert...."

"We have been expecting your call, Mr. Halthorpe."

Surprised at the no-nonsense voice and the attitude it conveyed, he thought, whew what am I letting myself in for here? It seemed like an easy touch, the way Braithwaite described his firm. I don't want to become involved with some penny-pinching johnny-come-lately millionaire. We never did discuss salary.

The soft female voice brought him back from his internal debate, "Mr. Halthorpe when can you begin your duties? You have a choice of staying in a flat near the aerodrome or the gatehouse at 'The Grange' Mr. Braithwaite's home."

"The place near the 'drome' would be just fine." Living in Braithwaite's lap would cramp my style, he grinned inwardly. "Would Monday be agreeable? Give me the weekend to move in."

"Monday would be fine. Is your passport in order? The office is located in the village of Dilsworth, near Chobham. From where you are the A3 would be the quickest route. At Esher take A317 to Ottershaw and from there the A319 to Chobham, drive through the town and about two miles further on you will see the road sign for Dilsworth. When you arrive in the village, ask anyone the way to the office. It's a large Georgian house on Murrin Street, everyone knows it. We'll see you here then at seven o-clock Mr. Halthorpe."

On the Monday he found the no-nonsense approach typified in his earlier telephone conversation carried over into the office. He spent the morning with Jonesy completing the paperwork associated with his hiring. The salary was generous. At lunch in the staff dining room he met the other members of the team. The young dynamic group, mocked by outsiders as the "Brains Trust," that Braithwaite had gathered around him, were quick to inform the newcomer of the humble beginnings of their boss.

5

Braithwaite at fourteen, large-boned, standing five feet nine inches and weighing one hundred and twenty pounds, had no trouble getting a summer job with Beadleton's leading demolition firm. The town of about forty-five thousand, south of Wandsworth had seen better days. In the aftermath of economic change, the firm was busy tearing down the old to make room for the new. His parents were not happy with their son's choice of summer employment. Nothing was said to Michael. He was a smart lad, getting top marks in school. Popular with his classmates, several of the girls thought he was "brilliant." His tousled taffy coloured hair, hazel eyes and his oblong face with its bony features they found attractive. Surely he could do better than labouring with a glorified junk man.

Michael was happy working with the salvage gang. The first few days on the job he spoke when spoken to, worked hard and never shirked any of the heavier work. This helped to allay the suspicion that perhaps he was a municipal spy, on the job to see if there was any hanky panky going on. He was different, his work clothes were clean and tidy, fresh ones every Monday. He wore sturdy leather boots not the shoddy shoes or trainers they wore. It wasn't uncommon for them to turn up for work not having washed and to have slept in their work clothes. The derelict buildings "squats" they lived in had no running water and if they cooked a warm meal it was done over a portable camping stove. Most of the workers were heavy smokers and by the time pay day came around they were out of smokes and groceries. Their sandwiches were usually bread and margarine; no cash meant no sandwich meat not even jam to go with the marg.

Pay days the gang dropped in to the nearest pub after work, "To get rid of the dust." Michael tagged along. Sitting in a booth, the air heavy with cigarette smoke and everyone talking at once, he drank it all in. He was having a great time. Plans were made for the assault on some, "smashin' piece o stuff's" virginity, by the younger ones. The older men discussed form, rattling off chapter and verse on the horse or dog they fancied.

Michael always had a cider. A non-drinker, the cider was a standing joke with the gang. His first pay day when he said he didn't drink gave rise to a noisy chorus: "What you don't drink? — Jeez a Bible puncher, next thing, he'll be trying to save us—and I thought we were gonna be pals - That does it I'm quittin'. I can't work with a bloke who won't down a pint— Look Mike you can't sit with us and not have a jug in your hand - He's right Mike, it lowers the tone of the group."

Looking around at the circle of serious faces, he decided he had better leave. Just when he was having a good time! He started to get up and was pushed down into his seat by two of the grinning drinkers. The serious faces fell apart in laughter. He joined in the fun and said that to keep up the high standards and the decorum of the group he would have a cider. This was greeted with whistles and shouts. A non-smoker, the gang soon found out that he could be "tapped" for a "sub" when funds were low. This ready access to funds at no interest was to test Michael's metal and was to be the breakthrough to full acceptance as a member of the work gang.

"Here's your money, you bloody shylock," and the money handed over with a playful push to emphasise that the loan had been appreciated. Michael found the inverted thank you's offered by his workmates odd. All of them were prompt in returning loans, but it was always accompanied by a disparaging remark. Puzzled and upset by this seeming lack of appreciation, he worried that it was because they didn't like him. Before the summer ended he had the answer. They didn't want anyone to think that they were being lah de dah, putting on airs. They were labourers and proud of it, not for them the effete manners of the "toffy noses." He enjoyed their rough, often racy humour and camaraderie.

"I can't pay yer this week, I'm skint." Heads came up, with pay packets in pockets the gang was getting ready to head to the local boozer for a couple of quickies. Looks were exchanged, Big Ed was giving the kid a hard time.

"You owe me ten bob."

"I told ya I'm flat stoney broke. Are ya deaf?"

"How can you be broke. I saw you get your pay. Gimme the ten bob!"

"I'll give you a belt along the side o yer 'ead you cheeky young bugger. I'll see you next week." Big Ed turned and started to walk away. Not a word was said by the others who were now all looking on at the "drama".

Yelling, "Gi'me my ten bob, you crook." Michael rushed at the big man. Caught off guard, never thinking that the kid would try and give him a hard time, Big Ed staggered and almost went down as he tripped over a pile of bricks. Michael, like a terrier after a bull, got in close and began landing blows on the other's chest. A couple of the wild swings with all his hard muscle behind them landed on the welcher's face. Shaking his head Ed started swinging, landing one on Michael's forehead. The next swing dropped Michael among the bricks. Ed wasn't finished; he would "sort out" this little gett. About to deliver a kick, he was stopped before his size twelve did any damage.

"Lift a finger and we'll finish what Mike started." Looking around at the intent faces, Big Ed turned to walk away. "Hey before you go, pay Mike his ten bob. Takin' advantage like that, you bag o shite. Here gi' me the ten bob and bugger off."

"Oh my jaw. Where is he?" A groggy Mike was helped to his feet to a chorus of approvals from his workmates: "Good for you Mike - Hey, you gave him a couple of good ones - You're OK," this last remark from the man who had shoved Big Ed when he was about to use his boots.

Not all the salvageable material went into the company's trucks. The foreman on the job picked over the lead, copper, iron railings and any other "good stuff" squirreling away enough to support his fondness for whiskies with beer chasers and willing women. Bricks were another source of cash in hand. Hobby gardeners, always keen to enhance their tiny plots, used the bricks to build walkways around their flower beds. The ornate wooden hand rails that had decorated the stairs in some of the older houses were always good for a few quid.

The foreman ensured that no one would "grass" him to the company by spreading the money around. He "divvied up" a percentage of the cash made in under the table deals with the regulars on the job. The result of Michael's sweat on the job and the "back handers" from the foreman amounted to a tidy sum. At the end of his first summer he had two hundred pounds in the bank and one hundred in a tin can hidden in his room. The hundred was mad money for use should a profitable deal come his way. Back at school with its endless homework, he longed for the work of summer and the cash it brought.

His Mum and Dad insisted that he complete his schooling. Mum was the law in the Braithwaite home. Dad enjoyed working in his garden or in the small hothouse built on the side of the house. Saturdays after supper, Mum and Dad would go to the Boar's Head where she would have a port and lemon and a gossip with her neighbours. Dad would put away a couple of pints while playing darts with his pals. Dad was office manager at Beadleton Metal, a family-owned metal fabricating company.

Michael worked summers with the wrecking crew until he left

school at sixteen when he became a permanent member of the gang. His Mum and Dad had ambitious plans for their youngest son, attendance at a good university being the primary one. He was adamant in his refusal to follow the path chosen for him by his parents. Most of the heated discussions on his future ended with Michael holding up his two brothers as examples of not having had a higher education.

"Mum, Joe and Bert are doing all right for themselves. Their kids, your grandchildren, don't look starved to me. Why can't I do as well in my job?"

"Michael don't talk such nonsense. You know very well they have good jobs, respectable jobs. You work for a junk...."

"Mum! I don't see where there is any difference between Joe's job as a plumber, and Bert's as a tool and die maker, and my chosen profession."

His using the word profession was a way of teasing his mother. At first, when asked by neighbours and acquaintances what line of work he was in, he would reply with a merry light in his eyes and a straight face, "The firm I work for specializes in landscape rearranging." This utterance was usually met with a nod of the enquirer's head and, "Mm must be interesting." If they asked for details, he would tell the enquirer, "It's not the sort of job suited to just anyone. Only a few choose to work in the field of landscape rearranging—it can be dangerous. Working for Beadleton Demolition is a hard difficult job, but somebody has to do it." When the enquirer realized that they had been "had" they shook their head and grinned or walked off in a huff.

Mum and Dad just didn't understand. He wanted to be his own boss. He held out against all the tears of his mother and the pleas of his father and stayed with the wrecking gang. He was making good money and he had a second source of ready cash. Weekends, along with Liam, a pal from the gang, who had an old banger of a car, they would scour the countryside, attend auctions in search of bargains which were then sold for a profit at car boot sales.

Working with the wrecking gang Michael met an assorted batch of characters. Besides the six who were regular members of the gang, there were the others. Depending on how big the job, the "extras" could number between eight and twenty. He enjoyed their company, their yarns of the bundles of loot raked in from their bold schemes. He never questioned the truth of their stories or asked why they were working as day labourers? He knew the yarns were just that and was also smart enough not to ask silly questions.

Inevitably there would be one of the extras who saw the fresh faced kid as ripe for picking. The scam usually involved some shady if not outright unlawful scheme that would double his investment. The approach was always made when none of the others in the gang were around. With regret dripping off every syllable, the bad actor would bemoan that he couldn't make a killing because of being short a few quid. A brief pause followed by a quick rundown of what was at stake and how easy it would be to grab it.

"The safe, open it with a hair pin." A few lousy quid was all that prevented the biggest robbery ever to hit the country from making headlines in the papers. After a meaningful pause, accompanied by a deep sigh the punch line would be delivered. "A few quid. I've got most of the cash, all I need is another fifty." Another pause, "I hear you have a few nicker put by Mike. How would you like to make an investment and double it in a night. Are you game? You wouldn't have to get involved. It's money for old rope."

Mike's response was always that he was saving up to send his sick grannie to a sanatorium in Switzerland. This answer usually spiked the tale of easy profit. Raffles would walk away after he acknowledged Mike's riposte with a knowing look, sometimes it was a shrug and a hint of a grin.

The hungry looks cast by a new man at the "doorstep" sandwich in Mike's fist prompted him to offer half of his second sandwich. Bert had joined the gang just before they downed tools for their midday meal. The offer was readily accepted and wolfed down. A tin cup of tea from Michael's Thermos was drunk with much smacking of lips. The newcomer was dressed in a much wrinkled business suit, expensive shoes, shirt and tie.

"Thanks mate. Would you have a fag on yah?"

"Don't smoke."

"Haven't had a fag in days. I'm skint. Fast women and slow horses."

"You're a bettin' man then. What happened?"

"Had this nice soft touch, floggin' used clothing, most of it going overseas. Money for old rope. Anyway met this woman in a pub one night, a smasher, she was some babe, believe me. She had it all, looks, in bed, great, knew all the twists and turns. She took me for every red cent. Crafty bitch had me buying her fancy jewellery and clothes, went as far as buying her a fur coat. That wasn't enough for the cow; she got into my bank book. And of course I wanted to show her off so we ate in all the best places. Bet on the ponies. There we were swankin' around the paddock with all the toffs. It was great — while it lasted. I ended up owing the bookies a bundle. When I paid them all off, I was broke."

Michael, at seventeen, thanks to his workmates, had a maturity beyond his years. Back at work, Michael looked at Bert, grinned and said, "She took off with the lot, the whole kit and kaboodle. You daft bugger. You should've known she'd scarper when the money ran out."

Bert paused in his shovelling and gave Michael a quizzical look and straightened up. Some of the other workers who had been listening to Bert's tale of good times stopped work, waiting. What would the new man do? Shrugging he answered, "Aint love grand?" and smiled. "I wasn't thinking, I was using my dick, not my head. What the hell! We had some great times. Not to worry Michael me boy just you wait I'll be back up there where the money is. I was born under a lucky star. I'll show the lot o' them."

At eighteen, Michael had a healthy bank account, thanks to his skinflint ways and a bit of luck. Living rent-free at home, his expenses were minimal. The flicks and fish and chips on a Saturday night, that was it. Liam usually tagged along, the two of them having spent the afternoon at an auction or a car boot sale. Occasionally, they drove around in Liam's old car, visiting junk shops, pawn shops and scrap dealers. The two of them in their constant search for "stuff" became the subject of much good humoured joshing from the other boot sale regulars. Their enthusiasm and the fun they had in buying and selling brought them customers who wanted to unload some stuff that had fallen into their hands and which they had no desire to keep. One such sale had far-reaching consequences for Michael.

"I hear that you two sometimes buy furniture and the like. I've got some, would you be interested in having a gander at it? It belonged to me Mum and the wife doesn't want it."

Liam looked at Michael and with a slight move of his head informed him that he didn't think they should bother with the furniture. Michael gave a slight shrug and asked, "How many pieces of furniture? Is there anything else? We don't usually buy big lots of furniture. Mind you we have been known to buy a couple of smaller good quality pieces."

"Tell you, I don't know anything about the quality. The wife says it's too old fashioned for our place. It's damn heavy too. Bloody hell, I thought you two would have snapped it up. One bloke offered me ten quid for the lot, said he would do it as a favour. It has to be worth more than a tenner."

"Well you may be right there, but we don't buy a lot of furniture. My advice is take the tenner and get rid of it."

"Hold on a minute Liam, not so fast. Surely we could have a look at it. It won't cost us anything. Maybe we can help the chap out and take it off his hands."

"Not me Michael. If you buy this stuff you are on your own. We'd never be able to sell it and where would we store the damned stuff, tell me."

"I'd like to see this furniture. Curiosity has got the better of me."

"Go ahead I'll look after things here. If you're daft enough to buy the stuff, I'll give you a hand to move it, but I'm not interested in buying it."

"Good, my car is out on the street. It's a half-hour drive." After driving for close to forty minutes, most of the way on country side roads, the driver pulled into a short laneway and stopped in front of a two-storey stone house. Pointing to a large shed beside the house he said, "The stuff is in there. I'll get the key."

Pulling open a half of the large door, Michael was surprised to find the shed filled with furniture. What have I walked into here? Jeez there must be enough furniture here to furnish one helluva big house. Well I suppose I had better go through the motions and keep him happy. A walkway had been left down the middle of the piled furniture. Walking into the shed, he could see that the furniture was in good shape, it obviously hadn't been stored for long. Opening drawers and examining the pieces that were at hand he concluded that the furniture was quality stuff and not as unwieldy as had been advertised by the anxious-faced man beside him. He never showed any more than a casual interest in the furniture, not even when he spotted an oak roll top desk at the rear of the pile. Now that would be worth a few bob. There are a couple of mirrors that look good.

"What do you think?"

"It's nice stuff, Mr….."

"Anders, call me Evan."

"As I said, it's well-made furniture. I'm Michael. I can take some pieces off your hands, but there is too much here for me to handle it all."

"The wife won't like that. She wants to get rid of the lot. Couldn't you see your way to taking it all, lock stock and barrel?"

"I'd like to help Evan, but where would I store it?"

Just then a young woman with a small child in tow joined them. "Don't forget that old chest goes too. I want everything from the old house to go."

"I can only take a few pieces Mrs. Anders. There is way too much here for me to handle. Have you considered putting the stuff up for auction?"

"Evan spoke to McDermid in town, but he is too busy right now to even come out and have a look at it. Seems there is some big country estate that he is appraising. The second one he went to for some unknown reason wouldn't listen to Evan, got up on his high horse and said he would come round in ten days. That was three weeks ago. Anyway I want the stuff out of here before the end of the month, that's final."

While Mrs. Anders was telling her tale, Michael listened with half an ear while he tried to think of how to get his hands on the few pieces he wanted. There was only one way he realized, and that was to buy all the furniture. It was the middle of the month, why couldn't he give them a few extra quid and leave it here while he tried to sell it? The desk and mirrors he knew, he could get rid of for a decent price. Taking out his wallet he looked at Evan and his wife and with a doleful face began counting five pound notes.

"I'll take the furniture off your hands. It's a gamble, but nothing ventured nothing gained, right Mrs. Anders?" His answer was a warm smile. "But, there is a but Mrs. Anders," this was in answer to the look that she gave her husband. "Let me store the furniture here until the end of the month; I'll pay you three hundred for the furniture and fifteen for storage."

A smiling Mrs. Anders nodded her head and said, "Just be sure you take that old trunk. It's over along side the house under the tarp. Take everything there, boxes and all, I want it all gone."

"That's a relief, now I can use my shed. Thanks Michael."

"We have a deal then Mrs. Anders, Evan is happy are you? Now comes the important question, who gets the cash?"

"She gets the money. I have my shed back, we're both happy."

The shed was emptied within days of the sale and Michael was richer by nine hundred pounds and change. He forgot about the old trunk and the two wooden boxes that were part of the sale until reminded by his father. They were cluttering up his shed and had been for weeks, he complained. There was no key for the trunk and the lids of the large boxes used to ship tea were firmly nailed. Dropping the large screwdriver he had used to break the lock, he lifted the lid of the trunk. There were clothes that when examined carefully were found to be old time uniforms, all neatly folded. The strong odour of moth balls made him sneeze. Laying the clothes out on the work bench, he looked them over. They seemed to be in pretty good shape. Under the last of the uniforms were a number of bundles wrapped in linen. Excited, he grabbed one of them and hastily un-wrapped it. What he saw took his breath away, a handsome coffee pot. Examining it he found some marks on the bottom, hardly breathing he looked closely at the marks. The pot was sterling silver, dare he unwrap the other bundles? What would he find? When his father came to see what, if anything his son had discovered, he saw a large tray with a tea pot, a coffee pot, a large jug sugar bowl and cream jug on it and all atop some old clothes.

"My gosh Michael, am I seeing things? It is silver, isn't it? Wait until your mother sees this. I'm going to get her."

With his mother bubbling with excitement and her appraisal of the silver service loud in his head, "Oh son it's lovely. It must be old, it's beautiful," he set to with quick hands to get at what was in the tea boxes. Throwing aside the top he cautiously put his hand into the sawdust that filled the box. His mother gave a squeak of delight when he produced a small plate. Taking the plate from her son she turned it over looking for the name of the manufacturer. There was no name, just some squiggles that upon closer scrutiny became Chinese characters. At least she thought they were, that or Japanese. The fragile plates with their delicate colours were like nothing they had ever seen before. After unpacking a few, Michael stopped. Looking at his mother he said, "What d'ya think Mum. This isn't your ordinary every day set of dishes. There is a small fortune here."

"I have never seen anything like this in all my life. Look, hold a plate up and hold your hand behind it and you can see the shadow of your hand."

"You're right, fantastic. There is no way that I'm to sell this stuff at a boot sale. Could I leave the stuff here for a bit Dad? Gimme a couple of days to make some phone calls. This stuff should do well at auction."

"McDermid would just love to get his hands on this stuff."

"Oh no Mum. I don't want any of the locals handling this lot. This is going to one of the big auction houses up in London. This is classy stuff."

A month later a twelve place setting of Ming china, with extras; a silver tea set; and several uniforms, went under the hammer at a well-known London auction house. After the sale Michael's bank account increased by sixty two thousand pounds. Some time later it decreased by two thousand. After hemming and hawing for days on whether to share his windfall with the Anders and having decided, there followed days of inward debate on how much to pay them.

When he handed over the money to the couple he explained that the stuff had sold for more than he expected. The Anders' were all over him in their appreciation of their "good fortune." Evan pumped his hand and repeated his thanks while his wife stood beside him beaming. Taking her husband's arm she said, "Now we can get that new stove and some nice things for the house."

Caught up in the excitement of their "windfall" they never thought to ask their benefactor how much he got out of the transaction. When Michael asked how the furniture came to be in their possession, Mrs. Anders said, "Most of the furniture belonged to Evan's mother. The roll top desk and some of the smaller items she got from a neighbour. Actually her neighbour had died, she was a widow, and the family didn't want to be bothered with the stuff."

"And where did the chest and two boxes come from?" he asked. Hoping that no questions would be asked about what was in them.

"The old boxes, they were part of the stuff that the family gave Evan's Mum. The neighbour's husband had inherited all of it from his father who had been in China as a young man. Again, thank you for being so honest. Most dealers would have kept the money and said nothing about it."

A week after the big deal, Liam quit the wrecking crew. He said, over a pay day pint, that he had joined the Army. With money in the bank, and Liam gone, Michael began to think seriously about going into business. He knew what he wanted to do. Prompted by Bert's yarns of the easy money he had made in the second-hand clothing business Michael decided to look into how the business worked. He got to know a couple of small timers who sold out of the back of their van and through them got to know where the full-time dealers were to be found. With this information Michael most weekends could be found mooching around the haunts of those engaged in the business. Slowly he got to be on nodding terms with them, and in time, got to know one or two quite well.

They were a secretive lot and while friendly and seemingly outgoing, they never even hinted at where they picked up their merchandise. That all changed the day he heard a dealer ranting to a friend about his bad luck in missing a great deal. When the dealer was alone and gazing morosely into his third cup of coffee, he walked over and asked if it was all right if he sat down.

"What's up Harry. You don't look your usual cheery self."

"Hello Michael, it's nothing. Nothing, I lost... aw hell forget it."

"If you say so Harry, but it doesn't appear to me to be nothing. I've never seen you so worked up. It has to be pretty important to get you this upset."

"You're a nice young man Michael, you're right. I've missed out on the deal of the year. Keep this under your hat. Last Friday I went out on a limb and bought a big shipment; had to borrow some of the readies to close the sale. Now two days later I get word of the deal of the century and I'm broke. It's all tied up in Friday's buy. The deal of the century, damn it."

"Can't you get a loan from one of your mates?"

"Michael you are an innocent. My mates would slit my throat to get their grubby paws on this stuff, it's quality."

They sat quietly in the booth, each with his thoughts. Harry gazing fixedly at the wallpaper and puzzling how he could get his hands on some cash. Michael fighting to contain his excitement realized, if he played his cards right he could be in business. Harry's concern at the loss was attested to by the deep worry lines on his face. How much would it take and could I handle it? This calls for finesse.

"You know Harry there is a way out of your predicament." I held up my hand as he was about to talk, "Let me finish. I don't think you will favour it, but you could walk away with a few bob."

"Well tell me, don't sit there and keep me guessing. What is it?" With raised eyebrows and a hard sarcastic edge to his words he continued, "I get it you are gonna put up the money — no interest on the loan. Don't keep me in suspense."

"Let me finance the deal for you."

"What? You haven't the kind of money it would take to clinch the sale. Thanks for the offer but you couldn't swing it. Naw it's over."

"Tell me, how much would it take."

"Can you come up with sixteen thousand? No credit, its money on the barrel head or it's all off."

"No problem Harry. I can get the money right now. Just say the word."

"Just like that," Harry said snapping his fingers. "No strings attached," with a wary look on his face. "C'mon Michael, what do you want?"

"I'll pay you the usual finder's...."

"You must be out of your mind. This is quality stuff Michael. No, no!"

"Don't be hasty now Harry. You didn't let me finish. The usual is ten I'll go fifteen. It's a lot better than nothing. Use your head Harry. Don't cut your nose off to spite your face."

"The fifteen, that would be fifteen percent of the sixteen thou, right."

"Of course."

"No I can't do it. This is quality stuff. A once in a lifetime deal."

"But I don't know that for sure — do I Harry? I haven't seen this wonderful stuff you keep talking about. Anyway, here's what I'll do, after all we are friends Harry. I'll go to seventeen percent and that's it, my final offer."

"No I'm giving too much away on this one Michael. You will have access to a prime supplier."

"I'm sure you aren't the only one who deals with this company, firm, whatever. So I don't think you have a valid argument for turning me down Harry."

"I disagree, I think it is a very good argument for saying no."

Michael, desperate to get a foot in the door of the rag trade, leaned back in the booth and smiled, "You are a tough old gaffer Harry." What to do, the old bugger wasn't budging, how to get him to say yes. Then he had an idea.

"This stuff, you are sure it's the best, quality stuff? Here's what I'll do Harry. I think you will like this. Fifteen percent of the profits I make from the sale of this quality stuff. Now you know how much of the stuff there is for sale and you must have some idea of how much it will sell for, so what do you say, fifteen percent off the top. A deal?"

Harry shrugged, "Make it thirty percent and we have a deal."

Secretly delighted, "Aw c'mon Harry, fifteen's fair. Let's shake on fifteen, it's a good deal. Don't forget I have to rent someplace to sell this quality stuff Harry. C'mon be reasonable."

Shaking his head, "That's your problem Michael."

"You drive a hard bargain Harry, you bloody tightwad. I'll go to twenty, but that's it. Shake on it."

"No, thirty or nothing." Tight lipped, a grim faced Harry shaking his head said, "I shouldn't do this, you know Michael, but you are a nice young man. Thirty!" Well at least I'll get something out of the deal, Harry thought. He's way over his head in this. He knows nothing about the business. He'll come running to me for help in selling the stuff and I'll clean up. Give him a few quid.

"I guess I'll have to think this over Harry." Secretly delighted at the way things were going, he slipped a forlorn look on his face and in his best "aw c'mon be reasonable voice" continued haggling. Thirty percent, was steep, but you don't get anything worthwhile cheap, he reasoned. With this deal I've got a toe hold in the rag trade. I'm in like Flynn. "How about we shake on twenty-five. Be reasonable Harry."

"I am being reasonable, thirty is fair."

"Oh all right Harry, thirty. Let's shake on it."

No one knew, not his parents, not the neighbours, not his pals, not even Michael knew that the handshake with Harry would open the way to a fortune. No one in his wildest imaginings would have forecast that a nondescript small store on a back street would be the first building block in an edifice, an empire that knew no international boundaries. The first heady venture was soon followed by the sale of used office equipment, used furniture, and antiques. Because not all his buys sold as quickly as he would have liked, they had to be stored. The prohibitive cost of such storage prompted the purchase of his own warehouse which earned a small profit from the low-cost rental of the space he didn't use. In time, he advanced to buying companies, newspapers, and overseas, radio and television stations. A ready ability to assess a situation and then to quickly make a decision on it was the key to his success.

His parents were not at all enthusiastic about his venture into the rag trade. To the voiced concerns of their friends on the street they smiled and shrugged, saying that the young sometimes had to learn a lesson the hard way. To their close friends they admitted that when Michael's funds ran out, he would get a decent job. One of the lots bought sight unseen in his wheeling and dealing turned out to be made up of army surplus clothing. When the lot went out the door in a hurry, he bought a second lot. When it too quick marched off the shelves, he rented a second store and in it sold only army surplus.

Rental of the second store, overnight changed Myrtle and Albert Braithwaite's outlook on their son's endeavours. Their savings, attentively put by and cautiously invested as a bulwark against possible hardships in their old age, were freely offered, but were not required. After eight months in business, his Mum and Dad's friends and neighbours thought that — maybe Michael would make a go of it. Once their initial doubts had been laid to rest Mum and Dad could become absolutely boring with talk of their son's business exploits.

One such occasion led Michael to take his parents to task and ask them not to talk in public about his business interests, particularly in the local. He explained that the competition in the rag trade was fierce. With tons of clothing being shipped offshore, the wise man didn't talk about where and when he was buying his job lots. They complied with his request, but were a little put out that now they couldn't quietly mention, while having a port and lemon or a pint in the Boar's Head, their son's latest coup. Business secrecy was and is today one of the company tenets all Braithwaite employees must honour.

6

Shortly after his nineteenth birthday, Michael moved out of his parents' house. The move was vehemently opposed by his Mum, who doted on her youngest. She was part of the reason for his moving; she still thought of him as her "baby," he found her motherly concern too much. He knew his Mum was happy with his success and wanted things to stay as they were, but he had plans. Michael's ambition, aspirations and dreams were not prepared to accept such a limited landscape. An unused area at the back of the army surplus store was, in consultation with his landlord, thought to be large enough to accommodate a one-bedroom apartment, the entrance to be through the office. Once all the forms were signed and permits issued, Michael and his pals, some of them in the plumbing and carpentry trades, set to with gusto to get the job done. The house-warming party three months later was loud and boisterous, spilling out into the store before the police told the party goers to put a lid on it.

Old habits die hard. Michael, whenever he could take a break, would jump on a bus and go to the town library and there he would sit in a quiet corner and forget his worries in planning for and dreaming of the future. Now, even with his own place, the library still called when he wanted to think a problem through or to lose himself in what if.... On one such visit to the library, his musings were set aside when a woman sat down at a nearby table. In profile, her pale features, firm chin and coal black hair had him staring. Full lips were pursed in concentration as she wrote on a pad.

When a library assistant brought her a couple of books, her face came alive as she looked up and smiled her thanks. Just then she looked over at Michael, and caught him gawking. Sitting two tables away, he came under the scrutiny of blue eyes in a face without need of artifice. A brief hesitation, long enough to see his face turn red, and she was head down writing. If he had taken a second look he would have also noticed a slight upturn at the corners of her mouth.

The lady was amused. She thought, one of the local yokels waking up from a snooze. If he comes over here, he'll get an earful. I suppose he is not bad looking in an animal sort of way. A big cat about to pounce and grab me. Well aren't you the romantic one, she mused with some sarcasm.

He guessed she was doing research of some sort. There was a stack of books on the table. She was making notes on a legal-sized writing pad in front of her. Embarrassed, he went to the shelves and pretended to look for a book. Keeping up the pretence he took a book from the shelves and sat down at his table. Thus camouflaged, or so he thought, Michael noticed the thin fingers, the firm grip on the pen, an expensive fountain pen, the way she pushed her hair away from her face. Her hand on her cheek as she obviously pondered some fact or statement she was reading; and then she busied herself with the pen.

When she got up to leave and happened to glance in Michael's direction, she thought, mmmh he can read. He does look sort of handsome in a—different sort of way. Now what does all that mean. Handsome in a different sort of way, spare me please. Studying has finally turned what little brain I have to mush. Michael watched her every step as she walked out of sight through the doorway of the reference section.

Determined to find out who she was, he followed and surreptitiously pointed her out to a librarian. The librarian shook her head. A woman who had blatantly listened in on the whispered question while waiting to have books date stamped answered in a superior know-it-all voice.

"That — young woman — is the daughter of our mayor. He's a lawyer you know, but doesn't practice. They say he owns most of the High Street." With such an attentive audience, the gossip couldn't resist continuing. "There was a big fuss last year when he bought property out in the country. Gossip was that he had secret information about a New Town that was to be built near here."

"What happened?" Michael asked.

"Nothing. Oh they had a big enquiry, quite a fuss in the papers. Mr. Oglethorpe is an honest man, I know. He is a warden at my church, St. Thomas', the big church on James Street. Besides why would he need to cheat anyone? Supports local charities, gave three thousand pounds to the church building fund. Everybody knows he's honest. A fine man," with this final pronouncement she departed with her books.

"Now you know who the young lady's father is," the librarian said with a smile and a shake of her head as she glanced towards their informant who was headed towards the street door. Michael nodded and smiled in reply.

"She had a great stack of books on the table. What is she researching?"

The librarian, titillated by the young man's interest in the pale young miss, leaned over the wide desk and in a conspiratorial tone informed him, "I believe she is using the holidays to swot for her year-end exams. Judging from the books she takes out it has to be a degree with great emphasis on English and History."

"Thanks, got to go."

Michael, busy with a new venture, second-hand furniture, quality stuff you understand, didn't have any time for library visits for quite some time. When he did have time, the librarian he had asked about the blue-eyed beauty recognized him and smiled as he headed for a quiet corner. The furniture business wasn't going as well as he had expected. He had things to ponder, to sort out, whether to quit and move on or work out a better sales strategy. An hour later, with no answers to his problem, it was time to go. Still deep in thought he walked slowly towards the door passing the desk on the way. The librarian, in her flights of fancy, thought that this young man and the mayor's daughter would make a perfect couple. She leaned over the wide desk, she just had to tell him.

"Hello. I have news for you. The young lady. She was in here yesterday."

When what she had said registered, he stepped quickly to the desk. "She's back! Still piling up the books, swotting away?"

"No, exams must be over now, she took out two books, mysteries. I suspect she's relaxing before she goes back to Reading." This last bit of news brought raised eyebrows and a questioning look to Michael's face.

"Yes, she is attending Reading University. Our know-it-all friend, you remember, volunteered the information. She said her parents weren't at all keen for her to leave home."

Just then the subject of their conversation walked through the door. As she approached the desk with an easy confident stride, he mused, I'll bet she plays tennis, maybe hockey. Michael took a couple of steps away from the desk and looked down at his shoes, looking up when she spoke.

"I'm afraid these are overdue, my mother asked me to return them. How much do I owe?" She opened her purse and began searching for small change. Finding none, she produced a five-pound note with an apologetic shrug.

With the cash drawer open in front of her the librarian, shaking her head, said, "I only have change for a pound. They emptied my drawer at lunch time, something about needing cash to buy a fixture."

Before she could say a word Michael, roused from his stupor of delight at being this close to her, volunteered, "Let me. Let me pay — pay me back later," he stammered.

The librarian's heart sang, this was perfect. When she saw the questioning eyes she hurriedly said, "I know this young man. He comes in here regularly. I'll vouch for him."

"Oh no I couldn't. I'll take the books back with me. Thank you," with a smile for Michael who could feel himself getting hot under the collar.

The librarian undaunted went on, "You can pay him back next time you are in the library. Leave the money with me if you wish." Carried away on wings of fantasy and with both of them red-faced, she continued, "He's a gentleman. A fine young man, you have nothing to be afraid of, he'll take care of things for you."

Outside, still flustered by the incident in the library, they stood not looking at one another and not sure what to do next. Moving away from the door, he stammered, "My name's Michael...."

"I'm Helen."

"I know, your dad's the mayor. I didn't know what your first name...."

"That's all right. I know what you mean."

They slowly moved away from the library. Michael, not wanting her to go, was cursing himself for his lack of social graces. He thought, what do I do now? Helen was also asking the same question. He must think I'm some sort of pinhead.

Then the light went on. "What do you say to a cuppa?" Pointing across the street to a sign which declared Robertson's Bakery and Tea Room, he rushed on, "They make the best sticky buns in town and their meringues, just great. What d'ya say?"

"That would be nice," and without looking for traffic, set off across the street as a double decker bus bore down on her. Michael grabbed her arm and pulled her back as the driver gave them a surly look and mouthed at them. The abrupt pull to safety caused Helen to stagger into his arms. Nose to nose they surveyed each other.

She smells nice. Gosh, she's skinny.

Julia and Ellen won't believe me. Picked up in the library; that's one for the book. They'll say I made it all up just so they won't tease me about men. The ones I don't have in my life. Michael holding her arm; they headed for the tea room. About to enter the restaurant, she smiled and looking pointedly at her arm asked, "Could I have it back, please?"

"Sorry. I didn't want you running in front of a bus — again. Thought it best to hang on to you."

"Escorting me across the street, like some Boy Scout doing his good deed for the day."

They collapsed into seats at a corner table laughing at the incident out on the street, both secretly excited at the closeness it had afforded. The fluttering somewhere in the region of the heart was the source of their unusual behaviour. Helen, while no shrinking violet, was not known for ready witticisms with strangers. Michael too had a ready wit when with his mates, but was not noted for witty chatter around young women. The situation was new to them and they were enjoying it to the fullest.

When the waitress walked away from the table, Ally said, "You pour." Watching her, he thought, she's beautiful.

"Milk and sugar?"

"No, black please." She offered him a scone.

"I hear that you are at Reading."

"Yes. English and History. How do you know about Reading?"

"My sources are not to be divulged."

"Aren't you the nosey one. Have you been following me? That day in the library, you were gawking at me."

"Gawking, never, admiring you from afar, yes." Sensing the colour flooding up his face, Michael changed the subject. "What are your plans when get your sheepskin?"

"Ah yes, a job. I'm not quite sure at the moment, but I have thought of teaching, preferably young children."

"Teaching, better you than me. Especially young...."

"Don't you like youngsters?"

"They're OK, but a roomful of them would drive me bonkers." Laughter was his answer.

"What do you do?" Obviously you're not in the teaching profession."

"I'm a man of many parts, a bit of this a bit of that."

"What sort of parts; Butcher, baker, candlestick maker?"

"I dabble in whatever comes to hand, providing I can make a few pennies. At the moment I'm selling furniture. Later I might go into antiques."

"Sounds sort of iffy, hit and miss. After all, the bills have to be paid"

"Right. The bills do get paid, but paying them gets a bit hairy at times, but nothing ventured, nothing gained. Anyway that's enough about me. Have you seen the show at the Alhambra?"

"What a dud! A waste of...."

"Pardon me, I enjoyed it. The scene where the girl, unaware she was talking to her boss, lambasted the firm, was funny."

"Well, yes it was kinda funny, but the movie overall was sappy and phoney. A waste of money."

A discreet cough brought them back to the tables and chairs, the empty display case, the waitress and the cashier waiting their departure. Engrossed in discovering what was behind the face across the small daintily arranged table they had entered a dimension removed from the ordinary, the mundane. The cough followed by the clock behind the cashier softly striking the hour, ended the magic.

"Six-o-clock, I'll be late. My mother will have a fit. I'm sorry Michael, I must run. Thanks for the tea." And she was out the door running for a bus which had stopped about fifty yards away to pick up passengers. He stood in the doorway unaware of the two standing at the cash register impatiently waiting for him to pay his bill. Marvelling at her easy grace as with long strides, she dodged around people. Stepping aboard the bus she looked in his direction and waved. After paying for the tea and cakes, Michael headed for the shop reliving every word and nuance of their time together. The beauty's name was Helen. An only child, her parents were very protective of her. They allowed her to attend university only because a maiden aunt who lived in Reading said she would be delighted to put her up. They would look back on their meeting and jokingly attribute their behaviour to temporary insanity.

When he got back to the shop, Jane was in the process of closing up.

"Thanks Jane. Sorry, I got tied up."

"That's OK Michael. Had a big sale while you were gone."

"Really. Good for you."

"Maybe I shouldn't say a sale, not just yet that is. Y'know that big new housing estate, out Fenner Street?"

"The one where the old jam works were."

"That's the one. Seems they are to include some furnished houses for pensioners in the project. The man who was in this afternoon said that city council is thinking of providing some of the furniture for them. Beds, dressers, wardrobes, that sort of thing."

"Sounds like a great...."

Not allowing him to finish, she hurried on, "He had a look at what we have in the store and said, 'good solid furniture, just what we need,' those were his exact words. Before he left I told him that if he bought in quantity we could give him a healthy discount." This was said in a whisper with eyes averted.

"Great stuff Jane, good for you. You did the right thing. We'll give a discount to anyone who buys big lots." Rubbing his hands together he chortled, this was the answer to the problem that he had been mulling over in the library. Thinking of the library brought him up short. Damn it, you dough head, you forgot to get her phone number. How stupid can you get?

Next day he had difficulty in keeping his mind on business. Blue eyes framed by dark shiny hair kept intruding on his thoughts. There was a big shipment of army surplus coming on the market soon which he was planning to bid for. The grapevine had it that while there was some clothing the greater part was thought to be mechanical, vehicles and the like. Michael wanting to know exactly what was up for grabs, had lunch in the Mare and Foal. While at the bar, having his usual cider, one of the regulars said hello and ordered a pint. In the course of their friendly chat a verbal list of lorries, their size and make; cars, light and heavy equipment was detailed in a low voice. Twenty minutes after Michael left the pub; the regular picked up his payment from where it had been hidden in the lavatory.

Armed with this inside information, Michael visited construction firms over a wide area and chatted with the owners. Some of the owners liked the terms offered by Michael and made tentative offers with a down payment on what he had to offer. A number of the firms were operating on a shoestring and were glad to accept his hire-purchase terms. All this before the shipment went under the hammer. The visit to the Mare and Foal also provided Michael with estimates of what the items would sell for. Armed with this information, Michael's strategy was to use the down payments as collateral when seeking a loan from his bank. The loan was needed to buy the heavy equipment. Storage of the vehicles was no problem. He arranged with a friendly farmer to store them in one of his fields.

Early one afternoon, after long hours of going over the books and with the walls threatening to fall in on him, he decided to go for a walk and free his brain of financial cobwebs. Lost in thought, he strolled aimlessly, trying to concentrate his thoughts on business and not on smiling blue eyes. Without realizing it his route had taken him to the steps leading up to the library. With the thought that she might be inside studying, he bounded up the steps and rushed through the door almost running to the desk. The friendly matchmaker was not on duty. Now what? Leave a note? Not much point, no one knew her. He left and dawdled back to the shop, stopping off on the way to visit the clothing store and check on sales.

There she was looking out at him from the front page of the local weekly piled on the counter of the newsagent's around the corner. Grabbing a copy he read: Mayor Maurice Oglethorpe, his wife Marjory, daughter Helen and Mr. Alfred Bottomeley, lead the Grand March at the annual County Ball at the Guild Hall. The more than three hundred guests were entertained at dinner by the Geoffrey Smythe Quartet. Afterwards guests danced into the wee hours to the sounds of Tom Flanagan's Melodaires. Reading the report of the ball, he discovered that Helen was now back at university after a brief holiday at home.

Caught up in the pressure cooker atmosphere of the furniture deal with the municipality and moving the military vehicles out of the farmer's field, he swore that there were not enough hours in the day for all he had to do. Late to bed and up early was the one constant in his life. The furniture deal, after a number of setbacks, was eventually sorted out and paid for. The bureaucrats with their forms and regulations had delayed the proceedings a number of times. In all the uncertainties of the sale of furniture to the city, and even after the sale was finalised, he found smiling blue eyes, soft pale skin set off by coal black tresses intruding on his thoughts at the most unusual times. He could be seated at a table making a proposal to a group that was worth hundreds of pounds and a smiling Helen would float across his consciousness, momentarily making him lose his train of thought. By the time the yellowed grass that marked where the cars, lorries, ambulances and motor bikes had been parked was returned to its pristine green, Michael was selling antiques.

Each new venture with its attendant profits had his father shaking his head and marvelling at his son's sure instinct for making money. His mother, while proud of his successes, was also apprehensive about them, fearful that her son's empire would come crashing down around him some day. With time being swallowed up by the needs of his business ventures, Michael no longer had time to kick a ball about in the park with his chums, join them in yelling on the local football team on a Saturday afternoon. Each new venture inadvertently widened the divide between his and their interests.

When he was able to take time off and visit with his pals he found that they had fallen into two camps. There were those who were glad to see him and those who were lukewarm in their friendship. The latter group claimed his newfound business interests had given Michael an exaggerated opinion of himself; he had become that dread of hard working folks, "big headed".

7

Every week it was his custom to read the headlines in the county newspaper, with attention being paid to the articles for sale column. A habit begun in his entrepreneurial early days — selling out of a car boot — kept him abreast of what was happening in the county. Quickly turning pages in his weekly ritual, he was stopped short. Was that her, he mused, as he turned back a page. There she was on the page listing the weddings and engagements. Oh no! It can't be. His heart fell into his stomach. Reading the print under the picture he sighed and straightened his shoulders. He was informed that she had graduated summa cum laude and was living at home. Once again they were nose to nose as the bus thundered by; again he sensed her perfume, her elegance. He was brought back to reality by a voice, "That will be threepence Michael."

Weeks went by and the few visits, stolen from his busy schedule, to the library were blank. The friendly librarian said that she hadn't seen the young lady since the day he had paid her fine. Living in the childish hope of meeting her in the library or on the street wasn't enough. He had to act, do something, but what? He couldn't just walk up to the mayor's door and ask, can Helen come out to play? Maybe she didn't want to see him. She might have forgotten about the gabby fellow who had treated her to tea and stickies at Robertson's.

The answer to the problem was found in the phone book. Listening to the burr of the phone he was tempted to hang up. She would have forgotten all about him. The voice in his ear said, "Oglethorpe residence." God, what if she was out somewhere, what to say?

"Miss Oglethorpe please," he muttered and had to repeat her name before he got an answer.

"One moment sir." The seconds dragged on into hours. Was she coming back? The sound of footsteps. What to say? Swallowing he waited his fate.

"Hello, Helen Oglethorpe. Hello, hello."

"Hello, it's me," in a too loud voice.

"Michael, how nice to hear from you. Are you still there?"

Wonder of wonders, she recognized his voice. Her question broke the fog of delight that had momentarily taken over his senses. "Yes. How are you?" Before she could answer, he babbled on. "Saw your picture in the local rag, you looked great. By the way, congratulations."

"Thank you. Now I have to look for a job."

"Any prospects?"

"Not at the moment. I've just begun to look around. Get my feet on the ground. Life will now be quite different. At school all I had to worry about was swotting for exams. Now the competition is for an interesting job. That's enough about me, how are you?"

"Me, I'm great. Been keeping busy. Staying out of mischief."

"That doesn't tell me much. What is it you do? You never did tell me."

"A little bit of this, a little bit of that. You could call me a gypsy of sorts."

"You tell fortunes?" The smile in her voice came easily over the wires.

"Cross my palm with silver and I'll read your hand lady. Better yet, what time is it, two-o-clock? Why don't we meet at Robertson's, say three-o-clock and I'll confess all."

Helen thought about the man she was to meet as she was getting dressed. This man was different. I want to get to know him, find out what makes him tick. Gosh he is good looking, handsome if truth be told. He makes me shiver when we're together. I don't care what he does. Actually he doesn't talk much about his work. What does he do? He could be a thief for all I know.

One thing for certain, he's nothing like the boys I met at Reading. Most of them were egotistic bores who wanted only one thing, to get into my knickers. Even some of the profs, randy old goats, were out to get you into bed with them. When you are in love, then it's alright to do it. Imagine going to bed together — lying naked in each other's arms. Oooh lovely. With a delightful laugh she stepped into black filmy knickers. Is there such a thing as love at first sight?

That day in the library, he was certainly gawking at me. And when I caught him in the act, he blushed. Pity it took so long for us to meet. Although then, as I remember I thought of him as — the word yokel comes to mind. But he is certainly no yokel. Now that we've met, I'd say he is interesting and I would love to get to know him better. Let's wait and see what happens today.

Watching her cross the street, running to dodge traffic, he thought, she looks great, fantastic. She was wearing a blue sweater over an open necked blouse, a nice skirt in a rich shade of red and sensible shoes. He wanted to rush out into the traffic and grab her in a bear hug, she was beautiful. She was beside him, her perfume, a whisper in the air, brought back that first time together and an emotion that caught at his chest.

He looks handsome, the most handsome man I know. His smile, oh it is just adorable. Take it easy, Helen old girl, best step lightly here. He is good-looking though. We make a good-looking pair. He's only two or three inches taller than me. Oh I'd love to grab him, kiss him right here in public. Now wouldn't that make heads turn! His greeting, "Well don't you look spiffy," was reward enough for the attention she had given to choosing her clothes. Happy colours, she thought. They portray my feelings exactly.

It took two pots of tea and seconds on the stickies for Michael to tell Helen of all the irons he had in the fire and the dreams of those as yet unfired.

"What I'm doing now is small time stuff. I want to get out there with the big boys, where the money is. More than the lolly though, there is the challenge to do something constructive. Take a firm that is going downhill and bring it back to full production. Provide jobs, pay packets for your ordinary everyday sort of people. That's what I want to do."

"Have you anything in particular in mind? Seems to me that there isn't much in the way of businesses you could take over in town. Then there is the financing. Taking over a business can be costly, even one going downhill."

"True, what you say is correct. What do you know about financing? Women are not supposed to be knowledgeable about high finance."

"Huh, that's all you know, Mr. Smarty. My father, before he entered municipal politics, dealt quite a bit in real estate. When I was growing up all I heard was talk of finances as he bought and sold properties. The story around town is that he owns most if not all the High Street."

"Is it true?"

"That he owns.... He might, I do know he owns several valuable properties around town. And yes, some of them are on the High Street. You were saying."

"Where was I? Yes, there are the two stores and the apartment...."

"You have your own place? Do you rent it or own it?"

"I rent it. I'd like to own it, but I can't afford to just now. Maybe some day. At the moment there are more pressing uses for my money."

"I'd love to have my own place. Just think, you could shut the door, kick your shoes off and unwind after a busy day. Listen to the radio while you prepared a meal. It would be great. Have friends over for a chat and a cuppa."

"Sounds great. But wouldn't you get lonely?"

"I'd get a cat," said with a mischievous grin. "Some day there might be a tall, dark, handsome fella around— maybe children. You should talk. Don't you get lonely in your gem of an apartment?"

"Sometimes, but...."

"There, it happens to us all. May I suggest a cat."

"Where was I, oh yes, use the businesses as collateral at my friendly bank. Now I don't want you to think I'm bragging, or trying to impress a lady, but I have a few bob tucked away in an old sock."

"Michael that's silly, keeping your money in the apartment. How can you be so silly. Ooops, pardon me, who am I to tell you...."

Laughing, Michael said, "I was just joking. The money is tucked away in investments — with some loose change in the bank."

"Do you really think you could take over a large business, say a factory manufacturing—oh, let's say for the sake of discussion, nuts and bolts?"

"Not if it covered acres and acres, but if it was your ordinary run-of-the-mill factory on about an acre of land, sure. I'd have a go. Mind you I would do my research: have an engineer check the building, have the property surveyed, look into the legal aspects of the offer, is there a market for the nuts and bolts and if not what could be manufactured in place of them, equipment and employee morale would be looked at closely. Duff equipment can slow you down. It can also kill people. Feel free to make suggestions."

"You have really done your sums, haven't you?"

"My Mum and Dad think that I have some magic system for making money. They marvel, their friends too, at my success. But having a plan and following trends is the secret of any success I have had to date. Mind you it helps when Lady Luck smiles at you."

Walking to the furniture and antique shop, it seemed perfectly natural for them to hold hands. She was delighted with the antiques. One piece in particular she fell in love with, as she put it. He almost presented it to her on the spot, she was so enthusiastic about the feel of the wood, the look of the little desk. Before leaving the shop to head to the clothing store, Michael took Jane aside and told her to put a sold label on the desk.

At the other store she was overwhelmed by the amount of military clothing and gear that was on the shelves. When told that there was great competition in the bidding for such stuff, her disbelief was summed up in one word: "Really?" Standing in his office, she wanted to know what was behind the door at the rear of the office. When it was suggested that she open it and find out, she gasped her surprise.

"Oh, what a perfect little kitchen. Everything in its place, reminds me of a yacht galley. And you keep it all so tidy. Now the question is do you cook in here?" said with a grin. "Can I have a look?"

"My castle. Step inside. Of course I cook and do the washing up, you cheeky thing. Its not huge as you can see, but it suits me fine."

Turning around slowly, she explored with her eyes before venturing on a closer inspection. "The furniture, it's beautiful. You must enjoy antiques. The sideboard is lovely. Where did you get those rugs? Persian aren't they? Fabulous colours. You certainly have an eye for colour and design. Did you do all this?"

"No, I called in the experts, my mother and a friend of hers. All I did was pay for the stuff. Mind you I had to say no a couple of times. Some pieces were a bit much for such a small place."

"What's in there?" she said pointing to the door off the living area.

"Have a peek, see for yourself."

"Mmmh, no bath. For a man I suppose a shower is OK. Me, I love to luxuriate in the tub. You have a fabulous apartment here Michael. I'm jealous, I'd love to have a place just like this."

Pleased at her frank admiration of the place he said, "It's not much, but I like it and it gets me out from under."

"Your parents? I know what you mean. They don't want to let go. Don't understand that you have to get away. I love my Mum and Dad, but I want to get out, away from them, live on my own."

"You too? It doesn't matter how old you are, they continue to think of you as a kid that still has to have its nose wiped."

"Graphic, but true."

Walking with Helen to the bus stop afterwards, they met her mother on the street. When introduced, Michael released Helen's hand only long enough to shake hands, which, along with the effervescent manner of her daughter, was duly noted and filed. When she told her husband about the young man she had met, his only comment was, "Do we know him?"

"His name is Braithwaite; ring a bell with you? Helen certainly enjoys his company. He seemed a nice young man."

'That's not the point dear. What is his background? All kinds of people are being admitted to universities these days. I suppose she met him at Reading."

"It's possible dear, but I don't think so. Helen wouldn't have kept news of this young man from us if she had met him at university." Maurice hadn't seen the way the two of them had behaved when she met them on the street.

"I thought Helen and young Bottomely were more than old school chums. There's a young man who will get ahead," Maurice said.

"Yes, I suppose he will go into the family business. Helen finds him somewhat pompous. He takes himself much too seriously, she tells me."

"Nothing wrong in that. Young people today are much too frivolous."

"That may be, but it doesn't apply to our daughter. She has a head on her shoulders. I sometimes think that we are much too protective of her."

"Now Marjory, don't go off on that tack again. We both know that the world outside our door isn't the safe, sane, law-abiding world of our day. We have to take care of our daughter."

"Yes dear I know that. I also know that she will have to live in that world and sheltering her from it won't help her cope with it."

"There is time for all that, for now let's just leave things as they are."

Helen was at a job interview when the little desk was delivered. Her mother, at first mystified by the delivery, signed the delivery slip and had the two men take it up to Helen's room. Walking down the stairs, she assumed that her daughter must have bought it and was planning to do some work in her room. It was not the sort of thing Maurice would buy, much too expensive; which gave rise to the thought, where did Helen get the money to pay for the little mahogany desk. When she came home, Helen would sort it all out.

"Your desk arrived just after you left. It's a beautiful piece...."

"What are you talking about mother, what desk? I don't know anything about a desk."

"It's no joke Helen. If you didn't buy it, who did?"

"Not me mother."

"It's upstairs in your room." As she said this, her mother started up the stairs. "Follow me young lady. It was addressed to you in big bold letters. The label was tied to a drawer handle."

And there it was, just as her mother had said: Miss Helen Oglethorpe in big black letters. Fingering the label she thought this looks a lot like the one in Michael's shop, could it be? The blush began below the collar of her blouse and progressed slowly to take over her pale features.

"Oh mother, it's a present," she said in a voice thick with emotion.

"My dear, a present. Are you all right?"

"Read the other side of the label. He is sweet."

Turning over the label she read: Affectionately, M. "And who is this M? Of course, it's the young man I met the other day. Well, well, Helen."

"I hardly know him, yet, oh I don't know Mum, I'm all mixed up."

Smiling her mother put an arm around her daughter's shoulders. She's no longer my baby; I can't doctor her emotions the way I did her skinned knees. This young man — he seemed nice enough when we met — has her in a tizzy.

Mum must think I'm an idiot acting this way. Drying her eyes, Helen faced her mother and said, "Should I accept his present? We've just met and he sends me the desk. It's expensive. And yet, Mum, y'know I feel as though I have known him for ages. Does that sound silly? When we're together — it's nice. I...."

"Yes of course accept the present. Men, some men give flowers, others perfume or perhaps a box of chocolates, but your Mr. M is an original and presents you with a desk. He must think...."

"What will he think? When I was in his shop I practically drooled over this desk. Feel the wood. It's beautiful, when you touch the wood it has a feel to it."

"It's obvious why he chose to send you the desk. Look at you, you're in raptures, talking about it. And it is beautiful."

"So it's alright for me to accept his present?"

"Yes, why don't you phone him now?"

Helen's acceptance of the gift was a definitive moment for Michael. The little desk also brought with it a shadow of worry to Michael that manifested in him becoming introspective and uncommunicative. Helen was slow to notice the change, but when she did she acted quickly to resolve the matter.

"Things have changed Mum. Michael, he's still attentive but there seems to be some underlying— oh I don't know— mood."

"Maybe it's business and he doesn't want to worry you."

"It's not business, no it's something else. I just know it."

"Could there be someone else?"

"No Mum! Whatever it is I'm to get to the bottom of it."

"Now Helen, be careful. If he wants you to know then he will tell you."

"That may be Mum, but I am going to have a chat with Michael."

So much for romance, she thought. We don't have fun anymore. Is it me or has Michael changed his mind? Oh how I wish things were still the same. Was it only six weeks ago we met? This can't go on, I love him too much. We've got to get this nonsense straightened out. I know what I'll do.

Picking up the phone on the second ring, "Hello...."

There were no preliminaries, "Michael we have to meet right away. I don't care what you're doing, we must talk. Business has to take a back seat to this."

He could hear heavy breathing, she sounded agitated. "Are you alright Helen? You...."

"Of course I'm alright," she snapped.

Surprised he said, "Fine, OK."

"Meet me in front of Robertson's, now."

"Right you are." The click of Helen's phone ended all talk.

Jeez! She's really got a head of steam up. I'd better get over there.

On the bus, she sat looking out the window unmindful of the city landscape, lost in thought. There's no backing out. This is something that has to be done. I hope he doesn't get the idea that I'm some sort of bossy female. Oh dear God, what have I done. What if he tells me to go to hell and walks away. Stepping from the bus, there he was waiting for her. Oh dear God, help me! I don't want to lose him.

Fear laid its clammy hand on him. Caught unawares by the sharp pain that seared his chest, he hesitated a moment.

"Hello Michael." He doesn't want to be here. I can tell by the way he drew back just now.

"Hello Helen." Let's get this over with.

"Let's find a quiet spot in Robertson's."

Sitting in an alcove and tea for two ordered, "No cakes or scones."

They sat not looking at each other. "What's happened Michael? Is there someone else? Tell me, I've...."

"Of course not; that's daft."

"Something has changed Michael. Is it business? Are you in trouble with payments? What is it, tell...."

"No! of course not."

"Michael, forget it, whatever it is; don't let it spoil our lives. Please!"

I've got to tell her, "When I was at school, I worked summers with a demolition crew. I had a great time working with them. Anyway, on pay days we would go to a pub for a couple of drinks." How do I tell her I'm impotent, she's always said she wants a family. "They were always on about getting me fixed up with a woman. It was a standing joke with the guys. The long and short of it was that one Friday they fixed me up with a woman."

He looked across the table at Helen, a plea in his eyes as the colour crept up his cheeks. Sighing, he continued, "She was a friend of one of the gang. She was a lot older than me." A shameful look matched his bleak eyes. "She had a room close to the pub; we went to bed. Nothing happened, I couldn't — do it."

"You poor dear. It must have been awful for you. How old were you?"

"Sixteen." She took his hand and gave it a gentle squeeze.

Taking strength from her touch; he tumbled his feelings and fears before her. "But don't you see, we won't be able to have a family."

"Michael you are so sweet." Smiling she went on, "I'm no doctor but I doubt very much you are impotent."

"But I couldn't do anything. Later it was the same. I just lay there. She tried to get me excited."

"What do you mean later? Did you do it again with this woman?"

No! it was Liam's sister Mary. She was high on something. I'd gone to meet Liam at his squat; he was off somewhere."

Red-faced and ashamed Michael recalled vividly the embarrassing scene: "As soon as I sat down, she grabbed me — laughing she said that she had never had a virgin — she stood there naked. Any second I expected Liam to walk in on us. When I couldn't do it she laughed and said I was a poof."

"And nothing happened this other time?"

"No."

"I'm not surprised, she literally attacked you. Of course you couldn't do anything." Leaning across the table she kissed him lightly on the mouth and with a smile in her voice said, "It'll be different when we do it."

Relief swept over him; her kiss was returned, a little off target, she giggled. "Michael we are putting on quite a show. One old dear behind you is about to have a heart attack."

Feeling light headed he said, "The pot's cold. Let's get fresh tea and some sandwiches, I'm hungry. You're wonderful Helen."

"I'm glad that's over. You're kinda wonderful too."

"Will you marry me Helen?"

"Yes!"

Three weeks later, Helen brought a young man home for dinner and set the mayor's orderly world askew. The young man was polite, if rather casually dressed. He was in business of some sort, antiques; there was something about clothing. Introductions were hasty, the mayor had been called away suddenly. There had been a fire at the municipal garage which the caller said looked as though it had been set. Apologizing for his hasty departure, Mayor Oglethorpe set off to examine the damage and maybe, just maybe a photographer from the county paper would be on hand to snap him in action. Election time was not far off.

Duty done, the mayor found his wife, his daughter and the young man, Braithwaite was his name, ensconced in deep chairs in the living room having a jolly good time by all appearances. On instructions from his wife, he made himself a sandwich of cold cuts, cheese and pickles in the kitchen. Enjoying the sandwich and with a mug of strong tea in front of him, he was joined by Braithwaite, who said right off that he had something important to say to him. Nodding his head, he waited for Braithwaite to begin.

At first the mayor thought there must be something wrong with his hearing. The fellow was asking — damn it, he didn't know anything about this upstart, and he wanted to marry Helen. Spluttering and coughing, he stood up and when Braithwaite made to slap him on the back he held up his hands and shook his head. Gulping down some tea he looked over at his wife and daughter who had just entered the kitchen in response to the noises.

"Marry my daughter! Good God man, I don't even know you. What do you do? Where do you come from? Were you at Reading with Helen?" The mayor took a deep breath prepared to continue. Cheeky young pup, he thought.

Michael didn't give him the opportunity. "Yes! I want to marry Helen. I love her. I was born and went to school here. I have my own business, at the moment it's second-hand furniture and antiques. We didn't meet at university, we met in town, at the library." This last statement delivered with a grin for Helen.

"And that's it, you have it all planned, but what does Helen have to say about this? — and you Marjory?"

"I want to marry him Dad," Helen smiled and went over to where Michael stood. "I love him and we want to get married."

The mayor, a surprised look on his face, and looking to his wife for support, muttered, "Did you know about this Marjory? You should have told me." The delighted smile on his wife's face spoke louder than any words she could utter in approval of the match. He quickly decided that it would be foolish to voice any opposition when his wife reached up and kissed Braithwaite. Turning to her husband she said, "No I didn't. It's a surprise to me too."

Two months after the "brouhaha in the kitchen" as Helen laughingly referred to Michael's meeting with her father, they were married. With her friends, she joked that she fell in love with Michael's apartment and the only way she could live in it was to marry the owner.

The newlyweds unpacking in a room in a guest house on the Isle of Wight found that confetti had been liberally scattered between the layers of carefully packed clothes. Helen made the discovery when she went to hang up a skirt in the wardrobe. Not satisfied with generously pouring the stuff between the clothes, the more devious had filled pockets and poured the bright paper fragments into dresses. The first sprinkling of paper was greeted with laughter, but when it became a shower faces darkened.

"This is bloody ridiculous," Michael exploded. Those silly buggers have gone too far this time."

"Stupid twits! I'd like to have them here in the room right now. I'd make them pick up every piece of the damned stuff — with their tongue."

"Great idea. Not now though, I want you all to myself, no sharing."

"Our first crisis," she smiled.

"We can't have this stuff underfoot. I'll go downstairs and get someone to come and clean it up. Back in a jiff."

When the maid entered the room with her brush and dustpan, she stopped and gasped. Looking at Michael and Helen, holding hands, she said, "This will take a while, maybe you should go out for a walk."

"Good idea, c'mon Helen, let's go exploring."

Strolling the narrow streets of Cowes the lovers didn't say much. They moved as though joined at the hip. Anyone who watched them for a few minutes would have seen they couldn't walk more than a few steps without touching.

Climbing the stairs to their confetti-free room after dinner, Helen said, "I think a bath is in order. Are you going to shower?"

"No I'm fine. You go ahead, I'll read the paper." Watching Helen pull her jersey over her head and then step out of her skirt, he marvelled at the supple flow of her body.

He desired to take her bra off and to stroke, to kiss her rounded soft breasts. He shivered. As he watched her move to the bathroom, he shifted in his seat. His stiffening member was making his present position uncomfortable. What am I gonna do, he thought. When she comes out of the bathroom. I don't think I'll be able to keep my hands off her. I don't want to spoil things, but bloody hell she's sure to notice the bulge.

When Helen came back into the room she was wrapped in one of the large bath towels. Holding the towel with both hands, she gave her head a toss to get her still damp hair out of her eyes. Looking over at Michael her eyes smiled at him. There was a whisper of apprehension in the air. Reaching over to the dressing table she picked up a brush and began untangling her hair. With each stroke the towel slipped a little lower. It was back again, the tightness in his crotch. Uncertain of what to do, he stood up to ease his discomfort and found himself walking towards the bed.

Falling to his knees beside his darling, he placed his head in her lap and slowly rubbed the soft, slightly damp skin, above her knee. Slowly he moved his hand further under the towel as her legs opened to allow his exploration. Suddenly the towel was jerked from under his head and frantic hands were pulling at the buttons on his shirt. As if on springs both stood up. Moments later Helen threw herself down on the bed in all her inviting nakedness. Michael caught up in his trousers as he struggled to get rid of them, bent over and lightly kissed the dark triangle awaiting him. The trousers in a heap, he got into bed. Helen moved over as he struggled with his underwear. Soft hands, trying to help, touched the head of John Thomas squandering his passion.

"I'm sorry. Oh Michael, I wanted so much to do this, and now. I'm sorry."

Throwing the soiled shorts out of the bed, he put an arm around her and pulling her close said, "My God, but you are beautiful." Moving his hand over her ribs he discovered a breast, a hard little button at its centre. "What's this milady?" in a whisper. Pulling the sheet over his head he marvelled at what he saw in the filtered light. Letting the sheet fall he kissed the delight nearest him and suckled, ever so gently, the erect nipple. Slight murmurs from his beloved as soft hands began exploring his body. Gentle massaging fingers made everything right and the first thrust was answered by a sigh. The end came in a shuddering gasp. They lay wrapped in each others' arms marvelling at the wonder they had found. Again and again, they rose on wings of delight, their coming together a fusion of their passion and their love. They slept.

The honeymoon over, it was back to business as usual, well not quite. Now the apartment became Helen's domain, a haven where business could be forgotten or discussed, depending on the needs of the moment. Socially too, life took on a broader, more eclectic, mix. At the mayor's table, Michael met the city's important people, the monied, (inherited), the cream of the legal profession, the bores with pretensions and of course their offspring. Michael and Helen invited them to their apartment in small groups. These intimate small dinners became a social event sought after by those in town who moved in the "right circles".

People found the young couple set a fine table and did not stand on ceremony. Dress was casual and the conversation was friendly, sometimes serious but never boring. The ultimate approval of course was to be accepted by the county gentry, the old families who could trace their lineage back centuries. Wealth did not ensure entry to this cliquish group. There were no rules, no votes were taken, entry was haphazard at best, usually on a whim. The Braithwaites gained acceptance from an unexpected source.

Brigadier Percival Wellington Gordon Pawley sat on the local bench. He was known as a stickler for protocol, and lawyers and clerks equally stepped lightly around the old man when he was on the bench. In court he was prone to hand down the severest penalty allowed under the law.

He was often heard to say, "I have no time for layabouts and rogues. They must be taught a lesson. Show them the error of their ways. Society must be protected, that's why we have laws."

Michael, busy in the office, heard the door open but didn't look up from the page of figures. Helen waited, fussing at his side until he looked up after jotting down the column's total.

"Michael, Mrs. Pawley phoned just now. Poor Myrtle, she is in a dither, their cook housekeeper fell this morning and she's in hospital with a broken hip."

"What has that to do with us. I'm sorry about the old dear's fall. But we're not in the catering business. There's nothing we can do."

"That's just it Michael, Myrtle was in a terrible state, almost crying. It seems that the Brig' wanted to impress some judge here for the Assizes."

"Surely if he wants to impress this visiting judge, old Percy could pay for one of the hotels to deliver a meal, complete with waiters, wine, the works."

"Alright he's not the friendliest person we know."

"Damned right! By the way I didn't know you were friendly with the huntin' shootin' crowd. Do you ride with the Hunt? "

"Michael! This is serious. Mum and Myrtle have served on a few committees together and the Brig. being on the bench has some dealings with Dad as Mayor. That's how we got to know them."

"Why should you help the old pratt. When your Dad introduced me to the old guy at that do in the Guild Hall, remember? He was barely civil, and now you want to go off and - do what? Cook for him?"

"If it were just him I'd agree with you, but poor Myrtle. I swear she was close to hysterics. Whatever the reason for the dinner, Myrtle wants it to be a success. She dotes on the Brig. She phoned me — she couldn't get mother — to ask if I knew of anyone who could take over at short notice and lay on a dinner for the judge and eleven others."

"Were you able to help?"

"No. Well yes, I volunteered to take over the kitchen for the day."

"So I was right. You old softy."

"I wish you could have heard her on the phone."

"OK, she was upset, whatever you say boss — softy," with a grin. "I'll drive you over to the Brig's place."

"That'd be super. I've some shopping to do on the way."

"Why don't I do the shopping for you? Drive you over and you can get started doing whatever it is you have to do, and then I'll beetle off and pick up your stuff."

When Michael arrived back at the Brig's, he found a number of jobs waiting for his attention. First there were potatoes and carrots to be dug up, brussel sprouts to be picked, lettuce, peas and beans to be gathered and washed. While Michael was busy in the sink, Helen was preparing her piece de resistance, Crown Roast Beef. In consultation with Myrtle who fluttered around the kitchen, Helen prepared beef barley soup, "Percy likes his soup full bodied," Myrtle said. A garden salad followed and the vegetables with the fish were nice and crisp. The roast beef, wreathed in mixed vegetables was served on a large platter with baked potatoes served on the side. Dessert was a light fluffy concoction of cake and cream. The maid (Helen) served the ladies coffee in the drawing room, while the butler (Michael) served coffee to the men in the library and afterwards passed the cigar humidor and then moved about with a lighter.

Several days after the do for the judge, the Brigadier came into the furniture store and asked to speak to Michael. "Good day sir."

"Hmurph, ah, I'm so damned embarrassed. Gad how could I sit there and not notice the two of you. Forgive my lack of manners Braithwaite."

"Michael, call me Michael."

'How can I thank you and your lady wife for the wonderful repast you prepared for Myrtle and me. Our guests...."

"My wife is the one who did all the fancy cooking and baking. I was just the pot walloper. Mind you we had a rare old time. We enjoyed helping Myrtle."

"Our guests were loud in their praises of Helen's culinary arts. I'm embarrassed, to think the two of you in my house waiting on table and I never spoke to you or your wife. Is Helen handy? Myrtle tells me that you have a nice little place at the rear of the shop."

"Yes." Nosey old bugger. "Why don't you come through and you can talk to her. In fact she is preparing lunch, why don't you join us. It's beef barley with melted cheese on toast. Jane, I'm going for lunch now."

The dinner and how it came to be prepared by "The daughter of the Mayor and her husband," became one of the Brig's boring after-dinner stories.

"Here was this young fella with a business to run and yet he left the business to help Myrtle. His wife, she is a dear, cooked a meal fit for a lord. And then, damn it, if they didn't serve the meal. Put on such an act that I didn't recognize Helen. Michael, a fine chap, played the part of the butler."

The ready response to Myrtle's cry for help had unforseen consequences for the young couple. The Brig, overwhelmed with their unhesitating response to his wife's cry for help, was loud in his praises of their generosity. The old man's cachet brought with it ears that now would listen to, and hands that would now help Michael in his business dealings.

A few weeks after Myrtle's rescue, the company Michael's father worked for declared bankruptcy. According to his father, the "Airy fairy schemes" of the two grandsons of the original owner ruined the business. Tipped off when he overheard a loud conversation between two real estate developers, Michael bought the company for a song.

A large lunch, a second bottle of wine followed by whiskies in the bar was their undoing. The two developers went on at length about their various projects. The one sitting on the other side of the partition separating their booths thought he was whispering when he told of the impending bankruptcy. Claiming to have the inside track he told his friend that the factory was to be demolished to make way for a large housing estate and with shops in the centre of the development. Unable to come up with the amount thought to be needed to close the deal, the speaker invited his friend to join him in the venture. The answer was no, his friend had too may irons in the fire.

In preparation for the demolition of the building, Michael had the factory stripped of all machinery and equipment, selling it overseas. When informed by his "inside man" that the development scheme had fizzled out; he talked with his banker. With the bank's money he refurbished the interior of the building and bought the latest in extruding machines and went into the plastics business.

The early months of the new venture were trying times for the owner. Added to the many problems of starting up a new business was an attempt by another company to put Michael out of business by undercutting prices. Short of cash, Michael couldn't meet the payroll. Meeting with the workers on the factory floor he appealed to them to tough it out with him. He walked back to his office with the workers' roar of approval ringing in his ears. In the office he was congratulated by his salesmen as they got down to working out a strategy that would keep production going.

Added to the problems at the factory was one at home. Helen's health was giving him cause for concern. She seemed to spend an inordinately long time in the bathroom mornings. When he mentioned his concern to his Mum, she gave him a funny look and said, "I'll drop around and have a chat today. I'm sure it isn't anything serious."

"You haven't seen her Mum. She doesn't look at all her usual cheery self. I'm worried. God I hope you're right and it isn't anything serious."

"Don't you worry son. It's likely some sort of woman's problem."

His concern blinded him to the twinkle in his mother's eyes. She had her suspicions, based on what Michael had told her she was certain that her son was due for a surprise. The surprise was delivered later in the day when Helen visited the office and invited him to tea at the nearby "caff." Sitting in one of the red vinyl booths, with mugs of tea in front them, the cause of his concern was explained.

"Oh Michael, you are a dear. Mum told me about you being worried. There is nothing to worry about. I'm, we're going to have a baby!"

"What! A baby!"

"Not so loud Michael."

"That's great. But what about your not feeling well? Is that because of the baby? You are OK?"

"Of course I am, I'm fine. It's called morning sickness."

"Why didn't you tell me sooner? You had me worried."

"I should have told you, but I kept waiting for the right moment. Then the morning sickness started and all my good intentions went out the window."

"I too have been keeping a secret. Now...."

"Out with it, what is this secret? Michael you haven't gone and bought another factory?" said with raised eyebrows.

"No, but I've have been looking for a larger place, the apartment's too small. Especially now with a babe on the way."

"We could manage. The apartment's cosy and snug, I hate to leave it."

"The place I've got my eye on; I think you'll like it."

"Where is this place? You haven't bought it.? Michael, the money, tell me you haven't bought the place. Money's spread pretty thin right now."

"Don't you worry about the cash. The place is going for a song. A house in its own grounds, lots of room for kids to play. My lawyer is taking a close look at the deal and is having an engineer look over the house."

"And where is this steal of a house?"

"Not far from here, over in Dilsworth."

Helen, five months pregnant, began choosing the decorations and colours for the nursery in their new home, The Grange, Dilsworth.

8

In his first two weeks on the job Robert learned a great deal about his employer's rise from rags to riches. He also found out that much of the work of Dilsworth Recovery was accomplished before noon. Afternoons the staff took to the phones and visited with the managers of the expanding Braithwaite enterprises. Also, hot tips on prospective acquisitions, who was short of cash or which company was on the brink of going bust were checked out and filed.

Robert took to the new job readily. Although on call around the clock, he didn't mind. After all, placing a bet was as easy as picking up the nearest telephone. The varied stamps on the pages of his passport told the story of his international flights with his boss. In his time away from flying he frequented, "The King's Head", a local pub, and there made friends with some of the regulars. One regular in particular caught his attention; she came in alone after work each evening, had one drink and left. Chatting to the barman, Robert found out that the "one-drink" woman worked for a firm of accountants in the village.

He would have to get to know the statuesque beauty. His opportunity came a month later upon his return from Canada, where Braithwaite had been laying the groundwork prior to making an offer to buy out a group of newspapers. Radio and television stations owned by the group were really what Braithwaite was after. Buying the papers was the carrot he held up in front of the shareholders in order to obtain their approval for the sale of the radio and television stations. Unusual for a Saturday, the bar at the rear of the pub was empty when he went through from the noisier public bar. The "Back Bar" was where people went who wanted a quiet chat with their friends or had business they wanted to transact over a drink.

Smacking his lips and speaking to the retreating back of the barman, "Mm mmh, just what the doctor ordered." She came in then, "Tom a customer. Hello. Your usual?" Robert standing with his head cocked in enquiry, his expensively shod right foot on the brass rail at the bar was ignored.

"Hello Tom."

"Yes miss, what will you have? The usual?"

"Not the usual, no Tom. I want a single malt Scotch. A friend has been babbling on about the merits of his favourite tipple. Would you do the honours Tom and choose one for me."

"May I, after licking my wounds, offer an opinion to the pretty lady Tom? Would you speak on my behalf with the fair damsel? Assure the lady of my impeccable character, my good deeds, dragons slain."

As Robert talked, the face of the young woman mirrored the thoughts going on behind her brown eyes. Looking at Tom askance and when he answered with a sly wink her eyes narrowed but not enough to hide the beginning of the merriment that despite her efforts slowly took over her face and ended in a merry laugh.

"While not an expert, there are a couple of malts that I have come to enjoy. Would you allow me to buy you your first malt? Tom here will vouch for me. Won't you Tom?"

A grinning Tom said, "He's quite harmless miss. And he isn't psychic, he is nosey though. I told him what your after-work tipple was."

"Will you let me buy this one?" a smiling Robert said.

"Should I Tom?" she asked with a gleam in her eye.

"Yes miss."

While Tom was pouring the drink, Robert found out that the confident young woman's name was Janice Scott and that she was an accountant whose company had recently moved to the peace and quiet of Dilsworth from the hustle and bustle that was London. That evening they went to a movie in Woking. During the next several weeks they spent together the weekends that Braithwaite wasn't airborne.

Robert and Janice were enjoying each other's company over a drink in the "Back Bar" when a voice from the past disrupted their friendly banter with Tom. Since their meeting, Tom had accorded them a special avuncular attention.

"Robbie, long time no see."

Robert's world tilted on its axis when he looked up to see Pete Mallory, a sly grin on his face. Speechless, a smile aimed at Janice, froze into an ugly grimace. "What are you doing here?" he asked in a throaty whisper.

"Looking after Jimmy's interests, as usual. You look good Robbie. I hear on the grapevine that you've had a couple of big paydays".

Robert glanced at Janice. In an attempt to disguise his agitation he pulled his shoulders back and shaped his mouth into what he hoped would pass for a smile. "A few quid, nothing much."

"If you say so Robbie." Draining his glass he continued, "I've got to run, see you around."

"What's wrong? You look so pale."

"It's nothing; I thought he was dead and now seeing him, here in the local. You will admit it is a bit of a shock."

I wish he were dead, he thought. Janice appeared to accept his explanation. Robert went through the motions of an attentive lover, but all the while there was the nagging thought thrusting at him, what is he doing here? Could it simply be coincidence, passing through and stopping off for a drink. God I hope so! Lost in a maze of thought, Robert was brought back to his surroundings by Janice poking him in the ribs.

"A penny for them Robert. You were away ta ta. Were you good friends?"

"No I knew him casually, we had a nodding acquaintance that was all."

If only that were true, he thought. If he tries to get me to bring in dope for Jimmy, I'll.... His thoughts were interrupted by Janice reminding him that they were to meet another couple in Woking for supper and a movie.

A few days later, Pete called Robert at work and said that they had to meet. When Robert said there was nothing to talk about, Pete was adamant that they meet. The meeting took place in a small restaurant just off the town square. Robert took his coffee to a table at the back and waited. Pete walked in about five minutes later. When he sat down with his coffee, he smiled.

"Why so glum Robbie? I hear things have been going your way lately. That was a nice piece of stuff the other day."

"Leave her out of it. What do you want?"

"Nothing. Not a sausage Rob old boy."

Resenting the familiarity and the mocking tone he said, "Why this meeting then? You want something and the answer is no! I squared my debts with Jimmy and you know it. No more...."

Pete looking around said, "Calm down, there's no need to get your knickies in a knot. I just thought", here he paused and smiled, "it would be nice to see you again and have a chat about old times. By the by Jimmy is a neighbour of yours now; old Jimmy is now a country gent, bought a farm down the road a bit from here. Decided the country life was the way to go, nice and quiet; comes down most weekends, a regular country squire. He's looking into some business interests down this way," this latter was said with a knowing grin.

Robert knew that whatever it was Jimmy was involved in he didn't want any part of it. The terror of clearing Customs, the fear clutching at his bowels every moment the dope was in his possession. The nightmares, they always ended with him being caught just as he was about to clear Customs. Oh God don't let it happen again, he thought. Not now when things are so good. "Tell Jimmy I won't do it. I know him, he wants me to get back into the courier business. No!"

"Relax Robbie, you're getting all steamed up about nothing. To tell you the truth, Jimmy is in a bit of a bind right now."

"I don't believe it. Jimmy with his back to the wall. If it is true, then I can't help...."

"Simmer down will yah," Pete snapped. His veneer of civility was beginning to peel under Robert's barrage of no's. Pete wasn't used to people saying no to him. "Jimmy needs cash, a big bundle and fast. All you have to do is give us some info. And you walk away with a handful of cash, a piece of cake old boy," Pete said sarcastically. Watching closely he could see Robert's thoughts mirrored in his face: puzzlement, doubt. "Some little bits of information, nothing to it and you will end up with a nice pay day Robbie," he said.

"OK, let's talk about it, this deal. No promises, the answer is still no."

Pete knew he had him hooked. "Braithwaite's son is in trouble at school. He was running a small-time betting operation and was caught at it."

"That doesn't surprise me. I flew him down to the Woking school from Scotland. He got in trouble there too. This must be the third or fourth school he has been expelled from."

"The fourth; what we want you to do is to find out what the arrangements are for the kid's move to his next school. Not too difficult is it Robbie?"

"All you want me to do is tell you when the brat will be heading...."

"That's it. Simple, phone the details to me," handing over a business card.

"That's all? There has to be more to it than that Pete. And what do I get out of the deal?"

"Hard cold cash, that's what you get Robbie old son. Do this for Jimmy; he won't forget it believe me," a serious faced Peter said. While thinking: gotcha, you dumb prick.

"Let's suppose I do this for Jimmy. Just suppose." With a sense of being in the driver's seat, Robert thought, the old sod, I'll make him pay. This time I'm in charge. He'll pay for what he did to me. Confident in his belief that he had Jimmy by the short and curlies, he said, "Tell him I don't come cheap."

"You'll have to sort that out with Jimmy, but I would guess that he would be good for — oh say a pay out of around sixty thousand nicker — at least."

"OK tell him I'll get the info, for eighty thou."

"Done, it's a deal."

"Don't phone me, I'll phone you."

"OK, OK, don't get your drawers in an uproar. Get the information asap and it's goodbye Pete, you wont see me around this place again."

Watching Pete's back as he left the bar, Robert thought, I handled that rather well. It would be easy to get the information. The kid's a menace he thought. Knowing the world Jimmy lived in, he suppressed any thought of what use the information would be put to. What the hell, it was none of his business.

As Pete walked out of the bar, he smiled. It was easy he thought. Like taking toffee from a kid; Jimmy will be pleased. Opening the door of his car he wondered what his boss's reaction would be to Robbie's fee for the job. Reporting what had taken place, Jimmy gave him a quizzical look and grinned when he mentioned the eighty thousand.

"We'll sort that out later Petey," was his only comment. "Now that we have that end of the business sorted out, we can get down to some serious planning. Horse and you can handle lifting the kid, we'll lift the van the day before. I'll take care of the plates. We'll need someone who can keep his mouth shut to drive the van. This is a first for me. We may end up in the 'Guinness Book of Records', hey how about that Petey," Jimmy said with a grin.

Pete agreed with a grin, and allowed that he had no one in mind as driver of the van. Pete knew Jimmy was desperate for the cash to pay off the bookies he had laid off with when he had more bets than he could cover with his own ready cash. If Jimmy didn't make good on his markers soon, he had been given six weeks to make good on the debt, then he would be having visitors. Looking at Jimmy pouring a drink from a bottle he kept in his desk, Pete marvelled again at the audacity of the scheme: kidnapping the Braithwaite kid.

Plans had been underway to pick up the Braithwaite kid, but the little twit had to go and get himself expelled. Some snot nose had squealed when he lost his tuck money on the ponies. The kid had really been a runner for the local bookie who in turn was part of Jimmy's far-reaching web of small-time bookies. When faced with a run of heavy betting, the small-timers laid off what they couldn't handle with Jimmy. In return they would place bets for Jimmy when the fix was in and he didn't want to show his hand.

Pete remembered the day Jimmy had first thought of the kidnap deal, the pleased look on his face, his smile beaming back at him from the mirror behind the bar at the club. Pete, Jimmy and the Braithwaite kid's bookie had been having a drink, when the bookie chuckled and went on to tell them that one of his runners was a rich kid at a fancy school.

When the small-timer left, Jimmy rubbing his hands together said, "Brilliant Petey that's what it is, brilliant. It'll get me out of this bloody awful hole I'm in and cash to spare. Planning is the key to this deal Pete, careful planning and we'll pull it off," a smiling Jimmy said.

"Pull what off," a bemused Pete wanted to know. "What's so brilliant Jimmy? Let me in on it."

"It's so simple Pete, we lift the Braithwaite kid, keep him tucked away at the farm, you and Horse can take care of that. We turn him loose when we get the money. Nothing to it."

"Do you think it will be that easy? Every copper in the country will be out looking for him. This guy Braithwaite is worth millions, has a lot of clout. How are we to get our hands on the kid?"

"Easy, security, if there is any at the school, is sure to be a joke. The kid isn't a royal or anything like that. I'll bet we could walk in tomorrow and lift him and be gone before anyone noticed."

"Sounds great Jimmy, but...."

"No buts about it, we can do it. You, Horse and a driver is all we need to pull it off. Just the four of us, we keep our mouths shut. The kid is sent home, not a scratch on him."

"Sure and tells the cops everything and we are nicked. They'll throw away the key on this one Jimmy."

"Shut up, just shut up, if you haven't the bottle for this say so and you can step out of the picture right now. It's what I have been looking for. The kid should be good for a million. Are you in? If not take a powder."

"I'm in. How are we to get our hands on the kid and stay in the clear? I suppose we could lift him at night, dope him and bundle him up." I didn't like the idea of an outsider working with us. "Why bother with a driver. There is always the chance he will shop us if he gets picked up for some job he pulls on his own later. What d'ya think?"

"You're right, the fewer people we have on the job, the better."

"You could drive the car and Horse and I would look after the kid."

"Why not; the three of us can handle it. You two make sure he has a pillow case over his head and can't see me." Jimmy hurried on,

"These kids, do they have their own room or do they share, two or three to a room. We'll have to check things out. I don't want any slip-ups."

You're right Jimmy, planning does the trick."

"Now you're with the program. Getting our hands on him will be easy, pick him up on his way to place his bets with my bookie. You and Horse wear balaclavas."

"Yeah we should have about an hour before he's missed. Possibly another half hour before any action is taken. By then we will have him tucked away in the loft at the farm. What about the money?"

"I have been working on that, I have a couple of ideas. Let me worry about the cash," Jimmy said. Jimmy saw the kidnapping as a soft touch, the means to get himself out of a deep financial hole — forty-seven thousand pounds deep. Acting out of desperation, he refused to look at the job with any but rose-coloured glasses. Failure to pull the job off would mean ruin. His club, everything he had punched and kicked for, would be in the hands of foreigners. If all went well, Jimmy would still be cock-o-the-walk on his patch and clear of the Russians, fuckin' foreigners.

Two days later Pete walked in on a Jimmy who was slouched over his desk in the small office at the rear of the club, a bottle of Scotch handy and a full glass in his fist. There were the remnants of a cup and saucer and a pool of coffee on the floor across from his desk. Jimmy, a disgusted look on his face jumped to his feet and kicked his chair back.

"The Braithwaite kid was nicked last night. I just had a phone call. He'll be thrown out of school for sure. The toffy noses who run the place won't want him contaminating the other little darlings. And now we're up shit creek, have to start all over again. Any ideas? Those leeches want their money now."

9

A sullen Simon Braithwaite was at that moment standing in front of the Headmaster's desk. This was familiar territory, the old man will fix things, a sizeable donation to some local charity and it would all be over. An anonymous phone call tipped the police off to Mike and his helper. Bundled off to the local police station by two grinning policemen, Simon was frightened at the thought of spending the night in a jail cell. The two policemen made no attempt to conceal their glee when they saw the Jamesbrooke crest on the bookie's blazer.

He was escorted back to school for a chat with the Head. "Braithwaite, you are a disgrace to the school. Your father is not available, therefore you will stay at Jamesbrooke until we are instructed by him what to do with you. Bookmaking, taking the tuck money of the junior school students, terrible, I am shocked at such behaviour. Your father will be most upset. You will not attend classes. You will be confined to the hospital. You will not communicate with any student or leave the school grounds. Do you understand? Very well then, go to your room and remove all your belongings to the hospital. Go!" pointing dramatically at the door.

Margaret Jonescu arrived at the school that same evening to escort Simon, the erstwhile bookie, home to The Grange. Waiting in the Headmaster's study she remembered how things used to be. Poor Simon missed his Mum. Michael too missed Helen. Their happy times together came to a sudden halt in the grinding metal of a deadly car crash. Michael buried his grief in long hours spent in business travel and late hours at the office. Poor Simon a lonely little boy, safe in the care of highly competent nannies, missed the fun times with his Mum and Dad. Jonesy recalled Simon began getting into trouble at the local school he attended, shortly after Helen died. The incidents ranged from fights in the school yard to talking back to his teacher. When the Headmaster told me that Simon would have to repeat a year, I knew that this was much too serious to keep from Michael. He had to be told. Acting on Michael's behalf I had been the one who listened to the recital of Simon's attention-seeking behaviour. A week after my visit with the Headmaster, Michael returned from a trip to Australia. I allowed him time to catch-up on his mail and then I dropped my bombshell. Michael was taken aback by my news. He sat quietly with his head bowed for what seemed like an eternity. I was about to leave when he looked up at me and asked if there was a private school, locally? When I said there was one, and that it had a good reputation, he told me to make the arrangements to enrol Simon in the private school. And now he's in trouble again, poor Simon. Jonesy's thoughts were interrupted by Simon being ushered into the Headmaster's study.

In the car, on the way back to the Grange all attempts at conversation by Jonesy were met by a sullen silence. She was familiar with the reaction of the boy, having acted as nurse-maid on the other occasions he had been expelled. "Simon your father has left instructions that you will stay in the house until he gets back from the Perth Bull Sales tomorrow. Take your cases up to your room. I suggest that you go to bed, it's late. Your father will want to see you at lunch. Good night."

Good old dad, Simon thought, off to Scotland to buy a fine bull, must improve the stock on the farms. He thinks more of his livestock than he does of me. Up with the birds, got to make another million, get the jump on the competition. He never has time for me, him and his hobby farms. Anyway who cares? He'll rip a strip off me and then pack me off to some awful school.

At sixteen, Simon was overweight but carried it well on his five-foot-ten inch frame. His imperious haughty manner; his defence against all comers, didn't sit well with his contemporaries. His casual way with money bought the company of those who would run and fetch for him.

Lying on his bed with his shoes on, he mused about where it would be this time. He hadn't liked any of the schools; all had insisted that pupils take part in sports. Cross-country and steeple chasing were not too bad. Running across open fields in the early morning certainly improved the taste of the breakfast porridge. Studying wasn't so bad, it could be fun. Old "Skinny" Skinner, the math teacher at "The Brooke" had been great. Even "thickhead" Burns had got through Skinny's classes with decent marks.

Still fully dressed, he woke up in time to see the sun poke its big bright face through the trees in the woods near the house. After showering he went and sat in the living room, knowing when his father came home there would be an awful row, as usual.

Instead of the expected angry outburst, his father nodded towards the breakfast nook off the dining room. "Simon," a pause, "Simon what the hell were you thinking of. I'm ashamed, taking money from the little gaffers in junior school. All you had to do was ask and you could have had the cash. What have you got to say for yourself?"

Simon wouldn't look at his father. The little snots were quick enough to line up for the cash when they won. Anyway, he had to take care of his interests, let one off and it would be all over. The bodyguard of hangers-on meted out the punishment to the late payers. Sometimes sports day helped them out. No one questioned a black eye after a rugby game.

"I hope your silence means that you are sorry for what happened. This time you have burnt your bridges. With what happened at the other schools I was prepared to give you the benefit of the doubt, give you a second chance— that fiasco at Ridgewood, and now this."

Simon stood up and was about to explain what happened.

"Sit down! I don't want my son taking advantage of others, quite the opposite. So here is what will happen. You are going to school in Canada. There you will learn to respect others and yourself."

As Simon attempted again to speak his father cut him off. "My mind is made up. As soon as I get to the office, Jonesy will start processing the paperwork and you will have a picture taken for your passport."

Sitting in the back of the company car on his way to the office, Simon's imagination took charge of his thoughts. Canada! Jeepers! I won't get home for holidays. I'll be all alone in some backwater; living with the Eskimos. No more excursions with Jonesy. Close to tears, he wallowed in self-pity. If his father noticed his discomfort, he chose to ignore it.

Good old Dad, his mind is made up, his steel trap mind is closed to anything I might say. Why Canada? Out in the ice and snow, I'll die of frostbite out there in the wilds. Simon in his anguish chose to ignore his father's business ventures in Canada. I'll run away from school, I'll show them.

At the office, Jonesy took charge and arranged for Simon to have an official picture taken and then told him to fill out the necessary forms. Simon did as he was told knowing from experience that Jonesy would not put up with any tantrums. He still remembered Jonesy grabbing him by the ear when he was thirteen and making him apologize to one of the women in the outer office after bumping into her hard in an open doorway. His excuse that he was in a hurry and wasn't at fault was met with a withering look and a further tweak on his ear.

"These are in order Simon," Jonesy said after examining the forms he had filled out. "Let's eat, I know a decent place in the village. Simon, your father is concerned about your behaviour, he worries about these scrapes you keep getting into. Well no one can say you aren't original, Simon the bookie," she said with smile in her voice. Simon looked up at her, a surprised look on his face. At lunch he quizzed her about the new school, wanting to know where it was in Canada, what was it that made this school in Canada so unique, so special.

"I don't know anything about the school other than it is in Canada. It is very highly recommended by business associates of your father's."

"Of course, that makes it just the place for me. His business pals said so. What about me, don't I get a say in this? It's a long way from The Grange; for God's sake it's in another country, thousands of miles away."

"This could be a golden opportunity for you Simon, wipe the slate clean, and show your father the stuff you're made of."

"He isn't interested in me, he doesn't care; all he thinks of is business, money, money and more of the blasted stuff."

"Oh Simon that's not true. Your father loves you very much. It's just, well between the two of us, he is not too comfortable expressing his feelings. Believe me young man your father does love you. This latest escapade has rocked him back on his heels."

On the drive back to the office the only sound heard was the faint hiss of the tyres on the road, wet from a sudden shower. Each kept the company of his thoughts. Simon marvelled at Jonesy's vehement defence of his father. Entering the office, they were greeted by Robert.

You wanted to see me Jonesy?" Robert said, walking with them into Jonesy's office.

"Yes, is the boss's plane ready to go?"

"There is a small wiring problem and the cabin sound system is acting up. Maintenance is fixing it right now. Tomorrow at the latest, they should have the job finished. Everything else is A-OK, ready for take off," he smiled.

"Good. Have the plane ready for take-off at short notice. Simon will be flying to his new school sometime this week or early next week."

"No problem, I'll start things moving at the hangar today. Where are we going? If you tell me where we're headed, I can file my flight plan today."

"Simon will be going to school in Canada. Where exactly has yet to be determined."

Robert's first thought was of Jimmy. Looking at Simon hunched up at one end of the sofa in Jonesy's office, he thought, what has Jimmy got in store for the kid? Best not to think about that. He gave his head a shake and in answer to a 'look' from Jonesy, said, "I'm on my way, see you all soon."

Leaning against the side of the phone booth, he listened to the phone ring several times then, "Yeah, what d'ya want."

Recognizing the voice as Jimmy's, he nevertheless said, "I have to talk to Pete, is he there? It's important that I talk to him right away."

"If it is important then you can tell me. Pete works for me. What is it that's so important?"

Unsure of how to proceed and frightened of what the rough voice on the phone could order be done to him, Robert blurted out, "The Braithwaite kid's new school is overseas...."

"What!" exploded in his ear, followed by a brief silence and then a series of bangs and the sound of breaking crockery. When the noises ceased, heavy breathing told him Jimmy was still on the line. "What do you mean overseas? Where the hell are they sending the little turd?"

"Canada. I have been told to get the plane ready to take off at short notice. That's all I know — for now."

"We'll be in touch," and Jimmy banged the phone down.

His hand still on the phone, Jimmy, oblivious to the wreckage around him in the overheated office, shivered. The initial six-weeks allowed him to pay his debts had been extended twice and now at eight weeks the wolves were howling at the door. Tonight at a meeting with the people holding his paper, he expected his pleadings for another week's extension would be met with cold stares and later, rough justice. If they let him live, the only way he could escape serious injury, was for him to sign over his restaurant and club to his two creditors.

"Where the hell have you been?" Jimmy yelled at Pete as he came into the office.

"What happened? It...."

"Never mind what happened. Did you know that they're sending the Braithwaite kid to Canada?"

"How would I know?" looking around the office Pete continued, "Robbie phoned?"

"And what do I do now? Those leeches want blood."

Looking across at Jimmy, Pete realized he was in a blue funk. He also knew that he would be out in the cold without Jimmy's muscle to back him. "There is the club, you could use it to pay them off."

"After all the sweat and hard times to get this place? It's a bloody shame, why me? I've worked hard to get here."

"There is no way you can get your hands on the cash?"

"No!"

Pete thought back to what he had done on behalf of Jimmy, standing aside while Horse went to work on a slow paying punter. With the club gone and Jimmy's muscle scattered, Pete would be in trouble. Then he had a thought.

"Y'know Jimmy there is a way out of all this. When...."

"Shoot myself, it's that or a wheelchair," he said bitterly.

"When you meet Niki and Yuri tonight tell them about the Braithwaite kid. You can bet your shirt that they have connections in the States who could help us out in Canada. They may even have connections up in Canada. It's worth a shot. The Russkies could be your answer."

Jimmy brightened and sitting up in his chair said, "You could be right," then he slumped back down, "Oh they would go for it, bet on it, but where does that leave me? Bloody foreigners, those two will take over and leave me with the shitty end of the stick. No, leave them out of it. We'll lift the kid before he leaves for Canada. I don't want those Reds walking off with it."

"Well good luck. How are you going to convince the bloody foreigners to give an extension on the paper," an exasperated Pete said. The situation he found himself in worried Pete, he knew that the Russians were just as likely to include him in their quick settling of accounts. Without Jimmy he was simply another heavy who could be bought for a few pounds. Gone would be the fancy suits, expensive women parading with him in the haunts of the moment frequented by crooks, musicians hoping for the big break, deviants of all sorts and the occasional slumming punter. Wrapped in the power lent him by Jimmy's ever present aura of intimidation, he could lord it over others without fear of reprisal. Goaded by fear, he forgot his usual deferent manner and angrily demanded to know what Jimmy intended to do.

"Grab the kid before he leaves, I told you. Get on the phone to Robbie and find out what's going on. We have to know the kid's movements. He doesn't seem to be the sort of kid that would sit around. He'll be looking for some action. I'll give you odds on it. Phone that poncey Robbie."

"Robbie calm down. I know what you said, but this is an emergency. I just heard the kid is going to Canada. Is he still in school or did his old man bring the bad boy home?" Pete said, sarcasm in his voice.

"He's up at The Grange and not allowed out of the house. Braithwaite landed on him like a ton of bricks. I told Jimmy, I still don't know when we take off. Look I'll call as soon as I know. I have to go."

Easing himself up on to the littered desk, Pete reported, "Nothing yet on the flight and the kid's locked up in the house. There is sure to be alarms all over the place."

"If we plan it right we can do it. Planning is the key to this."

"You're right, but we haven't enough time to plan things down to the last detail. It takes time to get everything in order for something like this Jimmy. I say bring the 'Reds' in and let them do the job in Canada."

"I suppose that's what I'll have to do. I'll have to cut them in for a share. I hate to think of those wankers getting more than I owe them."

"Right, but what is the alternative?" At this Jimmy gave Pete a hard look and nodded. "You will still have the club." This final argument convinced Jimmy to let Niki and Yuri in on the plan.

"Tonight, OK, I'll tell them. I don't like it, but I guess I have to." Sure as hell don't want to end up in an alley. "Sharing with those wankers, it's not right."

Pete heaved an inward sigh. Now we can get back to business. It was a daft scheme anyway. It's more in the Russkies' line of work.

10

Anyone seeing Niki and Yuri on the street would have taken them for pampered executives, which they were in a way. The Russians were part of a criminal empire whose soldiers battled in the underworld of the affluent West. Sitting at a table in a fashionable restaurant, the four of them presented a picture of men discussing business. Initially the Russians, conversing in impeccable English, kept the talk light and away from the subject of the meeting.

"Now to business Jimmy," Niki said. "We have been more than generous, but this is the end of the line. As you are well aware we, Yuri and I, are responsible to a hard task master."

"Who demands that the money owed him be paid. Which gives rise to the question, have you the money? A simple yes or no Jimmy," Yuri said.

"Let me explain."

Jimmy knew that the two men sitting across the table smiling at him wouldn't hesitate to break his arm or leg or kill him, all done with an efficiency born of practice. Money and the power that followed on its coattails was the disease that had inevitably eaten away at the hard inner core of unyielding and determined toughness that had given Jimmy an edge in fighting his way to the top of the underworld heap. Now he stood on the sidelines taking sadistic pleasure in what his underlings did at his bidding. The power, the money were on the line, without them he would be a target for anyone with a grudge or a wrong, real or imagined, to settle. Jimmy was frightened.

"Yes or no?"

"Hear me out, I can get the money, but you will have to help me get it." Taking a deep breath, he went on, "I was planning to kidnap this rich kid and buy my paper. Anyway the kid threw a spanner in the works. He was expelled from school, y'know thrown out, for making book. Some welcher grassed him. The upshot of all this is that the kid's old man is sending the little shit to a school in Canada."

Yuri looked at Niki and shrugged.

"His old man's loaded. He should be good for a bundle, a million at least. We are knackered for time, you see."

Niki held up his hand, "Get a grip Jimmy, I think I know what you are getting at, but slow down, take a deep breath and begin again."

Reaching across the table, Niki patted Jimmy on the shoulder. He was enjoying this, and in a quiet friendly tone said, "Go on." Niki was looking forward to destroying Jimmy, and he and Yuri taking over the club. The hard taskmaster they worked for was their former KGB boss.

"Sounds great. What do you want from us? It looks as though you have it all sewn up," Yuri said glancing with a knowing look at his partner.

"That's just it, the way things are we can't lift the kid. He's kept on a short leash. We can't get near him...."

"And you think we can, is that it Jimmy?"

"No no, not here, but you have connections in the States; couldn't they pick him up over there in Canada?"

"An intriguing idea," Yuri said looking at Niki with a question in his eyes. Both knew that a job of this magnitude would have to be cleared by the General.

"Say we agree to this scheme of yours. What do we get and when will you know of the flight plans for his departure? I presume that you have someone on the inside."

"He'll phone as soon as he has the info."

"This inside man, he is dependable? You trust him?"

"Absolutely, he's flying the plane to Canada." That ponce had better come up with the goods.

Ignoring the other two, Niki and Yuri, while eating dessert, carried on an intense conversation in Russian. Getting up to leave, Niki said, "We will be in touch," and with a grin, "Don't leave town Jimmy. Oh, and thanks for the meal, most enjoyable."

Jimmy spent the next two days never far from a phone, in an agony of moody frustration that erupted in violent angry outbursts, which could be triggered by the least inconsequential of incidents. After Jimmy kicked over two tables because his coffee spoon had a small water stain on it, Pete and the staff stepped lightly around him.

Niki reported to his boss — General Leonid Gerchinka— the day after the meeting with Jimmy.

"This could be a money maker Nikolaivitch, but we must be sure that things are as they appear."

"I understand comrade general. The man we are dealing with is well known to us. This is his method of paying off his gambling debts.

With your permission, we loaned him a large sum when he couldn't pay off on bets placed with him. He has a very profitable business, including a club."

"Yes, yes, now when will you find out when the plane takes off? I will make the arrangements to have the boy picked up. What you have to find out is when and where the plane will touch down. Also find out if there will be security personnel or others on the plane and what arrangements have been made when they arrive in Canada."

"Yes comrade general."

"How will our man get aboard the plane without arousing suspicion? There must be no slip-up."

"Yes comrade general. Alexei Stataspovitch will go aboard as a maintenance worker. The pilot will provide the cover story. Everything will be taken care of at this end comrade general."

"Yuri, the Jimmy deal is on. Our beloved comrade agrees. Now we have to ensure that nothing happens here to ruin the scheme. We have business to take care of comrade."

"Do you want me to phone Jimmy?"

"No, tomorrow will do, let him sweat, it's good for the soul I am told," Niki said, clasping his hands as if in prayer. They both laughed.

When Yuri phoned with the news that they would, "Look after the kid in Canada," Jimmy's first thought was one of relief, but next came anger at having to share with the damn foreigners. Now if that clown Robbie would get his finger out, and phone.

Jimmy spent the next week picking up the phone in his office on the first ring hoping that it was the call he was sweating over. When the call came, Pete was the one who answered Robert's excited whisper that take-off was on Wednesday.

"Jimmy will be happy to hear that, he's been going around here like a bear with the toothache. Is it just the kid and you?"

"Braithwaite's secretary will be along to baby sit the kid. She is also delivering some important papers for the boss. We get into Ottawa Wednesday afternoon which means it will be an early start."

"Is the school in Ottawa?"

"No, I've heard it is way out in the countryside, near Ashleigh, a small town west of Ottawa."

Pete, in a voice heavy with sarcasm wanted to know, "What's so special about the place? Is it one of those places where they send rich kids to be sorted out? Made into little gents fit to mix with high society?"

"Something like that. Be sure and tell Jimmy."

When Pete said that Robbie had given the OK, Jimmy grabbed the phone and relayed the information to the Russians. Now he could unwind. Pete would look after his interests in Canada.

11

An hour before takeoff Robert walked out to the plane.With him were two men, their overalls declaring they worked for AIRCOMmunications. With Robert completing his on board pre-flight checks, Alexei and Pete struggled out of their overalls and shoved them into a small locker at the rear of the plane. The supposed tool bag they had brought aboard provided their jackets and coats. Security at the small aerodrome was non-existent. Robert had mentioned casually when talking earlier with the tower operator that two maintenance men would be coming aboard to check the radios.

About to step into the plane, Jonesy saw that two men occupied seats at the rear of the cabin. She had never seen them before. Mmmh, where did they come from? Michael never said anything about other people coming with us. Robert will know. "Who are these men?" she demanded. "What are they doing here?"

Robert was prepared for any questions. "They are technicians. Mr. Braithwaite wants them to do some testing of the TV stations."

"Mr Braithwaite never said anything of this when he telephoned last night."

A sharp intake of breath, a nano second pause and Robert gained control. "I was told of their coming aboard when I arrived at the drome this morning."

"Was anything said about where they are going?"

His pulse racing, "No. Nothing was said about that. All I know is that they are going to Ottawa with you and Simon."

Jonesy returned to her seat, not altogether satisfied with Robert's answer. She was surprised that Michael hadn't mentioned the need for the technicians. Were they to join him in Seattle or work with the Valley Group in Ottawa, she mused. He usually kept her informed of what was currently happening in his endeavours. Still, she supposed, something could have come up at the last minute. Settling down into her seat she closed her eyes, she had been up half the night readying the papers she was carrying in her briefcase. She would hand them over upon arriving in Ottawa.

About two hours into the flight Simon found himself reading the same magazine paragraph for the third time. Giving in to the weights on his eyelids his head slowly dropped until he was resting on Jonesy's shoulder.

Simon awoke with a start, someone was chasing him down a country lane with high hedges on either side. They were so high and thick, he was in deep shadow all the time. Looking first at Jonesy, who was beginning to stir, and then at his surroundings, he realized the menacing force hounding him was only a dream. Undoing his seat belt he stretched and stepped through the door into the cockpit.

"What time is it Robert?"

"Coming up to one-o-clock our time, six-o-clock Canadian time. We crossed the coast about ten minutes ago. That's Newfoundland down there."

Stepping back into the cabin he saw that Jonesy was awake. Ignoring the two other passengers he said. "Is there any food? I'm starved."

"There should be something back in the galley. I'll have a look." Looking back at Simon she smiled, "Lots of goodies here for you Simon. Do you like smoked salmon? It's good on dark rye. I'll make you a sandwich. Here have a piece of cheese. Kill the pangs while I get things ready. Ask Robert if he wants a sandwich? Mention of food and I find I'm starving."

Half an hour later, with soft drinks to hand, they ate. The two maintenance men ate and talked in whispers at the rear of the cabin. Jonesy took Robert's sandwiches to him on a tray, but left the soft drink can unopened. Enjoying their food and with seat belts undone, they relaxed. Robert leaned back in the cockpit, savouring the smoked salmon.

Simon eased his seat back and took a sip of his drink. Boy, Jonesy knows how to make a sandwich; that was good! I suppose in a couple of hours I'll be at this new school. Hockey's the national sport. What sort of game is hockey? Sounds rather dull. Anyway they won't get me to play their silly game. I'll run away the first chance I get. Thumb a ride and head for the nearest town.

The technicians continued to converse, but now their talk was louder and punctuated by the noises of a card game in progress.

Robert noted the turbulence, which had been slight crossing the coastline, had become more pronounced. Although flying on automatic pilot, his hand resting lightly on the control column informed him of the change in the force of the wind. Shrugging mentally, he told himself there was nothing to worry about. Robert saw himself having a good time in Brazil. No more money worries, the sale of the plane would bring a bundle. He smiled, as soon as he was rid of Jonesy and the brat he would gas up the plane and file a flight plan for the UK. Off the coast he would head south. There would be no shortage of buyers in Brazil. About to open his can of soft drink, he dropped it and grabbing the controls, overriding the auto pilot, as the plane suddenly fell into a hole. Grabbing the mike he ordered, "Better get your seatbelts on, and keep them on until we are out of this rough patch." In the cabin, soft drink cans rolled around on the floor and puddles on the tables dripped sweet sticky beverage onto the clothes of the swearing occupants. Tidying themselves as best they could they settled into their seats and buckled up tight. An hour later Simon looked out his window and reported that it was snowing. Strengthening winds buffeting the plane took the pilot and passengers for a roller coaster ride through the sudden snowstorm. Jonesy and Simon, silent, their faces in a rictus of concentration as they clung to the arm rests.

The strong winds hammering the plane kept Robert fully occupied. His thoughts were of his own survival, the passengers were just so much cargo, a burden to be unloaded at the end of the flight. At the end of the flight he would be free of debt and have cash in his pocket. All he had to do was touch down in Ottawa, pick up his cash from Peter and walk away. There would be good times in Brazil. Pity about Janice. He had to look out for number one. Friends, even family, were forgotten in the haste to make good his escape.

Simon, hunched over his seatbelt his eyes closed, looked up when he smelt something burning. He jerked upright. There was a faint blue haze coming from the flight deck and wisping along the roof of the cabin. Next a series of tiny blue flashes in the open doorway grabbed everyone's attention. Simon, his lips forming an O, gave Jonesy a wide-eyed stare.

Jonesy, her eyes large in her white face saw that Robert was having a difficult time trying to control the plane. She could see the veins sticking out on his neck as he fought the monster the plane had become. She could see his lips moving and imagined him cursing his predicament. And then the distinctive odour of something burning brought fear to her eyes. Fear, bile in their throats, possessed them as the smoke thickened. Silently they clung to their seats wondering why the floor was no longer level. Suddenly there was silence, the engines—dead.

Outside the blast of the wind drove a blanket of snow before it, smothering the landscape in its icy embrace. Miraculously, the floor levelled off again, but just then the silence was pulled apart by the noise of the thin shell of the aircraft as it bounced several times before skidding over the terrain. To those sitting white-knuckled in their plush seats, the sound of the metal being torn apart sounded as if all the banshees from the "hell" of Irish story were on hand.

12

Pytor Mosigurskan was ready. He went over his set speech once more: Welcome to Canada Miss Jones, I hope you had a good flight. The limousine is over there. I'll get the luggage. Easy, he thought, then when Alexei helps me with the luggage I will explain to him what happens when we are clear of the city. Driving carefully, he parked the big car and walked across the road to the arrivals section of Ottawa airport.

Inside, he surveyed the area closely for any sign of a lounger taking an undue interest in him. Old habits die hard, he thought with a smile. There was no need for him to be guarded in his movements, no one knew him here. Not like the old days when before he took the airport transit way, he would have taken elaborate evasive action procedures to ensure he wasn't being followed. He walked over to a booth and ordered a coffee and bought a newspaper. The plane should be landing in about fifteen, twenty minutes. Being solely responsible to Moscow for the success of the pickup had caused a small nub of anxiety to rise in his gut. Usually he worked with a partner. I'll feel better when Alexei is here.

The planning had come from the General, he had simply followed orders. The rented RV was tucked away in a stand of trees off a dirt road near Brown's Lake. Ashleigh, the location of Simon's new school, was about twenty kilometres from the lake. The town of about five thousand people was the supply centre for a mixed bag of endeavours, including market gardening, farming, lumbering and tourism.

The General had decreed that only the boy was to be detained in the RV. All others were to be killed and their bodies dumped out in the bush. Pytor could imagine the cold hard voice of the General giving his instructions. Make sure the bodies are hidden well away from the highway. When the ransom was paid, the boy was to be shot and the RV set ablaze. By the time the cause of the smoke was located he would be on his way back to Ottawa and a plane out of the country.

The RV had been rented in Montreal by Pytor. Following the written instructions on a rough hand drawn map, he had driven the vehicle to its hideaway in the bush the same day Simon's final destination was known to the kidnappers. Pytor returned to Ottawa as a passenger in the car that had followed him into the bush. Nice and neat, trust the General, but Alexei should have been here by now. The tiny burr of anxiety that he had put aside now began to move to the forefront of his thoughts. Looking at his watch again, best not to get too concerned yet, the plane could be late for any of a dozen reasons. Dumping his empty coffee cup and the newspaper in the garbage, he sat down. There were only a few people in the area, two of them were in dark suits with peaked caps, obviously chauffeurs. There was no way he could find out about the flight. The plane should have landed by now. He would give them fifteen more minutes and then he would have to make a phone call.

Trying to lose the anxiety that was tightening its grip on his chest, Pytor got to his feet and began pacing up and down in front of the various rental company service desks. Looking around after a few minutes of pacing he decided better walk out into the main terminal and kill time at the magazine racks. When the fifteen minutes were up, he headed for a bank of phones. It was time to report to his contact and inform him that Alexei had failed to show. There had been no provision made in the General's plan should the plane fail to arrive.

There was no exchange of pleasantries. "There is no report of a crash along the route our plane was taking. Find out from the airport people why the flight has been delayed. Our information is that the plane left on time with our man aboard. Use a different location when you reply." Click and it was over.

"Ottawa International Airport, how may I help you?"

"I'm worried about a flight from England, a private flight. It was supposed to arrive here hours ago." Pytor had decided to play the part of the concerned relative.

"One moment sir, I'll connect you to someone who might be able to help you."

About a minute later and another voice said, "Tower Admin, Larry here. Sir, you want information on a flight from England. What's the flight number?"

"I'm so sorry but I don't know the flight number. All I know is that it left Dilsworth airport this morning at eight-o-clock their time."

"I am sorry sir, there is nothing I can do. Without the flight number there is no way I can help you, sorry."

"There must be some way to check."

"May I suggest that you phone Dilsworth to obtain the flight number and when you have it call me back. Without the flight number, there is nothing I can do, sorry."

Swearing under his breath, Pytor hurried towards a bank of telephones.

\+ + +

The administrator Pytor had talked with, decided on a whim to check on the flight. He knew a couple of the guys at Gatineau Flight Service Station. If the plane was missing they would know.

"Gatineau FSS."

"Hi Andy, its Larry. How's it goin'?"

"Uh oh what do you want now? The answer is no."

"Is that any way to treat a pal?"

"OK, how may I help you sir," with gushing insincerity.

"That's better. I just had a phone call from a guy asking about a flight from England. It originated at Dilsworth, those English names eh, weird."

"Flight number time of arrival, hey wait a sec, Dilsworth; Rescue Co-ordination Centre, Halifax, has started things moving on that one. The weather, its scary, snow and high winds moving slowly across Northern Ontario. A communications search will likely be underway."

"That's when you call the plane on available radio frequencies, check the ramp area here and ask the originating airport for the flight plan. Right?"

"That's it, right on."

"Suppose you don't get any reply to your radio checks, what happens? Do you get the search and rescue guys involved?"

"You're a nosey bugger. Next all potential landing sites in the area of responsibility are checked. What that means is that the police, and aircraft, if there are any in the air, are asked to check the sites in their area or on their flight path where a plane could land."

"Wow you guys really work up a sweat when the ETA of a plane is off. I'm impressed. Well thanks old pal, old buddy, I'll leave you to it." Hanging up the phone he looked across at the other man and young woman sharing the office with him and shook his head.

"Tell me, what happened. Is everything OK?"

"They aren't sure Phyllis, they are still checking. The weather was bad along their flight path, but you would think he would have gone above the weather or put down at another airport."

"If that happened wouldn't he have to notify Ottawa of the change in his flight plan. What about radio contact, emergency locators?"

"Nothing. You're learning Phyllis. Gone, disappeared, no signals, nothing since their last contact over the Atlantic."

"What now?"

"When the flight failed to arrive here and its vanishing off radar set off alarm bells and Search and Rescue were alerted. When the weather clears up, I guess they'll send the S and R boys along the flight path."

\+ + +

"Pytor here. No news of the plane. Without a flight number they couldn't help me. Do you have the flight number? With the number they would be able to help me, give me information on the plane."

"Shut up Pytor and listen. Just follow orders. Don't think Pytor, you were sent to do a job not to think. Call me in an hour and I will have instructions for you. One hour."

The man giving Pytor his orders knew that Moscow would have to be told, but before that was done he would make some checks on his own.

"Ottawa Terminal Control Unit."

"Hi. Supervisor Smedley."

"And you are sir?"

"Sinyavsky, tell Bill his badminton nemesis. He'll understand."

"Very well sir."

"Smedley."

"Hi there you old son of a gun, how are they hangin'?"

"Good, and how are you, you crazy Russian? It has been a while since I heard from you Mikhail."

"Right. You know how things are, work, trying to keep my head above the bills and taxes Bill."

"Tell me, I know where you're comin' from man. What can I do for you?"

"Trust old Bill, can't fool you. There is something, could you find out about a flight from England for me? A pal of mine was to have met a buddy here in Ottawa; he was flying in on a private jet. He waited around for an hour and a half and still no plane. The airport authorities wouldn't give him the time of day so he phoned me. Could you make a couple of enquiries?"

'Sure no problem. I'll need some details though, y'know flight number that sort of thing."

"Great, all I have is that the plane left Dilsworth, England, at eight-o-clock this morning, their time."

"Okey dokey I'll get on that right away. Still at the same number I take it."

"Yes, how long will it take? This friend of mine, he's worried, climbing the walls if truth be told."

"A couple of phone calls should do it. Gi'me half an hour."

"You're a real buddy, thanks."

Fifteen minutes later, Mikhail picked up his phone and heard, "Well I have to tell you, the news isn't good. You were right, they left on time, all the correct procedures were carried out in flight until they hit Newfoundland — sorry bad choice of word — then silence. They are overdue here in Ottawa and a MANOT has been issued by the Halifax RCC. All TCU's control towers and ACC's along their flight path were checked earlier. All replies were negative. It was then that the RCC out on the coast was contacted."

"Can you translate all that for me?" Mikhail said with a chuckle.

"Oops, sorry, I guess I did get carried away there. RCC is the Rescue Co-ordination Centre in Halifax, which is in charge of the search. Terminal Control Units and Area Control Centres are your TCU's and ACC's."

"OK but you left one out. What is a MANOT?"

"Right, pardon me all to hell buddy, it simply means Missing Aircraft Notice. What I have told you keep it under your hat. An announcement will be made all in good time, but right now don't say anything in public."

"Of course not, I'll tell my friend and it won't go any further. Thanks Bill, I owe you one. What happens now?"

"The search should get underway early tomorrow that is if the lousy weather lets up. A fierce snowstorm, high winds, some sleet, is moving slowly across Northern Ontario towards the Atlantic Provinces."

"What you are saying Bill is that there will be no rescue effort until the storm clears. Could the plane have flown off course or landed at another airport?"

"It's possible, but if that happened, the pilot would have reported the fact to the authorities; it's a rule. I don't want to scare you but for my money your pal's buddy is in trouble. Sorry about all this Mikhail, there is nothing we can do, it's in the hands of the gods. Haven't seen you in the gym lately, slackin' off eh."

"Too busy, my boss has been on my back for a couple of weeks now, do this do that, no time for badminton."

"Try and make it soon. I've been sharpening my game, you'd better come ready to rumble. I've been partnering with a Pakistani; man is he wicked! He wins most of the time. I can take him about one out of three."

"We'll see about that when I get back after this job is tied up neatly for the boss. Until then practice hard. When I come back look out. I'll take great pleasure in blowin' you away. I have to go, take care."

"Talk's cheap. See you Mikhail."

Before dialling the Moscow number, Mikhail thought over carefully what he would say to the General. "The plane did not reach Ottawa. The pilot followed correct procedure until Newfoundland. As per instructions he kept silent from then on. A snow storm with high winds in Ontario is moving towards the coast. As a result no search and rescue flights will be made until the weather clears. The storm is expected to last for twenty-four hours."

"Perhaps friend Jimmy changed his mind Mikhail. I'll have someone talk to him." Former general of the KGB, Leonid Gerchinka now without the trappings of his rank would never have been given a second glance on the street. Outwardly he looked like any one of a million Russians, a baggy suit in need of an iron, tie slightly askew, wrinkled shirt, maybe a clerk in some bureaucratic warren. Round pink-cheeked Slavic features, unruly thatch of white hair, five foot eight. In his youth he had been a champion wrestler which accounted for his wide powerful shoulders. His ordinariness at close quarters fell away, betrayed by his eyes, greyish blue, cold, unfeeling, killer's eyes.

Guile and the instincts of a hunted wolf that characterized his rise through the corridors of power were never listed in KGB records. Neither were the betrayals of fellow aspirants to power. Relentless in his stalk of high office and its attendant power, the milestones of his journey were the people he used and then forgot. The General took it all in stride; that is until the winds of change swept him off his high perch. A pall bearer at the death of Communism, the General went into business.

Having spent most of his adult life performing the mental gymnastics that were so necessary for survival within the secret world of State Security, Leonid was well equipped to conduct his shady dealings in the New Russia. Information carried over from the secret world was a scalpel in his toolkit of intimidation, one which he used with great care and precision. He was well aware of the route followed by senior bureaucrats when a promotion gave them access to departmental funds. Should greed or ambition supersede the Party's interests then at the General's direction the bureaucrat received an early morning visit from several stone-faced individuals. Shortly thereafter an amended departmental telephone list was published. Those still in power who had been naughty, but had been excused the early morning wake-up call, were always willing to show their gratitude. In his reincarnation as a leading gangster, the general was well served by a cadre of his former toughs and a network of informers.

Reporting on the interview with Jimmy, the interviewing committee's spokesman said there was no doubt about Jimmy's loyalty to the General. The quiet voice with its paradoxical undercurrents of menace and satisfaction noted that the interview had been difficult. The General smiled; well satisfied that Jimmy was in the clear and would no doubt recover. Still smiling, the General turned his thoughts to how the situation could be rescued — was it possible and if so how — and still have a payday. Pondering the problem, he reached for the box of Cuban cigars on his desk. Blowing smoke rings, he looked around his austere office.

Leonid led a very circumspect life; he had his orchids, cigars and Scotch. The orchids he tended lovingly in a climate controlled double-glazed conservatory attached to his modest house. They were his only extravagance, and perhaps an exotic Freudian link to his peasant origins. When he felt the need for female company, someone was always there to provide conversation and anything else he wanted. On such rare evenings the couple who saw to the preparation of his favourite foods and kept the house spotless, were given tickets to the ballet.

While not quite drab, the furniture and the decor could only be described as utilitarian. As a general, he had shunned the ostentation usual for someone of his rank. Although he no longer paraded in uniform complete with a chestful of medals, on the anniversary of the Great Patriotic War he saw no need to change the monkish austerity of his life. He still put in a full day at the office located in a building not too far removed from his old haunts. The major accommodation he had to make in his new job was getting used to the platoon of bodyguards who escorted him at all times. In the old days, the blue tabs on his uniform and his driver was all the protection he required.

Crushing the stub of his cigar in the large brass ashtray, he picked up the phone and curtly demanded "Get Niki at once."

"General."

"Go ahead as planned. Jimmy will call this man Braithwaite and say that we have the son. The price for his safe return is three million, a drop in the bucket to Mr. Moneybags. I want a team, including a sniper, on the ground to observe the pick-up. If the pick-up is compromised Jimmy is to be disposed of."

"Yes comrade General. You did say three million."

"Tell Jimmy the two million extra is interest on his loan," said with a noise that might have been laughter. "Ensure that friend Jimmy knows that time is against us and that he must act quickly. Should Mr. Braithwaite find out about our little deception, inform Jimmy that he forfeits his club."

13

She was home for good, no more school in Switzerland. Aware of the class barrier that ruled their world, he nevertheless kept telling himself that all would fall before their love. Some day he would take over the farm. They wouldn't be rich, but they would be together. Look at Mum and Dad, they were content. Would this summer be as wild as last year?

Alister MacKinnon was a good looking seventeen-year-old. Ally to his friends, got his hard muscles from helping his father farm three hundred acres on the Grant-James estate. On Saturdays Ally was the star forward of the Burnsbrae football team.

Fiona Grant-James and Morag, Ally's sister, were friends and had been since childhood. Home for the summer holidays, Fiona was around our house a lot. She and Morag often went riding out on the neighbouring hills, Morag on a borrowed Grant-James pony and tack.

Ally remembered how, last summer, he and Fiona found each other the Saturday night Alex Goudie treated them to a dram. Morag and Fiona being pals; it was expected that I would partner Fiona at the dance. Morag and Dougie, my best pal, were going steady. We all went outside at intermission, after several sets of Scottish Country Dancing the cool night air was just the ticket. Dougie and Morag wandered off and I was left with Fiona.

There was loud laughter at the back of the hall. Curious, I looked at Fiona and said, "Let's see what's going on." She nodded and grabbed my arm as she stumbled in the grass. Alex and several others were passing around a bottle of beer. When he saw us he waved us over. There were usually a few "screwtops" tucked away in the hedge at the back of the hall by those who preferred something stronger than tea or a fizzy drink at intermission. Alex tossed the empty bottle into the hedge and with a gesture produced a half-bottle of whisky from his hip pocket. Unscrewing the top he said, "Ladies first," and handed the bottle to Fiona.

She held the bottle for a moment and then raising it as if it were a glass she said, "Here's to your good health Alex and lang may yer lum reek!" Her ready acceptance of the drink and her entering into the spirit of the moment surprised the group. They looked on in silence while the laird's daughter downed a gulp of the whisky. Letting out her breath in a great gasp, she handed the bottle quickly to Alex, and began coughing. When the coughing fit ended she said, "That was super, great stuff Alex."

A grinning Alex looked at me and winked, "Anytime Fiona. Here Ally, it's your turn, have a swig."

As I handed the bottle back to Alex the band struck a chord, dancing was about to begin. The bottle was soon emptied and the group headed back to the hall. Fiona grabbed my arm as we started back across the uneven ground. As we approached the splash of light streaming through the doorway, she pulled my arm and said, "Let's stay outside a little longer. It's stuffy in there."

"Fine if that's what you want."

As we walked along the paved path from the hall to the roadway she still hung on to my arm. Nodding with her head towards the small wooden shed that served as a bus shelter she asked, "What's that at the side of the road?"

I didn't know what her game was. She must have known about the shelter. OK I'd play along and see what happened, "It's the bus shelter for people waiting for the bus into town."

"Oh, I see. Would there be a seat inside?"

What the hell was she up to?

"Let's sit in the shelter and get some fresh air. It's a beautiful night."

Sitting in the shelter, we could see the moon through the branches of the trees on the other side of the village green. There was enough light for me to see the profile of her straight nose and firm chin. In my mind's eye I could see her red hair, blue eyes and the dusting of freckles on her cheekbones. I had heard her described as a Celtic beauty.

Turning to me she said, "Do you ever think of leaving Burnsbrae Ally? Do you ever get…."

"Where would I go? What would I do? I know only farming; besides what would my father do if I left?"

"He'd manage. There's nothing to do around here. No excitement."

"True, but Dad depends on me, anyway what sort of job could I get in the city? There's no demand there for someone who can handle a pair of Clydes."

"When I finish school, next year, it's me for the city, London and the bright lights. Maybe go on to university, who knows."

We sat with our thoughts. I suppose Dad would manage without me. He could hire one of the local lads. Any one of a dozen I knew would be happy to work for him. There was always football. My team mates kept telling me I should have a go at turning professional with the county Northern Division team.

He'll stay here the rest of his life, what a waste. He's not bad looking and is a lot more on the ball than some of the others around here. That Alex Goudie, I can see him ending up a drunk. Ally he could make something of himself if he'd just get away from this dump. Aha, what's he doing? Well, well, at last he's putting his arm around me. What's to happen now? When I get back to school will I have a tale to tell? Is this where I lose it? The others, will they be jealous.

My arm slid easily around her slim body. Slowly I moved it up to touch her breast. Turning towards her I awkwardly kissed her on the side of her mouth. When she turned towards me our knees got in the way. Standing over her I pulled her to her feet and kissed her full on the mouth, tasting the whisky on her breath.

When he pulled me to my feet I thought of what one of the girls at school had said about finding her father and a neighbour, "Doing it against the wall in the kitchen." His busy hands were doing things to me, something was happening, I was all shivery inside. I grabbed his hair. It didn't take him long to undo my bra. His rough hand on my breast. As he began kissing my breast he began pushing my legs apart with a knee. Oh yes, do it, hurry, hurry, as I parted my legs, there was a gasp at the entrance to the shelter. A couple who had sneaked away from the dance were surprised to find their trysting place already taken. A nervous girlish giggle and they hurried off to find another less populated spot.

Bloody hell, just when things were going great. She looked great, excited. She fixed her bra. I gave her a quick kiss, "We'd better get back to the dance." The interruption had ruined everything. My underpants were in a mess. Damn it.

I fixed my bra and straightened my blouse and skirt. If only these two yokels had chosen some other place. I was a mess, a bundle of nerves. It was good, his hands on me. He looked dour and threatening. "Am I all right, presentable?"

He attempted a grin and said, "You're beautiful, smashin."

Anyway summer wasn't over. There would be other times. A dance was in progress when we went into the hall. Morag and Dougie, flushed from their efforts on the floor, joined us where we sat. Dougie with a silly grin on his face, I could have hit him, said, "You have decided to join us. Did you get lost?"

A grinning Morag didn't help by chipping in with, "Leave them be

Dougie. They were out looking for owl's eggs."

Owl's eggs! I giggled and gave Ally's hand a squeeze. The thought of prowling about looking for owl's eggs touched his funny bone too.

After that night at the bus stop she couldn't keep her hands off me. The first time was in the hayloft, we literally rolled in the hay. Morag and Dad had gone into town. It was wild, she was all over me. Afterwards we lay in the hay and held each other. She didn't want to let me go, but I had work to do. From then on we were at it every opportunity that came our way. We even did a stand-up in the stall of one of the Clydesdales I had just fed. What a wild summer it was.

We said our goodbye at the farm. She had taken the narrow right-of-way path from the Big House that brought her to the back of the steading and parked her bike out of sight. She knew where to find me. Mum had finished milking our lone dairy cow and gone into the house. She crept up behind me as I was turning the handle of the separator in the milk shed.

"I'll miss you Ally. It's been a super summer."

Standing behind me, she put her arms around my waist. Now with the cream streaming into its' container, I couldn't stop until the batch of milk had been separated. She grabbed my hand as the machine whined to a stop. I knew where she wanted to say her goodbye. She threw herself down on the straw and looking up at me, held out her arms and smiled. I knelt down beside her and she started on my buttons. I too was busy. After she left a sudden loneliness came over me. Could anything come of our wild horny relationship? Would she have anything to do with me when she comes home next summer? I headed for the milk shed and the washing up.

\+ + +

Lying in bed Ally hoped that this summer would be the same as last. Morag had mentioned that she had seen Fiona the other day, as she drove through the village. Ally was gloriously in love. It was his secret, his and Fiona's. His father's urgent voice from across the upstairs hallway dispelled all thoughts of romance.

"Out of bed Ally, we've to be at the Home Farm by seven-o-clock. His Nibs wants an early start. Get a move on, will you."

Today the tenant farmers on the estate of Sir Robert G.W. Grant-James, Bart., (His Nibs), were to gather at the sheep pens on the hillside behind the Home Farm buildings. The Grant-James estate was made up of fifteen farms, totalling more than 4000 acres, several square miles of heather and bracken and a stretch of river. The moor and the river earned a tidy sum annually from the sale of shooting and fishing rights. Each year, as part of their rent, the farmers sheared the laird's sheep.

Alister and his father met up with some of their neighbours on the mile walk to the Home Farm.

At the pens, some of the shearers were honing a fine edge to their hand-held shears. The bantering and bragging afforded by such an occasion made for a friendly day away from the farmer's hard graft on their hard-won acres. Alister and three of his friends had the job of catching the sheep and manhandling them to the open shearing shed where the shearers took over. They were the experienced old-hands, who would clip sheep for two to three hours with barely a pause. Alister, stripped down to his rough shirt, trousers and heavy work boots, welcomed the mid morning break for a mug of strong tea and a thick cheese sandwich.

Ken, one of the catchers said, "Hey Ally! Take a gander over on the other side of the shed. Isn't that the Grant-James girl? I suppose she's showing her pals how we do things down on the farm."

He almost choked on his sandwich. A warm smile framed by red hair. She was talking animatedly to someone in the group. He remembered her skin, soft under his rough hands, her sweet delicate features, blue eyes that spoke a language known only to him. It had been great. Now that she was home for good, dare he hope that they could pick up where they had left off? He hoped so. Two days ago they had met on the village street.

He remembered grabbing her as they had collided outside a shop window, her eyes, angry, as she struggled to escape his arms.

"Let me go, you great..., oh it's you Alister, and where are you off to in such a hurry?" said in a lighter, friendly voice as she snuggled closer.

"I'm late— the bus. Have to go Fiona."

"I just got home yesterday."

"The old man wouldn't let me away early."

"When can I see you?" I've been looking forward to saying hello Ally." Fiona remembered when she told her chums at school about her hols, no one would believe her. Now I'm home for good we'll really have fun. I can't wait to get him in the hay again.

Red faced he stepped back. "I don't want to miss the bus. It's an important game." Hell, I'm getting horny just standing here.

"Still the star of the local team?"

"I missed you. But I have to run."

"Who are you playing?" she shouted as he took off at a run.

"Achray, it's the season opener," shouted over his shoulder. On the bus he had been preoccupied with thoughts of last summer. The things they did. He was shaken out of his reverie when Alex Goudie hit him lightly on the shoulder and said, "Worryin' about the game Ally? They say they have a strong team this year."

Ken nudged Ally and brought him back to the present. "Ally! She's coming this way."

"Hello Alister," she smiled, and then turned to his pal Dougie, one of the catchers, "Hello Douglas."

Dougie grabbed the sheep Alister had been manhandling just as it was about to bolt. His grip on the ewe had slackened at Fiona's approach. His father, sweeping away the loose clippings around him, yelled, "Don't just stand there Ally, you dunderhead, I'm ready for another one."

A grinning Fiona, turned to answer one of the young men with her who wanted to know, "When do we see the stables? I came here to see your horseflesh."

"Oh that's the next stop on the tour ladies and gents. Follow me if you please," this latter said with a glance over her shoulder at Alister. As the group moved away Alister heard the one who wanted to see the horses say, "…lady of the manor, hobnobbing with the local yokels…."

"She's a fine looking lass. Wi' that red hair she'll have a temper, no doubt. Ah well Ally that is for someone else to handle, eh lad." MacKinnon senior had heard whispers about his son doing more than partnering the laird's daughter at local dances and after football matches. The laird and his kind would never allow Fiona to marry beneath her station. He knew the story of George Grant-James and his self imposed exile to America.

Alister, with eyes only for the redhead walking away with her friends, murmured under his breath, "Maybe."

Dougie nudged his pal, "Five minutes back o' the stables would sort out Mr. lah de dah, what'd you say Ally."

Ally nodded, his thoughts elsewhere. She had been on the sidelines at the Achray opener where she had met up with Morag. Following the game both teams and some of their supporters went to the local for a pint. Fiona was invited to join the group.

"What's yours?" Dougie asked Fiona. "Morag, the usual?" she nodded.

"Make mine a usual too, Dougie. It has been some time since we got together for a grand old natter, Morag. What have you been doing since last year?"

"Finished school, I'd like to go on to university, maybe nursing."

"Sounds great. Me I don't know what I'll do."

"Well yes, but university means going to Dundee and then there is tuition. It takes quite a bit of hard cash Fiona to graduate," Morag said wistfully.

Dougie, playing the part of the waiter with tray held high, placed it on the table and ceremoniously presented the girls with their half-pint shandies. Ally removed the two pints from the tray. Morag and Fiona hardly touched their drinks, a mixture of beer and a clear soft drink, they were having their good old natter. Their table was soon the centre of animated discussions of who should have done what during that afternoon's game. As they were starting on their second pint Dougie leaned over towards Ally, and with a sideways glance at Fiona said, "I didn't know we were so popular." His answer was a shrug and a grin.

That first Saturday was the forerunner of many. She was accepted as one of the team's more vociferous supporters and at games affected a long scarf in the team's blue and white colours. Fiona would pick Morag up in her vintage "baby" Austen around one-o-clock. Most of the Burnsbrae team's games were played on one of the pitches in nearby Aberlochry. The players walked or cycled to the match. A bus was hired for the away games. The players, some with their girl friends, and the core of diehard supporters would crowd onto the bus and head down the road to the game.

After the game win, lose or tie, everybody headed to the nearest pub or if the home team had a favourite hangout the visitors would join them and have a beer. Rarely did this fraternising result in anything but loud bragging. On the occasions when someone was invited outside to settle what had become a heated discussion, calmer heads put a lid on it. After the ritual couple of pints had been downed the women would check their watches and begin to talk of food.

The teams would leave the pub in small groups and head for their favourite fish and chip shop. The visitors, no strangers to the town, their team having played in the league for years, knew where to get the crispiest fried fish, the largest portions, the thickest slices of white bread slathered with butter and the most satisfying cup of tea to finish the meal. Afterwards they might wander the streets killing time until the early evening flick. After the film the local palais de danse was the next stop.

Somewhere around midnight back on the bus and depending on the quantity of beer downed by the passengers a sing song to shorten the journey homewards or lights out and silence broken by an occasional hand slap or smooching noises. It was on one of those away jaunts two weeks after their bumpy meeting that Ally and Fiona's relationship got back to where it had left off the previous summer.

The game against long-time rival Tulibartun Thistle had been a struggle. Play was disjointed; they couldn't follow through on the opportunities handed them by the opposition. In the last minute of play the Thistle scored on a fluke, the goalie skidded on the grass and the ball, just out of his reach, blasted into the net. On the bus home, conversation was desultory and ceased when the bus driver doused the interior lights as soon as they left the built-up area.

Aboard the bus Fiona and Ally chose the seat along the back of the bus. There were empty seats on the return trip, courtesy of the die-hards who had stayed on in Tulibartun to drown the game results. Fiona leaned over and kissed Ally full on the mouth. When he returned the salute, she put her legs up on the seat and leaned back into his arm. "Did you miss me Ally?"

"I did, oh God I did. The first weeks after...."

His words were smothered as she found his mouth and kissed him. Her inquisitive tongue aroused him. Breathless, "It was awful back at school."

As his hand found her breast, she eased forward helping him undo her bra. She shivered as his tongue caressed her nipple. As the night, momentarily swept away by the bus' headlights, rushed in behind the bus to reclaim the road, the lovers were only conscious of each other. Swept up in a frenzy of desire, of passion, they were lost to all, but each other. Unaware of time or place, they escaped embarrassment only because the driver yelled, "We're home folks. Wakey, wakey," minutes before he switched on the interior lights. Time enough for clothes to be rearranged.

After saying goodnight to the other passengers, the four stood outside in the clean night air muttering a few words about the weather and agreeing to meet in the afternoon. Taking Ally's hand Fiona looked at Morag and then Dougie.

"Would you mind if I had Ally all to myself tonight. I haven't ...."

A grinning Morag said, "Nae bother, we'll manage." When she saw her escort glower, she poked him in the ribs. "It'll be fine. It's some time since I had a ride on the bar of a bike. It'll be fun."

"Super, thanks Morag, you too Dougie."

"Great, you're a couple of pals."

"Think nothing of it pal," Dougie said, sarcasm heavy in his voice.

Morag gave him a push to where his bicycle lay against the side of the bus garage. Looking back over his shoulder he said, "See you tomorrow."

Ally raised his hand and followed a silent Fiona to her car. Driving through town nothing was said, Fiona was busy with the gears. Clear of the town, the headlights burning a hole in the night, Ally remained silent reliving again the feel of her lips, her breast, her tongue. Looking directly at Fiona he said, "Back in the bus, jeez, we were almost caught with our pants down."

Fiona laughed. "If we had, oh my, what would the neighbours say?"

"The old biddies, I can hear them now."

"The pair of them, shameless. That MacKinnon boy, he seemed such a nice young man. You know what they say, still waters ...."

"Young hussy, she'll come to no good. Mark my words." They

laughed.

Both stared ahead as the countryside, ghostly in the weak lights, passed along each side of the little car. Each, savouring the excitement of the bus ride.

He can't just leave me like this, she thought. He has to do it.

Oh my balls. We can't do it in the car; we'll have to do it on the grass.

The silence was broken after they passed through the gateway to the Home Farm and the Grant-James house. "Maybe it would be better if I hoofed it from here Fiona. We don't want anyone at Big House to see me and gossip.

"Good idea Ally." While agreeing, she did so with the mental reservation, only after they did it. Although excited by the emotions of the evening she realized that it would be best not to take any chances. If her parents found out about Ally, there would be hell to pay. And that would be the end of their wild love making. Dowsing the lights, she allowed the car to come to a stop under a large tree, well over on the grass at the side of the driveway.

They turned simultaneously and faced each other. She smiled and edged towards him. The small car with its gear shift and brake between the front seats meant there was an effective barrier between them. He sidled over as far as the handles allowed and sitting on one hip on the front edge of the seat clumsily reached for her. Met half way by an eager Fiona, they kissed. Their ardour set the little car to rocking crazily. The tight quarters didn't allow for anything but a kiss.

"This is no good Fiona, let's move." She was quick to act on his words. She met him with open arms when he walked into the dark under the large oak. Leaning against the car, their early frustrations were assuaged. They coupled in a spasm of sheer animal lust. Again they coupled, and again, before they were satiated. Their clothes dishevelled they lay on the tatty blanket taken from the back seat of the car and slowly regained their senses. Nothing was said as they stood up together and sorted themselves out. Moving to the front of the car they stood side by side, holding hands. Nothing was said until Ally leaned over and softly kissed Fiona's eyes.

Turning to face him she whispered, "Oh Ally."

Also in a whisper he replied, "My love," and smiled.

They separated. Ally stood in the driveway and waved as Fiona drove away; not knowing that their early efforts in the little car had been observed.

Each side of the driveway, for about half a mile from the gateway, was heavily wooded and was much favoured by Bert Mackay, the local poacher. The rocking of the car surprised the late-night traveller who had stopped when he saw the lights of the car turn into the driveway.

He stood hidden in the shadows. An urgent motion of his hand and his dog stood motionless beside the statue of her master. Well, well, he thought, what do we have hear? When the car door opened he whispered to his constant companion, "Gyp its young MacKinnon the fitba player. And there's herself on the other side. I wonder, was he trying for a goal in the wee car?" The watcher chortled as he moved towards the ornate iron gates, "Won't we have a fine tale to tell, Gyp old girl. Ally and Fiona rockin' the boat and then some," he whispered as he headed home with his night's haul tucked away in his poacher's pockets.

Ally stood watching the car disappear into the night. Dog tired, he stepped out for home whistling "Hamilton House" his favourite reel.

What the poacher saw was soon common knowledge. With much shaking of heads and wise nods it passed quickly by word of mouth, losing nothing in the telling.

"That spoilt Fiona and young MacKinnon. Mark my words, she'll get herself in trouble, just you wait and see."

No good could come of such brash flouting of the class-conscious conventions that still ruled all their lives. While some wondered where the young people of today were headed, others marvelled at the bold Ally having it off with the laird's lassie. Fiona was cast as the headstrong temptress, with Ally playing the role of the helpless lover, led astray by her wiles. The more generous folk opined that it would be all over by Fiona's next birthday. They knew that the affair would be ended once the folk up at the Home Farm got word of it. Fiona would be whisked off to visit some distant relative. None of Ally's team-mates wanted to see their star forward and his girl have to bow to "class". They, in their youthful optimism wanted things to be different—dreamers. The unspoken reality of their different backgrounds would in time strike out at them and end the affair.

Ally's parents knew that Ally and Fiona were "palling together" at football matches, but that was all; there was nothing serious between them. How could they be up to — well you know. They were always with Dougie and Morag. Mrs. MacKinnon eventually concluded that something more than the occasional kiss was going on between the two.

At first she never stopped to ask herself why Ally spent so much time out in the steading after the milking. Other hints she had were: an occasional whisper of perfume on Ally's work clothes, Fiona's bicycle in a shed at the back of the steading and no sign of Fiona. When she mentioned her concern to her husband, he pooh poohed the thought, declaring it was only a summer fling.

"He's a sensible lad. He'll come to his senses. Anyway she'll be going off to university in a while. Let them be, woman."

Her suggestion over breakfast that he talk to Ally was met with a vehement, "No! He knows what's what. There is no way they will have him up at the Big House. Fiona'll be gone in a couple of months. Mark my words. Stop worrying."

Washing the breakfast dishes, Ally's mother smiled fondly, remembering the birth of her son in the bedroom upstairs. The midwife had handed the small bundle to her and the doctor had said, "A fine brawny lad, Mrs. MacKinnon." He'd been an easy birth. Once he got his legs he was into everything. He was a little tinker. She chuckled remembering the time he fell into the drainage area behind the milking cow. Covered in cow dung, he was yelling his little heart out. Oh what a mess! Then there was the time he played hooky from school and went wading in the burn. That was a hullabaloo, oh dear, he got his backside warmed that time. He did well at school. He would come home — pleased as Punch— and tell me that Miss MacKay had him read one of his classroom exercises to his classmates. Once he got his nose into a book, you had lost him. Another time I caught him trying to ride a calf inside the steading. My, if his dad had found out!

And now he is all grown up. A kiss and a hug isn't going to make this affair go away. There's not much I can do, not much any of us can do. Ally, Ally, you'll get hurt. She sighed as she dried the last dish. I wish I could do something.

Unaware of the stir their affair was making in the neighbourhood, the lovers revelled in their intimacy. Twice, when Fiona's parents were up in London, she sneaked him into her bed. The excitement of tip-toeing up the back stairs and down the creaky corridors of the old house was a fillip to what was to follow. The large bed between them they threw off their clothes, their glances speaking eloquently of their desire. In bed, wrapped up in each other briefly before hands began to explore and arouse, then it was wonderful, such ecstatic pleasure.

Standing outside the back door, her kisses warm on his lips, he heard the key turn in the lock. What a night, didn't get much sleep, damn it, it was great, he thought. Looking at his watch he realized that he would have to hurry to reach home in time to feed the beef cattle before his mother got up to milk the lone Ayrshire. Sunday was just another day on the farm. He took off at a trot.

Walking towards the house after feeding the livestock he passed his mother in the courtyard. Neither spoke, he nodded and his mother shook her head. Despite her concern, a twinkle came to her eyes. Upstairs in his room he carefully hung up his only suit in the wardrobe and scrambled into bed bollock naked. He went to sleep, the smell of Fiona on him.

During the week, the manual labour that kept the farm functioning kept his hands busy but left his mind free to wander dreamy byroads. They could get married. Fiona was of legal age, they would get married. Mucking out the byre, feeding the beef cattle, working in the fields, it didn't matter what he was doing, he could relive the weekends and escape the boredom of hard work. Memories of the Christmas and birthday parties up at the Big House came back. Then he hated it when he was dragooned into dancing with the Grant-James girl, her and her frilly frocks and her lah de dah ways.

Now he lived only for the weekends when he could hold that Grant-James girl in his arms. Dancing with Fiona at the George Hotel after a home game, she confided that her father had received a letter from a long lost relative in America. "He wrote that he would like to visit, his 'ancestral home', it seems that he will be in London on business in a couple of weeks."

"What is the connection this Yank has with your family?"

"Daddy told me a little about it. Way back when, sometime in the 1800's, one of great-grandfather's brothers got a local miss in trouble. The upshot of the scandal was that they married and sailed for America".

"Good for him. He stood by his girl."

"I'd heard whispers of the American branch of the family. But to leave his family and go off to the other side of the world, I don't know if I could do that."

"Sure you could."

The matter was dropped when Dougie and Morag joined them at the bar.

Fiona reported later that the American had arrived and had made a hit with everyone. "He was very interested in the family history and we, he and I, went for walks around the estate. He was only here for a couple of days. He was very impressed with it all. He left for London Thursday."

"Of course he was impressed, look who he had for a guide. I'd like to meet him and clue him into what's what; you're my girl, right," Alister said with a grin.

"Oh don't be so dopey. He's married, has four children, all of them at university. He's very keen for us to go over and meet them"

"Are you to take him up on his offer? What did your father have to say?"

"The two of them hit it off right away. Daddy's not your hail fellow well met sort of person, but yes, they appreciated each other."

Fiona too had been impressed and excited by her cousin Earl's description of life in America. She wondered what it would be like to maybe go to university in the States. Earl when speaking of his children had used bright colours to paint the picture of their life at university.

Nothing more was said about the overseas visitor. Ally and Fiona, entangled in their emotions, were unaware of the gossip making the rounds of the district. The surprising thing was that no one at the Big House got word of the affair. Ally's parents deep down in their secret thoughts knew that their son and Fiona made a fine couple— to hell with convention. Overriding this inner rebellion was the knowledge of the certain disappointment that awaited their son. There was the whisper in their minds that the laird, if he so choose, could turn them out of the farm at any time. The resolution came a few days later, the result of a transatlantic telephone call. Few were surprised that the affair ended, but most were surprised, some devastated, by the aftermath.

The two lovers were tucked away in a quiet corner of the upstairs bar at the George, not saying much, enjoying each other and holding hands under the table. Fiona casually mentioned that the transatlantic telephone lines had been busy since her father received a letter from America. "It had something to do with business. Daddy thinks it is worth looking into."

The following week on the bus to an away game Fiona told Ally, "Daddy's going to America on business, something to do with the letter I told you about and an offer Earl made when he was here. Mummy and I will join him for a holiday; brother James is otherwise engaged and so will miss out this time."

The following week Ally broached the subject of the trip to America. "When will you be going? I was hoping we could go away for a few days together. The club's organized tickets and transport to the World Cup next month in France. We don't have to go to the games. Just the two of us Fiona, it'd be great."

"Oh you know I would love to, but this is a once in a lifetime opportunity."

"Fiona, we could make this a once in a life time opportunity too. Let's get married; we could get married at a registry office. Say yes Fiona. I love you. Marry me and we'll take off for the States."

"Alister stop, I love you too, you know I do, but my family, give me time to win them over. This is all so sudden."

Surprised by the ardent proposal and somewhat thrown off balance by it, she panicked. A part of her was flattered, but marriage was not on her agenda.

"I like the way things are, please Ally, stop. Oh Ally I can't, Mummy and Daddy, I can't up and leave them, not like that, please."

The anguish in Fiona's voice, her pleading eyes, stopped Alister's impassioned entreaties to venture into the unknown with him. She came into his arms. Clinging to Ally, in a flash of insight, realization came to her; the visit to America would be the perfect out. Eloping was not the way out of this predicament. University beckoned.

A week later they said goodbye. Intuitively, his Celtic heritage nagged at him that this was the end. He put a brave face on his premonition as Fiona said, "It's not as if I'm leaving for ever. The three weeks will pass quickly. I'll write, send you a postcard."

With the promise of return still in the air, he couldn't silence the inner voice that told him this was the end. Their brief time together in a quiet lane in the early evening was filled with electric silences. As Fiona drove away down the lane and back to the Home Farm, Alister thought, no more, I'll never see her again. Scrubbing at his eyes with a clenched fist, he thought, it's all over, this is it.

Time fled before him as he carried out his many day-time tasks, but the nights. Time crawled, each minute an hour as he lay in bed and relived the fun, the passion of his time with Fiona. His mother wanted to grab him and give him a hug, but no, he was beyond motherly cuddles, Ally was on his own in this.

The letter arrived two days before Ally and his team mates were to depart for the World Cup football games in France. The stamp told him it was from Fiona. The tone of the letter was subdued and informed him that she was to stay with her relatives in Seattle, Washington, and had enrolled at the University of Washington. Well great for you, Fiona, he thought. What happens now? Chin up and all that stiff upper lip guff, he thought bitterly. He flashed on thoughts of heading south and losing himself in a big city, Glasgow, Edinburgh, London. Ally put on his usual face for his pals, but underlying the facade he was disappointed and bitter. Why, was the question foremost in mind; she could have gone to university here at home, why? Unaware of the thunderbolt that had knocked Ally off balance, his team mates were surprised when he got into an argument with a passenger on the ferry. Ally's black mood continued ashore, his team mates, including Dougie, kept their distance. Two days after the first game of the Cup series Ally didn't appear for the usual get together at the evening meal. He had taken to leaving alone early in the morning and was not seen again by his mystified team mates until evening. He was still missing when they staggered back from their night on the town. Assuring themselves that he would show up in the morning with some tale of a "shack up," they headed for the stairs and bed.

Dougie, vehement in defence of his pal, shouted after them, "Ally would never cheat on Fiona; c'mon you know how daft he is about her."

"Well then what has happened, could he have been robbed?"

The question hung in the air. Everyone stopped on the stairs and looked back at Dougie. They knew that something was amiss with their star forward, but none of them knew about Fiona's letter ending it all. Since Fiona left for the States, Ally had been in a bind. As soon as she was back all would be well; they could live with his odd behaviour.

"Jeez, he had a fair bit of cash on him. I hope you are wrong Ken. He could be beat-up and lying in some back street."

"Let's not jump to conclusions; I still say, despite what Dougie says that he is shacked up and having a good time."

"Yeah, me too, he's in bed with some tart he picked up."

Likely in some boozer. Last night he had a pretty heavy load on. I heard him staggering up the stairs."

"Yeah, he woke me up; it was late."

"Maybe he's shacked up for the night. We'll hear all about it at breakfast." was greeted with derisive laughter.

The discussion went on as they climbed the stairs; with Dougie adamant that Ally wouldn't cheat on Fiona.

14

Ally was already in bed. In his wandering around the city he had passed what appeared to be an old fort, its massive gates hiding what was within. When he found himself passing the fort for a second time he stopped to read the plaque on the wall: Bureau d'Engagement — Legion etrangere — Ouvert jour et nuit'. About to continue his slow moody meandering, he was stopped short by someone stepping around him to hammer on the doors. Curious, he waited to see what would be revealed when the doors were swung open. Inside was an ordinary cobbled courtyard, but the figure with a hand on the huge door was not an ordinary everyday sort of person, he wore the uniform of the French Foreign Legion. Pictures of mounted Arabs attacking a desert fort flashed into his head. What the hell, she's gone, I'll never see her again, what have I got to lose — he entered the courtyard.

Looking around at the grey stone walls of the courtyard, Ally was reminded of the farm buildings at home. Turning to see what was going on behind him, he was in time to get a brief glimpse of the quiet street just before the heavy wooden door thudded into place. Making sure the door was barred, the smartly turned out legionnaire nodded at them to follow him. The thud of the door, loud in the courtyard, sharpened Ally's awareness that he was leaving all that he knew and was familiar with, for the unknown. To hell with Fiona, anyway it can't be that tough. The only furniture in the room was a bare wooden table with a soldier sitting in the only chair; he stared at Ally with unblinking eyes.

"I want to join the Legion."

"Why?"

Surprised by the question, he said the first thought that came to mind, "To see the world; for adventure, see exciting places, travel."

"I think you should go away and think again English," the soldier said in accented English. "You sign a contract for five years. The life is tough; make a mistake, the punishment is swift. Sign the contract and you belong to the Legion."

Surprised by the soldier's candour, Alister said, "I want to join, I've nothing to lose."

Muttering, the soldier heaved himself out of the chair and beckoned Ally and the other candidate to follow him. After tramping down echoing corridors and up a winding stairway, he led them into a barrack room. Two-tier bunks took up most of the space in the small room. Several of the beds were occupied. Four men sat on the edge of their beds, and using a suitcase as a table played a game of cards. Pointing to a couple of bunks, the soldier left them. Sitting down on his bunk, Ally had a good look at the other occupants of the room. They were a mixed bunch, two of the card players were dressed in suits with slicked-down hair, obviously a couple of "wide boys". The others, including the other two card players, were a scruffy unshaven bunch. A couple with mops of long hair had him scratching his head as he imagined the tangled mess a haven for all sorts of creepies.

Ally tossed and turned on his straw-filled mattress and dreamt of cake and ice cream. Mrs Grant-James was a pain in the neck. Every year at Christmas she would run around at the Big House, making sure we were all having a good time. The scoff was great, but before we could get to the goodies we, the children of the tenant farmers on the Grant-James estate, had to play daft games. I was too old for this sort of nonsense, I was sixteen, but Mum and Dad insisted I go and look after little miss know it all, Morag my sister.

After eating we lined up at the bathroom where Mrs. Grant-James supervised us as we washed off the traces of our sticky buns that we hadn't licked off. After hand inspection we had to dance. Dancing in the village hall was great fun, but up here at the Big House, it was all lah de dah.

Dougie Johnston, my best pal, and I were in the same set; Morag my sister was his partner. Mrs. Grant-James told me to partner Fiona. Before she turned the grammy on, Mrs. Grant-James read the movements we would follow in the reel. Fiona, ignoring her mother, was busy talking to Alison Goudie. The dance was an easy one. We had taken it at school. I suppose "Dancie Munro," had written out the "cheat sheet" for her Nibs.

Our set was a schemozzle. Fiona didn't know what to do, so I had to push and pull her through the dance. It was great fun pushing the laird's daughter around. When the music stopped, I bowed and thanked her, as we had been taught, she smiled and gave me a funny sideways look.

Before the next dance was called, I saw Fiona and her mother having an earnest conversation at the gramophone. Whatever it was all about, Fiona stood with a smug look on her face, while her mother searched through a pile of records. Finding one she turned to the room and clapping her hands to shut us up, announced, "The next dance, a quickstep, is a ladies' choice."

A quickstep, Dancie didn't teach us quicksteps, it was strictly Scottish Country Dancing, where the boys were on one side and the girls on the other side of the set. A quickstep — you had to put your arms around a girl. The only girl on the floor was Fiona. She's coming over here. I sidled away from Dougie, hoping that she would pick him. No, it was me she was after. I can't dance a quickstep. I could feel my face getting red. "May I have this dance?" What to do? I suppose I could refuse, but then I got my back up. She was paying me back for pushing her through the last dance. Well bloody well let her.

The music filled the room, all eyes were on us. Suddenly I had two left feet. We stood, she smiling, me like a window dummy. Somewhere, above the rushing in my ears, a voice called, "Show us some of your boogie, Ally." It was Morag referring to my efforts in the kitchen at home when listening to jazz on the radio. My Mum and Dad shook their heads at me doing my steps, but it was fun. Sometimes I would grab Mum and twirl her and step around her in time to the music. It was always good for a laugh.

The fuzz in my head cleared. Staying well away from her feet, I started to move — surprise, surprise, Fiona moved with me. It was great, when the music stopped we found that several of the more venturesome girls had partnered each other and joined us. Unconsciously I put my arm around Fiona's waist as we walked off the floor. When I realized what my hand had done I quickly dropped it to my side and red-faced, thanked my partner.

Giving me an enigmatic look, she said, "That was great fun."

That was the first time I really saw Fiona. She was seventeen. Before, she was just a girl I had to be polite to and dance with when her mother insisted.

A week after the party, Morag was barely in the door when she announced that Fiona had shown up at the weekly dancing lessons in the church hall. The jigs, reels and strathspeys of Scottish Country Dancing were popular in the district. Dancie Munro conducted dances Friday nights in the village hall.

"Look at your partner, smile. When you lead down the dance, remember, it's a dance not a gallop. Don't grab for your partner, take her hand as you would your Mum's best china, carefully."

I'd had to miss the weekly dance class because of a farrowing sow. By the time she was finished there were twelve little pigs snuggled in the straw beside her. Breeding pigs was my idea. Sheep and cattle were the usual livestock in the district. Dad had loaned me the money for my experiment. If all went well we might go into pigs on a larger scale.

I was my father's right-hand man on the farm. Between us we ploughed, sowed and harvested three hundred acres with a pair of Clydes and an old tractor. We were one of the three farms on the estate that had some hill acreage on which we ran about a hundred head of sheep. Dad was the shepherd. When I left school at fourteen the road I would travel had already been chosen. Outside of farming the only other jobs in the district were blacksmithing or joinery. Working as a blacksmith would have been interesting, but Dad needed me on the farm. My wages were my room and board and a few bob for pocket money.

The next week, Morag and I were off to the dancing. Parking our bikes at the back of the hall, Morag said, "It looks as though Fiona is here again." Pointing she said, "She must have talked her brother into joining her. That's his bike."

Before she went back to school in Switzerland, Fiona attended a Saturday night dance in the village. After the dance, Dougie and I, at Morag's insistence escorted her and Fiona up the tree-lined driveway to the Big House. Fiona insisted we park our bikes and join her for a "cuppa." Morag and Fiona were old pals. Morag, having been conscripted to keep Fiona company when they were little. Morag an independent little girl held her own with Fiona who, in the early days of their playing together, wanted things done her way. From this early friction, perhaps because of it, a lasting friendship developed.

Dougie and I sat on a couple of stools and chatted. He asked how my pigs were doing. He didn't think much of my experiment, we had argued about this several times.

"One of my sows has twelve growing pigs suckling her. The other one shouldn't be too far behind her. And then instead of two pigs Dougie I'll have lots of little pigs."

"Just remember smart arse these same little pigs have to be fed."

"That's no problem, after they're weaned, we'll feed them on the swill from the George's kitchen."

"Well well aren't you the clever one Ally MacKinnon! And how did you manage that?"

"Nae bother at a', I spoke to the manager and that was it. Before I sell them the little porkers will be fed an oat and bran mash to finish them for market."

"Maybe we'll try pigs up at our place. But first, let's wait and see you don't lose your shirt on this daft scheme of yours."

"Nothing ventured nothing gained Dougie me lad. The other day there was an ad in the Farmer's Weekly about growing mushrooms. This firm will buy everything...."

"Mushrooms! My God Ally, you've finally gone round the bend." Shaking his head he said, "Mushrooms, come off it Ally, you're pulling my leg."

Grinning Ally said, "That's right, I sent away for more information."

"Where will you grow your mushrooms, you daft bugger?"

Before he could answer Morag said, "It's all ready, quit your gabbin' and come and have a cuppa."

While yarning about old times, Fiona and Morag had opened cupboards and raided the contents of the huge frig and prepared a midnight snack of biscuits, cheese and cake. All laid out on the big kitchen table. Fiona was the only one fully at ease, the rest of us were just a wee bit apprehensive. What to do should the housekeeper or the cook come marching into the kitchen. Worse yet, what if her mother waltzed into the kitchen. Cycling home, after tiptoeing out the back door, the last words Fiona said kept repeating in my head, "I'll be home for the summer. Good night Morag, Dougie — *Ally!*"

15

There was someone dancing on the tin roof of the tractor shed. Banging a pot with a lid and yelling, a soldier marched into the room. Realization of where he was jolted Ally fully awake. During his three-day stay at Fort de Nugent, Ally was on his feet at six-o-clock. After a wash and shave with cold water, it was time to eat. After a breakfast of coffee and a croissant, Ally cleaned toilets, picked up cigarette butts, and in general was kept busy doing all the shitty jobs (corvee) around the Fort. On the third day, a Friday, after a hurried meal and with much shouting of vite, vite, they were herded aboard a night train to Marseilles.

At Aubagne, headquarters of the Legion, Ally and the twelve others from Paris were joined by a large group from the several recruiting offices across France. Shouted at by a commanding figure in a black kepi, the new arrivals were persuaded with hearty shoves from his two helpers to form up in two ranks. Names were called and after all had been accounted for they were marched off to breakfast, coffee and a slice of bread, no seconds.

After breakfast all their personal belongings were taken and they were only allowed to keep what cash they had. Hot showers followed. In their new quarters they were crowded in bunks three-tier high, making for eighteen bodies in each small, but clean room. The issue of clean denims were also welcomed. He began each day with the hope that today would be the day he would hear an English voice. Fights were commonplace, especially in the dining room. Food, apart from breakfast, was good but not served up in overly large quantities.

The candidates, when not being herded to one test or another, were left on their own, unless grabbed by an NCO to do some grubby chore. An early breakfast, then began the task of finding out who among the rag tag bunch would be selected as suitable for service with the Legion. A thorough medical examination was part of the winnowing process.

Waiting with a dozen others on benches in a cold antiseptic room, Ally puzzled over what they were waiting for. After about half-an-hour a soldier came in and told the group to undress. Those who didn't understand French followed the example of those who did.

One by one the naked recruits were pointed at and then escorted into a room presided over by a man in a white coat. Ally's arm was grabbed by the soldier who gestured for him to get up on the examining table, and the medical exam began. Gestured to get off the table, he stood expectantly beside it not understanding what white coat was saying. The soldier bent over and pointed at Ally to do likewise. Surprised at what happened next, he was still red in the face when he left the room. Dressed and it was back to waiting. The soldier joined them, read several names from the sheet of paper in his hand. Ally's was not among them, he had passed the Legion's tough medical.

Early next day, he was hauled out of his bunk and shaken awake by a soldier who kept repeating the same phrases, each time delivering them more forcefully. Standing slack-jawed in his underwear, he didn't understand what was being yelled at him. He came to his senses when the shouter motioned him to put his pants on and follow him. The shouter gave him a shove towards the door before he had his shoes laced. He spent the day fetching and carrying for the cooks.

Ally, after his day of trying to understand and then follow the mimed orders of the grinning cooks, was not in the best of moods. All he wanted to do was crawl into his bunk. When he arrived at his bunk, he found it occupied. He tapped the shoulder of the occupant, a dark-skinned, solid looking individual. He was answered in a foreign tongue; the intent of the message needed no translation. He was being told to "bugger off."

Instantly he grabbed the intruder by the shoulder and hauled him clear of the bunk; in the process smashing his head on the metal frame of the top bunk. Dazed, the interloper, held firmly by Ally, struggled to get on his feet. Changing his grip, Ally belted the guy on the jaw and dropped him unconscious on the floor. About to climb into his bunk, he paused, turned back to the prostrate body and gave it several hearty kicks on the upper arm and shoulder, all the while yelling and swearing. The card game continued.

Next morning, Ally, enjoying a quiet smoke, saw the Italian leave the group he was with and walk towards him. While still some distance from Ally, he pointed and said something. Ally stood his ground, his gut in a knot. Taking a last drag on his cigarette he flicked it towards the guy. Hell, if he was about to get into a "barney" with this guy he might as well show a bit of class. After all, as the only Scot present, there was the no small matter of national pride.

To the onlookers Ally appeared to be unconcerned, but behind the nonchalant mask he waited, a wound-tight spring, oiled by adrenaline, ready to strike. Someone in the group the intruder had left shouted, and he turned round to face them and made a gesture. Stamping on the flicked butt, he continued towards Ally, all the while talking in a quiet voice, with a smile on his swarthy face. Ally wasn't fooled by the smile; he was close enough for him to see the cold hard eyes. A sudden thought, what if he had a knife? Fear curdled in his gut, but was overtaken quickly by a resolute calm. This daft bugger would take some stopping; best keep him at arm's length.

Ally waited, leaning against the wall, ready to explode into action. When he, still with a smile pasted on his face, was close enough for Ally to smell him, he raised his fists. This was it. Ally stepped quickly aside, intending to land one on the intruder's jaw. His manoeuvre surprised garlic breath, whose booted foot, aimed at Ally's family jewels, grazed his leg. Quick on his feet Ally moved behind the kicker and gave him a boot in the arse sending him crashing into the wall he had been leaning against.

Shaking his head, he turned, and teeth bared came at Ally again. Taking a couple of steps backwards, Ally waited. The wild eyes of the other guy warned Ally his attacker was out for blood. No doubt thinking he had the kid on the run, he charged. Gone was all caution, the attacker wanted to hurt to maim the kid.

Ally stood his ground, his heart in overdrive, and when it looked as if he would be run over, he moved. With all his one-hundred-sixty pounds behind it, he kicked the Italian in the goolies. Clutching his balls, the Italian doubled up in pain. Bent over he was an easy target. Ally swung and connected with his attacker's chin. It was over; the Italian collapsed in a heap.

Next day he was on the alert for a rematch. At the end of each week the process of selection took its toll. In Ally's room there were only two others left. Taking tests were a regular part of life in the Legion. Later tests would determine the candidates' knowledge of weapons, physical fitness, map reading (day and night travel) unarmed combat, shooting and all the other skills of a legionnaire.

Also, there was the "examination" by the two hard faces from the internal security unit. The "Gestapo" vets each candidate's background and has the final decision on whether he stays in the Legion. He remembered the reaction of the one in the grey suit when he gave the same answers as he had in Paris. Shaking his head, he spoke to the other, who snorted, and raising his eyes heavenward muttered something about les anglais sont fous.

Of the thirty or so recruits who had walked through the gates of Quartier Vienot three weeks earlier, only Ally and twelve others were left. Before transferring to the training regiment at Castelnaudary, they were marched to a room where tape recordings in a number of languages explained that they would be signing a five-year contract, and once signed there was no reneging on the deal.

Next stop was at the quartermaster's where he was issued a large bag into which he stuffed all his equipment (paquetage), which included a dress uniform complete with red and green epaulettes, blue waist sash, and white kepi. And of course boots—two pair of les Rangers. Life now took an abrupt turn to the left. Enroute from Aubagne, a recruit taking life easy and having a smoke with his feet up was the template for what would be a constant element in their training.

The poor sod never knew what hit him. The corporal in charge lit into the lounger yelling at him. Failing to understand what was being shouted at him he sat his face blank, his feet still on the seat. This was too much for the corporal. Grabbing a handful of clothing, he yanked him to his feet and slamming the amazed recruit into the side of the bus, continued his rant. Ally, sitting beside the culprit, attempted to get up and move out of the way. He was rewarded with a back-handed smash to the jaw and a warning look from two glowering eyes.

At Castelnaudary Ally and the others joined the engages volontaires waiting to be transferred to a farm out in the back of beyond. Here, way off the beaten track, volunteers would be shaped to the Legion's mould. There was no idling while waiting for enough candidates to make up the platoon. A super-sensitive corporal kept them all occupied: cleaning toilets, scrubbing floors; the floors were clean enough to eat off. Next it was picking up every piece of scrap paper, no matter how tiny, dog ends (cigarette butts) too.

Their first morning at the farm, the forty volunteers were handed pails, mops, scrubbing brushes, and bar soap and began the work of giving the buildings a thorough going over. All had to be immaculate. Every piece of wood was scrubbed white, every kitchen utensil shone. As with fine steel, the volunteers were hammered and tempered in a fire, one fuelled by tradition and heroic deeds. Those who had fought and died under the Legion's banner were held up to the volunteers as role models, worthy of emulation. There was no let up in the harsh treatment meted out for mistakes. After the initial blows to the body, punctuated by a rave in which your ancestry was recast in ribald terms, the punishment could range all the way from extra duties to several hours of la pelote.

\+ + +

Running around with two bags of sand in a pack which had the straps replaced with heavy-duty electrical wiring was no fun. Sergeant Mendoza went on a rave about the condition of my rifle and gave me an hour a day for six days. The torture had been refined. The runner, me, at the shrill command of the NCO's whistle, had to do a forward roll, crawl on my guts or hunker down and march in a crouch. The number of blasts on the whistle ordered my action. After pelote there is appel, and if things are not to the duty NCO's liking there is further punishment. Was it really necessary to hammer at us day in day out the way they did? Bastards!

Dust on the edge of your bed, equipment folded incorrectly, to wearing unwashed denims, brought down the wrath of a corporal. They enjoyed having us crawl around in the dust and shit as punishment for the sin of not getting it right. Washing our denims, usually around midnight, was the last chore of the day. Issued with two of everything, each had to be spotless to remain in our locker. A spot, real or imagined, and it all ended up on the floor.

Pride of place in our locker was given to our kepi blanc, which was centred between our red and green epaulettes. Still volunteers, we had to earn the right to wear the white kepi; then and only then could we call ourselves legionnaires. It remained in its plastic covering while we sweated, were pummelled, marched almost to exhaustion, all with the sole purpose of earning the right to wear the revered kepi, emblematic of the legion's gallant past.

With the privilege of wearing the cherished kepi went the daunting task of upholding the grand traditions of the Legion. And when called upon to make the ultimate sacrifice, to do it unhesitatingly and with style, as did those who rest in faraway places. The haunting melodies of their ghostly marching songs, the old hands say, can still be heard in the former outposts of the Legion when the moon is high and a soft wind blows from the south.

If someone pulled a major boner, not only the culprit was punished, the section too had to get down in the dirt and take its lumps. Peer pressure was a great motivator for the clumsy and slow learners. Push-ups were a favourite with the NCOs, who after ordering the section to get down and do twenty, would themselves join in and do the twenty with us. After a few weeks, push-ups were no sweat. Not to be outdone in their efforts to get the platoon in top physical condition, the corporals came up with push-ups to music. Oh yes the music was when you clapped your hands while in the prone position. There were bloody faces before this too was mastered.

At Aubagne we were a collection of individuals, there was a wariness in any social contact. This attitude continued at the farm for a few days. A camaraderie, founded on our communal hardship, began to show itself early on in our stay at the farm. In the mornings, nods were exchanged with a few saying, "hello Johnny" to me.

Our first month at the farm went quickly. Time flies when you're having fun! We were always on the move. A corporal screaming at us to get out of our bunks at five-o-clock was our reveille; washed, shaved and with a mug of coffee and a slice of bread for breakfast, we were ready to start our day that didn't usually end until midnight. The dodgers at headquarters and the training staff, crafty sods, knew how far they could push us. There was a line they knew not to cross, they wanted to bend us to the Legion's way without damaging the goods.

To mark the end of our month in hell, we were let off the leash. Spiffed up in our uniforms complete with blue waist band and epaulettes, we paraded at dusk. The regimental band had been transported to the farm for the occasion.

The undercurrent of excitement could have been cut with a bayonet. Bare-headed, we marched to where a huge bonfire and flaming torches lit the darkening sky. Called to attention, we stood looking straight ahead as Commandant Auger, in a clear ringing voice, reminded us of our oath of honour and fidelity and then led us in singing Le Boudin, the song of the Legion.

Then the magic moment; we were authorized to don our kepis. We had been holding them behind our backs. Gathered around the fire we sang the songs we knew and the commandant and the staff entertained with some of the songs we had yet to learn. And of course the boys in the band put on a show for us. The cooks too did their part and gave us a slap-up feed. At the end of the party, buses transported us to base camp. It was a night I'll never forget. When I think back to that night I get the shivers.

Next day, we were granted our first leave. Accompanied by the NCOs and an officer we ate lunch at a restaurant in town. After the meal, we were on our own until midnight. Spotting a boozer in the early evening, I decided to try the French beer. Inside there was a lone legionnaire standing at the bar and a mixed bunch of Germans and Spaniards at tables towards the back of the room. I nodded at the blonde guy and went over to the bar. After a couple of drinks, he looked over and pointing to my empty glass gestured he would buy me a beer. I nodded and thanked him.

Before we left at about ten-o-clock we had put away a few beers. Both of us had picked up enough French in the school of hard knocks to be able to swap basic information about ourselves. He was a Finlander, our names, and what we thought of the NCOs. Matti and I were sharing a snack when loud voices at the back of the room brought our heads up. Over at the German's table they were pushing one of the guys and demanding he get to his feet. Finally he downed his beer and stood up. Clearing his throat he began to sing. Wow he was good, and then the group joined in. It was great. They were still at it when we left. Thick-headed next morning, I didn't get out of bed quick enough for the corporal who proceeded to throw my carefully folded kit on the floor. Leave was over.

In the early days it had been difficult to follow my philosophy of keeping my eyes and ears open and my mouth shut. Once and only once did I object to a corporal kicking me. We were into our seventh week of hard training, when I lost it. Punishment for striking an NCO is severe, but I didn't give a damn, I was fed up and wanted to smash his face in.

We had halted, on our way back from a hike with full kit, to sort ourselves out and make an entrance at the farm. I failed to make the smooth crisp drill movement Geller demanded. He came at me with his fists. The last straw was his ill-aimed kick, meant for my arse, it caught me on the side of the leg. It wasn't any more painful than a dozen others I had been given by him and others, but I'd had enough. To hell with this, and stepped out of my rank and called his name. He stood still while I carefully put my rifle down. A grin on his face, he stripped down to his shirt and motioned for me to do the same.

We stood facing each other, about eight to ten feet apart on the rough track about half a mile from the farm. All was quiet, our section was the only one in the immediate area. He motioned me to step closer. Geller tore into me and gave the section a demonstration of unarmed combat, and me, the hiding of my life.

At appel, after inspecting my kit, he winked at me as he moved to the next bed. I wondered, was it his way of saying no hard feelings Johnny? All Brits in the Legion are called Johnny, don't ask me why. Striking an NCO is a cardinal sin in the Legion and requires the sinner to do penance for forty days in the guardhouse and hours of the punishing pelote.

Until I picked up enough French to fully understand what was being yelled at me, I was treated as a punching bag. Pride was what kept me going. My mother always said I had a dour streak in me three-feet wide. I'd show them, they wouldn't get the better of me, the bastards. In time I got it into my thick head that the purpose behind the punches and kicks was the Legion's way of preparing us for the hard life that would be our lot once our four-month basic training was completed.

Toughened by our daily hikes and jaunts around the gut-wrenching combat course (parcours de combattants), at the end of three months we were pulling together as a unit. No longer did we dither when ordered to name the parts of our weapons. Now we could name the parts and strip the weapons while blindfolded. Our singing too had improved; now there were no more punishments for not following the melody, or botching the words.

On the march a song would often be called for. It wasn't enough to sing, you had to sing with spirit— or else. By the time we started our fourth month of training we had quite a repertoire. The songs with their haunting melodies were a Legion tradition and were part of the training program. The songs, it's weird, but they sent shivers up my back; there was something about them that made you hold your head up, you were proud to be a Legionnaire. I know it sounds daft, but that's the way it was. Some distance from the farm we would halt for a few minutes and get our kit straightened before resuming our march, but now at the regulation eighty-eight steps a minute. The long unhurried step of the Legion — and sing!

Finally it came to an end. We were ready to take our place in one of the Legion regiments. I didn't fancy the cavalry; driving around in a tank wasn't my idea of soldiering. The regiment I really wanted to join was the paras, but only the cream of the crop were sent to the 2nd Regiment. I wasn't that daft about jumping out of an aeroplane, but your wings brought extra pay, and on top of the money you were one of the elite. Ready to go at a moment's notice.

Parading for the last time at Castelnaudary, we waited to find out where we would be sent. My name didn't come up in the names called out for the cavalry. Great. But it was the same when the infantry guys were called. Where am I going? After all I have been through don't tell me I've failed. Bloody hell, I gave it my best shot! I wasn't the only one whose name hadn't been called. There were about a dozen of us— and then the light went on, we were the guys posted to the paras!

At Calvi, we new boys were put through the mill. The NCOs set out to make sure our life was hell. It was more of the same, punches and kicks, only more intense. Three to four hours' sleep a night. Grinding marches, intensive unarmed combat, weapon inspections, usually in the early hours of the morning were our lot. After parading before the colonel to receive our wings, things changed. I was now one of the lads. It had all been worth it. There was no let up in the discipline. No excuses were allowed, should you appear on parade not properly shaved, boots not polished, with a dirty weapon, or untidy uniform.

16

Alister MacKinnon threw a log on the open fire in the large room of the cabin.After years of living in cramped quarters in bunk and boarding houses he marvelled at the spacious rooms in his new home. It had been a good day; the trip to Miskimin for supplies. Driving had been easy on the highway, but the mile of bush road had been a challenge. Where the snow had formed drifts, it had taken several charges with the 4 x 4 to batter his way to the cabin by the lake. The wind in the trees the only sound, he poured a generous measure of amber liquid into a glass and sank into the wing chair by the fireplace.

Taking a sip of whisky, he thought how lucky he was to be alive. There had been exciting times along the way. Here he was safe in his own place, no one around to bother him. Settled comfortably in the chair he rolled the whisky around his mouth. Whisky abetted by the blazing fire soon had Ally nodding off. The empty glass slipped from his hand and made a small sound as it came to rest on the small table beside the chair.

Bleary eyed and stiff, he stretched. Jeez what brought all that on. That's all water under the bridge. The good old days, yeah. Fiona,— we certainly caused a stir— I bet she married well. Yank and Wayne, did they stay in the regiment? Blondel got over his wounds, he'll be a captain for sure, maybe a commandant. The jump at Kolwezi, whew that was a dicey do. And Blondel's parents; the cigarette case was a nice touch. Walking over to the sink he rinsed the glass and headed for bed. Grey ashes were all that remained of the earlier warm blaze.

Next morning when he opened the cabin door, he was greeted by a tiny avalanche of snow cascading onto the hardwood floor. Alister cleared the doorway with the shovel kept indoors for just such a happening and then tackled the snow around the pile of logs on the porch. Banging logs together to remove the snow, he soon had an armful. As he carried the logs indoors, the wind-sculpted patterns in the snow were a brief distraction. After breakfast he put a big log on the fire and went outside to check out the snowmobile. As he closed the cabin door, an odd sound - air escaping from a balloon, a giant balloon - grabbed his attention. The noise was explained when a plane appeared from behind the tall trees near the lake. Jet engines silent, the plane was only feet above the snow swept lake ice. The pilot, seen fleetingly, was wrestling with the dead controls. The plane hit the ice near the edge of the lake, the aluminium skin of the plane screeching like a banshee in protest as the rough ice and then the stony shore tore at the metal. Snow spumed upwards around the plane as it tore a wide path through the bush.

Even as he took all this in, his legs were already pumping through the hindering snow between him and the shed. The engine kicked over on the fourth try; babying the motor, he eased the snowmobile out of the shed and into the snow. The wind-driven snow that had blocked the front door was here, near the beach solid enough to provide quick access to the lake ice. Once on the wind-swept ice, he saw the plane was partially on its side, one wing slanted towards the sky. The right wing had caught on a big rock causing the aircraft to tilt over partially on its side. Gunning the snowmobile he wondered what he would be likely to find once inside the plane. Following the path made by the plane as it skimmed with wheels up across the lake and onto the rocky beach, Alister halted in front of the jet and surveyed the damage. The door into the plane was blocked by trees. He had to act quickly, there was no time to get a chain saw and cut the trees down. The danger of exploding fuel tanks was something he tried not to think about.

The rocks and trees in the jet's path had opened up the front of the plane as if by a giant hand. The pilot was a mess, held in place by his harness. Exposed to the elements, he was tipped over at a grotesque angle. Blood from a gash on his head was oozing down his jaw to drip from his chin. Leaving the engine running, he moved to where he could get his gloved hands on the shards of twisted metal. As he carefully pulled at the jagged metal he became conscious of small noises that made him pause and listen carefully. The ticking and clicking noises he quickly realized were the engines cooling and not a bomb. The adrenaline rush set his senses on a fine edge to where thought was translated into quick action. Paradoxically, the adrenaline changed his perception of time to a slower, more casual measure. Within this paradox he floated with only one task, to get the people inside the aircraft to safety.

Setting his feet firmly, Alister kept up the pressure to pull apart enough of the metal to get safely inside. A popping sound and a piece of the fuselage broke off in his hands. Mindful of the spears of metal he climbed up on the twisted broken remains of the cockpit. Hanging on as best he could, Alister began pushing metal aside with his booted feet. When most of the metal daggers had been blunted he set about getting people out and away from the wreck. Crouching, he took the pilot's weight on a knee and releasing his safety harness gently draped him over the co-pilot's seat. The pilot was in a bad way. His breathing was laboured. His right arm was hanging at an odd angle. His legs appeared to be OK, scratches and superficial cuts where his pants were ripped.

Thinking out loud he said, "That's the best I can do for you right now Jim. Now to see if there is anyone else back there." As if in answer to his query, Alister heard noises in the cabin. He suspected that whoever was back there would at best be in need of first aid but more likely the services of a doctor. Alister shouldered the door aside and entered the cabin where everything was askew. Thank God the seats haven't broken loose, was his first thought. Just inside the door, a teenager was struggling to release his seat belt, a woman next to him appeared to be unconscious; she wasn't moving, but he saw her chest rising and falling regularly. The boy, at last able to release his seat belt buckle, collapsed against Alister.

"Easy does it young fella, take a couple of deep breaths. You're doing fine. There doesn't seem to be anything broken, can you move?"

"I think so," he said, as he felt his legs and arms.

"That's great, what I want you to do is to help the lady out of her seat belt and then get her outside, see if she's OK, any broken bones. Do you think you could do that? It would be a big help."

"Sure. I'll help Jonesy."

"Is there anyone else aboard, besides you two and the two in back?" The noises that had alarmed him initially were no more. It was quiet inside the aluminium carcass of the plane.

"No only the two at the back."

"Well I had better have a look at them."

One of the men, blinking and looking around muttered, "Keep an eye on the Russkie," and began to struggle from his seat belt.

Turning around, Alister said, "Grab all the warm clothes, blankets, anything to fight the cold and get out of the plane, quick." A thought that the gas tanks might explode returned to loose tiny maggots along his spine. "Quick get outside. Grab anything warm and get out." As an afterthought he told them, "Follow the skid marks back to the cabin, it's warm inside." Scrambling through the shambles of luggage, clothing and blankets that had been emptied from the storage bins, he shook the Russkie, "Time to go, wakey wakey, let's get you out of here. C'mon, c'mon, let's go big guy."

Stirring, the man looked up at Alister with dull unfocussed eyes. He put his hand up to his head and groaned. Bending over to get a closer look at the man's head, Alister was pushed away with some force, but not before he saw the lump on the right side of his head. Obviously he had struck his head on the side of the aircraft as it went over when the wing caught.

"C'mon Ivan time to go, this junker could go up any minute."

Pushing Alister away, the big man undid his seatbelt and struggled to his feet and head down scrambled to the front of the plane. The man and the woman were floundering around in the snow picking up the blankets the boy was throwing to them. Pushing the boy aside, the big man crawled through the opening and jumped down into the snow.

"Well done young un. Do you know where the first aid stuff is kept? I don't have much. What's your name?"

"Simon. This is my dad's plane."

"Have a look for the first-aid box Simon; there should be one in the cabin." Alister moved to the rear of the aircraft where amidst the broken dishes and clothing that had been flung about he found a box marked with a red cross. Kicking aside the debris and opening cupboards yielded nothing more in the way of medical supplies.

With the box under an arm he said, "OK Simon, let's get the hell out of this mess, grab those blankets and throw them out, watch the sharp metal, step on them and you're good for stitches. Be careful, we have enough on our hands without anyone else getting banged up. Help me Simon, he's in a bad way."

No one had thought to ease the pilot to the ground and try and make him comfortable. Dazed, frightened and with the cold chilling their very marrow, all they could think of was to get out of the plane and cover up against the wind. Gently easing the pilot through the shattered nose of the plane, while taking care to avoid the razor-sharp pieces of fuselage, had Alister sweating in spite of the cold. Lowering the pilot head first onto the snow he ordered Simon to grab him by the shoulders and slide him into a sitting position. Looking at the others standing together he shouted, "Don't stand there, I told you to get the hell out of here. The cabin is only two or three hundred yards away. I said move it, get outta here. Just follow the skid marks. Now Simon we have to get this guy under cover quickly, he's about all in. Hold him until I can get the snowmobile closer."

The big man was sitting on the snowmobile, head bowed. The others stood around him having moved only a few steps at Ally's shouted instructions. Alister grabbed the big man's shoulder and pulled him to his feet. Hanging on while the man he had named Ivan tried to shrug him aside, Alister gave him a push towards the cabin. He staggered a few steps and then continued down the path made by the skidding plane. The others followed. Alister slowly eased the snowmobile over beside the pilot whose teeth were chattering uncontrollably.

"All right Simon, now to get this one on old Betsy and it's off to the cabin. You take his legs and see what we can do." The pilot, his clacking teeth for all the world sounding like a death rattle, appeared to be sound asleep. The illusion was shattered by a scream. Dropping his burden in surprise was the cause of another scream that caused the crows to object and take flight. Looking into Simon's pain filled eyes, Alister softly encouraged him to help get the pilot on the snowmobile. There were no more screams.

"You hold him until I get on the machine. I'll look after him until you get aboard, OK?"

"Sure, I can do it. This cold, let's get out of here, I'm freezing."

"Good man, hang on and we're away," moving off, Alister slowly increased the speed. The injured man couldn't take any more knocking about and the best route was to angle up the snow-covered beach towards the cabin. The two men and the woman were slipping and sliding their way there. The ice-topped snow made for hard going.

At the cabin door he let the motor idle and looking at Simon said, "Now to get this guy inside and see what we can do for him." Each with an arm around his shoulders and holding a leg apiece they carried the pilot indoors.

"Gently Simon, here in front of the fire is the best place. I'll get him settled, you bring in the first aid stuff, all of it."

As Simon turned to go outside the others crowded through the door, the big man leading the way. All three, rubbing their hands reached out to the fire. Alister removed his snowmobile suit.

"Gimme some room. You'll have to move. Move damn you, this guy needs help."

The big man did not move. He looked at Alister and planted his feet firmly where he stood. The other two moved aside, the woman offering to help.

Standing up, Alister said, "You'll have to move Ivan, I need room in front of the fire to work on the pilot. Look, grab that table and bring it over here. Great, thanks Simon, just set the boxes down there."

Reluctantly, the big man assisted by the woman moved the pine table near the fire. Looking at the big man with a quizzical look, Alister reached down and caught the pilot under the shoulders, the implication being that the other would take his feet and help get the pilot onto the table. This was done to the noisy laboured breathing of the pilot.

"Let's have a look at his chest, his breathing doesn't sound right."

Surprisingly the big man, whose eyes were now clear, smiled and said, "Of course," and began to remove the pilot's jacket, but gave up when a scream from the injured man startled everyone. Taking a knife from his pocket, the big man cut the clothes apart and then gently removed them. While this was going on, the pilot was grinding his teeth and making unintelligible sounds deep in his throat. At first glance there didn't appear to be any cause for concern with the appearance of the chest area. And yet, Alister mused, when we moved his upper body, here and at the plane, he screamed in agony. Gently probing with his fingertips in the area above the heart he felt a slight lump. Probing further he discovered a thin hard core under the bruising. Looking up at the others, their querying eyes begging to be told what was wrong, he shook his head.

"I don't know what is wrong here, but whatever it is, it's serious. There is a little lump, here above the heart. My guess is that something, a piece of metal, maybe glass, has pierced his lung."

"Where is the cut, the wound?" this from the man in the well-tailored suit. "He's out, bumped his head on something."

"You're sure?" the woman asked. Alister nodded. "Well in that case we will have to get Robert to a hospital," she said.

"That's right, the sooner the better. Whatever is in there has broken off under the skin. You can feel a small hard part at the centre of the lump."

"How will you move him to hospital?" the big man asked. "I don't think he will survive the journey."

"We have to try. The hospital in Miskimin is well equipped, they'll look after him out there."

"I don't think he should be moved. He will come round in time, He should be kept warm, he will be fine here in front of the fire," the big man said, a harder edge to his voice.

"We have to get him to Miskimin. He'll die if we don't," Alister said.

"He will never get there alive. Tell me, how will you keep him warm? Here it is warm. Tell me, if he has a piece of metal in his lung why isn't he bringing up blood."

"Believe me, in time he'll be bringing up blood. Listen to his breathing, it's shallow and laboured, a sure sign of lung damage. We'll wrap him up in blankets and hitch up the sled. He'll be OK."

" Everybody stays here," the big man ordered loudly.

The others, warming themselves at the fire, glanced at the speaker, he had their attention. Glancing at one another but refusing to look directly at the speaker they stood, silent onlookers. Then collectively their faces mirrored their awareness, it was as if a light had gone on behind their dull eyes. An undertone of menace could be felt in the cabin.

The big man, aware that he was outnumbered, smiled again and said, "I want to help Robert as much as you do. It is best to leave him here. We can look after him. I'll go and get help, the snow doesn't frighten me. I am used to winter. It won't take lo...."

"Simon get the blankets. I'm the one to go. I know the country. You would get lost out there."

The big man's eyes narrowed, his lips tightened to a thin line as he walked towards the cabin door. His head bowed, he appeared to be in deep thought. Turning abruptly he threw out his arms and appealed to the group. "What do you think we should do? I say he stays. My friend here says, 'he goes'. Let's vote on it. Agreed?"

17

"Forget the vote. We have to get him to hospital. I agree with Mr....," she said looking over at Alister.

"Alister MacKinnon, call me Ally."

"Very well Ally. My name is Margaret Jonescu, but I answer to Jonesy. Simon you have met and this is Peter Mallory, or so he tells me."

The big man chimed in with, "And I am Alexei."

"The mystery man. Alexei and Peter spent most of the time hobnobbing in the rear of the plane," Jonesy said.

"You have an active imagination Miss Jonesy," Alexei said with a smile. "We were just yarning, playing cards, to pass the time. It was a long flight."

"Let me tell you Jonesy, you are barkin' up the wrong tree," an agitated Peter said.

"Now that is settled, let's get this guy bundled up and ready to move." "There will be no bundling Ally. Robert stays here with us."

"We'll see about that. Hand me the blankets Simon."

"What right have you to decide whether Robert lives or dies?" Jonesy demanded in an angry voice.

"This gives me the right, Jonesy," Alexei said holding up a gun. "Now shut up all of you. Everybody sit down."

Jonesy, her eyes ablaze, took a step towards Alexei and stopped when he motioned with the gun that she had come close enough. "You can't leave Robert here! We have to get him to a doctor. Can't you see he is hurt. He'll die...."

Peter, with a derisive sneer, said, "Yeah poor old Robbie, how do you think we got on the plane, you silly cow. Robbie's one of us and he stays here!"

"Sit down Jonesy. We can't argue with a gun," Ally said.

"No one will get hurt. Just do as you are told. Peter search them for weapons." Pointing at Ally, "you first."

It was obvious that the Russian meant business. Best do as ordered and wait for an opportunity to turn things around.

"Now over there on your knees. Jonesy you're next." When she too was on her knees beside Ally, Alexei said, "Better check little Simon too, Peter." When Peter pushed Simon, Simon whipped round and swung a roundhouse punch at the grinning Peter. Surprised, Peter ducked and muttered, "You little shit." Coming up out of his crouch and setting himself firmly on his feet, he hit Simon on the chin. The boy went down and Peter got in one kick before Alexei interrupted.

"Enough Peter, don't damage the merchandise. We need him in one piece for now."

"The little gett, I'll fix his lordship right proper, later."

"Later Peter, now get out there and have a look around and see if there is any place where we can lock them up." I have to get to a phone, he thought. Mikhail will have to report to the General.

"What's the rush Alexei. What can these clowns do, you have the gun."

"Outside and have a look around. Now!"

"I'll freeze to death out there."

"Put on one of the suits in the cupboard, you have several to choose from. Do it!" Alexei's voice took on a hard edge, "I want them locked up."

The General won't be happy with the way things have gone.

"All right, I'll go. No need to get your knickers in a knot,' Peter mumbled as he moved to the cupboard.

He was back in a few minutes. "Found the perfect place at the back of the house. It's some kind of storehouse."

"Can we lock the door? Are there any windows, a chimney?"

"No; the door opens out. We can fix it."

"I'll have to take a look. Get something to tie them up with."

Peter's search of the cabin turned up a drawer full of pieces of string. Choosing several thick pieces he proceeded first to tie the ankles of the three and then their wrists. Stepping back, he pushed Simon over on his side with his foot

"Now for a tour of inspection Peter."

When Alexei shut the door, Alister waited a few moments before saying in a low voice, "Simon, no more wild swings. We'll have to be patient, take it easy if we are...."

"Those two are going to kill us," Simon said in a voice shrill with fear, "You heard him, 'don't damage the merchandise for now'. What does that tell you?"

Jonesy, fighting to smother her fear, said, "We have to fight back. Simon's right, Ally."

"Shut up both of you. Sure we have to fight back but now isn't the time. We have to wait, be patient."

"Have you a plan Ally?"

"Nothing concrete, but believe me we'll get out of this in one piece," he said, while thinking that there was obviously an organization behind Alexei and that he would not act against them without orders from his masters. Of course if Simon attacked Alexei and was killed then Alexei would have no reason to keep anyone else alive.

"Listen Simon ...," Peter barging through the door followed by Alexei put an end to Ally's warning not to do anything foolish.

"We found a nice snug cell for you. Untie their legs and get them outside," Alexei ordered.

Knowing that it would be deathly cold in the unused cold-storage shed Alister said, "How about some blankets, its cold out there."

"Pick up the blankets we brought from the plane, there are enough of them to keep you cosy," Alexei said and grinned.

"Our hands are tied. We can't pick up the blankets," Simon said in an angry voice.

"Of course you can. Pick them up and let's get you in the shed. I'm starving, when we come back we will eat."

At the mention of food Peter raised his eyebrows and stroking his stomach smacked his lips, "No prisoners allowed in the dining room."

The prisoners, under the watchful eye and gun of Alexei and urged along by a grinning Pete, stumbled through the snow to the shed. A spiteful shove from Pete brought them up hard against the wide shelves along the outside wall of the storage shed. Ally took note of the sturdy table against the far wall and the gap in the shelves on the wall next to the cabin before the door was slammed shut. They were in darkness. The thunk as the strong wooden latch fell into place was followed shortly by the sound of nails being hammered into wood. Further hammering conveyed the message that the latch was being reinforced at the top and bottom of the door. Ally realized that Alexei must have found his tool box and nails on the floor of the cupboard where the winter gear was kept. They stood clutching their blankets, blind to what obstacles lay underfoot.

Simon with tears in his voice said, "We're going to die. I know it. They'll shoot us down."

"Shut up Simon. Stop your whingein' and pull yourself together, now isn't the time to come apart at the seams." Alister knew that now was not the time for sympathy and a light touch.

"Leave the poor boy alone, he's frightened."

"Well that makes two of us Jonesy," Alister replied. "Put your hand in my right pocket."

"What for?"

"Go on, put it in my pocket."

Her reaching hands found clothing and before she could begin her search for the pocket Simon said in a whisper, "It's me." She jumped and bumped into Alister. "Oh dear, pardon me," and continued her search.

"You have the right one this time. Good, now slide your hand into my pocket. There's a small knife on my key ring. That's it, be careful."

After much effort, "I've got it." Jonesy was glad that no one could see her efforts. She could feel the blood rising to colour her face.

"Good, now hold the knife firm. I'll open the blade, hold tight. There, now cut the ropes. Here, can you feel my arm. That's it, great stuff. A nice steady sawing motion should do it. Careful, just the rope, if you please Jonesy."

"I'm sorry, I'm sorry." Dear God! Will we leave here alive? I hope Alister can think of a way to get us out of here. That smarmy Peter and the other one, he frightens me.

"Now the same trick for Simon. I'll cut yours, then we can sit down and take stock of what we have to do."

When Alister's groping hands found the string around her wrists and freed her hands, she grabbed for Simon and hugging him whispered in his ear, "You have to be brave Simon. Your father will have begun the search for us. It's just a matter of time." The words sounded hollow in her ears, but she knew that she had to give the boy something to hang on to.

"She's right Simon. We have to hang tough. Your old man will be out looking for you and Jonesy. Bet on it."

"How can he, he doesn't know what happened."

"Your no show at Ottawa will start the ball rolling," Alister said. "Your flight plan, filed in England, is the answer. All he has to do is backtrack on the route." Even as he comforted the boy, he knew that it would be some time before the search and rescue operation got underway. The driving winds would, in no time, bury the plane under deep snowdrifts. A flight plan on a map appeared as a line drawn from A to B, but in flight was subject to the vagaries of weather and instrumentation.

"What's to stop them from killing us after they get the money? Our bodies — what's left of them after the wolves ...." he shuddered and didn't finish the thought.

"Your father is smart Simon, he'll know what to do. I'm sure he will find us." Even as she was reassuring the boy, she realized that it would be hours before anyone was alerted to their danger. The crash had made them show their hand earlier than intended. The sealed papers she carried were to be delivered after she had seen Simon settled in at his new school. No one from the school would be at the airport.

She assumed that none of the lawyers awaiting the papers she was carrying would be aware that something had happened to their flight. While no one outside the cabin knew their lives were in danger, the authorities certainly would know that something had happened to them. Thank God the others couldn't see her face.

"Let's get ourselves over to the table."

Slowly they inched through the blackness. One hesitant advance after another and Alister reaching ahead with a foot found their target. "Ouch," from Simon when his head struck something hanging from the ceiling, reaching up he found a large metal hook. "Now we have a place to sit and plan our next move."

"What can we do? They're going to kill us. How are we to get out of this place?" Simon said with a quaver in his voice.

"Good question Simon, but never sell yourself short. Maybe they will do us in, but I don't believe that we should roll over and let them."

"Alister is right, we have to think things through, not panic. We'll think of something," she ended lamely.

"We have some time to come up with a plan of attack. It's the Russian we have to be wary of, he's the dangerous one. Pete can be bought. After they eat, it is likely they will fall asleep in front of the fire. After all that's happened they will be dead to the world in no time. Just to make sure that is what happens let's wait a bit before we go exploring."

Her senses, heightened by the silence and the clinging blackness, became aware of the faint noises niggling away at the edge of her hearing. "What's that? It sounds like someone talking. I heard something," Jonesy whispered defensively.

"Me too," Simon said. "Coming from under the floor."

"Under the floor? Simon, are you sure? I'd swear they're outside, along one of the walls. There, did you hear that loud clang?"

"Yes, there are other noises too, maybe voices. What do you think Alister?" Simon asked.

"Ssh!" Alister who had been listening intently said, "The sounds are coming from the cabin. Pete or Alexei dropped a pot or some such on the floor. That was the loud sound you heard."

"Will they be able to hear us?" Jonesy asked.

"It's possible, but only if we talk as loudly as they are doing now. And they are banging pots and pans around. There must be some part of the wall that isn't as well insulated or it's thinner, maybe a hole someplace, for us to hear the noises from the kitchen."

"If we only had a light, even matches, we could search for the thin part of the wall," Simon said. "They left me my lighter and cigarettes. Let's see whether there is a weak spot in the wall." Scraping noises and tiny sparks, but no light. "Damn it, my lighter is out of fuel. Anybody else smoke? With or without a light. I'm to have a look at the wall, you stay on the table."

"No, quit years ago. Be careful Ally."

Ally slid off the table, and began shuffling towards the wall. The two on the table could hear Ally muttering to himself as he tapped the wall. The muttering stopped, he was making his way back to the table.

"I'm not sure but the gap in the shelves may have been a door from the kitchen into the shed. In the old days this would have been used to store vegetables, pickles that sort of thing, hang venison, which would explain the hook you hit earlier Simon. The wall is rough plasterboard and over time has become soft. We should be able to cut a hole in it."

"That'll take forever with that thing you have on your key ring," Simon said with defeat in his voice. "Now I suppose we wait until after they eat?"

"What now?" from Jonesy when Alister hoisted himself up on the table.

"They won't hang around washing up. With their bellies full they'll settle in front of the fire and pass out. All we need is a hole big enough for me to get two or three fingers in it and we can pull the wall apart."

"Ripping the wall apart will wake them up, that is if they are asleep as you predict."

Sliding off the table he answered, "The plasterboard is soft, it'll break without too much noise. All I need is a small hole and we're on our way." Faint noises and mutterings told the pair that Alister was at work on the wall. The going was slow, the knife blade was about an inch long. The mother-of-pearl-handled knife was a keychain ornament, not a functional tool. Still the hole was almost large enough for him to insert two fingers. It wasn't enough. The hole would have to be worked on. Periodically he had to stop and wipe the sweat from his brow. The need to work quietly and quickly with the tiny tool and the realization that it could break if handled roughly had him in a fever of sweaty trepidation. With three fingers in the hole, he was able to crumble the edges until he had a hole large enough to take a hand. Applying a steady pressure he broke off a piece with no trouble and no noise. Using both hands he broke off a large piece which alarmed Simon and Jonesy with the slight popping sound it made. The next piece of wallboard which was partially nailed to a wooden stud made a cracking sound as it parted from the stud. Gasps from Simon and Jonesy joined Ally's muttered curse.

In unison they whispered, "Take it easy!"

"That's one for the good guys. Jeez, sure as hell hope they didn't hear that! It was loud. We'll soon know if they did."

"They must surely have heard that," Jonesy said. Her thoughts were running wild, I hope they don't beat me. Oh God, they'll rape me then kill me!

"I hope not Jonesy. We'll soon find out if they heard anything. I'll wait a bit before ripping out any more. The wallboard is on the damp side and crumbles easy enough. It's only where there's a stud that it makes a noise."

After an interval, of about ten minutes, and with no sounds coming from the other side of the wall, Alister got to work again, carefully breaking off chunks of wallboard by pushing and pulling each piece until it fell away from the wall. When he was finished he guessed that he had an opening about three and a half feet square. The wallboard had been nailed to either side of what he supposed was a doorway. When he told the others what he had done they urged him in excited whispers to begin ripping apart the one remaining wallboard that separated them from the kitchen. He shushed them to silence

"What next? How does this help us?" Jonesy asked.

"Break down the other wall. You said they're sound asleep. Let me help you," an excited Simon said.

"Stay there. I can manage this. We have to be careful. They have the gun so easy does it Simon. Stay there. There is some sort of insulation, I'll soon get rid of it. Then we wait for a bit and assess the situation quietly and calmly.

Simon in an angry whisper sputtered, "Why not do it now? You said that the two of them are likely sound asleep by now. Give me the knife!"

"Now seems like as good a time as any, Ally. I agree with Simon."

"Surprise is the only thing we have going for us, right? Breaking down the wall will alert them, and don't forget Alexei has the gun. This wasn't supposed to happen out here in the bush. My guess is that you would have been picked up on the way to your new school."

"So, that doesn't change anything here. Let's do something now. This waiting in the dark is driving me crazy," an agitated Simon said and got to his feet.

"No, we are still locked up. Hear me out. Alexei works for someone, and he will act only on orders from that someone. The crash has forced his hand, what is he to do? The first thing he has to do is to get to a phone and clue his boss in on what has happened here. After a night's...."

"How can you be sure? Seems to me you're taking a big gamble...."

"My life's at stake too Jonesy. There are still a lot of things I want to do. If we panic now, we're all a goner. Mark my words, he'll be off in the morning looking for a phone." After a brief pause, "With the Russian gone we have only Pete to deal with. He doesn't have a gun and there are three of us."

No one spoke after Alister's evaluation of the situation. Although wrapped up in blankets and protected from the elements by sturdy walls the cold slowly wormed into their bones. Jonesy's thoughts strayed from the concern of the moment, temporarily easing the tight knot of fear in the region of her solar plexus. They would be rescued, she just knew it. Michael would find them. A little maggot of doubt slid across her thoughts. Would she ever see Michael again? Oh how she loved him, but he was all business.

Hired by Michael as his secretary, she remembered how eager she had been to make a go of her first job after graduation from secretarial school. She enjoyed the give-and-take of the office. The foremen from the factory floor had ready access to the boss's office and she was the guardian of the door, they joked. A shadow of a smile crossed her face as she remembered the first crisis at the plastics factory. They had all assembled on the factory floor for the announcement. Michael had told them that he couldn't meet the payroll. He explained that he was short a few thousand and that it would be a week, maybe ten days, before he could pay them. The workers had been wonderful. He went on to say that the shortfall was caused by another firm attempting to squeeze him out and take over the company. The news brought angry shouts from the workers and when he asked if they would tough it out with him, they roared their agreement.

Later, it might have been hours or minutes, the only sound the quiet breathing of the three prisoners and the occasional small sound as they moved to ease their aching bodies, Alister spoke up. "Tell me Simon, I'm curious how come you find yourself in this situation? Is your old man really wealthy enough to pay a ransom for you?"

"It is none of your business why I am here or whether or not my father is wealthy."

"Spoken like a real toff. I guess your old man is rich, well good for him. Of course you don't have to tell me, but as I said I'm curious. C'mon, we have nothing better to do right now. It will help to pass the time. You tell me your story and I'll tell you mine. C'mon let's hear it." Ally's seeming curiosity was a ruse to get the boy to talk and in talking steer him away from giving in to despair.

"If you must know I was on my way to school, a new school."

"What happened at the old school? Even I know, Simon, that school started some time ago, September to be exact. Why the change, huh?"

"You don't have to say anything Simon, to Alister or to anyone. It's behind you; time to turn the page, forget what has happened."

"Now I am really curious, Jonesy. What did he do that was so terrible that he had to leave Merry Old England?"

"I am sorry Simon."

"It's OK Jonesy. Sorry, Miss Jonescu."

"Call me Jonesy. Now is not the time to stand on ceremony."

"I took bets...."

"You ran a book— at school?" Alister said incredulously.

"I had an agreement with the local bookie," this said with a touch of pride. "The milkman was my contact. I'd take the bets and give them to him and he would then take them to the bookie. Next day when he delivered the milk he would also deliver any winnings that were owed."

"So what burst your bubble? The 'Headie' want more cash under the table or should I say the desk?"

This brought a snort from Simon and brief chuckle from Jonesy.

"No the headmaster went off the deep end when he found out what was going on. One of the boys in the junior school had a big win with his first bet. So the greedy little toad bet all his tuck money the following week. The little snipe thought he had found the goose that laid the golden eggs. His horse wasn't in the first five. When he came to me asking for his money back I told him that he had bet on a loser and his money was gone.

"Someone, the little stinker who lost if you ask me, told the police, and Mike and I were picked up the next morning. We were having a chat, we often did, in the bushes at the side of the driveway when the police drove up."

"Why'd you do it? Surely it wasn't the money?"

"Of course not, it was the excitement, putting one over on the school. I don't know why, but they never liked me. It was the same at the other schools. I always tried to be friendly. It was OK for a while then they would change and I was on my own again. Well not strictly on my own, there were some who chummed around with me."

"Did you never stop and ask yourself what made the other kids change?"

"Why should I, they were the ones who changed, not me."

Jonesy, protective of Simon said, "That's enough! We have other things to think about. It's none of your business Ally what Simon did or didn't do at school. His father wants only the best for him, which is the only reason for sending him to school in Canada."

Jonesy's defence of his father surprised Simon. Her coming to his aid too and the emotion behind the words was the greater surprise. Were Jonesy and Dad? He shook his head, no it was all business with them.

"OK, OK Jonesy. In my former life I worked on a newspaper, so being nosey comes naturally. How many schools have you attended? Several schools and you never stopped to wonder why the other kids didn't like you? C'mon Simon, you want me to believe that the other kids were wrong, every time?" Listen to me, Alister thought. Now I'm sounding like a pulpit thumper or trick cyclist; dry up MacKinnon, leave him alone.

"They were the ones who changed, I didn't, why should I? I was never stingy with my tuck money. I was always the one ready to accept a dare. The others, for instance, were scared silly to borrow a bike and ride it back to school."

"When you say borrow a bike what exactly do you mean?"

"Borrow it, there were always bikes lying around. On Saturdays farm workers biked into town from around the district."

"But that wasn't right Simon," Jonesy said. "Think of the farm workers having to walk home. How would you feel if someone borrowed something of yours without permission? You wouldn't be overly pleased about it."

"It wasn't stealing, they got their bike back. It was a game really. I only did it a couple of times," he said defensively.

"I suspect that the farmers would have changed your mind about it being a game if they had got their hands on you. Did you never stop to think that maybe the other kids thought you were a bit — over the top — and were scared of getting into trouble because of your daft exploits? What happened when you were found out in one of your escapades?"

"The Head would bawl me out and then it was six of the best. Later my father would pay a visit and leave a cheque with the Head and that would be the end of it."

"Until the next time, eh Simon?" Alister said.

Simon sitting between Alister and Jonesy on the not too roomy table was not happy with Alister's candid assessment of his behaviour. Who does he think he is anyway? He has no idea how hard I tried to be pals with the others. I almost got caught the time I sneaked into the chapel and hid the cross and the candlesticks in the pulpit. They were chicken, all of them, but I did it on my own. For days afterwards I was sure something bad would happen to me. Lucky for me the minister never said a word about it to anyone; why would he do that? Taking bets, whew that was scary, fun too. Sneaking out before the masters got the school out of bed.

Mike the milkman always cracking jokes: Top o' the mornin' Simon me lad, and what's on the me-n-u today? Something with more sparkle than that Arctic Star in the third at Doncaster yesterday. Maybe if he had had a few sparklers up his arse I wouldn't be skint today. Or the way he carried on after a particularly loud fart: he would give a little jump followed by quick darting sideways glances, a quick glance over his shoulder and then come close and whisper, I think I'm being followed, should I get Scotland Yard on the case?

The unlikely pairing came about by accident. Simon sneaking out of the dorm to check on whether the robin's eggs in the nest he had discovered were hatched. The nest, found by accident, was his secret. The nest in a bush at the side of the footpath that followed the driveway was hidden from the school by a bend in the driveway. The milkman had stopped and asked, "Are you alright son?"

Jealous of his secret, he answered abruptly, "Of course I am."

"Pardon me all to hell, I thought maybe you were in a bit of bother."

Simon taken aback at the milkman's attitude was at a loss for words.

Stepping down from the van, the milkman walked over to where Simon stood. "Well then young 'un what's the attraction? Cat got yer tongue?"

Simon stood his ground, he didn't want this intruder to share his secret. He seemed to be friendly enough, his bantering easy manner came as a surprise to Simon. Adults, when they deemed to speak to him, usually spoke in a formal, stilted condescending way.

"Aren't you the gabby one. What's up? Tell old Mike. Get it off your chest." While talking, he pulled a cigarette package from the pocket of the waistcoat under his white jacket. Opening the pack, he proffered it to Simon. "No thanks."

The milkman about to light his cigarette, jumped back from Simon. With his hands up as if to protect his face he said, "Gawd, it talks. It's real."

Startled, Simon gaped open mouthed at the grinning smoker. A chuckle bubbled to his lips and quickly became a laugh. And so was born a friendship. Mike would regale Simon with yarns about the people on his route. Whenever Simon could sneak out of the dorm, they met at the site of the robin's nest and while Mike smoked, they chatted.

One morning Mike mentioned he had won a few quid on the dogs. A curious Simon wanted to know what he meant. When told about dog racing, an excited Simon asked Mike to place a bet for him. Word soon got around the school that Braithwaite was placing bets with the local bookie. When queried by some of the seniors, he agreed to place their bets and so became the school's bookie.

Simon smiled wanly in the darkness. No more laughs with Mike. The people on the other side of the wall meant business. They were after money. What would happen after they were paid off was anybody's guess. I hope Ally has the answer. They must know that we are overdue. They should have planes and people out searching for us. They must — please, please God, help us, please I don't want to die.

Alister was aware of Simon's torment. Poor little bugger, a cheque for a few thousand wouldn't buy his way out of this one. Easing around to the end of the table to give himself and the others more room, he closed his eyes. He came to with a jerk that startled the others. "It's OK, I fell asleep. It might not be a bad idea to get some shut eye. The shelves should be strong enough."

"Sleep!' a disbelieving whisper from Jonesy. "How can you even think of sleeping in a situation like this? You are impossible Alister."

"Well excuse me Jonesy, but sleep seems a good idea to me right now. And for your information I have slept, like a baby I might add, in circumstances that were way beyond this. You have led a very sheltered life Jonesy. This experience will be something you can brag about to your grandchildren."

"Believe me I won't want to talk about it ever!" Jonesy said in a fierce whisper.

"Well it's me for some kip." Alister moved away from the table. "Damn it!" as he stumbled over blankets on the floor. "Here I'm taking a couple, you two can divvy up the rest. There must be three or four. It's cold."

Simon and Jonesy heard him muttering and when he swore, they guessed he had bumped his head when crawling onto one of the shelves. This was followed by some shuffling noises as he arranged blankets and himself for sleep. Later unintelligible mutterings and movements signalled Ally was asleep and perhaps dreaming.

18

On his feet and waiting for the green light Ally stood in the door of the C-130 transport and flexed his legs. The four-hour flight from Kinshasa was about to end. Below, the Katangan "Tigers" were rampaging through Kolwezi.

Looking down along the side of the aircraft he could see the airport — the drop zone — about half a mile ahead. As the first flight-path markers appeared below he tensed, ready to go; he knew it would take a hearty heave to get clear of the plane with all his equipment and then get sorted out for a landing.

With the need to get on the ground in a hurry, the planes were flying in at six hundred feet. Ally had barely enough time to check his chute and get himself organized before he hit the deck. Sorting out his kit, he stamped his feet. It was great to be able to stretch and feel the ground under his feet. Before moving out from the drop zone, groups of Tigers had to be dealt with before the regiment could begin its assigned tasks.

Cuban trained, the rebels had stormed across the Angolan border in a convoy of jeeps and trucks determined to take back Shaba Province. Undisciplined, the heavily armed rebels, in a frenzy of blood letting, rampaged through the city, leaving their innocent victims where they were slaughtered.

As they advanced from the drop zone, the sound of gunfire, some of it heavy weapons, came from their front. Ally's section was on the left flank of the company which had been given the task of clearing the Old Town. Advancing through the built-up area the stench of death was everywhere. Bodies lay where they had been shot. Men, women, children, some hacked to death, were stark witness to the blood lust of the Cuban-trained rebels.

What had been neat well-cared for bungalows with enclosed gardens were now burnt-out wrecks. Broken furniture, clothes and family treasures scattered indiscriminately outside the doors and windows was further evidence of the rebels running amok.

All was quiet in their immediate area. Ally, front man of the section, was excited. With the possibility of sudden death popping up from behind a garden wall or hiding around the next corner, his only feeling was of exhilaration. A burst of automatic fire from just ahead and bullets were spanging off the metal wall of a shed across from the section. Holding up his hand to halt his chums, Ally turned to the corporal and put a finger to his mouth, and motioning again with his hand for the section to stay put, he advanced along the iron fence which was almost hidden by a high hedge. Taking two men with him, the corporal ran across the road, ready to cover Ally's back and to engage any rebel flushed out by him. Ally took a careful look around the end of the hedge.

There was a rebel standing in front of a group passing a bottle around. Obviously the one on his feet had loosed off a few rounds. His mates were hunkered down interested only in the contents of the bottle. With a finger on his lips, Ally waved the rest of the section forward, and looked across at the corporal and motioned him to stay where he was. Pulling the pin of a grenade, he stuck his head out, and with an underhanded throw heaved the grenade at a target as yet unseen by the others. Shouts from around the corner and bottles breaking preceded the explosion. Ally killed the shooter before he had run more than a few steps. The smell of liquor puddled in the blood of the six rebels whose shredded legs and bloody torsos — caused by a better-safe-than-sorry second grenade— lay round the corner, filled the nostrils of the section as they went on their way.

Ahead of the intersection a two-storey building commanded a view of the area. Corporal Gesner, in charge of the section, decided to have a look inside. A sniper or a rebel machine gun on the second floor could do a lot of damage. Ordering two men to the back of the building, he grinned and headed for the ornate door of what was obviously some sort of office building. Ally, close on the heels of the corporal, found they were in a hallway with stairs leading to the other floor.

Detailing four men to "examine" the ground floor, he went upstairs followed by Ally and two others of the section. Weapons at the ready, their search for rebels began at the top of the stairs. All the doors were closed and most of them were locked. Para boots proved to be effective door openers. Clearing each office was a matter of moments. Offices with doors unlocked tightened the gut up a notch; this might be the one with rebels inside.

Half-way down the corridor, they made their first find. Opening the door of a small cupboard, Ally was astounded to come face-to-face with two cowering wild-eyed women. Their whimpering cries brought

Gesner on the run. As he charged into the office, grim faced and weapon at the ready, the women began to scream. Clinging to each other they tried to get further into the shallow cupboard.

Surprising Ally, Gesner reached for the women, and uncharacteristically put out his hand to pat one of them on the shoulder. He made soothing sounds, the sounds you would make to quieten a baby. Their faces slowly mirrored their return from the edge of madness. Stepping out into the office they broke down and cried. Sobbing, the two woman reached for the corporal and clung to him for dear life. Gesner's arms took on a life of their own, fluttering about their shoulders. At a loss of how to react, he gave Ally a perplexed look.

Outside, and continuing down the street with the women in tow, they rendezvoused with Lieutenant Blondel, the company commander and the rest of the company. In their sweep, so far, the company had rescued fifteen civilians. Blondel, young and not long with the Legion, was eager to press ahead and continue the task of bagging Tigers. A graduate of St. Cyr, the French military college, he had committed himself to the Legion. The top six graduates of St. Cyr are given the choice of serving all or part of their military career with the Legion. Turning, he pointed to the three nearest legionnaires, and after giving them detailed instructions on how to get to the holding area for civilians, sent the civilians off with their escort.

Ally didn't know the other two, they were replacements. This was their first action. Being the ancien, Ally took charge. Candidates are told to watch the old hands and learn from them when campaigning and in barracks. Organizing the civilians in two ranks he told one of the guys to take the front of the queue and the other one the rear. Before moving off, he told the civilians that at the first sign of trouble not to bunch up and to immediately hit the dirt. In an effort to make light of the situation, he quipped their clothes could be easily cleaned or if not then easily replaced.

Blank stares greeted his lame joke. Ally felt sorry for the civilians, as they shuffled along with their heads bowed and their pain-filled eyes taking in their surroundings in darting frightened glances. In a sudden intuitive flash, it came to him why he was able to ignore the nightmarish landscape they were walking through while the civilians were overwhelmed by it. The harsh treatment and punishing discipline of the Legion recast him in a new mould, one that was hardened mentally as well as physically, enabling him to rise above the carnage all around them in the Old Town.

At the holding area, Ally found that groups of civilians were arriving, some under escort, some on their own. The medics were run off their feet as they attended to the wounded. Those whose wounds didn't show were left to the solicitations of less damaged friends and acquaintances. Taking leave of his charges after seeing them lose themselves in a large group, he headed back the way they had come, anxious to get back with the company and get involved.

A brief halt to light a cigarette and names were exchanged. Sporadic gunfire punctuated the silence. No order was needed; their training took over. Ally led and Albert followed a short distance behind. Giorgio on the other side of the dusty street watched their back. Approaching the area where they had left the company, voices up ahead — friend or foe— in one of the yards slowed their advance. The speakers were out of sight, hidden by the thick the hedge and the flowering plants that crept over it.

Signalling for silence, Ally moved ahead slowly, the others keeping watch. Silence. Were the speakers still behind the fence waiting for Ally, Albert, and Giorgio to get closer; or had they gone? A long burst of automatic fire bore witness to their presence. Instead of waiting for their target to approach them, the Tigers, hidden by the thick foliage, had decided to take the fight to the three legionnaires. Waiting until they couldn't miss, the bullets ripped into Giorgio. He went down, his hands clutching his guts. Ally, followed by Albert, made a mad dash across the street. There was nothing they could do for Giorgio; he was a goner. Taking cover behind a burnt-out car, they had time for a couple of breaths and then the bullets started flying again, still from the same spot.

This decided Ally. Pulling the pin from one of his grenades and spitting on it, he heaved it towards the shooters. His ears ringing from the explosion, he ran towards the hedge which was now in tatters, and double tapped those who were still alive. Albert, close on his heels, yelled and fired shots to Ally's left. Whirling, Ally loosed off a couple of shots and saw them hit the rebel in the chest, but still he came charging at them. Suddenly the life went out of the Tiger, and he collapsed a few feet from their boots.

After clearing the bungalow, they went out and attempted to pick up Giorgio and to place him in the shade. Almost cut in half, they had to use the jacket of the rebel who charged out of the house, and wrap it around Giorgio's mangled guts. Gently, they carried him and laid him under the lone bush in the garden. Gathering up the tattered remnants of clothing, they threw them over the body in an attempt to keep the swarming clouds of flies away.

Alert for signs of danger, they lit up and sucked the smoke deep into their lungs. After a couple of drags, Ally wandered over to the bodies of the rebels. Ignoring the clouds of flies disturbed by his poking boot, he bent over one of the torsos and picked up a sub-machine gun; it had a fully loaded mag.

An approaching vehicle had them instantly alert. Loud voices betrayed that it was not friendly. After a quick look through the tattered foliage, Ally directed Albert to take care of the driver and any others in the cab of the approaching vehicle. Ally hunkered down at a hole in the hedge a few feet to Albert's left, ready to step out into the street and shoot up the truck from the side; they waited.

A hasty look while getting into position told Ally there were about eight or ten rebels in the back of the small open truck. Looking across at Albert, he gave him a thumbs up, which was returned with a grin and a shake of the head. Laughter and shouts getting louder prompted Ally to risk a quick look. Slowly the truck rolled to a halt in the middle of the intersection. One of the rebels was leaning over the side of the truck, relieving himself. His mates were standing up and sharing a bottle while they hung on to the metal framework welded to the body of the truck to allow passengers to shoot while on the move.

Their senses dulled by drink and whatever it was they were smoking, Ally emptied the mag of the sub-machine gun before the three still alive realized the danger they were in. The survivors tumbled from the rear of the truck and ran, the truck between them and the avenging legionnaire. Albert, proud of his marksman badge, picked them off before they made it to cover. After killing the three occupants of the cab, he had crashed his way through the hedge ready to take on any runners. Adrenalin coursing in their veins, Ally and Albert approached the truck slowly. No saying what a wounded rebel lying in the truck body would do. Staying clear, they carefully examined the bodies sprawled in the truck. Slowly, slowly they moved closer. One of the bodies moved, a foot caught on the side of the truck fell with a thump. The body moved once more as high powered bullets smashed into it. Ally and Albert lowered their weapons and moved to the truck. All was still. Moving to the front of the vehicle, Ally hauled the three dead bodies from the cab while Albert cleared the truck body.

After loading Giorgio and the rebel weapons aboard the truck and with Albert driving and Ally standing up in the back, they went looking for the company. Spotting movement ahead, Ally thumped on the cab top and shouted to Albert to slow down. Using the binoculars taken from one of the rebels, he surveyed the action ahead. Hitting the top of the cab again he said it was OK to go ahead. Albert leaned on the truck's horn to warn that the occupants of the truck were friendly. As soon as they came up to the rear of the company, Ally asked where the lieutenant was. A sergeant gave him directions.

Jumping down from the truck, Ally reported to Blondel. The lieutenant, grinning, noted that he hoped they hadn't paid much for their transport. His grin vanished as Ally began his report. The lieutenant stood still, looking down at the ground as he heard what had happened. Looking up at Ally, who had been joined by Albert, he said, "Well done, you two." Walking over to the truck, he looked at the dead Giorgo wrapped in his shroud of bloody bits and pieces of uniform. In a voice little more than a whisper, he commented it was one of the replacements and that it was his first death in the company. Walking away from the truck, the young lieutenant was all business. He was responsible for a company. There were civilians to search for and rebels he had business with.

Ally and Albert back with the section never said a word about their set to with the Tigers. Remembering, Ally gave the bodies lying in the back of the truck a brief thought: better them than me. He saw again the result of his weapons training; the bullets finding body mass as he went about the task at hand.

Midday, the following day, the Old Town was free of rebels. At dawn that morning, the remainder of the regiment jumped and took part in clearing the New Town of the rampaging rebels. In the New Town the going was tougher. Rebel armoured cars and heavy weapons gave the legionnaires a hard time, but didn't prevent them from killing rebels and rescuing civilians. Blondel's company breached the defences of the native quarter and got down to the task of clearing the area house by house. Here the rebels were fierce in their defence of the area. Blondel was continually on the move between sections. On one of his visits he found Ally's section held up by a particularly determined group of rebels, who, safe in a solid cement walled building controlled their area with a heavy machine gun. Two men in the section were wounded by the murderous fire. The defenders appeared to have an endless supply of ammo.

Ally and the corporal, deep in conversation, were unaware of the lieutenant's approach until Albert nudged Ally. Breaking off their conversation, Corporal Gesner saluted and reported. In answer to Blondel's question, the corporal explained that they had been discussing how to get at the rebels and that Ally had proposed a solution. While the section held the attention of the rebels, Ally with extra grenades supplied by the rest of the section would carry out an attack on the strong point.

With the lieutenant shaking his head and looking dubious, Ally put forward his plan of attack. Pointing to a narrow laneway that led off the dusty road, he explained that he would follow it until he could approach the strong point from the rear or the flank. With the element of surprise in his favour, he told the lieutenant that he had a good chance of success.

Crouched down behind a couple of straggly bushes, Ally examined the target. He didn't like what he saw. The rear of the building was a blank wall broken by what appeared to be a large, heavy metal door.

Ally, to get at the door, would have to cross about forty feet of open ground. And then would he be able to open the door, should he get to it in one piece? Looking around and seeing no sign of movement, he decided to see if there was an entrance at the side of the building.

Charging across the open space, the bag of grenades thumping against his hip, a sudden thought; what if the pin of a grenade popped? There wouldn't be much to pick up; he would be scattered all over the place. Taking deep breaths, he stood beside one of three windows in the side wall. The wall was about fifty feet long, and the rear wall about thirty feet wide. What could be so important that it had to be kept in such a large cement building? Let's find out. Listening and not hearing a sound from behind the glass, he wiped the dust from a couple of panes and looked into an empty room. The next room held pieces of equipment. Trying to visualize the inside of the building, he closed his eyes; likely there was a passageway on the other side of the rooms he had examined. Would it lead to the front of the building where the heavy machine gun in a window pinned the section down? Cautiously, he looked into the third room. This was the one. There were several empty bottles on a table in the centre of the room.

If he was right about the passageway linking the rooms, then would this room give easy access to the front of the building and the rebels? How to get into the building? The metal-framed window was latched inside by a couple of handles. Using the butt of his rifle, he clenched his teeth and tapped the glass. Nothing happened. A second heavier tap and the glass cracked. Two minutes later he was inside the strong point. Through the door he could hear the heavy sound of the machine gun, and opening the door, the sound of small arms.

Rifle at the ready, he crept down the passageway, halting at the first of two doors that led off the passage. Outside the door an iron rail went along a concrete walkway which was about three feet above the floor. The gunners were in plain sight, busy tending their killing machine. Taking his time, Ally looked the place over and noted that in addition to the belts of ammunition there was a box of ammo next to the gun. Closing the door, he started towards the other one. A door at the end of the passage opened and a rebel walked towards Ally. Unarmed, the rebel in a moment of panic stood still, and just as he wheeled quickly to go back through the still open door, Ally fired. The rebel dropped and lay still, he wasn't going anywhere. Frozen momentarily in panic, Ally waited between the doors for the rebels to come charging through, in answer to the racket in their rear. Thirty seconds passed, forty seconds, nothing happened. The shot must have been drowned out by the weapons firing out front.

Taking a deep breath he moved to the door and carefully opened it. Everything was as it was before; the gunners occupied with what was going on to their front. Without looking, a rebel tossed an empty bottle behind him. There were already a number of empty bottles smashed and scattered behind them. Ally was where he wanted to be, close to the gun and the box of ammo.

Holding the door ajar with his foot and getting ready to use the grenades, he saw that four steps led from the concrete walkway to floor level. Senses attuned to what he was about and bolstered by adrenaline, the most inconsequential trivia were noted and filed away in his consciousness. One of the rebels sported a gold wrist watch; another had a collection of gold and silver necklaces around his neck. The one behind the gun had a beard and his hand, the one resting on the gun, bore witness to his penchant for rings.

Taking two grenades from the bag, he tucked one under his arm and pulled the pin on the other one; he paused before heaving it. He had the second grenade on its way just as the first exploded. If any of the rebels survived the first blast the second certainly finished the job. Deafened by the noise, he clung to the wall. The force of the explosion blew the metal door inwards, slamming it against the wall. The blast caught in the confines of the passage blew him off his feet. Dazed and bruised, he picked himself up and checking his rifle staggered towards the doorway. Standing in the doorway, still dazed and shaky on his feet, he looked out at the wreckage. The cement wall was cracked and in several places the reinforcing rods poked through. A bundle of rags and the twisted remains of the gun were all that was left.

Staggering down the steps, he crossed the floor eager to get away from the dust and the smell of cordite. Outside he took a deep breath. At the sight of Ally bent over in a fit of coughing, the section shouted their approval. Corporal Gesner appeared to be saying something, his lips were moving but Ally couldn't hear a word. Shaking his head he pointed to his ears. Shaking his head again, he moved closer to Gesner and yes he could hear faint sounds. Gesner's order to move ahead came loud through the ringing in his ears. By the early afternoon only small groups of rebels remained to be winkled out of their holes. Civilians didn't argue when the authorities offered to fly them out to safety. Belgian troops had taken over control of the airport.

During the six days of fighting, rebels in increasing numbers left Kolwezi and headed for the Angolan border, leaving the city relatively quiet. Using their own vehicles and any others they could lay their hands on, the regiment began the job of routing out the pockets of rebels still active in the rough country beyond the city. Travelling over dirt roads fighting patrols moved out into open country and began searching for rebels.

Ally sitting in the back of one of the four jeeps in the patrol, hung on with both hands as the jeep bounced its way over the terrain. Those not in jeeps were bounced about standing up in the back of the patrol's two commandeered trucks. Blondel called a halt at the foot of a small steep ridge. Several wide gullies running at an angle up the ridge were a noticeable feature of the terrain. In one of them only the upper body of the legionnaires leaning against their jeep could be seen. Joined by Corporal Gesner, Blondel motioned to Strelski in the second jeep to follow, and they started out to climb the ridge and put the binocs on the surrounding country. Taking the easy way, Blondel angled up the ridge in line with a gully.

About half-way up the ridge he stopped and was in the act of using his binoculars when it happened. Heavy automatic fire came from the top of the ridge. Something tore into his legs knocking him to the ground, hard. When he regained consciousness he could hear moans and cursing coming from somewhere nearby. When he tried to get up a voice ordered him to stay where he was. It was Strelski saying Gesner was dead and that he had been hit in the leg, small calibre stuff, a couple of rounds, and was OK. There was a burst of automatic fire and bullets kicked up the dirt around them. Seconds later, another long ragged burst and more little fountains of dirt showered his uniform.

Blondel, slowly shaking his head in an effort to clear the cloud that threatened to blanket him in unconsciousness, looked down at his legs. His right thigh was bleeding and his left leg above the knee was a mess of torn flesh. Not yet feeling any pain, he mused that a high calibre bullet had done the damage. Slowly the realization of the difficulty of their position came to him through the fog seeping into his brain. With an effort, he fought it off and forced himself to look around. About ten feet from where Strelski lay he saw a break in the ground.

Ordering Strelski to follow him, he attempted to head in the direction of safety, just feet away. His face in the dirt, he tried to pull himself forward with his elbows. Pain knifed through his body to burst in his head, and then blackness. Pulling himself up into the light, he looked around. Dazed and in pain he heard someone talking. Fighting off the pain, he listened, the voice sounded familiar. It was Strelski. Slowly the sounds became words. Strelski was ordering him to stay down and not move. Rifle fire was coming from somewhere below him. Lying in the dust with fists clenched, he slipped in and out of consciousness.

When the lieutenant went down, I yelled, "take cover," and jumped into the nearest jeep. For a moment I thought the damned thing was to roll over, but no I made it into the gully that gouged up the slope near the guys. I had to gear down. Although angled across the side of the ridge, the gully was fairly steep. Crouched over the steering wheel, I was screaming in my head, C'mon move you fuckin heap of junk, move, move, faster, I've got get up there on the double. Finally I got up to where the bodies lay. One foot on the ground and the jeep began to roll backwards. I goosed the gas and this time put on the hand brake.

All was quiet up on the ridge. Bastards, they were waiting for me to pop up and attempt a rescue of the downed Blondel and Strelski. This was where things were likely to get dicey. I couldn't sit on my arse and do nothing; the guys needed help, and quick. These clowns up on the ridge were likely high on something. Whenever a rebel head popped up, the guys below let go a couple of rounds. To hell with it, I'd have a go anyway. Strelski was closest, I'd grab him first and then go for the lieutenant. I was scared. My heart was going to beat the band. All it would take was one guy — tucked out of sight— up there to aim before he pulled the trigger and I'd be a goner. Crouching, I took a couple of steps backwards. This was it. I charged at the wall of the gully, aiming for a partly exposed stone. Merde! The stone gave way and I went head first into the dirt.

Getting my feet under me, I scrambled over the edge of the gully and all hell broke loose. They were pouring the stuff at me on full automatic. Grabbing Strelski's boots I dragged him to the edge of the gully and shoved him over the edge. Chased by the devils of expected bullets ripping into me, I went for Blondel. There was a dark stain on the ground beside his left leg. The wound was a raw, red pulpy mass. He needed medical attention and fast. The rebels kept blasting away. Thank God they were lousy shots. Any moment I expected one of these clowns to remember his training and drop me. My luck held, I was alone with my fear. This wasn't the time or place to practice my first aid so I grabbed his combat jacket and hauled him over to the gully and heaved him over the edge to join Strelski. As I slid into the gully, I felt something pull at the leg of my denims.

Strelski with his back against the side of the gully told me, "Gesner's dead, he got it in the head. See to Blondel, I'm fine. The bleeding has stopped. Small calibre stuff, went clean through the fleshy part of my leg. See to the kid, Johnny." The lieutenant, white-faced and unconscious, had lost quite a bit of blood. Keeping my head down, I got out my knife and cut away the bloodied uniform on his left leg. Using pieces of the trouser leg knotted together as a tourniquet, I got the bleeding stopped. A chunk of his left leg, the fleshy part above the knee, was blown away. I had seen worse. The bone was exposed, but it appeared to be OK. Broken bones complicated things.

His right leg had a neat hole through the fleshy part well above the knee. The bullet must have tumbled after drilling his right leg. He would pull through providing we could get him to hospital soon. Stuffing a couple of field dressings into the mess of his leg, I used some of the uniform I had cut away as a bandage. He never once groaned or moved while I was doctoring him. I was beginning to have second thoughts about him pulling through. He seemed decent enough. A bit too concerned with living up to the tough life and traditions of the Legion. He would get over it — soon, assuming he wanted to stay with us after this.

Looking over at the silent Strelski, I asked, "Are you all right?" His answer was a nod. He nodded again when I asked him if he could crawl to the jeep. Poor Blondel objected to my hauling him the few feet to the jeep. His groans stopped, but not the grinding of his teeth, when I leaned him against the front wheel of the jeep. Poor bugger, the noise he made bothered me more than the occasional shot from the top of the ridge. Strelski, through sheer will power, had managed to get on his feet at the rear of the jeep. He was one tough geezer. I scrambled back beside him and boosted him into the jeep where he lay in a huddle on the floor. Now to get the lieutenant in the front seat and we were off, back down the gully. He never made a sound as I manhandled him into the front seat.

The rebel guns were quiet. Were they on the move? Leaning Blondel against the dash, I whipped round to the other side and with one hand on the wheel I put the gear shift in neutral, released the brake and grabbed Blondel before he fell out of the jeep. He was in a bad way, white as a sheet. I doubted if he would make it. Back with the section, I yelled for someone to come and give me a hand with the lieutenant. We lifted him out and laid him gently against the side of the gully. Two others picked up Strelski and put him down beside the lieutenant. White faced and obviously in pain Strelski checked his rifle was free from dirt and said he would look after the kid while we did the business with the rebels.

While wanting to get the business over with quickly, I forced myself to slow my racing thoughts. Slow down, use your head. Taking a couple of deep breaths, I pushed my fear aside.

Yelling at the platoon to mount up, I crowded into a jeep. Standing up, I yelled for the two jeeps in the rear of the column to turn and attack the ridge from the flank while we attacked from our side. Engines howling in protest, we set out to take on the shooters. If my jeep mates hadn't been quick and grabbed me, I would have fallen over the back of the jeep. Hammering over the rough ground, we hung on for dear life. The madman at the wheel was obviously in a hurry to get round the end of the ridge and take on the rebels. The two beside me were cursing the driver in French with lapses into Hungarian and Spanish.

Waving for the charging jeeps to spread out we headed right at the rebel vehicles. The rebels were scrambling around their vehicles, pushing and shoving one another. They wanted to leave. Two of the small trucks had a heavy machine gun mounted in the body. No rebel attempted to use them against us. If they had, the outcome of the battle might have been different. Slamming on the brakes just in time to halt at the edge of a shallow ditch, the driver, followed by the guy beside him, jumped out and took cover. The three of us in the back pitched head first over the side into the dirt. Spitting dust, head pounding, heart banging away, I took a couple of breaths. I had to get things sorted out before they got away.

We were about forty feet from the trucks. Several rebels had managed to get aboard the trucks; there were four of them. Those on the ground were screaming at one another as they fought to climb aboard the trucks. The only way out was down the ridge. We had to act before that happened. Racing truck motors, crashing gears, they were going to get away. The bastards had to pay, they didn't shoot us up and get away with it. I was madder than hell at these clowns.

Dieter, the guy next to me, I saw had a couple of grenades; "Gimme the grenades." Gripping them firmly, I had him pull the pins and yelled, "Hold your fire;" and I was off and running. I couldn't afford a repeat of my earlier balls up, so I ran to where I had no trouble stepping out of the ditch. Determined that they wouldn't get away, I charged right at them. The nearest truck jerked forward. The rebels crouching down in the back of the truck were yammering and banging the top of the cab; they wanted to get out of here. I slammed into the ground just as the grenade exploded. An over handed throw as I lay there, and the second one exploded between two of the trucks. A couple of the lads followed me and their grenades did the trick. The four trucks weren't going anywhere. Spitting dust I got to my feet and went to check if any of the rebels on the ground were alive. Not one, the guys had done a good job.

On the way down the ridge, we stopped to pick up Gesner. Blondel was still unconscious; Strelski too had flaked out. They required medical attention on the double. My poking fingers brought a groan from Strelski. He must have been more seriously wounded than he claimed. His right pant leg was soaked in blood. Bandaging him as best I could, I called one of the truck drivers over and told him he would have to take the wounded and Gesner back to Kolwezi. Ordering three of the truck's passengers to go back with him, I told the others to get aboard the remaining truck. I urged the driver to make the best possible time between here and the road and once on the road to go for broke. Whether the wounded would survive the journey was a gamble, but it was one that had to be taken.

With Blondel and Gesner gone, it occurred to me there was no one in command. Why not, I had a fair idea of the area we were supposed to patrol. Ally, lad, it looks as though you are the man in charge. This fuck-up doesn't mean that the patrol should be abandoned. It's up to me to take over and finish the job. No one objected when I ordered them to mount up. Albert asked me if I was OK, I nodded. I felt faint, but wasn't about to admit it. I felt tired, lethargic, but shook my head and climbed into the lead jeep. We were on our way. For some time the sky had been darkening, some freak of the weather. I felt a hand on my arm just before the sky went black.

The antiseptic whiteness of it all, the figures, their movements seen through fine gauze, I thought I had bought the farm. The tubes stuck in my arm clued me in. Blondel, Strelski and I had been evacuated by air the day after the "do" up on the ridge. My wounds weren't that serious, but as we were all soon to be going back to Calvi, it was decided that I travel with the wounded, which suited me just dandy; although at the time I was in no condition to debate the matter.

After five days in hospital, I was discharged as fit for duty. I had been lucky, the bullets had only gouged my right thigh. Reporting at the company office I found that the company had just left on an extended training exercise. I had the barrack room all to myself. Until the company wheeled into the barracks three weeks later, I was the office dogsbody.

There were several fresh faces in the crowd. Luigi and Hans, coming out of the showers, gave a shout when they saw me. When I asked where Yank and Wayne were, Luigi said they were still in the showers. He gave Hans a questioning look. Hans answered with a slight motion of his head. Both looked like the cat that ate the canary, in a word they were smug about something. But whatever it was, they weren't about to let me in on their secret. I noticed the new guys whispering among themselves and looking our way. What the hell was going on. I checked my uniform, my fly.

What was it that had them whispering? If Yank knew, he wasn't telling. And he too had a satisfied look on his face when he nodded hello. Next morning I was still in the dark. On parade I was ordered to the barracks and to get into my dress uniform, vite, vite. When I reported back to sergeant Kluga, he gave me the once over and said, "You'll do." Marching across the parade ground I began to get a little concerned. We were heading for Captain Feydeau's office. In my experience a visit to his office meant trouble. In the outer office Kluga gave me a closer inspection and without a comment marched me into the inner sanctum.

Feydeau was a hard man. He earned the respect of us all by often joining us on our twenty mile cross-country jaunts. When displeased, his light blue eyes changed from their warm sparkle to twin drills boring into you. I knew this from first-hand experience. Halting two paces from his desk, I saluted and reported, and stood waiting for the axe to fall. Whatever it was, I'd shut up and get it over with as quickly as possible. I could just see the short cropped blonde hair on the top of his head as I looked straight ahead and waited. He looked up at me and smiled, maybe this wasn't to be a bollockin after all.

When he stopped talking, I stood there dumbfounded. Did he say that I was to be awarded the Croix de la Valeur Militaire? What the hell was this all about, the bloody thing was awarded for bravery. There must be a mistake. Stammering and stuttering, my protest was just a meaningless babble of sounds. Laughing, Feydeau banged his hand on the table, and as he got to his feet he said something to Kluga. He rattled it off so fast, I couldn't understand what he said. I certainly understood what Kluga was saying as we marched back across the parade ground. The little shit bawled me out for my tongue-tied performance.

A week after my faux pas, it was back to the old grind of living rough out on the Corsican hills on company training jaunts. Some of which had us stumbling around in the dark on night marches. Hunched around a fire, eating your sardines, after a gruelling day in the mountains, there were rare secret moments of inner wonder when all was still and the moon was high in a cloudless sky. But no matter where we were, or what the conditions were, we had to wash, shave and polish our boots before we could have our breakfast, a slice of bread washed down with black coffee.

Back in barracks and standing at attention beside our beds, we were told that General Lejeune would pay us a visit in two days. Before then we were to scrub the barracks down and get our kit sorted out and in shape. As the star of the upcoming inspection I was excused most of the clean-up corvee. My time was spent in rehearsing for when Lejeune would plant a couple of wet ones on me. Why do the French have to make such a fuss over a medal?

On the great day adjudant chef Uhlrich, gave me the once over and nodded his approval as I stood rigid in front of the company office.

"No mistakes out there," he said nodding towards the parade ground. "Better use the lavatory MacKinnon. You have about thirty minutes before anything happens sergeant, take it easy for a bit."

Gussied up in our dress uniforms, we took our ease, and waited, and waited. This waiting is worse than the bloody fracas that got this whole thing on the go. Sergeant Kluga, glancing at his watch, moved in close for a final inspection. Taking a pace backwards he grinned and said, "You'll do, you look— smashing, old chap." The surprise mirrored on my face at the remark brought a chuckle from Kluga. Now to have the banty rooster of an NCO mimicking English and being friendly was a shock to the system. The band marching to the head of the bataillon stopped any further thoughts about the sergeant. As we started out to keep my date with the General, the band began to play. Behind the band they marched, heads up, eyes front, confident, disciplined, tough, men of the 2eme Regiment Etrangere de Parachutistes, I was proud to be counted one of them.

During the protocol of readying the battalion for the General's eagle eye, Ally was wishing himself anywhere but where he stood. The sooner this is over the better, was foremost in his thoughts. Although it had all been rehearsed, Ally remained nervous. Would he grab him and plant a great big smacker on each cheek? Whew, what'll I do? Do I kiss him back? If the lads back home could only see me now, they'd laugh their bloody heads off. His thoughts took flight when the voice of the adjudant-chef commanded recipiendaire Legionnaire MacKinnon, 141242, to march to the reviewing stand.

And in the same parade ground voice he ordered the regimental colours, be marched to the reviewing stand. Ally halted six paces from the six-inch high small dais on which the General stood, flanked by the commandant and the other officers in the official party. At a command from the General, the adjudant-chef stepped forward and in his gravelly voice read from the document in his hand.

The Croix de la Valeur Militaire for conspicuous gallantry in the field is awarded to Legionnaire MacKinnon, 141242, 2eme Regiment Etrangere Parachutiste.

In the early morning of May 22, 1978, a fighting patrol commanded by Lieutenant Henri Claud Blondel, came under heavy fire from a group of rebels armed with automatic weapons. Uhlrich then went on to detail what happened.

Taking the medal with its red and white ribbon from adjudant chef Ulrich, General Lejeune smiled and pinned the medal on my uniform. Placing his hands on my shoulders he went through the motions of kissing me on both cheeks. His grey eyes inspected me closely as he shook my hand. "Lieutenant Blondel's family are here today and want to meet you. Your leg, how is it now?"

"Fine, thank you general."

"You led the survivors with élan MacKinnon." Smiling he turned to the commandant, "Lebras you have a future sergeant in this young man." He stepped back, it was over.

As I saluted the General, I wondered what the hell did Blondel's family want with me. Kluga set me straight, he told me to report to the guardhouse for my pass and to hurry. There was a taxi waiting for me at the gate.

+ + +

No one asked me whether I wanted to meet the Blondels. General Lejeune had decreed that the regiment have the day off. I couldn't join my pals for a beer, oh no I had to visit the family of my company commander. So here I was standing in front of the Mirabelle Hotel watching my taxi move off into traffic. I didn't want to be here, anyway, why all the fuss? Oh God let this be over soon. Straightening my uniform and setting my kepi at an angle, I marched into the hotel foyer. The foyer with its fancy furnishings stopped me dead in my tracks, what do I do now? The guy behind the desk would help me.

The elegant young man behind the reception desk turned quickly and stepped through the doorway of the small office behind the desk. After talking to someone he again faced the loungers in their deep chairs. I noticed Mr. Elegant's bored look had been replaced by a pleased smirk. The loungers' surprise at this invasion of their territory, by a common legionnaire, quickly gave way to annoyance. I swear you could hear their thoughts: A legionnaire indeed, this was too much. We are people of affluence who value the privacy and service offered behind the ornate doors of the Mirabelle.

What to do? I stood there like a bump on a log, with the people in their chairs giving me the evil eye. I imagined they were thinking: Who let this guy through the door? I suppose I reminded them of the things they wanted to forget, at least while they were on holiday. They were looking around and muttering to one and other. Where is the concierge, the manager? A heavy-set moustachioed individual came out from behind the desk and hurried towards me. It was goodbye Johnny, I was about to get the old heave ho.

He was halted by lieutenant Blondel, "MacKinnon, hello. Let's go upstairs. My parents' rooms are on the first floor."

I saluted. Smiling, the lieutenant leaning on his cane, returned the salute. Climbing the stairs, I saw that Blondel favoured his left leg.

At the first floor landing I asked, "How is the leg lieutenant? Giving you a bit of bother?"

"Sometimes, and all is well with you?" Before I could answer, we were at an open door halfway down the wide hallway. The grey-haired man, slight of build, bright intelligent eyes behind glasses, about five feet ten inches, a bounce in his step, greeted us with a big smile.

"Father, may I present Legionnaire MacKinnon." We shook hands and then if Dad — teary eyed— didn't plonk a wet one on each cheek. Hanging onto my hand he pulled me into the room.

"My dear, this is the man who came to the rescue of Henri."

What to say. Talk about being embarrassed; I could feel my face getting red. Blondel's Mum was a nice-looking woman. She was as tall as her husband, full figured, a nose with a hint of the patrician and smiling blue eyes. With arms outstretched, she stopped about two paces from me.

"But you are only a boy — so brave."

Flustered, I didn't know what to do or say. Mum took charge;

taking my face in her hands, she thoroughly kissed me and then taking my arm, we walked over to the booze all lined up on a small table.

"A drink Mr. MacKinnon, whisky perhaps?"

I nodded, not quite sure what was expected of me in this unfamiliar situation. While Mum was pouring a man-sized drink, I rubbed my cheeks. I took a sip of my drink. Mum said, "Mr. MacKinnon tell me what happened when Henri was injured?"

"Call me Ally, everybody does, that or Johnny."

"Very well — Ally. What happened that morning? I would like to know. Henri just mumbles when I ask him."

"Nothing much, we were attacked by rebels and we fought back. The lieutenant was wounded, that's it. Oh and we got him safely to hospital."

"Oh Mr. — Ally, please tell me what happened. I know it sounds awful but I have to know. I want to know what happened to my boy. He has changed."

Blondel was no help, he shrugged. Well I thought, better tell Mum what happened and then I can go.

"It was just another patrol. A group of rebels were on the loose in our patrol area, and were shooting up anything that moved. This particular group, Intelligence reported, was led by a particularly nasty fellow.

I then went on to give Mum an edited version of what happened. She and her husband gave me their full attention, as I spun my yarn.

"You risked your life to save our son. We are in your debt," Mr. Blondel said quietly.

"I was thankful the rebels were such poor shots."

A concerned look on her face his mother asked, "Were you frightened?"

"Frightened, I was scared sh...," I stopped, realizing where I was. The lieutenant waved a hand for me to go on.

"You could have been killed. You were very brave. It makes my blood run cold thinking about it," she said.

"Any of the others would have done the same. I got there first."

I turned at a slight noise behind me and found a young woman looking at me. She was a looker, nice dress that showed off her slim figure. I guessed she was maybe a few years older than me.

Blondel said, "My sister Madeleine. Legionnaire MacKinnon."

I gave a stiff little bow — if the folks back home could see me now! She smiled and sat down and and surprised me.

"I expected someone quite — different. Please excuse me, but I thought you would have been taller, bigger."

The Blondels were really nice, they made me feel at ease. I laughed and said, "I'm not much to look at, but the uniform helps."

Madeleine smiled and went on, "My brother refuses to tell us anything about what happened. He speaks well of you, but nothing else. You make light of your actions, I suppose we will never get the full story, Legionnaire MacKinnon."

Her father said, "We are indebted to you Mr. MacKinnon. The medical people tell us that if you hadn't applied a tourniquet to Henri Claude's leg, we would have lost our son. Henri Claude is our only son and someday will have sons of his own to carry on the family name."

"Father, please! Thank you Ally, but for you, my career would have ended that morning in the scrub. You saved my life, thank you."

When will they stop making such a fuss, I remember thinking. All this song and dance was a bit too much for me. Just then a knock at the door got our attention. The door opened and in waltzed a waiter pulling a trolley. A second waiter with a trolley came into the room. Mum directed them to a large table at the side of the room and they transferred covered dishes from the trolleys to the table. The two guys lit little spirit heaters under the larger dishes. There I was sipping my second Scotch — acting the toff — and starving; anxious to get at the groceries.

The wines with the meal, the whisky and now the better part of a large brandy down the hatch, I wasn't feeling any pain. In barracks your past, particularly any talk of family, is not a subject of conversation. I'll blame the booze. When Mrs. Blondel asked about my family, I rattled on about farm life and playing football for Burnsbrae.

All good things must come to an end they say. When it was time to go, I thanked Mrs Blondel, "For a great time." Then it was handshakes from the men and kisses from the women, Madeleine gave me a feathery one on the cheek.

"Ally, before you go my husband has something for you. A...."

"A small token of our appreciation. Please accept this cigarette case; from all of us. We are indebted to you for our son's life."

The shiny case was inscribed: Legionnaire MacKinnon — A Gallant Scot. What the hell, why all this fuss. "Thank you. There was no need to do this. I only did what any of the other lads would have done."

"Ah yes, that may be so, but you were the one who saved my son's life," Madame said, and kissed me again.

In the taxi on the way back to barracks, I had a good look at the cigarette case. Mmh, nice gift. At the barrack gate, I made sure I was all present and correct before marching into the guard room to hand in my special pass. The duty sergeant gave me a cold stare and a nod of dismissal in answer to my smart salute.

With the regiment excused all but necessary duties, I knew where to find the guys. Before I left for my date, the guys gave me a hard time. I had no idea of what to do when eating in a fancy restaurant.

Venditti and Huskau warned me not to drink from my finger bowl, not to slurp my soup, and to ask for food to be passed instead of making a grab for it.

In the foyer I saw a crowd around a bare table watching two guys arm wrestle. You could have cut the haze of cigarette smoke with a knife. I wanted to have a beer with the guys before lights out. Hell, one of the straining drunks was Yank, he was always bragging about how fit he was. There wasn't much to him, skinny, but as strong as a horse. He was wrestling a heavy-set German. Eyes shut his face screwed up in a teeth-baring grimace it was obvious the German was giving him a fight. And if further proof was needed the corded veins in his neck told of his effort to best the German. It was over, Yank yelled and jumped to his feet holding his hands over his head like a boxer. The loser, a dour look on his face, nudged one of the cases of beer at his feet towards Yank.

Yank handed me a beer. The guys wanted to know how it went. After admitting that things went well, the food was first class, I shut up. The afternoon was mine and I didn't want to share it. The generous friendly atmosphere that had surrounded me in the Blondel suite was something to be treasured.

19

A moan from where Ally slept startled Jonesy, who was having a struggle to stay awake. Maybe it wasn't such a bad idea to try and get some sleep. Simon, soon after Alister made his decision, had stretched out on the table and seemed to be asleep, in spite of his earlier fears. Stretched out beside the boy, she arranged her blankets as best she could and put her arm around the blanketed Simon.

Her thoughts wandered briefly across a landscape far removed from her present peril. Her parents, what were Mum and Dad doing? Then she remembered it would be morning in England. Mum would be getting Dad breakfast. The office, soon though, there would be lights and people; a brief smile touched her face as she remembered the give-and-take in the office.

Cuddled into Simon's back she closed her eyes to journey off into fuzzy lethargic state. In this dreamy landscape, death was her companion; the death of Helen Braithwaite. Michael had gone to pieces at the death of his wife. They were so in love. Simon, seven at the time, escaped the heart-breaking grief of his dad, but the loss made a difference in both of their lives. Michael buried himself in work. Simon, when at home, was in the very proper care of a nanny. Gone were the good times, the games with his mother, her sense of fun, her laughter snuffed out in a terrible road accident.

\+ + +

Helen, when she came to the office, brought with her an air of quiet authority. When she put in an appearance, it was to insist that Michael take her to lunch at an expensive restaurant. Invariably her visits were made when a particularly important transaction had become fractious, charging the atmosphere in the office with an undercurrent of apprehension. She remembered him saying after one such visit, "She's my compass Jonesy."

She remembered being her willing partner in buying surprise presents for the staff Christmas party. How she helped a gawky young woman get settled into her first job. Showing me what to do, and what was expected of a secretary when her boss was setting up a new plastics factory. Those were great times. Getting the credit for ideas that we had discussed and at her suggestion I brought them forward at meetings. Now, as Michael's personal assistant, any suggestions I make are my own. His readiness to listen to the ideas, the concepts of others and to spend money on the ones that intrigued him was one of the major reasons for his success. Having been with the firm since day one the staff come to me for answers when they have a problem. Referring to me as "Britannica" when they assume I am out of earshot. If they could have seen me back then, green as a cucumber. Not a clue about what to wear, makeup was a dab here, a dab there, I was a mess. My knowledge was certainly not encyclopaedic.

My parents were so proud of me. Our Margaret has a job with that new firm, the boss's secretary. The feeling was not reciprocated. My snobbish pride refused to acknowledge my humble family origins, the sacrifices they had undertaken to send me to secretarial school. The day of my twenty-first birthday my snobbery was severely bent out of shape. First, Helen and my Mum planned a surprise party for me. At the party my Mum showed a side of her personality that was new to me. She and Helen worked easily together. Mum had us all in stitches with her funny stories of growing up on a farm. The party was a huge success. Helen insisted that because there was more room "the do" be held at The Grange.

Secondly, Michael stopped as he was hurrying out of the office to tell me, "Your Dad has a head on his shoulders. Your Mum and Dad are coming over to the house on the weekend. Your Dad has some ideas I want to talk over with him".

My Dad, the cobbler, talking business with my millionaire boss, it was mind-boggling. Looking back it shouldn't have been. Dad was an avid reader, technical, adventure, biography and scientific subjects were all grist to his inquisitive mind. Mum was forever chiding him for leaving his library books underfoot.

Shortly after the party, newspapers became the subject of quiet conversation in the office. One of the two local weeklies was having financial difficulties and was rumoured to be for sale. Word was that the owner of a small group of county newspapers was looking to expand his holdings. Rumours about the sale were many and varied; of hard information, there was not an iota. The newspaper deal was a great time for me; I was at the centre of all that went on. In fact, I was the one who brought the sale off. It all began in the ladies' loo at the

Saturday night dance in the Meridian Hotel.

There I was sitting minding my own business when two women burst through the door. One of them was declaring in a loud voice that her boss didn't appreciate her. Apparently he had handed her the draft of that week's editorial an hour before deadline. She had my sympathy. What she said next was what made me decide that Loud Voice and I were to get acquainted. Her bombshell was to the effect that she couldn't see what all the fuss was about when his brother was bent on selling the paper. In answer to her friend's question, Loud Voice said that she had typed up letters to and taken phone calls from someone at the Journal. Stepping up on the toilet seat I was able to get a look at the two of them as they headed for the door.

Downstairs in the dance hall, I spotted my target and made sure that we bumped into each other. We were both without partners. Her friend's boyfriend had shown up as arranged. She invited me for a drink. In the bar we swapped tales of ungrateful bosses, had a couple of dances with young men who had a line of guff that had us laughing when we compared notes back in the bar. When she left about ten-thirty we had arranged to meet and take in a flick on Wednesday. She confided to me that she had a date who was picking her up in his car.

Within two weeks I knew her family history. Her father drank too much, her mother was a moron, her brother had a good job and was engaged to a slut. When Eunice told me that she was secretly engaged to the brother who wanted to sell the paper, I almost laughed in her face. When she told me that her lover had arranged to meet secretly with representatives of the Journal, I had a talk with Michael.

The other firm never had a chance. The clincher was Michael's guarantee that the paper would be printed locally. The other firm's papers were all printed at a central location. This was the sticking point, the owner didn't want the printers to lose their jobs. I got a raise out of the deal, congrats from Michael and my first glass of champagne at a special staff meeting. What was that?

\+ + +

Alister came to with a start, and realized where he was when his head struck the shelf above. Sliding off the shelf, his probing hands touched something soft. A startled Simon sat up on the table. The abrupt movement brought Jonesy fully awake.

"Wh wha, what's going on? Oh my back."

"They're on the move Jonesy. Noises from the kitchen." With the plasterboard and the insulation gone the noises from the kitchen were louder than before. The three of them waited expectantly in the dark Would Alexei take off on the snowmobile?

Jonesy was the first to speak after the sounds in the kitchen subsided. Leaning over she whispered in Ally's ear, "Now what do we do, those two crooks have had breakfast. And by the way I'm hungry. The smell of that bacon!"

"Only the best in my kitchen," Alister whispered. "Uh oh, sounds like they've got the snowmobile wound up. Alexei is off to check with his boss."

"You say Pete will likely be left to hold the fort and he will be easier to handle than the Russian?"

"I think so Jonesy. We have to go in there fast. If we can do that I'll take care of Petey. There are no screws in the wall so it's safe to say that there are no shelves to hinder us."

"Let's do it now," from Simon. "There is no way we can tell what is going on in the cabin. Now is as good a time as any Ally. What do you say Jonesy?"

Jonesy remained silent.

"I think you're right Simon. When Alexei comes back things are likely to happen. He will have been in touch with his boss and been told what to do."

Simon, hopping from foot to foot, was desperately eager to be doing something, anything. "Why wait, let's do it now. For all we know they may have taken off and left us to die here in this stinkin' shed. Let's do it."

"Not so loud Simon. OK, here's what we'll do. The two of us will smash a hole in the plasterboard. I'll go into the cabin first, you follow, no hesitation, jump right in. OK Simon? Let's do this right."

"OK, OK, what are we waiting for? I'll be right behind you Ally."

"Not so fast. Put your right foot flat against the wall. Do it," in a fierce whisper. Ally placed his left foot beside it. "Now when I say go, draw back your foot and we are on our way. Keep kicking until we have a hole big enough for me to crawl through. Go!"

20

The ringing of the telephone startled the three men hunched around one end of the table that filled most of the large room. The insistent ringing brought the youngest of the trio to his feet. "You were told to hold all calls." A brief pause, "Oh! put it through. It's for you Mr. Braithwaite."

"Hello, Braithwaite."

"Michael, how are you? When was that plane of yours due to arrive in Ottawa?"

"Hang on a minute, with the difference in time it should have touched down by eight-o'clock, Wednesday morning, eight-thirty at the latest.

"That's what I thought. In that case your Miss Jones should have been at my house some time ago, it's now two-o-clock and I have had a couple of phone calls from their lawyers."

"Correct, Jonesy knew how important the papers were. Something must have happened. And you are saying that she hasn't shown up with the papers?" a tiny stab of fear pricked his heart. He would be lost without Jonesy. She was more than a personal assistant, she was a friend.

"I thought it best to phone you first Michael, before making any enquiries. No need to stir the pot if there is a perfectly sound reason for the delay. You know of course that I cannot go ahead on the deal without the information that you were sending with Jonesy. The newspaper part is sewn up but I need the documents to close the radio and television side."

"Thanks for the call Dave. Leave this with me and don't mention it to anyone. Hold them off as long as you can. I'll get back to you as soon as I have some information." Moving back to the table, he asked, "Is there a small office I can use? There are some calls I have to make."

"Why don't you stay in the boardroom? I'll get you hooked up with an outside line. We'll leave you to your calls."

Alone, he leaned back in the chair. Surely if there had been an accident the authorities would have notified him. What could have happened? What to do? For starters phone the airport in Ottawa and take it from there.

"Ottawa International Airport."

"A plane I own is overdue at Ottawa by six hours. The plane left from Dilsworth aerodrome Wednesday at eight o'clock in the morning and should...."

"Excuse me sir, but how do you know that the plane is overdue here? There are several things that could have happened. It might have...."

"I know the plane is overdue. My staff had on board important papers for delivery in Ottawa. The person who was to receive these documents has just phoned me to say that he has not received them. He has had no communication from the person carrying them."

"Could the papers have been stolen sir? We have no report of a plane down in this area."

"No, no, no, I trust my messenger implicitly. Before I go, my name is Michael Braithwaite, the plane is owned by Dilsworth Recovery. If you hear of any news please let me know. My number is 555-0236, the area code is 206. Call collect and ask for me."

"Got that Mr. Braithwaite, your company is Dilsworth Recovery and call collect, yes I have the number, certainly sir."

"Hey Phyllis, did you say Dilsworth?"

"That's right Richard, why?"

"I had a call earlier about a plane that left Dilsworth, England, and didn't show here as scheduled. How did this guy on the phone sound; did he have an Eastern European accent?"

"No this guy was English, y'know they way they talk. He was phoning from Seattle. This guy said he was the owner of the plane, a Brampton-Naismith."

"Not my guy, he was phoning from here in the airport. The S and R boys have it now and will begin a search as soon as weather permits."

"My guy said to call him collect if I heard anything. For my money that makes him the genuine article not some looney calling in to create a stir. I'll call from an outside phone when I go on break."

"OK, be my guest. When you are in the doggie doo for stepping out of line don't say I didn't warn you."

"Mr. Braithwaite, at last, I thought I would never get through. About your plane, a fellow worker took a call earlier from someone enquiring about it."

His voice betraying his concern he said, "I don't know of anyone who would be interested in the arrival of my plane."

"Definitely, my friend wouldn't kid around about that sort of thing. Someone with a European accent phoned and said he had a friend on the flight and that they were going on a trip. My friend was told that the flight from Dilsworth never reported to flight control in Newfoundland. A snowstorm with high winds is in the area of your plane's flight path. It's pretty widespread and is slowly moving out to the coast."

"So what you are saying is that the plane may have been forced down because of the storm."

"That is the worst case scenario, Mr. Braithwaite."

"You have gone to all this trouble to help me and I don't know your name."

Uh, oh I hope Richard was wrong about the doggie doo, "Cunningham, Phyllis Cunningham."

"Miss Cunningham I am very grateful. Have the authorities been notified?"

"After the first enquiry Search and Rescue were informed. But there isn't much they can do until the storm blows over."

"Thank you again Miss Cunningham. My son and a very good friend are aboard the plane. Would you, would it be possible for you to do me a favour, without getting into trouble with your boss?"

"Depends, what is it you want me to do? Is it legal?"

The question was greeted by a chuckle. "It is all above board. What I would like you to do is to hire a chopper and have it waiting for my arrival."

"I can't do that Mr Braithwaite. I haven't the kind of money it would take to hire a helicopter and...."

"I'm sorry, no no, I will send you the cash. I can have it there within the hour, would twenty five thousand be enough to start things off?

She gasped, "Good grief, are you for real? Could you really do that? I have to tell you I'm just an admin assistant. I've never done anything like this before. I'm on my lunch break, I'm calling from an outside phone. They don't like us to use the phone for personal calls." Take it easy Phyllis, she chided herself. You are babbling on here like teenager on her first date.

"Miss Cunningham, I don't wish to make trouble for, but if you could help me I would be eternally grateful. Should I talk with your boss?"

"Let's leave him out of this. Sure I'll help. It's not the sort of thing I do regularly. I'll do it." Caught up in the excitement of this departure from her routine duties she was eager to get on with the task.

"Good, now how will I get the cash to you? It will be in bills, which means it will be a fair sized package."

"That's OK, no problem." Wow! Am I dreaming, is he really gonna send me twenty-five thousand in bills? God!

"I'll have someone from my bank in Ottawa bring the money to your office. The reason the money is in bills is so that you can pay as you go. I suggest that you begin phoning as soon as I hang up."

"Certainly, the money, send it to Ottawa International Airport, Admin Office second floor for my attention. I'll phone them and have someone bring it over to me."

"Very well, that's what I'll do. You have my number if you get any static about this don't hesitate, give me a call."

Placing the phone carefully in its cradle he sat still for a few moments before going to the door and beckoning the two men chatting outside to come into the boardroom.

"I'm sorry gentlemen, but something has come up that demands my immediate attention."

"What's this, some sort of smart bargaining move? You can't leave, we have a deal on the table." The young man thumped the table so hard that the ash trays on it rattled. Looking at the older man, he said, "He can't do this." The young man wanted to sell and with his share make a start on his own. For him the sale meant no more having to toe the family line.

"Easy Earl, yes he can. We were just talking, nothing concrete."

"I'm sorry, this came at me out of the blue, believe me...."

"Sure. Believe you, why should we? Why now Mr. Braithwaite? You led us on, we thought you meant business. It was all phoney, some strategy of yours to get a better deal."

"That's enough Earl! Please excuse my grandson Mr. Braithwaite. I must say I was under the impression that we were headed for a deal."

"We were, we are. This is an emergency, something I must take care of."

"Is there anything I can do to help — book your flight?"

"Thanks, a regular flight won't do; I'll rent a plane. If only my own plane were here."

"What is this sudden emergency, tell us Mr. Braithwaite?" Earl asked his words thick with sarcasm.

"It's nothing to do with the Grant-James Group, that's all I can say at the moment. I have to go."

"How long will it take you to clear up this emergency? When can we expect you to return to the table?"

"Good question and a fair one I might add, Mr. Grant-James. Unfortunately the situation I find myself in at the moment doesn't have a time frame. This one is a seat-of-the-pants situation, sorry."

Unable to cover up his disappointment, an exasperated Earl looked at his grandfather and said, "That may be Mr. Braithwaite, but we have had other offers on the deal. What do we do while you are off flying by the seat of your pants. We have had a separate offer for the television stations." This latter statement brought a shake of the head and a glare from his grandfather. "We want to close this deal. We prefer to sell the papers and the stations as a package, right?" looking at his grandfather, who nodded.

"I'm sorry about this. It is something I have to attend to. This is something I can't delegate. I have to deal with this problem myself. Sorry."

"I'm sorry that you have to go. We were making progress. We have covered a fair bit of the groundwork."

"That makes two of us, Mr. Grant-James. It's too much, I know, to ask you to hold off until I can get this emergency behind me." This was directed at Grant-James in the hope that he could convince the other family members to put the sale on hold. "I understand your position. Excuse me, I have to get to the airport."

"I guess the deal's off granddad. We can't wait around for Braithwaite's problem to be solved. The family is chompin' at the bit."

When the door closed behind Braithwaite, the patriarch of the Grant-James Group scolded his grandson. "There was no need for that last statement. Something has come up. It was obvious he was scared. My guess is it is something to do with his son who is always in trouble. If you had read the report on Dilsworth, you would be aware of his propensity for getting into scrapes."

"What now? Damn! I should have listened in on an extension."

"No you wouldn't. That's not the way we conduct business. We could weather this bad patch Earl, but no, everyone wants to sell. Tighten our belts, cut back on our own spending, but no one wants to swallow that medicine. Whatever happens, my guess is that he will be back, mark my words young man. Listen in, I never heard of such a thing. I should cuff your ear you young whippersnapper," followed by a friendly push. "That's enough."

"There is no one out there who is likely to come close to Braithwaite's offer. What can we do now gran'dad? I thought we had him hooked."

"First things first, nothing is to be said to the family about his sudden departure. He left to consult with his banker, that will be our story. The mention of his banker should keep things quiet with the family. You and I will, I think the expression is kick back, do nothing until we find out more about Braithwaite's hurried exit."

Before leaving the Grant-James Building, Braithwaite asked the receptionist on the main floor for the Yellow Pages telephone directory. He was successful on the third phone call.

"I want to rent a plane — a Lear, great— for a flight to Ottawa,

Canada. Certainly, check with the Mercantile. Get the damned plane gassed up and ready to go." Looking at the receptionist who was listening in to his conversation, he smiled and asked, "Call a cab for me please. I'll be at the airport within half-an-hour. Have someone at the main terminal meet me and ferry me over to your hangar. The name again is Braithwaite, thank you."

Next he dialled the number of the Mercantile Bank of Seattle and had a brief conversation with the manager. Then followed a longer conversation with the manager of the Dominion Commercial Bank in Ottawa and arranged for the transfer of funds to Phyllis Cunningham. Reviewing the situation in the taxi, he couldn't think of anything further that had to be taken care of. I suppose the flight time will be about five hours. Damn, a lot can happen in five hours. What could have gone wrong? The plane was checked out not that long ago. The weather is bad, could be ice on the wings, oh hell it could be any number of things. I'll just have to sit tight until Ottawa.

Within an hour of receiving the phone call the jet with Braithwaite aboard was airborne. The moment the seat belt sign went off, Braithwaite went forward to the flight deck and spoke briefly with the pilot before handing him a piece of paper. After glancing at the paper the pilot nodded and gave thumbs up. Bending closer to the array of instruments before him, the pilot made some adjustments. Looking up at Braithwaite hanging over his shoulder he nodded and smiled and began talking into his mike:

"Spokane Centre, this is Executive Leasing, Alfa-Golf-Foxtrot-Papa-Seven-One-Niner-over."

"Executive Leasing, Alfa-Golf-Foxtrot-Papa-Seven-One-Niner this is Spokane Centre over."

"Spokane Centre, passenger requests a collect telephone message be sent to One Eight Six Five Six Seven Two Eight Niner Three, Dilsworth, England. Message reads: 'Seattle discussions on hold. Ottawa requires a visit. Ottawa contact Six One Three Two Three Niner Zero Zero Two Seven Braithwaite. Read back. Over"

When the message was read back, Braithwaite took off his head set and sat down. If they go down in the kind of weather Cunningham talked about they will never survive; hypothermia will do them in. I read somewhere that it is quite painless, you fall asleep and never wake up. Shaking his head to rid himself of such morbid thoughts, he told himself to smarten up and think positively.

His thoughts turned to Simon. It was a Saturday, his fourth birthday. Helen had invited some of the neighbours and their children over for the celebration. Other incidents returned to kindle the fires of memory: his first bike, pushing him, the shouted instructions to keep pedalling; the fun the three of them had on weekends. Then the crash, things changed. Poor Simon, he missed his Mum so much. It took both of us a long time to get over it. I sometimes wonder if Simon is over his Mum's death. Jonesy will look after him, she seems to be able to get through to him. Thinking of Jonesy brought a picture of her vividly to mind. God if anything happens to Jonesy I don't know what I'll do. This thought jarred him to the sudden realization that he wasn't thinking of her as a friend and confidante. This feeling was different, it tugged at the heart.

An hour out from Ottawa he had the pilot contact the Ottawa tower. There was still no report of a plane having been diverted to another airport. The B-N seemed to have flown into a Bermuda Triangle somewhere off the coast of Newfoundland and failed to come out. Before the plane had come to a full stop he was at the door waiting impatiently to get out and begin stirring people and things up. Grim faced he strode away from the plane to be met by a Customs officer and the airport manager. Sitting comfortably in a deep chair in the manager's office and looking out over the snow-covered landscape edging the runways a black feeling of despair swept over him.

"Are you all right sir? Is there anything I can get you Mr. Braithwaite?"

"I'll be fine. It's nothing. The trip; and I haven't had much sleep. Don't bother, I'm fine now, whatever it was is gone." The black mood persisted though and resurrected the darkness of that other time when the light was lost . Dear God I pray that they are still alive. Simon's face came to him briefly before it disappeared under a wall of greenish water. He was frightened. Dear God, let them be safe! I don't know what I'd do if I lost them. They've got to be alive please. Struggling up out of the overstuffed chair he came to a decision. The best way to fight this mood was get up and about, do something. It had always worked in the past.

"Thanks for the coffee; now to get on with the job. Outside there should be a chopper all gassed up and waiting for me. I think I'll go and find it."

"It's parked a little way from the main building. I think it would be better if you stayed here in Ottawa, Mr Braithwaite, until we have more information, something definite to work with. There's a lot of geography between here and the coast. It will take a major effort to cover the ground."

"Damn! Of course you are right, but it is damn frustrating to sit here and know that your son and a dear friend are out there and you can't do a damned thing to help them. What's the word on the weather between us and the coast? Any improvement?"

"It's moving slowly out to sea. I'll be notified as soon the S and R boys get the go. You are top of my list, I'll let you know what's happening. Why don't you get some sleep, you look all in. This is a tough time for you. It is not likely that anything will happen for at least twenty-four hours."

"Well, I suppose it would be the smart thing to do. All I have to do is convince myself of that. Is there somewhere here at the airport where I could get my head down, a couch in an office somewhere? Y'know this chair is very comfy," said with a thin attempt at a smile.

A telephone call was all that was necessary and he had a room in a quiet corner of the airport building. The four small rooms were used by pilots of private planes who had to make their pre-flight checks at an ungodly hour of the dawning day in order to be ready for their bosses' early morning departures. He lay down on the narrow bed fully clothed. Half an hour later he was asleep.

Struggling in the deep drifts of a windswept snowy wilderness, Braithwaite fought to find out who was behind the elusive voice. Suddenly a hand on his shoulder, the voice was near "Mr. Braithwaite, Mr. Braithwaite, a phone ...." He sat up in bed, wide awake, "Have they found the plane? Are they safe?" Looking at the figure standing on the other side of the bed, he said, "Well out with it, tell me where are they?"

"It's a phone call, sorry Mr. Braithwaite. They're still on the line. They said they would hold. They must talk to you, no one else. They got quite excited when I told them you were asleep and couldn't they call back later."

Walking together down the narrow corridor Braithwaite wanted to know, "Did the person say who was calling?"

"The caller gave his name as Roger. It's from England, your head office I think. He said it was urgent that he talk with you right away. He was sure upset about something. The desk in the corner, I'll be down the corridor if you need me."

"Hello Roger, what's going on?"

There was a brief silence and then, "Mr. Braithwaite, Simon's been kidnapped. We've had a call from the kidnappers."

"What! Kidnapped, that can't be! The plane failed to show here. Have you contacted the police?"

"No, no that was one thing the kidnappers said would result in Simon disappearing for good, was how he put it. Three million was what he asked for and then he hung up."

Falling into the chair beside the desk, his mind became a tangle of black thoughts. They must have hijacked the plane. Would they kill Simon and Jonesy? Maybe, oh no! maybe they are already dead. Why did I send him to a school in Canada! Oh God I pray they're alive. God, please. If anything happens to them I'll never forgive myself. Noises from the telephone brought him back to the task at hand.

Slowly his practical no-nonsense self took command leaving behind the funk that had threatened to take hold of him. "I'm fine Roger. Yes I'm fine now, it's all right. The first thing we have to do is to get moving on the money. You know what to do at the bank. I want to know what is happening the minute it happens."

"About that, I think we should arrange for a secure line. He was very emphatic, keep this in the family or else, was how he phrased it."

"Thanks. Did he say anything about Jonesy and Robert?"

"No, he only mentioned Simon, referring to him as 'the kid.'"

"It's all very strange Roger, I'm phoned in Seattle and told that the plane has gone missing which brings me to Ottawa, and now this. Is there a connection? The plane could be tucked away at some quiet airstrip here in Canada."

"The call was from England, local I think. They want the money in used bank notes, no high denominations. The voice, it was mean. The threats, he meant them. Sorry Mr. Braithwaite, you have enough on your plate."

"I'll get a secure line fixed up here, you look after your end. When they phone, ask to talk to Simon, insist on it. Call our friend in security; I don't care how much it costs. Have him put a trace on the phone call. To hell with the regulations, I want my son and Jonesy back safe and sound. Keep me informed." I suppose I'll have to sit around and wait. The bastards. I'd like to get my hands on them. God, I hope Jonesy and Simon are all right. If they hurt them in any way .... Here his thoughts trailed off. He got to his feet, murder in his heart. "Bastards," he muttered and sat down, the cubby hole of an office didn't allow for pacing.

21

In another small office, where a red leather sofa and chair and glass-topped cherry coloured desk took up most of the space, Jimmy refilled the tumbler and put the whisky bottle back in the desk drawer. Jimmy, acting on instructions relayed from Canada, had made the phone call demanding the ransom. Well pleased with how things were going, he put his feet up on the desk. When told that the kid had been grabbed, the flunky in Dilsworth almost filled his pants. Jimmy chuckled in recollection of the reaction at the other end of the line. When told that it would cost his boss three million, the reaction was disbelief: "Good grief. What'll I do? I'll have to get in touch with the boss."

The second call, made from a different public telephone tomorrow, would give the details of how the money was to be handed over. The order from the Russians was to let them sweat a bit. The bastard Ruskies were in charge, he had to do as he was told if he wanted to keep the club. Finishing his drink, he went down the corridor and into the club, his club. When this was over he would settle things with the Russians. Nobody took the piss out of The Baker and got away with it. Looking over the early evening diners from his table on its raised dais he caught the eye of a waiter and waving imperiously, had his complete attention as he ordered dinner. Thinking about the next day's phone call the corners of his mouth lifted in a pleased smile.

"Have you got the money? Small notes." At that moment there was a loud clattering noise, the flunkie had dropped the phone. Jimmy was enjoying this, when he came on the line he was subdued and sounded scared.

"I'm afraid we haven't been able to get all the money, we...."

"Don't get lippy with me sonny. Get the money today or its goodbye kid. Understand!"

"I'm sorry but we simply can't get all that money at such short notice. It takes time. We have most of the cash. We are about five hundred thousand short. We'll get the money just give us a little more time. That's all I ask. How do we know that Simon is still alive, that you haven't killed him? Let me talk to him."

"You can talk to him when we get paid. Not until then, we're taking good care of him. The kid's fine."

"Mr. Braithwaite has ordered me not to pay the ransom until I talk to Simon."

"All right then you can talk to his little darlin' when you have the cash. I'll call later today."

When he heard the click at the other end of the line, Roger looked over the desk to where the security man was fiddling with his equipment. "Anything Roy? Where the hell is he phoning from? Did you get a trace?"

"The background noise tells me he is using a public call box. Not quite enough time for a trace. Have you thought of taking up acting? Your scared rabbit routine, marvellous."

"I'd like to get my hands on him for five minutes. I'd sort him out."

"Use it next time, our friend on the phone is not very bright. He might get too cheeky for his own good and give us a clue to his location."

"I have to phone the boss." He was answered on the first ring. After reporting what had transpired, he asked, "How far do you want me to push insisting that I talk with Simon Mr. Braithwaite?"

"It's asking a lot Roger. You have to tread a fine line here, not too pushy but again not too easy. Can you do it? Try and buy us some time. Give security time to get a fix."

Putting the phone down Michael sat at the desk in the small office. God I hope he is still alive. Poor Simon, Jonesy will look after him. They have never made any mention of her. Is she dead? Could they have got their hands on Simon without anyone knowing? But how could they do that? This waiting, it's so damned frustrating. Another night pacing, waiting for the phone to ring.

The ringing of the phone brought Roger's head up off his chest. Wide awake he looked over at the security man, who nodded. He picked up the phone, "Have you got the...."

"Before we talk of money, Mr. Braithwaite has instructed me to talk to Simon before any discussion of money."

Taken aback by the change in the flunky's manner, Jimmy could only sputter and mumble his instructions, "The money...." he got no further.

"First I must talk to Simon, Mr. Braithwaite was quite firm on this. The boy could be dead for all we know. What's the problem?"

Jimmy was at a loss, what to do, this wasn't part of the plan.

Braithwaite's flunky was supposed to hand over the money without any fuss. The Ruskies wouldn't, they wouldn't kill the kid. Leave me in the shite all tied up for the old Bill to nick me. The Reds were in it for the money, they wouldn't do anything to cancel the payday. He said the first thing that came to mind, "No problem. The kid isn't here. I'll phone you later." Back in his office he phoned Yuri and explained in no uncertain terms what had happened. The information was relayed to the General. After a brief pause, the General resolved the matter.

"He will have to fake it. Tell Jimmy to have someone impersonate our Master Braithwaite and he is to say one word, Dad, that's all. Then have him mumble some gibberish. While this is going on fake a scuffle, chairs going over maybe a glass or two broken. Then you say, now do you believe me, you heard, he is very much alive.

Reporting on the phone call, Roger was hesitant about how best to pass on to his boss his feelings about Simon's message, if it could be called that. Braithwaite immediately picked up on his reluctance to speak and wanted to know what was going on.

"There is something you are not telling me Roger. Spit it out, let's have it all, the good and the bad."

"Mr. Braithwaite it's a feeling I have. It didn't ring true, the phone call sounded phoney, staged. It's just a feeling."

"What was said? What did Simon say? He's all right, and Jonesy is she with him?"

"That's the problem, Mr. Braithwaite, he only said one word 'Dad' and then there were sounds of a scuffle and that was the end of it, the conversation. There were some garbled sounds and then the kidnapper came on the line and said how much more proof did we need to confirm that he was fit and well. Remembering your earlier instructions I told him that one word wasn't enough and that I wanted to talk to him right away. He came back and said that was impossible as Simon had been knocked out in the fracas."

"You did what you had to do Roger, thanks. What instructions did he give you about the ransom?"

"He was most explicit. He wants it in three suitcases."

"I trust you Roger to handle the exchange. I have to go on the assumption that they are alive. All we can do now is to wait and see if I did the right thing. Keep me informed." I hope to God I did the right thing. I'd pay double the ransom to get them back. Are they dead, in a ditch somewhere? Michael alone with his thoughts, unpleasant thoughts, Roger's report didn't bode well for the safe return of Simon and Jonesy. This waiting around is driving me up the wall.

22

Alexei came awake slowly. Oh hell, I'll have to go out in that awful weather. Looking at his watch, he saw it was six-thirty, it would soon be time to get to a phone and report what had happened. Fully clothed he stretched and yawned and stood up and stepped into his shoes. Throwing a blanket around his shoulders he went outside, where standing a few feet from the door he relieved himself. Shivering, he slammed the door shut and grabbed a couple of logs from the big box beside the fireplace. Placing the logs and some kindling atop a wad of newspaper he took a wooden match from the box on the mantle and stepped back as the kindling began to crackle. Pulling the blanket around him, he settled into one of the large chairs.

As the flames took over the dry logs; his thoughts meandered some of the byways and trails he had travelled as a servant of State Security. He had never lived his dream of having coffee in a Parisian café with Franscoise. What a woman! She certainly put me through hoops. The memory brought a smile to his face. That first time we met, it was after a football game and we had gone back to the dormitory. University student huh, hindsight is always twenty twenty. She fooled me, the bitch. When she introduced herself, again he smiled and shook his head.

"My name is Alexei Stataspovitch, you are from France, the accent."

"Yes, aren't you the clever one Alexei Stataspovitch. Now let me see, where do you come from? Ah yes — but of course — you are from the mountains — let me think — from the small town of Svertstok in the Ural Region."

Alexei slack-jawed and wide-eyed, was momentarily bamboozled and then he saw the look in her eyes and a smile taking shape at the corners of her mouth.

"I'm psychic. Cross my hand with silver and I will tell your fortune Alexei. Paper will do if the amount is large enough," she grinned.

Alexei aware of the others crowding around, self consciously allowed her to hold his hand. Her hands were incredibly soft, sitting close together on the floor he could see that her sparkling eyes were brown, the blonde hair, the soft pink in her cheeks, her straight nose. She was not at all like the girls at home.

Alexei was enjoying himself, nothing like this had ever happened before. Here was a beautiful girl sitting beside him with eyes only for him. When he tried to free his hand she grasped it tighter and gave him a playful push.

"No, no, I must read your hand. Let me see. You will have a long and distinguished career in government, ah yes I see it now, with lots of travel, most of it abroad. You will marry and have a large family and your lifeline tells me that you will die an old man in your bed."

"Who told you that I'm from Svertstok. The town isn't that small, fifty-five thousand people. It is an important railway junction and mining centre."

"Of course and don't forget the timber."

Surprised at her knowledge of his home town, he sputtered a reply, "You're not psychic who told you?

"Huh! I come from Caen a city with ten times the population of your village. No one told me, I'm psychic."

"But of course," said in an attempt to mimic her accent.

"Touche. Are you at the university?" Not waiting for an answer she went on, "I enjoy these small parties; you can really get to know people, the soul of a country, of Mother Russia."

"Well, well, fancy that, and why this interest in Mother Russia? You are French and yet your Russian is good."

"Only good? I thought it was perfect."

"Not quite, there is a slight French lilt on your tongue."

"For your information Mr. Cleverness, I have been given the special privilege of studying at Moscow University. I am here on a secret mission." Here she furtively looked around and whispered in his ear, "My task is to steal your upright Russian soul and baptize you in the one true faith of good times and fun."

Growing up within the puritanical structure and rules of the System, Alexei fell readily into the trap set for him. The System with its insistence on conformity provided the blinders which kept him and the nation's young on the straight and narrow path towards the New Communist Man.

At first it was in the Octobrists where the rules urged youngsters to study hard, love their school, respect their seniors, love work and be congenial. It was more of the same for the Pioneers who if they wanted to succeed had to study diligently, be disciplined, love to work, be courageous and not be afraid of hardships. All evoked with evangelical zeal.

He may have thought of himself as a man of some experience, but when set against the wiles and intellect of a clever and motivated woman, he was lost. They parted in the early morning hours. In class he was taken to task by one of his professors for his daydreaming. It wasn't until he was walking home after classes that he realized that he did not know how to get in touch with Franscoise. He hoped that she would turn up at one of the games, soon he hoped.

She was unlike any other woman he had known in his limited sorties into the world of women and intimacy. There had been the usual scuffles and groping back home in the park, at school and once in the hay on a visit to a commune. Franscoise wasn't like the girls back home. She was bright, great fun to be with. It was obvious that she was highly thought of; she must be an important Party member in France for her to obtain permission to attend Moscow University. Foreign students attended Patrice Lumumba University. Alexei, pleased with himself and the situation he found himself in, allowed his canny peasant good sense to be subverted by a smile and a cheeky manner.

Franscoise, when she reported to her superiors, was ordered to frequent a particular hotel bar; the hotel was reserved for foreigners. The Alexei operation was on hold while she became friendly with a member of a trade mission, a more pressing assignment.

Franscoise enjoyed her time with Alexei; the job was uncomplicated. It was obvious he was taken by her, but that was supposed to happen. He was young, he would get over it, they always did. This new assignment would not be as easy. Her experience with trade delegates was that they, feeling free of all restrictions and with all their expenses paid for, wanted to party. They could be delightful companions on the street, but once in the bedroom, look out. Demanding in the bedroom, and should their demands, no matter how perverse, not be met, they would often take their frustration out on their companion of the evening. The committee preferred — before the trap she was the bait for was sprung — that things get a bit rough. The tape of the incident when shown in all its graphic detail brought lover boy to heel quickly.

What she did, she looked upon as just a job, better than the streets where she had worked before being picked up by the KGB. Her French communist parents had immigrated to the Soviet Union in the late forties. Ten years later, disillusioned and much wiser, they found when they tried to leave the country there was no way out. The State would never acknowledge that all was not well in Utopia. With no job, no apartment, deserted by their friends, overnight they became lishentsy, (people deprived of their civil rights). Social pariahs, they subsisted in the criminal nether world of Moscow. Her father used his skills as an engraver to forge documents for his underground neighbours. Her mother, a pharmacist, made love potions and cure-alls for the gullible from herbs and plants she gathered on trips to the country.

She had been neatly conned into the work by a smooth-talking Armenian. He picked her up in a club where she had an arrangement with the owner to use one of the rooms on the second floor. They spent the night in his apartment, whose size told Franscoise that this man had money. He was either bribing some official or he had political connections, and at a fairly high level. When she woke up that first morning, there was a note on the refrigerator inviting her to stay for the day and they would go out in the evening. She was to choose the place.

The Armenian, ardent in bed, and easy with his money set her up in her own apartment. When he asked her to accommodate one of his customers, she said yes. Why not, he was generous and she always had a good time with him when he was in Moscow. Shortly after this, the mask was removed; it became official, she was working for the KGB.

Alexei had come to the conclusion that he would never see his delightful French companion again. Mooching through the park in the quiet of dusk after a heavy session in the library, Alexei heard his name whispered, turning quickly he saw there was no one behind him. There it was again, who could it be? Was it? Dared he hope, it was—Franscoise stepped from her hiding place in the shadow of a lavatory doorway.

"Look at you standing there with a funny look on your face. Alexei aren't you glad to see me? I missed you."

For a moment Alexei stood speechless, a silly grin on his face. "I missed you too, where were you? I looked all over for you, didn't know what to do."

"Here I am, I'm back, so what do we do tonight?"

"There's a lecture tonight at the Potemkin Club, I was gonna go," Alexei said lamely. To his surprise, she readily agreed. They went to her apartment where Franscoise worked wonders in the kitchen. The meal, served with wine, was right out of the pages of a gourmet cookbook. He was rather overwhelmed with the meal and the apartment, both were beyond his experience. The furniture was dark rich browns with the occasional lighter coloured piece. The paintings and decorations on the walls were a mixture of icons and abstracts, the latter starkly framed to set off the artist's work. The mixture of old and the new on the walls and in the furniture, strangely enough, had a pleasing ambience. The carpets scattered about the three-room apartment added to the overall effect. Alexei was so taken by the size of the apartment and its furnishings that he never noticed that there were no family photographs in any of the three rooms.

While busy in the small kitchen, Franscoise had noticed his gawking at his surroundings, and with a hidden smile invited him to feel free to look around. Alexei, although considered by his professors a brilliant student, retained a rustic naiveté which at times bordered on the gauche. The beautiful Franscoise with her charm had banished his powers of rational thought. He accepted without question the apartment with its expensive furnishings.

After the lecture — The Psychology of the Socio-Economic Strata in the American Workplace — they sauntered through the park. Walking hand in hand Alexei was removed to another planet, everything had a rosy hue. He was brought back to reality with a bump when they arrived at the door of Franscoise's apartment. He didn't want to leave her.

"Will I see you again Alexi? Why so glum? I thought we had a good time tonight. It was so nice to see you again."

"Me too, it was good. The meal was first rate. I don't want to leave you. I've never met a girl like you," he blurted out in a rush of youthful emotion.

"Thank you Alexei, I'm flattered." Mindful of her purpose in getting close to this young man she took his hand. "Tomorrow and the rest of the week I have to work late. Could we meet here Saturday? We'll have supper and go out somewhere nice. Do you like the ballet? Come over at about four o'clock."

His mood did an abrupt about turn and a beaming Alexei agreed that four o'clock would be just perfect. Grabbing her by the shoulders he kissed her on the cheek and quickly walked away, a spring in his step. Lying in bed with fantasies dancing in his head, he knew he was the luckiest man alive. She wanted to see him again, maybe. Dared he think that he would be allowed to go back with her to France? Sitting in the sun drinking coffee while an envious world walked by. Strolling the streets of Paris arm in arm. He fell asleep in the early hours of the morning, and as a result missed his first class and was late for his second.

"Oh ho, where were you last night Alexeiovitch? There is a woman somewhere in the picture. The bags under your eyes and the bright gleam in them tell their own story," his friends joshed him. "Is the French one back in town?" At this Alexei blushed to the delight of his classmates. After classes he had to undergo a gauntlet of taunts about his French date as he begged the use of class notes. With an effort he settled down to his studies. Each school day seemed to be made up of twice the usual hours and the nights were filled with wishful thinking, hopes and fears. Alexei was in love.

Early for classes Saturday morning, he sat alone in the large-tiered lecture room with thoughts only of Franscoise and the coming evening. He made only cursory notes in each of his three classes. His thoughts, butterflies in the sun of his infatuation, flitting from one dream to another. Hurrying from the last lecture of the day, he took his usual route through the park. The trees were beginning to bud, the grass was greening, it was great to be alive, he thought.

Alexei dawdled through the park going off his usual footpaths to explore the areas beyond his hurried unseeing walk from school. Checking his watch, he sat down on a bench under a tree and lapsed into a daydream. Today was different, the excitement rose in his blood. Yet in a corner of his practical, everyday sensibility, there lurked doubts. Could life really be this wonderful, his pessimistic Russian soul asked? Such thoughts he thrust aside before they could rise full formed in his consciousness, but he could never banish them. They sneaked out from behind his infatuation at the most inopportune of times.

A much surprised Alexei admitted to Franscoise that he had enjoyed the ballet. "I think my pleasure in the evening was in large part due to my companion," he said with a shy grin. When reporting to her masters afterwards Franscoise was told to begin the second phase of her assignment: to bed Alexei and find out what his political leanings were from their pillow talk.

Six months later, a sizeable dossier on the likes and dislikes of Alexei Stataspovitch was placed on the desk of Major Yegorin of the KGB. Opening the top file, he began to read. The French whore certainly earned her keep. Wouldn't mind a few hours in that fancy apartment of hers myself. Several hours later, having read the mass of paper originated by paid informers, party activists and the vigilantes supervised by the Komsomol, he made a decision. Taking out a blue folder from a desk drawer, and using the notes he had made while reading, Major Yegorin began completing the forms it contained.

Towards the end of his second year in university,Alexei was asked to take part in An Examination of Altered Mind States — Methods and Means, a program sponsored by the KGB. His task was to keep detailed notes on the people being used in brainwashing experiments. Daily he was witness to the memory-destroying effects of extensive electrical shock treatment. Referred to as deprogramming, the treatment left the people experimented on in a zombie-like state. This was followed by an equally long process of reprogramming. They must have done something terribly wrong for them to be included in the project. After treatment they would be much better citizens, he rationalized.

After four months of enthusiastic note-taking and about to begin his third year of studies, Alexei was invited to a meeting by two of Major Yegorin's underlings. The result of the meeting had Alexei saying goodbye to his football-playing chums and transferring to a military academy. The transfer in itself was unusual, but to a military school, had his friends uneasy. Had good old Alexei been spying on them? The transfer was a cover for his move to a secret training establishment in a quiet forested area not far from Moscow.

The good old days, Alexei thought! Green as grass and ready for mowing. When it happened, he had been heartbroken, poor me, he thought. In the process of putting the Franscoise affair behind him, a harder, cynical edge was burnt onto his personality. A graduate of the KGB's school of black arts, his motto was get them before they get you. One thing about the liaison that he remembered with fondness was the sex. She was a specialist first class in bed. She was all woman.

He wandered through his years of labouring in the Indian sub-continent on behalf of his masters. Starting out as a lieutenant, his diligent work there saw him rise quickly through the ranks to colonel.

Whether it was running a business as a front for his subversive activities, bootlegging or dealing in drugs or weapons, he was always careful in siphoning off a modicum of the profits for his retirement fund. His years posing as a renegade Albanian Muslim in Afghanistan were particularly satisfying in a monetary sense. In the narrow streets of certain sections of Kabul he was well known as a purveyor of quality Russian weaponry, secretly supplying the rebels with guns and ammunition sold to his agents by Russian soldiers. Pocketing the money, he then informed government intelligence the route the gun runners would take into the hills. Most of the arms confiscated in such raids found their way back into Alexei's control; a few for appearance's sake were displayed beside the corpses of the rebel gun runners. Those were great days.

Working free of the oversight of the embassy KGB section, his orders were received direct from Moscow. His radio was set up in a warren populated by families who lived on the rough edge of life. The maze of winding alleys and narrow streets that served the area was Alexei's security blanket. Anyone following him could be readily lost in the maze. Should the follower be seen a second time, then a neighbourly chat and cash would take care of the matter; a knife thrust in one of the darker alleys.

His greatest coup, the one which earned him his papakha, the peaked cap with the unsightly looking large top, worn by colonels and above, was the theft of a large shipment of American weapons destined for one of the rebel factions.

Because of the dangers of the route into the hills and it being impassable to motor vehicles, the weapons were to be transported by donkey and on the backs of the rebels. He smiled at the memory. Informed of the shipment and the route it was to take, he set out to find a way to use the weapons to his advantage. How could he turn them against the people they were being shipped to?

He found his answer in a conversation overheard while drinking tea in one of the caravansaries he frequented. The travellers, resting for the night in Kabul before moving on, brought with their merchandise all the gossip of the journey from Pakistan. One item of gossip provided him with all the information needed to steal the weapons. It was simplicity itself; use the Afghan philosophy of an eye for an eye, and the guns and rockets would never reach their intended destination.

Blood feuds were part of the Afghan cultural landscape. The gossiper, relishing the attention being paid him by the locals crowded around him, told them in dramatic detail of the blood feud between the smugglers and a clan which supported another faction in the war against the Communist government. Blood had been spilled and honour must now be satisfied.

Two weeks later, in the desolate landscape of a narrow mountain pass, the weapons changed hands. The attack came in the pre-dawn hours when the body is at its lowest ebb. Silent figures moved from their hiding places and went about the business of avenging one of their own. Twenty of the smugglers were dispatched without a sound. The alarm was given when a smuggler awoke to answer the call of nature. About to scramble to his feet, he raised his head and saw the guards had been changed. The replacement, a boy, was crouched down with his back to a rock. There was something odd about the way he sat. Sniffing the air, he got to his feet—blood. Alarmed he came fully awake and realized, too late, that what had struck him as odd was the boy's rifle was not in his hand. To an Afghan his rifle is a part of him and is always to hand.

Before he could give the alarm a wraith rose up beside him. Their deadly pas de deux with bloodied knives punctuated by grunts and gasps awoke the camp.

When the sun reached into the pass, the caravan had gone, only the dead — forty seven bodies — were left, lying in the twisted postures of their violent end. Overwhelmed by larger numbers, the smugglers were able to only take ten attackers with them to Paradise.

Alexei stored the weapons overnight while the rebels celebrated their avenging raid. While the rebels were enjoying such delicacies as sheep eyes and goat brains the commander of the Russian Special Forces (Spetsnaz) acting on orders— priority rainbow— from Moscow had his men examine the American weapons. The next day the weapons were loaded on donkeys and were on their way to the rebel's base camp.

Strange though, the grenades exploded before they could be thrown, ammunition exploded in the barrel or blocked the barrel by misfiring, rockets went astray, occasionally wheeling about and killing the firer. No one would use the weapons. They lay gathering dust in a small hut until a Russian gunship blew it up in an attack on the village.

+ + +

Arousing himself from his reverie, he stood up. Moving into the kitchen area of the open concept cabin he turned on the tap and began filling the kettle. Something on the floor snagged his attention. A piece of the wall was sticking out and there were small pieces of wallboard on the floor. With an ear to the wall he stood listening, nothing. Picking up several of the small pieces he stood unsure whether they were fresh or he hadn't noticed them earlier. If dislodged recently it meant the prisoners had freed themselves quicker than he had estimated. Alexei thought he had lots of time to get to a phone and report. Ally's toy knife changed the schedule; there was no need to search for a protruding nail or a sharp object.

Why not let them go on thinking that they could escape? Why stop them? The wall was solid enough to keep them occupied for quite some time. He daren't tap the wall, to do so would alert the prisoners. They can't have done much damage, we would have heard them if they had been breaking through the wall. While they're busy I can get out to a phone and get things organized to get out of this mess. I should be back long before they break the wall down. Anyway, if they do succeed, Peter can take care of them one at a time as they come through the wall. A grinning Alexei put the kettle on the propane stove and went silently to warn Peter of the escape attempt.

Peter awoke with a start and started to lash out at the figure shaking him awake. Alexei grabbed his shoulders and held him down on the bed until he stopped his struggles. Leaning over, he told him quietly of the escape attempt and in a fierce whisper told him not to do anything to warn the prisoners. Peter wanted to smash the wall down and shoot the lot of them; arguing that was what was to happen anyway, why not now?

Still whispering, Alexei said, "The General has an investment in this venture. The ransom first, then we take care of the prisoners. Don't do anything foolish Peter," this in a menacing voice. "If we fail, all our lives are forfeit. If this situation is to work for us we must exercise caution and think things through before we act. Who knows, we might need them to get us out of a hole."

"OK, OK, all right. What do we do now?"

"We let them think that they have a chance of escaping. They can't do us any harm Peter.

"I'd like to sort out that Simon."

You'll get to settle accounts before we go. I have to get to a phone."

"How long will you be gone? There's three of them Alexei."

"You can do it Peter. Don't worry, you have the advantage of foresight."

"I must inform certain people of what has happened. MacKinnon mentioned a town nearby. He was to take the pilot to a hospital there."

"Is he still alive? Will he recover?"

"Don't worry about him, he's as good as dead. Before I leave we'll dump the body somewhere out of sight. But before we can do that I have to find where MacKinnon stores his gasoline. You don't want me stranded out in the bush, now do you Peter?"

"Why not let me go? You have the gun. What can I do if they come through the wall?"

"They won't come through the wall. Let's have breakfast. You get things organized in the kitchen and I'll look after getting gas for the snowmobile."

The wind from across the lake whispered of more snow as it swept around the cabin and outbuildings. Astride the snowmobile, Alexei repeated what Peter was to do should the prisoners come through the wall. "If they come at you a solid blow to the head should stop them. That is Ally and Jonesy. If you kill them there is nothing lost. But if the boy attacks you strike him hard on the shoulder and then use your fists. Don't damage the goods Peter."

Alexei proceeded with caution until he got the feel of the snowmobile. Once clear of the cabin, he stayed in the centre of the road and increased his speed .It was easy driving the snowmobile, he thought. All I have to do is stay in the centre of the open area marked by trees on each side and keep going. When I reach this town or village I'll have to be careful, very careful. I suppose everyone will know MacKinnon, where he lives, what he does. Better make sure the gun is out of sight and hope I don't have to use it. A shot would likely bring the police and probably the whole town down on me. Most of them are likely to have a weapon of some sort, hunting rifles at least.

Looking around him, he found that the landscape had some things in common with his native Ural region. The crisp air, the cold, the snow highlighting the dark trees, reminded Alexei of home. He could smell — a trick of imagination — the summer pine forests around the family dacha. Would he ever see his homeland again? The big house atop a slight rise at the end of the cul-de-sac lined with the larger than usual houses of the local apparatchiks. And the small park where the neighbourhood children played.

He remembered the rough and tumble of growing up in a large family, a smile creased his face, four boys and three girls. His father, mayor of Svertstok and his mother, chief administrator at the local hospital, were Party members. Ambitious for their large brood, they saw to it that the correct path to success was trod by their children. It was unusual for people like them, intelligentsia, to have a large family. Those envious of their favoured position in the local apparat referred to them as the boar and his sow.

Alexei first came to the attention of the KGB because of his nimble footwork on the football field. He began playing football as an Octobrist and continued as a Pioneer and upon joining the Communist Youth League was asked to play for one of the Spartacus society's junior teams.

Spartacus is the national sports association of those who work in trade, communications and other services. There are nine such associations: Dynamo is allied with the KGB. In the local soccer league, Dynamo always fielded a strong team. The championship trophy bore ready evidence of this, Dynamo being listed more than any other team. The two most recent championship games saw Spartacus win over Dynamo, thanks to the stamina and clever feet of team captain Alexei. After considerable backroom haggling and after a number of vodka bottles were emptied, he played on the championship Dynamo team the following year.

He was, although the third born, the first boy in the family and therefore became the family's champion in the schoolyard. His brothers and sisters never knew the fear of having to obey a bully's quirky demands. He saw it all again, the schoolyard brawl that had set the mark of the fighter on him.

Alexei's team was ahead three to one in a pickup game of football. The pitch was an area that paralleled the schoolyard. The playing field was marked off with their jackets as were the goals. A lanky twelve-year-old, quick on his feet, he was heading towards the goal, there was no one in front to stop him, an easy goal. Aiming to shoot the ball just inside the goalpost, he drew back his leg intending to send the ball rocketing past the goalie for his second goal. It never happened, he fell rolling in the dust, his leg seized with pain.

With his team-mates' screams of foul a counterpoint to the derisive laughter of their opponents, he scrambled to his feet. Dusting himself off, he was pushed by a fourteen-year-old who began yelling at him, the same boy who had kicked his leg when about to score a goal. In a reflex action, Alexei pushed the big boy who staggered back. Surprised, he swung a roundhouse punch at Alexei which grazed the top of his head. Putting his head down, Alexei charged at the bully, his arms flailing. Before the bully could react, his nose was bloody, and in his haste to back away from his attacker he tripped and fell.

In no time the schoolyard was empty, everyone wanted to see the action that was causing the hoots and yells over on the football field. Slow to get up, the bully touched his nose and looking down saw blood on his hand. Gingerly, he touched his nose again and feeling the blood sticky on his fingers he let out a roar and aimed a kick at Alexei. This was an unforgivable breach of the rules. Only girls used their feet in a fight. Alexei charged in again and catching the bigger boy off balance knocked him to the ground. The bully lay where he fell.

He was a long way from home and the days of his youth. Pursing his lips he wondered where he might be now had he not gone to university in Moscow. Probably cutting a wide swathe as a local apparatchik in Svertstok where he had been marked for advancement in the Party. As a boy he had toed the Party line, never questioning any of its directives. This unswerving loyalty had earned him a place at Moscow University, and an ear for languages brought him to the attention of KGB recruiters.

University had been a challenge; his first time away from home and the sanctuary of his family. At home, he knew his place within the System. Because of his parents' prominence in the local apparat, he was accorded much more leeway in his manners and actions than most of his peers. Pitched into the hurly burly of university life he was, at first, overwhelmed by the manners and mores of his fellow students, most of whom were from large urban centres.

That first year he had only taken part in extra curricular activities that were in support of his psychology studies. Lonely in the crowded corridors of the university he looked forward to his grandmother's monthly parcels. Carefully packaged, they were filled with her baking and with the delicacies there would be a long rambling letter detailing all the happenings in and around home. He loved his babushka; she was always there to treat his scrapes and bruises and later a ready listener to his problems. Alexei never tired of reading the letters, which became tattered by year's end.

On a brief holiday he found that his life at university now set him apart from his contemporaries. They still played football in pick-up games and sometimes drank too much, but there was a change in his and their interests. Their horizons were limited to Svertstok while his were unlimited. He found the life and pleasures of Svertstok stifling. At school there was always something new, challenge, debate, new and interesting friends.

Saying goodbye to his grandmother at the railway station, he felt a little bit ashamed at being glad to be going back to school. Back in Moscow, he found that the beds next to his in the dormitory had been allotted to two first-year students. They were from the same town. One of them had a record player and a collection of bootleg jazz records. Most of the time, the music was filtered through large earphones. Occasionally they were mislaid and when this happened, Alexei complained about the raucous foreign sounds. This led to a heated discussion as to the merits of the foreign music. Alexei declared "the noise" was a classic example of the depraved culture in the West. He stated that it wasn't music, it was plain and simple a cacophony. Later when the slanging match on music finally ended, they discovered a mutual interest, a love of football. From then on the three of them were inseparable, Alexei playing the part of big brother.

Life away from home was no longer time spent between letters. That second school year he and his dorm mates were aggressive forwards in their play for one of the few intramural football teams. Team sports received little if any attention although physical training was a must for all first- and second-year students. They were the team's star players and as a result were always welcome at the reprise of the game.

It was at these discussions that Alexei's quick wry wit was discovered, gaining him access to a widening circle of friends. The get-togethers began in the changing room at the gym and then gravitated to the dormitory. Football gave the players an escape from the hard grind of studying. Alexei, like his fellows, had to earn good grades in the mandatory five courses each semester. Added to this was the time and effort required to participate in the affairs of the Young Communist League. Alexei knew that membership in the Komsomol and then the Party were mandatory requirements for advancement within the System.

It was after a football match that he met Franscoise Allard, whom he assumed was a student, a very pretty French student. Her screams of support for the other team caused a few heads to turn. In the dormitory after the game she sat down beside him and introduced herself.

23

Alexei lost in his memories didn't notice that the snowmobile was no longer centred between the evergreens. He realized he had drifted of course when the snowmobile came to an abrupt stop in the snow-filled ditch. Jumping clear he fell in the snow as the snowmobile slowly tipped over on its side. Struggling to his feet, he righted the machine. Now what, he thought. The engine had died. Was there a reverse gear he could use to get the machine back on the road?

The motor started easily, and standing in the ditch, Alexei, a steady pressure on the throttle, pushed as best he could and slowly got the machine back on the track. I'm sweating like a bear in summer, these suits are warm he mused, as he undid a zipper at his throat.

When he came to where the snow-covered road formed a T junction with the highway, he hesitated briefly before turning right. Driving on the verge of the road where the passage of the snowploughs had packed the snow to an icy hardness, he twisted the throttle wide open.

He knew he had made the right turn when he saw the sign, Miskimin. Easing off on the throttle, he saw the first houses up ahead as he came around a bend in the road. Slowing down further he crossed the bridge on the outskirts of what looked to be a small town. Most of the houses appeared to have been built without benefit of architect or plan; wooden boxes on a cement basement. That some were larger than others was the only difference; all were built of wood. Crossroads with Levesque's General Store on one side and the Gold Star Hotel & Restaurant opposite marked the centre of the town. He continued slowly down the highway hoping to find a public telephone.

Nothing, patting the pocket that held his automatic, he turned the snowmobile and headed back the way he had come. There was nothing else to do but park and make a phone call from the store or the hotel. Standing at the door to the store and looking out over the veranda rail, he saw the street was still empty. The noise of the snowmobile hadn't attracted any attention. Let's hope the lack of interest continues inside, he thought, as he pushed the door open and set a bell to ringing.

Putting his hand in his pocket he looked around, expecting someone to come to the counter. He could hear voices coming from an area behind the counter. Looking around, Alexei saw that the shelves were filled with the multi coloured packages, plastic containers, bottles and tins found in a grocery store. Towards the back of the store the shelves were taken over by clothing and hardware. Turning back to the counter, he saw that a glass-fronted case in the passageway behind the counter contained several rifles, a shotgun and boxes of ammunition. Still no one came in answer to the summons of the bell. The voices continued their monotone. Striding to the door he gave the bell a prolonged ring which was answered by a figure bustling through the passageway.

"Hello and what can I do for you today?"

"Hello. Have you a public phone I could use? There was no sign of one on the main street."

"We don't have one, but you're welcome to use our phone in the house."

Alexei wanting to keep his conversation private, said, "I couldn't do that. I wouldn't want to trouble you. Would there be one in the hotel across the street?"

"Yes there is one in the hotel, that is if you can get to it without being bothered by the drunks." With a new face to talk to she prattled on. "The gang from The Falls are over there. They're sinking a mine shaft up near Dixon Falls. They're always picking fights; two of them are in jail. They work out in the bush for a month to six weeks and then come into town and go on a bender."

"Thank you, I'll take you up on your kind offer. It's a long distance call; I'll reverse the charges."

The call from Mr. Shabashnik was readily accepted, the operator unaware the name he had given meant moonlighter in Russian and informed the listener in Ottawa that the caller was one of Leonid's operatives, "Yes, who is calling?"

"Alexei, the package has been delayed in transit. I am phoning through the kindness of a store owner in the town of Miskimin in Northern Ontario. The delivery system broke down. Matters here are being controlled, but a quick exit is requested. The package remains intact but there are other elements that may be problematical."

Alerted by Alexei that the call could be overheard the voice asked, "Can you deal with the problem or should I send help?"

"Yes, what I need is transport; here in the next twelve hours."

"What is the weather like in your area? Could a plane land?"

"The weather is not good. There is a break in the snow but the winds are bad and there is a promise of more snow. The pick-up will have to be by road."

"The road conditions and the distance make it difficult for a vehicle to get to you in twelve hours. Our driver is out of town on a trip and is expected back here soon; however the roads are icy and he could get into trouble on the way. We will try for sixteen, but it could be twenty-four. Can you hold off the problems for that time?"

"Yes. My immediate problem is that I have no telephone and no other way of communicating with you. Because of this we will have to make the arrangements for the pick-up now."

"Go ahead."

"When the transport arrives here, in Miskimin, he will drive about five kilometres out of town to where a side road goes off to the left. He will have to be careful not to miss the road as it is under a couple of feet of snow now and there is likely to be more snow by the time he gets here. My helper will need a snowmobile to get in and out of the area. Tell him to look for a telephone or hydro pole with duct tape wrapped around it; the side road is beyond the marked pole. That's it, now to get back to the cabin."

Putting the phone down, he looked around the room. It was a large kitchen with part of it used as a sitting room. The woman was settled in a chair, only the top of her head visible, obviously entranced by a day-time program, the source of the talk he had heard when out in the store. The room was untidy, newspapers on the floor beside a second large chair, knitting on a small table beside the woman's chair. A chrome-legged table with cereal packages on it and four matching overstuffed vinyl covered chairs, one with a towel thrown on it, completed the picture of an easygoing housewife's warm friendly domain.

Alexei caught up in the atmosphere of the place, flashed in memory to another kitchen where the pots and pans were scrubbed spotless, the rich smells of cooking, and baking filled his imagination; bright in his mind's eye, stood his babushka, mistress of it all, his mother at work.

The woman rose from her chair. "Did you get through OK? A storm like this can bring down the lines."

"Yes thank you, I appreciate your help. I would like to buy some heavy tape, strong enough to seal heavy boxes."

"We have that stuff in the hardware department, have a look back there."

With his purchase in hand he was at the counter when the door opened and in walked a policeman. The policeman smiled at the woman and said, "Hi, how are you Mrs. Levesque? It's cold out there."

"Hi Ted. I'm about to put on a fresh pot of coffee, can you stay and have a warm up? Turning to Alexei she said, "How about you, like a cup of coffee, one for the road eh?" without waiting for an answer she returned to her kitchen. Believing that attack is the best method of defence Alexei was the first to speak.

"Hello, you are right about the weather, terrible," his head swimming with conflicting thoughts, what to do if the young policeman asked probing questions. Would his cover story of staying with MacKinnon, an old friend, be believed? In weather like this a stranger simply didn't drop into town out of nowhere for some shopping at the local store.

Ted, two months on the job after graduating from the Ontario Police College, Aylmer, thought another one of those mining hard rocks. Ted had been involved in the arrest of both miners who were awaiting trial in Timmins. This guy looks OK.

"Is that your machine out front?"

"Yes." Now what, Alexei thought.

"The glass on your front light is broken. You'd better get it fixed."

"What d'ya know, never noticed it, must have been when I went into the ditch on my way here. Good, I'll get it fixed, thank you."

"You should get it fixed right away. Bernie'll fix you up. Go out the door, you'll see the garage sign on the other side of the hotel."

Just then Mrs. Levesque arrived and conversation was stilled while they doctored their coffee. She returned to the kitchen and came back with pieces of cake on a plate. Pushing the plate towards them she urged them to "Try a piece, made it after Bill left for work this morning."

Youth deferred to age and held the plate out to Alexei. The two men enjoyed the warm cake in silence.

"Thanks Mrs. Levesque," Ted said smacking his lips. "The icing tastes different, you've added something, anyway it tasted great."

"Have some more Ted, you too," this to Alexei.

"Thanks, but no thanks, Mrs. Levesque, two pieces that's enough for me."

"Me too, the cake was delicious, the coffee excellent, thank you. Now I must be on my way."

"Bye Ted, see you tomorrow. Excuse me sir, excuse me, the tape in your pocket."

Alexei pulled up short. He was about to follow the policeman through the door. "Of course, forgot all about it, excuse me." Mindful of the gun in his pocket he carefully unzipped his snowmobile suit and pulled out his wallet and handed over a $20 Canadian bill.

The wind whipped at his face as he stood for a moment on the porch. When he tried to start the snowmobile he found that the cold had seized up the engine. Despairing that he would ever get the engine started, it finally coughed noisily into life. Sitting on the machine he debated whether to do as requested or forget about getting the light repaired. He decided in favour of the repair. In twenty-four hours a lot could go wrong; better not to have the police breathing down your neck.

The sign announced in large orange letters on black: Smyth's Garage.

"Hi, bit blowy out and what can I do for ya. Saw ya over at the store."

"The light on the front of my snowmobile is smashed. Can you fix it, replace it for me?"

"Let me have a look at your machine, then I'll be able to tell you."

Without bothering to put on a parka or even a cap, the roly poly mechanic ambled out to inspect the damage.

Back in the warmth of the snug little office, he said, "You're in luck, it just happens that I have some second hand stuff in the back shop that should fit your machine. I'll go and check it out."

Half an hour later, Alexei, his mind at ease, was on his way back to the cabin. Twenty-four hours and he would be on his way south with the goods safely bundled up and out of sight. It would be impossible to travel with the others. They would have to be disposed of at the cabin. While waiting for his Ottawa helper, he would have a look around the cabin, maybe MacKinnon had an ice drill. It wouldn't take much time or effort to drill a hole in the ice and dispose of the bodies. Cruising along at a steady speed he began to wonder whether he had passed his marker pole. With no odometer on what passed for an instrument panel, he could only guess that he must be getting near to where he branched off for the cabin. When the snowmobile tracks marking the T-junction slid past, he let the snowmobile coast to a stop. Turning around Alexei made his way back to the nearest hydro pole. Throwing away the cardboard that had held the tape he surveyed his handiwork. He should see that easily enough, he thought, as he increased his pressure on the throttle. Alexei eased the snowmobile off the highway onto the side road and opened the throttle.

24

Powered by pent-up feelings, their boots drove a hole — not large enough to crawl through — in the wall. Both went to work, cursing as they rampaged at the broken wall. No one on the other side of the wall could ignore the noise. Desperate to gain the kitchen, Ally began pulling at the broken edges of the hole. Pete's sure to be out there waiting for us after all this racket. I'll have to be quick. Shouldering Simon aside, he made a crouching dive, was through and lying on the kitchen floor. Rolling over, he saw Pete, club in hand, coming at him. The blow landed on his leg just above his bent knee.

The pain searing through his knee wrenched a scream from him. A frightened and desperate Pete, with the scrap piece of two by four raised high, was coming at him again. An attempt to roll clear got his legs tangled up in a kitchen chair. The blow meant for his head glanced off the chair, but still had enough power behind it to send spears of pain down his arm and up into his head. Alister tried to stand up, but fell in a heap. The blow to his leg had rendered it useless. The look of desperate triumph that lit Pete's eyes told Alister that nothing could be left to chance if he was to thwart the next murderous attack. Alister, enveloped in an inner mist of madness, got his weight on his good leg. Where were Jonesy and Simon? Where were they, screamed loud in his head.

Pete, confident that the fight had gone out of Alister, stepped back and hefted the two by four. Grinning, with club raised, he moved to get behind his victim. Alister, head down, didn't move but watched Pete's feet closely. Inadvertently Pete moved closer to his victim with each step. When he stopped and set his feet, Alister knew Pete was getting ready to deliver the killing blow. Alister threw himself at Pete's ankles and the intended deadly blow fanned the air as Pete went down. Muttering incoherently Alister, pushing with his good leg, got his hands around Pete's throat. Banging Pete's head on the floor he snarled again and again, "You bastard, I'll kill you."

Screaming, high pitched, frightened, why doesn't it stop. Someone was trying to pull him off Pete. The screaming changed to a noise in his head. It changed shape, took form, a name — it sounded like his name, it was. As the mist slowly evaporated, sanity returned. Jonesy was screaming his name and trying to pull him off Pete. Simon, an iron frying pan in his hand, was standing open-mouthed, eyes wide and a shamefaced look on his face. Pete was out cold.

"Sorry. I got stuck in the hole, a nail. Sorry Ally. Some helper, sorry."

Taking in the despondent look on the boy's face, Ally managed a smile, "It's over Simon. These things happen. We took care of him."

Finding no broken bones, Alister got up slowly on his good leg and hobbled around the room trying to get his sore leg functioning fully. When he could put his weight on the leg he moved over and looked at the unconscious Pete.

"He'll live, there's rope out in the barn, will you get it for me Simon? I'll keep an eye on him, when he comes to he may still have some fight left in him."

Zipped into a snowsuit, Simon headed for the door. Outside, without snow shoes, he made slow going through the deep snow. In the barn, he found the rope readily, about twenty feet of it hanging from a nail in the wall. Closing the barn door, he headed for the cabin. He stopped and listened, it sounded like a snowmobile, whoever it was he was in a hurry. Was it Alexei returning to kill them? Standing in the knee high snow Simon panicked and fighting the hindering snow headed for the cabin. He was halfway to the cabin when the snowmobile came from behind the trees along the top of the ridge.

Alister stood in the doorway motioning Simon to fall and hide in the snow. Too late, the noise of the engine changed to a whisper as Alexei took his hand off the throttle. He allowed the machine to move slowly ahead for a few yards while surveying the scene. As Simon continued to flounder towards the cabin, Alexei revved up the engine and began a wide turn to head back the way he had come.

"Damn the son-of-a-bitch, may he rot in hell. He's a crafty sod. It'll be dodgy for a while until we get our hands on him Simon. We can't have him on the loose. The bastard will have to be taken care of."

"How the hell can we do that?" an irate Simon asked. "We don't have any guns, not even a knife. Anyway he's gone. It's likely he will head south, get out of the area."

Jonesy who had just joined them said, "Can't we get in touch with the police and let them deal with him?" a quaver in her voice.

"Forget the police Jonesy. He has to get rid of us. He can't leave until he has. You and Simon, barricade yourselves in the cabin. Don't open the door for anyone but me. My guess is that he will stay out of sight until it's dark then he'll make his move. I don't intend to wait here for him. I'm going after him. He may pretend to be seriously injured in order to get you outside, remember he has a gun."

"Well I know that," an exasperated Simon said. "How are you gonna stop him? With your bare hands?"

"If I have to, you cheeky bugger," said with a grin. "Old Ally has a trick or two up his sleeve. I have something tucked away in a hidey hole in the barn that should give me an advantage."

Simon and Jonesy, nerves tight as a bowstring, looked out a window and scanned the area around the cabin for any sign of Alexei returning. When the cabin door banged shut behind Alister they both gave the lie to their apparent calm acceptance of the danger. Jonesy gave a squeaky trill of fright and Simon ashen faced and lips trembling almost fell as he turned to face a grim-faced Alister. Buckling a belt around his waist to which was attached an oddly shaped wooden box he said, "This should even things up a bit."

"What is it?" a puzzled Jonesy asked.

"A gun, that's what it is Jonesy."

"A gun?" from Simon.

Reaching for the pair of snowshoes hanging from a porch pole he continued, "It's an old Mauser pistol. The wooden holster can be attached to the gun and hey presto you have a nice little rifle. If I get within a hundred yards of Ivan, he's a goner. You two get inside and stay there until I give you a shout."

Alister set out at as fast a pace as the snow shoes allowed and headed for the trees along the side of the dirt road. From the cabin the road turned left up a slight incline. At the top there was a sharp right turn where the road disappeared behind the trees that lined the low embankment. The embankment petered out about a hundred yards from the turn in the road. Alister moved about fifty yards beyond the turn before heading up the incline. Close to the road the trees were thicker, and in places the scrub bush was dense. Figuring that Alexei wouldn't stray too far from the cabin, Alister wanted to scout the terrain before he took any action. Making the most of what cover there was, he kept going for the protection of the trees. Would Alexei park the snowmobile out of sight and move out to the edge of the trees and ambush any pursuer? Taking off the snowshoes and cradling the Mauser, Ally carefully advanced through the heavy scrub bush and then on elbows and knees made his way to the edge of the embankment; there was no snowmobile in sight.

The attack came from behind, to Ally's left. Alexei aware of the terrain knew Ally could only come from one direction and crossed the road as soon as he hid the snowmobile. A whisper of sound had Ally rolling in the snow to escape his attacker. The first bullet lodged wood splinters in his face. As he continued rolling, he tumbled feet first over the edge of the six-foot drop, the second struck his cigarette case. The bullet had enough power to slash a deep cut down his gut. On the way down he struck his head on the thick root of a tree stump.

Alexei advanced warily to view his handiwork, the body lay there a silent token to his marksmanship. He brought the Tokarev TT33 up and was about to make sure of the kill, with one in the head, but decided he had better conserve ammunition. The box mag held only eight rounds and there were two more to be taken care of. Scrambling down to the body he prodded it with a boot; he was dead. In a hurry to put an end to the disaster, he turned abruptly and headed for the cabin. He would be glad to have the whole thing over and get back to the easy life of the streets.

\+ + +

Simon and Jonesy stood at the door and watched Alister for a moment. "Well that's it Simon, we had better get inside and barricade the door. Do you think he'll come back, Alexei that is?"

"I hope not, I hope Alister kills him."

"That's a bit drastic Simon. I do hope Ally captures him. He is a thoroughly bad piece of goods I agree. Better still, I hope the police get him."

"Don't be daft Jonesy, we're in this all alone. The police, if they come, it will be after we're found dead. Shot by that bastard out there." Simon in the confines of the cold storage shed had come of age.

"Oh! Simon, we can't give up hope. Even if he does come back he won't be able to get at us. Alister said that no matter what sort of sob story he gives us we are not to listen to him. We will be safe behind the barricaded door."

"What's to stop him from coming through one of the windows. They're just ordinary glass."

"Now that's a good idea Simon. We will barricade the windows as well as the door. Let's get inside and get to work. Don't forget, Alister is armed and Alexei doesn't know that."

"Let's hope Ally shoots him with that old whatever it is, in the box. I hope to God he kills him."

Alister would come back and save them. He had a gun. This couldn't be happening, it had to be a dream. There was no lock on the cabin door. Jonesy kicked the door with a sensibly shod foot and said, "C'mon Simon, we can't stand here like ninnies and wait to be killed." They stood face to face, frightened but determined. "Let's pull the old finger out and get organized. That Russian gangster isn't to get the better of us. We'll show the bastard what sort of stuff we're made of.

Give me a hand here, we'll use this apology for a sofa to block the door."

Simon galvanized into action by the metamorphosis of the soft-spoken Jonesy to this loud-mouthed virago grabbed one end of the heavy old sofa. When the sofa was in place, Jonesy began stripping the sheets off one of the beds. With the sheets filling her arms she walked to the kitchen and began pulling the large headed pins from the cork board on the wall beside the sink. She folded one of the sheets in half and stepping up onto a chair proceeded to pin it over the windows that faced out onto the porch. When she was finished all the windows had similar makeshift blinds. About eighteen inches of each window was left uncovered.

"If he can't see in he can't shoot at us. Now that table, place it in front of the side window."

The preparations for the return of Alexei had a calming effect on them. Propping the table on its narrow end Simon grabbed a broom and jammed it against the table. If he came in through the window they would have time to react and defend themselves.

"Have we missed anything Jonesy? I can't think of anything else"

"I think that's it. If he tries to come through the windows, he'll get caught up in the sheets. We are as ready as we will ever be," said with a shrug and a grimace.

Now with nothing to do but wait, imagination captured his thinking. Maybe Alister had killed him. Would the shots be heard here in the cabin if he had? I hope he's lying out there in the snow, dead. If he comes back we're done for. A mental picture of Alexei coming through the window in a shower of glass tied his stomach in knots. Please Ally, kill the bastard, blow his head off.

Jonesy too was lost in a maze of conflicting thoughts. She wanted to get out of this terrible predicament alive. If Ally could only wound him, please God I don't want anyone to die. He has to come back, we can identify him. Maybe he wont, but if he does, he will kill us. I hope Alister stops him somehow. I hope he kills him, he shouldn't be allowed to live. He's a monster. Oh God forgive me, what am I saying? I don't want to die. Kill him Ally!

There it was, they both heard it at the same time, the sound of an approaching snowmobile. Who was driving it? Was it Ally? Was it Alexei?

"He's coming Simon. He won't get me without a fight. Where's the club that awful Pete had?"

"There must be a knife or something we can use to fight him with. I'll have a look in the kitchen. Take the butcher knife and give me the club. It's too heavy for you Jonesy."

The sound of the snowmobile died. After a brief pause, they heard the crisp sound of someone walking on frozen snow and then the hollow sound of footsteps on the wide porch. Alexei was coming to get them. Hardly daring to breathe they stood in the middle of the large living room, waiting. All was quiet outside. A slight noise at the door, he's outside!

"Please help me, I'm bleeding. Your friend is with me. He's been hurt. We had a fight. He's in a bad way, we need a doctor. Simon will you go and get the doctor?"

Simon while aware of the duplicity of Alexei and yet at the mention of Ally being hurt he was uncertain how to react. He looked at Jonesy and made as if to move towards the door. Jonesy grabbed him. Shaking her head she held a finger to her lips. When he attempted to pull away from her grip on his shoulder, she mouthed, "Remember, Alister warned us that he would try something like this. Go to the window and have a peek outside."

"I know you are in there. For God's sake help me to get Ally inside, he's in a bad way. I need help. Do you want your friend to die? He would help you if you were in trouble, help us, please."

While Alexei was pleading for help Simon tiptoed to the window farthest from the door and lifted the edge of the makeshift curtain and saw Alexei standing alone in front of the door hunched over and favouring his left arm. There was no sign of Alister. Shaking his head, Simon tiptoed back to Jonesy.

"You were right there is no sign of Ally. He seems to be hurt, his left arm," he whispered.

Nodding, Jonesy whispered, "He could be faking an injury or maybe Ally did beat him up, but whatever happened out there he stays outside."

"Jonesy help me, I'll die if you don't do something. Do you want Alister to die? He can't take much more of this cold. Please help us, look I'll give you the gun, just let us in out of this terrible cold, please. Talk to her Simon, I can't do you any harm."

Simon looked at Jonesy with a question in his eyes. She looked back at him her eyes cold, lips in a determined thin line, chin up and shook her head.

"This is not the time to be a nervous Nelly, Simon. Remember he'll do anything, anything to get inside. He can't let us leave here alive, you know that."

Simon turned away, a confused look on his face. Jonesy caught his arm and pulled him to face her.

"It's him or us Simon. I for one don't want to die here in this wilderness of snow. We have to find a way to beat him at his own game. We have to think."

"You know what I'm thinking. He has us locked in here and we can't do a damned thing about it. Why not open the door just enough for him to give us his gun and then we let him come in."

"Don't forget we don't know whether he really is wounded or is pretending to be hurt in order to get inside. He could have a pistol, maybe a knife tucked away somewhere."

"OK, how about this then, when he comes through the door I bop him over the head with the club that Pete had, that would stop him and then we could tie him up and leave on the snowmobile."

"I forgot about Pete, he's very quiet. Maybe he's dead. Better have a look and check the knots, although I think Ally did a thorough job of tying him up."

Pete hadn't moved from where Alister had propped him against the wall near the fireplace. He didn't appear to be breathing. They exchanged frightened looks. Jonesy quickly knelt beside the comatose Pete and put her hand on his chest, she could feel it rising and falling rhythmically.

"Whew, thank God he's OK. For a moment I thought he was dead."

"Are the knots still tight? I don't want him to come to and escape."

"Don't worry Simon he's trussed up like a stuffed turkey. We're safe from him. It's the other one, him outside that I'm worried about. As you said, we are prisoners in here, we have to think of some way of getting out and going for help."

25

Under the snowmobile suit, unseen by Alexei's hurried glance, a pulse throbbed even as blood slowly darkened the clothing under the heavy suit. Trying to lift his head up from the wet pillow he became aware there was something running down his cheek. Fighting off the black cloud threatening to envelope him he moved a hand to his face. The hand was dropped when it touched a bunch of sharp needles. The cloud enveloped him. Struggling his way out of the fog, he moved his head. He couldn't see, he was blind. No he could still see. Slowly he moved a hand over his face; again the stabbing needles. Ally struggled to get away from the cold wet stuff. Semi-conscious, he rolled onto his back and darts of pain overrode briefly the hammer blows at the back of his head. Struggling to his knees and grasping a bush he stood up. Dazed he looked around ... what was it he had to do? There was a woman; she had a kid. A few stumbling steps before the darkness captured him again.

Alister crawled out of the dark fog and looked around. The thumping in his head, the pain in his chest, were threatening to send him back down into the depths. Something, some fact was trying reach his consciousness, slowly at first it began to trickle to the forefront of his brain. There was a Russian somewhere ahead. Maybe he's at the cabin. I've got to get back to the cabin. Simon and Jonesy?

Getting slowly to his feet, the gun dangling from his right hand, again he went in search of the elusive cabin. Still groggy from the knock on the head, he stopped, and looked down at the gun. The box on his belt, funny bloody holster, mhhh it fits. Where did I pick up this antique? A memory of a too bright sunny day was at odds with the snowy carpet he was stumbling about in. Fastening the top of the holster loosed tiny spears of pain behind his eyes.

\+ + +

Memory, keyed by the pain, gave him his answer; we were on a sweep in Chad, near the Sudanese border. We were after some rebel the Intelligence guys were keen to have a chat with. Dismounting from the trucks outside the village we set up a cordon around the place, mud dwellings around an oasis.

My section's job was to capture him, dead or alive. A wide track through the middle of the village was the only street. Access to the rest of the village was by a series of narrow alleyways and paths. Our sergeant, a tough old dried prune of a guy, had in his fifteen years in the Legion picked up a few crafty dodges. Before the house search began he ordered four of us up on the roofs. Our job was to prevent any escape across the roofs should our man decide to do a runner. Things were going along nicely; it was easy to jump across the alleyways, when a hullabaloo started in a house ahead of Dierckxsens and me. Kraus and Stellenberg were a couple of houses over from us.

We could hear women wailing, kids crying. They had flushed him, would he make for the roofs? My partner jumped to the next house and kept going to the next one, where we guessed all the noise was coming from. I stayed where I was and hunkered down ready to back up my partner. The other two moved towards the noise. The sun was beginning its march across the sky, it would be another shitty day in Chad.

The prickling began somewhere at the top of my spine and rose slowly up my neck. My gut lurched, he was behind me. The noise up ahead was to distract us while he footed it across the roofs. Turning around I saw him leap over an alleyway. I shouted and took off after the bastard. On the run I loosed off a couple of rounds to warn the others I heard shouts behind me.

The fleeing rebel never looked back. I yelled at him to stop. He kept going. I wasn't gaining on him. He was going to get away. The orders were "dead or alive". Stopping dead in my tracks, I took a breath and loosed off half a mag. When I got to him a cloud of flies were buzzing around the hole in his back. Dierckxsens and the others, pounding across the roof tops, were shouting to those below that Johnny had shot the rebel. When I rolled the body over with the toe of my boot, I saw he was holding a funny-shaped wooden box in his hand. When the sergeant made it to the roof, the box was out of sight in my pack. Back at base camp, I discovered a Mauser pistol inside the box, which when attached to the Mauser gave you a rifle, small but deadly.

\+ + +

Jeez it's cold, where has the sun gone? Opening his one good eye he found himself lying in the snow. With an effort he realized where he was. There was something he had to do. On his feet, he set out for the cabin. Still not clear about what he was supposed to do, he knew that whatever it was would take place back at the cabin. Each step hammered dull bolts of pain up into his head while pinpricks of light flashed behind his eyes.

He had to get back to the cabin. Jonesy and Simon needed him. They were no match for the Russian. His breathing came in short hurried gasps. Prompted by the strident voice in his head to get back to the cabin, he ignored the red hot poker on his chest. Something was to happen at the cabin and he had to be there to stop it. He had to stop it — keep moving — the cabin.

On his knees at the top of the ridge he could see the cabin silhouetted in the snow. There were no lights in the cabin; had the Russian — Alexei killed them? He was all alone in the moonlit snowy landscape. Hurrying to get to Jonesy and Simon he tripped and fell, tripped and fell. Each fall thrust red hot needles into his chest. His howls of pain were only loud in his head, in the cold night air they were eerie croaks. He kept going towards the cabin.

+ + +

Alexei straightened up at the door and headed for the shed in the trees, and from there would keep a watch on the cabin. Who knows, maybe they would be stupid enough to try and escape if they thought he had gone. While at the door, he had lifted the latch and put his weight against the door. Whatever it was they had blocking the door it was heavy enough to stop him from opening it.

The moon was high in the sky when Alexei left his hiding place. In the interests of moving silently he had stripped off his nylon snowmobile suit. Checking to see if there was any movement of the sheets covering the porch windows — nothing. He moved on, heading for the cold storage shed at the rear of the cabin. It had come to him in a rush: they had found a way into the cabin, therefore why couldn't he get into the cabin the same way.

He had come prepared for what he had to do. Using the short rusty piece of cast iron pipe he had found in the shed he began to prise the planks loose that earlier he and Pete had nailed in place to lock up their prisoners. Slowly, carefully he applied pressure, nothing happened. Changing the position of the lever he put one foot on the door, took a deep breath and pulled and kept up the pressure. Without warning he was flat on his back in the deep snow. The noise of the nails separating from the wood made him pause. Satisfied that all was quiet, he worked the bottom board loose without a sound; two down and one to go. Because of the length of the piece of pipe he was unable to get the purchase needed to remove the board quickly. After several sweaty attempts, he could feel the board moving. With aching arms he finally worked the board loose.

The way was now clear. All he had to do was move with caution. The safety off, he shoved his pistol into the right side pocket of his jacket. Pulling the door open he stepped inside; his hand found the shelves and he moved to the gap in the shelving. After carefully exploring the gap with a hand and finding no obstruction he moved slowly into the black hole. When his hand found the rough edge of the opening he grinned. It wouldn't be long now. He had planned on getting rid of the bodies under the lake ice, but now with the pick-up just hours away, he would leave the bodies in the cabin and with Simon in tow hide near the rendezvous until Pytor arrived.

Alexei ran his hand round the edge of the hole in the wall before carefully crawling through into the kitchen. Standing quietly, breathing slowly, he waited until his eyes adjusted to the dim light of the cabin. The bright moonlight provided a modicum of light to the centre of the large room but there were areas of shadow that could prove dangerous. With a light touch, he felt along the wall of the kitchen with his left hand. His right held the pistol. There were no hanging pots or utensils to betray him.

As he moved away from the hole his boot came down on several small pieces of wallboard with a slight crunching sound. He let out his breath slowly and waited with his back against the kitchen wall. Slowly, he scanned the shadows. There didn't appear to be any darker areas within the shadows to indicate where an attacker waited. He surveyed the large room several times. Where are they? I would have heard them if they had moved out — maybe not. Could they have heard me pulling the nails and decided to get out while the going was good?

Well, there was one way to find out, and after all, he had the gun. He inched his way out of the kitchen area; no sign of them. Where could they be? There was no place to hide in the cabin and the shed was four walls and no secret doorways. He stood still, a faint scratching noise behind him, whirling round he had only time to loose off a quick shot at Simon, who with club raised high over his head was all set to cave his head in. The club brushed his left arm as Simon collapsed at his feet, holding his leg. A grim-faced Alexi had time only to think that the next bullet, a head shot, would.... He never completed the thought. A fireworks display of lights exploded in his head and then he noticed the bright light at the end of the passageway.

The mushy sound as the metal poker connected with Alexei's head was loud in the darkened room. A grim-faced Jonesy connected a second time with the poker as the body was falling. "You've killed him.

Oh dear God not Simon. I'll kill you, kill you." Jonesy, her actions the combined result of rage and fear was about to bring the poker down again on the head of the dead Alexei when Simon's plea for help arrested her in mid swing.

"Jonesy! he's dead. Can you stop this bleeding? Help me, please Jonesy."

Slowly her eyes began to focus; the red mist to dissipate. She shook herself and looked around the cabin. When her eyes came back to Simon and the dead Alexei, she said, "Oh my God I've killed him. Oh my God!"

"Jonesy, help me. He's dead. My leg, whew it hurts. Help me Jonesy."

"You poor boy, of course, of course, please forgive me. Poor Simon." Dropping the poker, she moved quickly to the fireplace and picked up a piece of kindling. At the sink, she grabbed a couple of dish towels and a knife. Kneeling beside Simon she used the knife to saw away at the trouser leg around the wound. Muttering under her breath, she examined the wound. "It's not too serious Simon. A flesh wound. No tourniquet needed. I'll use the dish towels to stop the bleeding." Working quickly she folded up a dish towel and placed it over the gash. The second one she used as a bandage to hold the first one in place. Examining her handiwork she decided it would do until the doctor arrived. What am I saying? There are no doctors for miles around. Just then there was a scraping noise outside the cabin door and then a faint thump.

"I'm busy," she shouted, unaware of the incongruity of her response. The noise came again. "Oh all right, in a minute, I'm coming."

Simon whispered, "Maybe it's Alister. Could it be the police? I hope its Alister. Maybe Alexei didn't kill him."

"First things first. How does that feel?"

"Fine, it's OK. Have a look, see if it's Alister."

"All right, all right."

Jonesy had no problem moving the heavy old sofa from the door, her muscles were still fired with the adrenaline that had carried her through her ordeal. As she lifted the latch, the door gave way under the weight of Alister. She was able to grab him before he hit the floor. She got both hands under his arms and dragged him, groaning, over to where Simon was propped up against a large armchair.

Propping Alister beside him she saw the toothpick like sliver in his eyebrow and the dried blood on his face. Looking closer she spotted the holes in his snowsuit. Undoing the zipper, she tried to slip the top of the suit off his shoulder, but stopped when Alister cried out in pain. To her inexperienced eyes there seemed to have been a great loss of blood. Just then Alister opened his eyes.

"Hello Jonesy. This is some sorry bloody mess. We have to get out of here. Have you seen Alexei? What happened to Simon? Is he OK? We're not safe here. I'll help Simon. Crank up the snowmobile, hurry."

Alister paused for breath. When he tried to continue, Jonesy said, "Shut up and take it easy. Neither you nor Simon is in any condition to travel. First things first, I'll attend to that eye of yours. Anyway," looking over at Simon, "How am I to get that brute of a thing started. Damned thing is likely frozen solid."

"I'll go Jonesy. My leg is OK now, the bandage is fine. Just let me get on my feet. I'm OK."

"You can't go in your condition! What if you fall off, tell me, what then?"

"I won't fall off and I'm going. You can't handle, as you said, 'that brute of a thing.' Honest I'm fine. The quicker I get out there and start the engine the sooner we will get away from this place."

An exasperated Alister broke in, "What are you two ninnies babbling on about. We have to get Alexei. You idiots, he's out there waiting for us. C'mon let's...."

"Alexei won't bother us," Jonesy whispered.

"That's him on the floor. He won't bother us. Jonesy took care of him!" Simon quickly explained what had happened.

"Now to look after that eye. I'll get the stove going and heat some water." Placing the steaming kettle and a bowl on the rug she gently touched the area around the sliver. "Well it has to come out Ally. Are you ready for this? I'll have to pull it out. It could be painful."

There was no answer, Ally indoors and out of the cold relaxed and fell into another black hole.

Conscious again, "Hey what's going on? What the hell are you doing Jonesy?"

"She's removing the tree from your eye Ally," Simon said in an attempt at making light of their situation.

"That's it, its out. Now some hot water and we'll clean you up. There you go, finished."

"Whew, that was a little on the nippy side Jonesy. Thanks."

Later with Ally asleep or passed out, Simon, clinging to a chair arm pulled himself upright. He clung to the chair fighting off the swirling fog in his head that was threatening to knock him down. He swayed and almost fell. When his head stopped spinning, he hobbled painfully to where the snowsuits were. Grabbing at one, he looked over at Jonesy and gestured for her to help him. She slipped the left leg of the suit over his injured leg while Simon clenched his teeth. The right leg was no trouble. Standing up, he swayed, dizziness threatening to floor him. "Now to get that damned machine out there started." A bullet of pain swirled him down a black hole. Conscious, Simon found Jonesy kneeling beside him; her wet cheeks testament to her concern. "Simon, oh Simon. Your father will be so proud."

To reach the snowmobile, Simon, with Jonesy supporting him, had to fight for every step. Pain, dull, and incessant threatened his will to go on. I've got to make it was the thought uppermost in his mind. Ally and Jonesy are depending on me. I've got to do it. I've got to do it. Get help. Time had no meaning. Pain was alive in him and progress was measured by the number of times it took control and he had to pause and fight it off. I made it. He pulled himself up onto the seat and sat atop the brute. How long he sat there he didn't know.

He was brought back to the task ahead by Jonesy encouraging him to start the machine. Straddling the bulky seat he pushed the pain aside and settled on the seat and wiped the sweat from his face. Hanging on to the handlebars, he fiddled with the controls. Listening to the low growl of the snowmobile's engine, Simon thought, lucky for me it didn't take much effort to get it started. After a couple of jerky trial starts he was able to control the "beast." Looking at Jonesy shivering beside him he nodded and was off. When she reached the cabin the sound of the snowmobile was a faint purr in the snowy landscape.

Not quite sure whether he could handle the machine, Simon went ahead with caution. Alexei's trips had packed the snow into an easy-to-follow trail. Once he got the feel of the brute he increased speed. Shortly after leaving the cabin the cold began to take a toll. Unfamiliar with snow suits, he had not zipped up the bottoms of the pant legs. Jonesy, concerned with trying to avoid causing any pain, had not paid attention to the flapping bottoms when she helped put the suit on.

Slowly the cold took over his lower limbs until his legs felt like logs. The woollen gloves he had found in the pockets of the suit were no protection from the bone-chilling cold. As the pain took over his hands, he thought, to hell with this and gave the throttle a savage twist. Speeding over the packed snow, each little bump no longer brought pain to his leg; the bitter cold his anaesthesia. His mental faculties were slowly succumbing to the insidious cold. Continually he came to with a jerk and had to remind himself to pay attention, stay on the track. In the lost intervals, each one longer than the previous one, he travelled a landscape peopled by the ghosts of what might have been.

Things would have been different if Mum was still here. She was great to talk to. Always knew what to do; knew the answer when you had a problem. Jonesy says she was funny, kept Dad from getting too serious about work. Old Arbuckle said she was as tough as steel, but every inch a lady. They were a handsome couple, a great team. He was talking to Jonesy after the funeral, he was almost in tears. Jonesy kept blowing her nose. I never told anyone about what I'd heard. They never knew I was on the other side of the hedge. We were wandering in the garden after the funeral. People kept patting me on the head and murmuring at me. I wanted to get away from them all.

The cold no longer bothered him. His hands and legs were simply lumpy attachments. The sun was warm on his back as he stepped lightly over the stile. This was the last leg of the two mile cross-country run. He knew there was no runner ahead of him, but still, he kept up his driving pace. He wanted to rub the noses of the other schools' runners in the dirt, particularly that snotty Guy Lodge from St. Paul's.

Another school, a tall boy pulling a small boy behind a building; uh oh, the Bean has some junior at his mercy again. Walking quietly up behind the tall boy who was giving his full attention to trying to separate the junior from his arm, Simon gave the bully a violent shove. Staggering, he let go of the small boy and whirled to meet the attacker. His uplifted arm struck Simon full on the side of the head. Shaking his head, he bored in at the bully and pinned him against the wall with his forearm. Anger focussed, twice he punched the bully in the gut. What was it Alister said about the others not liking me? That I was over the top with my daft exploits. They didn't want to take on the Head and the teachers. Borrowing a bike to get back to school in time was risky. If caught it would mean a thumping from the owner, but it was exciting. The cabin, that was different, jeez the Russian had a gun. It had been scary back there.

The cold, the mesmerizing endless track unwinding in front of him together with the sound of the engine at times left him disorientated. When the track suddenly disappeared into blackness he came to with a start. In time to see the snowbank charging at him he attempted to turn aside, but was betrayed by his stiff arms. The snowmobile ploughed into the snow at an angle. The engine died as the machine rolled over. Locked in place by the machine he closed his eyes. It was nice and warm, this was great.

26

Constable Ted Czapla on his way to Timmins with a prisoner saw a shape at the edge of the road. Slowing down, he put on his brights. It was a snowmobile with a body pinned under it. He put on the roof lights and stopped. Looking to see that the drunk in the cage was OK, he got out of the car. Bending over the body he gently ran his hand over the leg — no broken bones — what's this? Mmh bandages. Something's happened out there in the bush. Better get him to the hospital. Moving quickly he righted the machine and dragged the boy over to the car. Getting the boy into the front seat was a challenge, care had to be taken in moving the bandaged leg. The drunk had fallen asleep. Moving the heater control to high he turned and looked at his passenger. He radioed Corporal Jerry Baird, detachment boss and reported the incident and that he was on his way to the hospital.

"The kid's in a bad way. Hang on Jerry he's coming to."

The boy, obviously in pain as feeling slowly came back to his extremities, began to whimper. Shortly afterwards his eyelids fluttered open.

"Take it easy, we'll get you to a doctor. Easy, easy," this as the boy tried to pull himself upright in the seat. Ted couldn't understand what the boy was mumbling incoherently as tears streamed down his face. He understood the tears having experienced the excruciating pain of circulation returning to cold-numbed limbs. The babble of sounds rushed meaningless into the warm fuggy air of the cruiser. One word only, Alexei, made sense. Pulling himself into an upright position with great effort the boy took a deep breath and after several attempts slowly began to talk coherently.

"There are — two — in the cabin. Jonesy saved me — fine — needs help. Robert the pilot."

"Where is this cabin? How many people are injured?"

"Ally's been shot — Jonesy — looking after him." After a pause, he continued in a rush to get the information out, "The pilot, I think he's dead. The plane crashed near the cabin."

"One guy's been shot, I've got that. This pilot you mentioned, what about him and this guy Alexei, is he still alive?"

"Alexei is dead, Jonesy took care of him. The pilot, blood all over his face." With his words now spilling from him and his voice rising in pitch, he continued. "You've got to do something."

When Ted reported that there had been a plane crash and one of the two people at the cabin was a gunshot wound the corporal's voice, even through the radio static, had a harder edge.

"Take the kid to the hospital. Next organize three or four snowmobiles and get into the bush and find these people. Has the kid told you where they are?"

"He mentioned a cabin. I think it must be that new guy, MacKinnon's place. He moved to the lake from Timmins about three months ago. Where I found the kid there were snowmobile tracks heading off into the bush. I'll follow them and report back as soon as I have any info for you."

"Good, and Ted, be careful there could be someone still on his feet and armed. Take it nice and easy. As soon as I have things squared away here I'll join you. Wait! Make sure your volunteers are armed, rifle, shotgun, whatever, but armed. I'll notify the transport people about the crash and talk to the young fella. You go ahead and find out what happened at the cabin. Take care."

After leaving the boy in care of the doctor on call at the hospital, Ted began rounding up his helpers. The first door he knocked on was Bernie Smyth's. He knew that Bernie owned a snowmobile and maybe, just maybe, there might be one or two newly repaired machines in the garage which hadn't been picked up yet by their owners. No such luck. Bill Levesque, about to leave for work, nodded and reached for his snowmobile suit. Bernie had his machine cranked up and ready to go by the time he climbed the hotel steps. Bill wouldn't be far behind. No one asked questions or hesitated when they saw who was asking for help. Joe Green owner of the hotel and his wife Marilyn, were having their first coffee of the day when Ted strode into the kitchen.

"Hello Ted, everything OK?" Something was up, the look on Ted's face

"I've just taken a young lad to the hospital, he'll be OK, I guess. I picked him up on the highway."

"One of the guys from the mine? Drunk?"

"No, no, nothing like that. He told me there has been a plane crash out at the lake and that MacKinnon has been shot."

"MacKinnon, he bought the place about three months ago. Worked for the paper up in Timmins, he told me. Gimme a sec Ted to get my stuff together and I'll be right with you, the snowmobile ...."

"No Joe, you stay here. What I want is your machine and the tow buggy to bring the wounded guy out. The drunk, could you let him sleep it off in the lobby?"

"Sure, no problem. I'll get the buggy hooked up; take off as soon as you're ready. It's gassed up."

Ted reported to Cpl. Baird that Bernie Smyth and Bill Levesque were going along with him. Before the police cruiser was locked and left in the hotel lot, Ted transferred the emergency supplies in the trunk to the buggy. With Bernie in the lead the small convoy lost no time in getting to the side road. Bernie didn't slacken his pace on the side road. The quicker they got to the cabin the sooner they would be able to assess the damage and sort things out. Ted bringing up the rear was going over what he would have to do in the variety of scenarios flashing in his head.

God, I hope the wound isn't serious. The other one — Jonesy, the kid said he was OK. He said Jonesy took care of Alexei. More shooting? Who shot the wounded guy? When we get to this cabin wherever it is, it looks like we will find blood and guts all over the place. MacKinnon, he seemed like a nice enough guy when I met him at Levesque's. Said he had been a miner at the Gypsy Lode, never mentioned anything about working for a newspaper. Was he into high-grading gold and some of the big boys down below had it in for him for some reason? Maybe he was short-changing them in some way. If he was high-grading then that means the Mounties will have to be called in.

Ted in his short time in the North had heard stories of how some of the businesses in the area had been founded on the illicit trade in gold. In the underground maze of stopes, drifts and raises, a secret economy held sway. The gold mined was usually not visible to the eye of the men who drilled and blasted in the stopes. However those lucky enough to see high-grade gold veined in the ore face never questioned their good fortune. Finders keepers, was their law.

Bill Levesque's father had been a miner. Bill had some wild tales to tell of the bad old days when there was no security, or very little, at the mine head. Then the high grade could be smuggled out in a lunch pail. Miners stepped off the cage and headed home. Now the miners change and shower on mine property and walk naked in front of a guard station to get their street clothes. But still high-grading goes on. The timid sell it underground, the venturesome take it out on their own.

A shout from Bernie made Ted aware of his surroundings. There were trees atop an embankment on his left. Copying the others, he eased up on the throttle. The cabin was just ahead. Everything looks OK so far, he thought. What's inside is any one's guess. That looks like a woman. The kid never mentioned a female. Don't tell me this is a domestic. Please Lord not a family set to, not that. When Ted cut his engine, the only sound was Bernie's and Bill's boots crunching in the snow as they joined him. She had been crying; her hair was a mess. Dressed in lightweight clothing, she stood shivering on the porch, her arms tight across her chest.

"He's inside — Ally. He's been shot, lost blood. Hurry he needs a doctor."

She's had a rough time, better step lightly here. "It's OK ma'am. We'll look after him and you." Looking around as he stepped towards the porch he saw the wing of the downed plane a beckoning finger in the snow. Pointing, he told Bill: "Ride over to the plane at the end of the lake and have a look inside. We'd better make sure that everyone has been rescued. Now ma'am let's have a look at your friend Ally."

"Thank you. I've been so afraid that no one would come. I tried to make him comfortable. He fainted, again, just after Simon left. Where is Simon? He's alright?"

"Simon's OK. He's in the hospital in Miskimin."

"Thank God, he's safe. I was so worried. Thank God!"

"My name's Ted. I'm with the OPP." Noting the questioning look on her face he continued, "The Ontario Provincial Police, ma'am. Bernie and Bill are helping me." Inside the cabin, in the light of his torch, just beyond the wounded guy someone was stretched out on the floor. Was this the killer Alexei? "Bernie let's get some light in here; take down the sheets at the windows."

Ted saw that the body lying at his feet was the guy he had seen earlier in the store. Pointing at the body Ted said, "Is this the guy who shot Simon?" and with a nod in MacKinnon's direction, "and this guy, you say his name's Ally?" At her nod, he continued. "Simon's OK. It's MacKinnon we have to take care of. How about stoking the stove and putting the coffee pot on while we look after your friend?"

"I'm afraid I don't know where the coffee is kept. You see after the plane crash Alexei kept us locked up in the shed at the back."

Working at getting the groaning Ally's snowmobile jacket off, Ted asked, "How many aboard the plane? Are you sure that all the passengers got out? What happened? A fire, ice on the wings?"

"There was no fire. Some smoke and that was it. Whatever it was, it caused the engines to conk out. Ally got us out of the plane and brought us back here. We all got out. Simon helped Ally with the pilot."

"So the pilot was injured. Where is he then? Do you know if he sent out a distress signal? Is he in one of the rooms?"

"That's what made Alexei show his true colours. Ally wanted to take Robert to the hospital. But Alexei with his gun took over."

"Stop right there. Let's hear it from the beginning. Alexei is dead ...."

"Yes, I killed him. He was going to kill Simon. I hit him with the poker. It's over there beside him."

Just then Bernie broke in, "It sounds as though there's somebody in one of the rooms. It could be the pilot."

Ted exasperated by the mass of garbled information and feeling a bit over his head snapped, "OK take care of it. Now ma'am, let's hear it from the beginning. The pilot was injured, OK, but where is he? Is he in one of the rooms?" At that moment Bill barged through the door and informed them, "There is no one in the plane. It's one helluva mess inside."

"No, Peter is in the room. We had to tie him up. He was helping Alexei."

Shrugging his shoulders and giving Bill a quick sceptical glance, he was about to try again to find out what had happened when Bernie called, "There is one in here — tied up. He looks the worse for wear. You'd better have a look Ted."

"Coming, look in the other rooms. The pilot has to be here somewhere, Bernie. Now ma'am, think about what happened here and when I come back we'll sort things out."

Looking down at the bound man, Ted said, "On your feet Peter." Grabbing him by the shoulders he pulled him upright. "I'm told that you are one of the bad guys. Is that right?" Not waiting for an answer he checked for concealed weapons. "Leave him tied up. Haul him into the next room and dump him in one of the big chairs. Keep an eye on him. According to the woman he was up to no good."

Back in the main room he saw that the woman appeared calmer. She had done something with her hair. She sat up straight, hands in her lap, her anxiety, her concern and the mental bruises of her ordeal tucked away behind a mask of calm efficiency. Ted knew that this time he would get the full story.

Speaking softly she told of the crash and what had taken place after the rescue by MacKinnon. When telling of how she had dealt with the murderous Alexei, she gave a long shuddering sigh and wiped at her eyes with a finger. She explained that MacKinnon was wounded while attempting to prevent Alexei escaping.

When questioned about the whereabouts of the pilot she shook her head and pointed at the bound figure in the big chair. "Peter should know, he was Alexei's little helper as we found out to our sorrow. Right Petey. It's my guess that the two of them were all set to kidnap Simon. Dear God, his father, Mr. Braithwaite will be heartsick. We must get word to him at once. Tell him..."

"Later, Simon's OK. I've got to get MacKinnon out there as soon as possible. The father will be notified once we get straightened away here at the cabin. One of you get a pile of blankets and we'll head back to Miskimin with MacKinnon. We've wasted enough time, let's roll."

"Hey what's goin' on here Jonesy? Who are these guys?"

"You passed out Ally. Everything is under control. These two men are helping me. My name is Ted Czapla, I'm with the police, the OPP. Bernie will take you to the hospital in Miskimin. They'll take good care of you."

"I know you, Bernie, you're the owner of the garage. Alexei knocked me down but I'm not out. Gimme a hand Bernie." Bernie moved quickly to the wounded man and got him on his feet. Slowly they made for the door. Ally was obviously in considerable pain. He bit down hard, ringing his lips with blood as he fought to deny the pain a voice. Sweat beading his forehead, a groan escaped his tight control when Bernie and Ted lowered him into the blanket-lined buggy. Jonesy wrapped also in blankets was next. She stretched out beside Ally and the two of them were snuggled under more blankets.

"They should be warm enough under the blankets. Get to the hospital as quick as possible Bernie. Jerry should be out there. Tell him what happened. Bill will follow you out."

At this Bill objected. "I'll have a look around for the pilot. You can take care of this guy. Write up your notes or whatever it is you do at a murder."

"No way Bill. Should anything happen, you'll be there as backup."

"Nothing is gonna happen; it's too cold. C'mon Ted, let me help you."

"For all I know there could be a dozen guys out there waiting to finish the job. Why do you think I had you bring your rifles? I'll be OK. Get outta here. You can come back with Jerry."

Standing in the snow, his shadow long in the early morning light, Ted watched the snowmobiles until they were out of sight. Ted closed the door and walked back to sit down beside his prisoner.

"Where have you hidden the pilot? Not much point in keeping it a big dark secret Pete? We'll find him. Where is he?"

"Alexei had the gun, he took care of Robbie. I had nothing to do with it. Straight up, not a thing."

"Did he kill him?'

No, I don't think so. He said Robbie was so far gone, there was nothing we could do for him. He said that he would leave him outside and let the cold finish him off. He took him outside when he left to phone his boss."

"So, you were an innocent bystander, Alexei did the dirty work."

"Look, I'm no angel, but killing, not me mate."

"You don't know where he is?" Not waiting for an answer Ted

went outside in search of the missing pilot. Half an hour later he was back. Shaking his head he said, "I found him back of the shed. Your pal Alexei wasn't kidding."

"No friend of mine. I was just along for the ride. I was looking after Jimmy's interests. I don't work for the Russians." Ted decided to ignore this latest piece of information and began to question Pete. Under Ted's easy questioning the sorry tale unfolded: unpaid gambling debts, kidnapping as the proposed method of payment and the subsequent deaths. When Pete ended his version of what had happened, Ted looking at his watch found that the day was well on its way and also that he was hungry. His day had begun in pre-dawn darkness and it looked as though it wouldn't end until nightfall. His stomach made growling noises, reminding him of the hearty breakfast eaten before he took off with the drunk.

What was that, could it be Jerry? Hurrying to the door, he threw it open. Several snowmobiles were charging towards the cabin. A heavy sigh escaped him. Now things will get sorted out. Not wanting to show the nervous tension that had kept him on edge, he made light of their arrival, "Nice to see you guys but I have to tell you the party's over. Hi Jerry. I've got a guy inside all tied up and ready for delivery to Timmins. There's a body inside and another one out back of the barn. The woman Jones — I sent her out with the wounded guy, MacKinnon — said she had to kill the stiff to save the young guy."

"The kid, he's the one you found on the highway."

Ted nodded and Jerry continued, "Where is the second body?"

"The second one is the pilot — was the pilot of the plane out there at the end of the lake. The body's behind the shed."

"Did you check the plane for survivors? How did he die?"

"I sent Bill to check the plane as soon as we arrived. The pilot died of exposure. The Russian, the one inside, left him back of the barn. He had been banged up bad in the crash." Jerry didn't say anything and Ted went on with his report. "There isn't much damage inside the cabin. There's a hole in the wall which leads into a storage shed at the rear of the cabin. That's where the dead guy and the prisoner held the woman and the kid and MacKinnon prisoner. From what I can make of the statements I have taken, the plane crash made Alexei and Pete show their hand sooner than intended. The plane was headed for Ottawa, where, as I understand it, they were to kidnap the kid."

"Inside with you. Let's get in out of the cold." Inside, Jerry directed the rescuers to stay by the door. Producing a tape measure he and Ted began the work of measuring the room and the distances between the grim reminders of what had recently taken place in the cabin. When they completed their task he drew a rough sketch of the room and the details of the crime scene.

Pointing to the hole in the wall Jerry said, "That's where the door used to be. Old Dan kept a side of venison in the shed through there. His kids must have blocked the door. They sold the place when they moved down below. Yeah Dan was quite a guy. I'd come in here couple of times a winter to check up on him. The old bugger refused to go out and stay with his kids. My last trip in here I found him outside stiff as a board. Heart attack, he'd been out at the wood pile."

"What now Jerry? Can we remove the body? And there is the other guy. We could wrap them in a blanket and take them out in a tow buggy."

"First, Ted, I'd better have a look at the pilot, then I'll decide what has to be done. It looks like a straightforward case but let's have a second look. We don't want to upset the Inspector now, do we?"

The body lay behind a pile of scrap lumber at the rear of the barn. Bending over the thinly clad body, Jerry examined it carefully. "There is a small tear in his shirt in the area of the heart, nothing else. He was alive when MacKinnon hauled him out of the plane, right?"

"That's what the man said, Jerry. He wanted to take him to the hospital in Miskimin. The dead guy pulled a gun and with the help of the prisoner locked them all in the shed. Which reminds me; the stiff went out to town and reported to his bosses. When he came back here, they had escaped, and at that time he and MacKinnon had their shoot-out up there in the wooded area."

"OK Ted, I think I have a pretty clear picture of what happened here. You can fill me in on the other stuff later. Let's get this guy over to the cabin and get him and the other one in a buggy and get them out to the hospital. The coroner will no doubt take it from there. Make sure you write up all the gory details. You'll need them for the inquest."

"What about the woman?"

"Yeah what about her?"

"She killed the Russian."

"Oh that, I don't think there will be any fuss. I'll have a chat with the Crown Prosecutor. If it was up to me, I'd give her a medal. It was self defence."

The sad procession of six snowmobiles led by Jerry sped over the snow hurrying to beat the approaching night. Ted, guardian of the frozen bodies, brought up the rear. Their noisy arrival at the hospital was witnessed by the lone nurse on duty. Willing hands removed the bodies from the snowmobile buggy and on to handy gurneys. Covered with a blanket, the bodies were left on the gurneys in a small storage room to await the attentions of the coroner.

"Well that's that, thanks guys, really appreciate your help. C'mon Ted we'd better check on the survivors. Would you two mind keeping an eye on the prisoner for a few minutes more?"

Walking down the short corridor, they were beckoned into a room by the woman. Two of the four beds were occupied.

"Hello, how are you, OK?

"I'm fine Ted, thank you."

"Jerry this is Miss Jones, she..." here Ted paused at a loss for words.

"I'm the one who killed the Russian. I had to, he shot Simon; luckily he didn't do much in the way of harming the poor boy. I'm sure he was out to kill both of us. That's Simon next to the wall, he has been a regular trooper in this horrible affair. The other one is Ally, he went after Alexei and ended up almost getting killed by that awful, that awful gangster. As you can see both of them are sound asleep. I told the nurse I'd watch over them. She has her hands full with a couple of newborns."

The calm matter-of-fact presentation and her ready acceptance of having killed the kidnapper had Jerry thinking this woman is either one tough cookie or she is buttoning up her emotions and will fall apart when all this catches up with her.

"My name is Jerry Baird, I'm in charge of the investigation. Ted is working with me. We'll have to get a detailed statement from you, Miss Jones. Not now, later, after you've washed up and had a meal."

"My name is Jonescu, Margaret Jonescu. My boss calls me Jonesy which leads people to believe my name is Jones. Incidentally, I telephoned my boss from the hospital. I knew he would want to know what happened. It so happens he is in Ottawa and is flying up here. He should be here early tomorrow."

Recollecting the phone call, she smiled, remembering the relief in Michael's voice when she told him that she "Didn't have a scratch."

27

When told there was a phone call for him, Michael, expecting to hear Roger with the latest on the kidnap, let out a yell when he realized who was phoning: "Jonesy it's you. Where are you? Is Simon there?"

"Simon's fine, he's in good hands." Not wanting to alarm Michael, she hurriedly went on, "He's sound asleep in a room down the corridor."

'Corridor, where are you, is he all right? Oh God if anything should happen to him. I don't know what I would do Jonesy. And you?"

"I'm fine, not a scratch."

"Oh God! I'm glad to hear that; to hear your voice. Where are you? I thought you and Simon had been kidnapped. Roger phoned me...."

"Their plan almost worked. Your son saved the day. He's a fine young man Michael. He certainly redeemed himself up here in this cold wasteland. He's comfortable and safe in bed." She went on to tell him the highlights of what had gone on since taking off from Dilsworth.

"This chap MacKinnon, is he with you? I would like to talk with him, thank him."

"That will have to come later. They are both asleep."

"Well in that case I think I'll have the chopper jockey earn his keep and drop in and say hello Margaret."

Michael was elated at the news and wanting to share it, he jumped up; he was alone in the small office. Grabbing the phone, he had to share the news with someone, he dialled a number: "Miss Cunningham, Braithwaite here, good news, the best; just got off the phone with my secretary. The plane is down in Northern Ontario, near Timmins. I'll be leaving within the hour. I was beginning to think I'd never see them again. Thanks for all your help, you were great."

"It was nothing, really Mr. Braithwaite. I enjoyed the challenge. I still have your money, where do you want me to send it. There's almost twenty thousand in my desk drawer."

"Not to worry I'll have someone from the bank pick it up." Talk of money brought back the other transaction he had been dealing with. The damned crooks never had Simon, they were selling me a bill of goods. The bastards! Well I'll fix their hash. Picking up the phone he dialled Dilsworth. When Roger came on the line he told him what had happened.

"Here's what I want you to do. Follow the instructions of the kidnappers to the letter. Inform the police of the bogus kidnap. Cooperate with them fully."

The police were not amused that they hadn't been brought in on the kidnapping from the beginning. After some mutterings about what should have been done, the police took charge and set their trap. Fiddling with his equipment, the policeman looked up and said that the call hadn't been long enough for him to get a trace on it. All he could say was that like the other calls the background noises told him that it was from a public phone. Roger, warned not to let his voice betray his feelings, played the part of the dutiful employee carrying out Braithwaite's orders.

It was the same hard voice. This time with a cocky edge. "Have you got the readies then? If you want to see the boy, do as yer told."

"I have the three million. The money is in three suitcases. As you requested the money is in small denominations."

"Good. Here's what you'll do. I want you to put each suitcase in a bag, a strong bag and tie it up with rope. Make sure the rope is good and tight. Got that?"

"Yes."

"Take the A247 out of Woking. Where the road goes over the A3, stop there at three on the dot and throw the bags over onto the edge of the southbound lanes."

"Where will Simon be?"

"Your precious Simon will be sitting on a bench in Dilsworth Municipal Park. After you get rid of the cash, stay there for twenty minutes; give us time to get clear. No slip ups, follow orders and the kid'll be safe."

Eager to get his hands on the money, Jimmy ignoring his own instructions, arrived at the flyover a few minutes before three. He stopped the car short of the bridge and waited with the engine running. Not much traffic, lucky for me, he thought.

When the bags came flying over the side of the bridge, he put the car in gear. With his head full of thoughts of revenge, he failed to notice that there was no traffic in either direction. Jumping out of the car and grabbing the bags he ran back to the car and threw them in the front. With the engine howling in protest he pulled out onto the highway heading for the first exit and back home with the loot. What's this ahead; a pile up? No, what the hell? Slowing down and looking around he saw some activity at the side of the road. They were in uniform, was that guns they were holding? Slamming on the brakes he brought the car to a screaming halt about two hundred yards from the police roadblock. "You fuckers, up yours! You'll never get me." Madness coursing in his blood, he wheeled the car around and headed back the way he had come.

Some distance beyond the bridge, another roadblock. Easing his foot off the accelerator, he saw the armed police waiting. Realization engulfed him, this was the end of the line, he was nicked; never, he vowed, I'll kill the bastards. They can't stop me. Jimmy's fear of being locked up, of life behind bars, drove him to one final desperate act. Jimmy didn't want to live if all he had lied, cheated, punched and kicked for was lost.

The madness that had been brought to blossom at the first road block burst to full flower now that he saw what was ahead of him. Screaming "Fuck them all! Have a go Jimmy! Show the wankers how to do it. They'll remember me."

Stopping the car he rolled down the window and thrusting his arm out he gestured and yelled, "Up yours, wankers." Laughing insanely, he reversed at speed for several hundred yards. He came to an easy careful stop. With his knuckles white on the steering wheel Jimmy launched the car on its final run; smashing into the road block at over one hundred miles an hour.

Examining the grotesque caricature, all that was left of Jimmy, taken from the wreck of the Bentley, the medical examiner noted the trauma to the chest. To his assistant he said, "He was dead before the petrol tank went up."

"Do we know who he was, Doctor.?"

"A small-time crook who got too big for his britches was what the superintendent told me. He was known as Jimmy The Baker, the super said."

"That's an odd nickname for a hard man. I wonder how he was lumbered with a name like that?"

"Would you get me a cup of coffee."

28

The helicopter set down gently in a storm of snow, whipped up by its downdraft, on the outskirts of Miskimin. Michael ran to the waiting police car.

"You're Braithwaite, the kid's dad?"

"That's right. Is Simon all right?"

"Sure, he's fine. The doctor said he'll be up and about tomorrow. His leg will be sore, but there's no permanent damage, the doctor said. I'm Ted Czapla. I found your son on the highway. He was in bad shape, the cold. He had driven from the cabin to get help for the others."

"When can I see him and Jonesy? You're sure they are both all right? No broken bones or other injuries?"

"Jonescu is baby-sitting your son and MacKinnon. He was wounded too. I guess it'll be a couple of days before the doctor lets him go." Answering the rapid- fire questions shot at him by Braithwaite, Ted detailed all that had gone on at the cabin by the lake.

When Ted pulled up in front of the hospital's main door, Michael jumped out and bounded inside. Hurrying down the short corridor, he stopped at the desk. The nurse who was doing some paperwork said, "And who are you? Not so much noise, you'll wake everyone up."

"Excuse me nurse. I am anxious to see my son. My name's Braithwaite."

Just then, Jonesy came out into the corridor to see if it really was Michael she heard talking. She whispered, "Michael, he's in here." He whirled at the sound of her voice and with a great grin on his face dashed to her and lifted her off her feet in a fierce hug.

Surprised at the show of affection, she clung to him.

Whirling her around he put her down and holding her at arm's length said, "Oh Jonesy! You're all in one piece."

The concerned look on her boss's face loosened the hold she had been keeping on her emotions. She collapsed in his arms, shoulders heaving, sobs tearing at her throat and tears streaming on to his borrowed parka. "Oh Michael, it was terrible." Between sobs she poured out her pent up feelings and told him what had happened. "We thought we were all going to die out there in the snow. I was so frightened. I had to kill him Michael. He shot Simon."

Holding Jonesy tight, he stroked her hair. "Shh, shh, I'm here, I'll look after you. Poor Jonesy it must have been awful for you. Poor dear. My love. Shh, I'm here now, shh."

Slowly she gained her composure, taking the offered handkerchief she wiped at her face. Blowing her nose, she looked up at Michael. "I'm being an awful ninny." Her answer was a smile and a hand taking hers as they walked into the room on tiptoe. Looking down at his son he thought, "Thank God he's not seriously hurt." Reaching out, he lightly touched the pale face. God I don't know what I would do if I lost him. Wiping at his eyes, he turned to leave the room and found himself being eyed by the man in the next bed.

"Hello."

"Hi, how's the kid? Hi Jonesy."

"Jonesy tells me that my son is fine and in good hands here. And you, Mr. MacKinnon, how are you. I owe you a lot."

"Nothing. You owe me nothing, not a sausage." Woozy from sedatives he went on, "I've been a damned sight worse. Big Wallie smiled when that bastard went for me." Ally turned away and closed his eyes.

With a last long look at his son he took Jonesy's hand and they walked out to where Ted was waiting for them at the desk. "How is he, Miss Jonescu?"

"Still sound asleep."

"That's good to hear. He's a lucky young fella. No frostbite the nurse said. When I picked up him up he was pretty far gone. And how about you Miss Jonescu, do you feel up to answering a few questions?"

"Couldn't they wait?"

"I'm fine Michael. I would just as soon answer questions now and put the whole thing behind me. Go ahead, Ted, isn't it? Am I to be charged with ..." Here her voice dropped off to an awkward silence.

"No, I don't think so. Jerry is to have a word with the Crown Prosecutor. This won't take long," pulling out his note book he asked his questions. He went over the attack by Alexei in detail and closing his notebook said, "Thank you. Coffee's on; Mrs Green said to bring you over for breakfast."

"Sounds like a great idea Ted. Hungry Jonesy?"

When they arrived at the hotel they found that Ted's helpers and his boss were all in the dining room .

Someone said, "Marie, two more customers for that stuff you call coffee."

Mrs. Levesque, helping out in the kitchen, bustled about getting the coffee.

"That's enough from you Bernie Smyth. If the coffee is so bad, why is it then that as soon as I sit down for my ten-o-clock pick-me-up, who should walk through the door? You guessed it folks."

A grinning Bernie, electing himself group spokesman, introduced the group to the latecomers. Several tables had been pushed together to make one large enough for all to sit down together. Marilyn Green, followed by Marie Levesque, each brought in a large stack of pancakes.

"The sausages and eggs are on the way." Looking at the newcomers Marie smiled and said, "Around here Bernie is known as a man who enjoys his food. On fishing trips they always pack extra groceries when Bernie's along. Right Bernie?"

The easy friendliness around the table brought a change to Jonesy's features; worry lines, a mark of her terrible ordeal, softened. An easy smile tugged at the corners of her mouth as she looked at Michael. Taking note of the change in his companion, Michael joined in the friendly banter.

"Bernie you have competition, I'm so hungry I could eat a horse, but I'll settle for some of those pancakes and bangers and eggs."

The easy talk continued throughout the meal.

"Mrs. Green thanks for breakfast," Michael said. "Jonesy and I will need rooms Mrs. Green."

Rising from the table Michael thanked everyone for his help. Refusing the offer of a ride from Cpl. Baird, he and Jonesy walked back to the hospital. When they looked in on the patients, both were asleep. An hour later, after a walk down the highway and a quick tour of the town, Jonesy and Michael flew to Timmins and shopped for essentials. Upon their return to Miskimin they settled into two of the big chairs in the lobby and not saying much enjoyed each other's company. After the evening meal, Mrs. Green showed them to their rooms.

After a brisk walk to aid in the digestion of another breakfast fit for a lumberjack, Michael and Jonesy found the patients awake. Each declaring that he felt fine and wanted to leave the hospital right away. The nurse equally adamant, insisted only a doctor had the authority to discharge them.

"Well hello Simon. Glad to know that you're in fine voice. The nurse is only doing her job."

"Hello Dad. Ally and I have things to do back at the cabin."

"Never mind about that Simon, I'll soon get the place tidied up. You will want to be with your father."

"I certainly want to be with him Mr. MacKinnon. I'm afraid I've been neglecting my son. This affair brought home to me how much he means to me."

Simon gave his father a wide-eyed wondering look, which did not go unnoticed by Jonesy. Looking first at Michael and then at Ally she said, "Why don't we all go back to the cabin and help sort things out. There's a lot of work to be done. If we all chip in and help it shouldn't take too long. I'm sure you wouldn't mind a little help with the work Ally."

"Not at all. I think it would be great if the three of us — and you too Mr. Braithwaite— got together. After all we've been through it would be great to get better acquainted."

Before any further discussion could take place the nurse appeared, "There's a phone call for you Miss Jonesy, long distance."

"I expect it's Roger, I had to phone him to get your number in Ottawa."

"Jonesy, you OK? How's Simon?"

"Simon's fine Roger, we both are. He's with his Dad. He is to be discharged today."

"That's great, now to business. The Valley Group have withdrawn; they now say that they want more time to examine our offer against others they have had. I suspect they got a bit antsy when you didn't show with the papers."

"But I thought that the newspapers were all sewn up. Did they take them off the table too?"

"That's right. The deal is as dead as a doornail."

"That leaves the Seattle bid our only iron in the fire at the moment."

"That's right, although it too may be in jeopardy. The boss had to leave just as he was getting things underway in Seattle. He dashed off to Ottawa when told the plane was way overdue. It was his first meeting with the Grant-James Group, so things there might still be OK, I hope so anyway."

"Anything else I should pass on?"

"Nothing, that's it — half a mo Jonesy, there is something. Tell the boss that the kidnappers are in the nick. The number one gangster blew himself up in his Bentley."

"Thanks Roger, I'll tell Michael the news about the gang."

Back in the room she told of the loss of the Canadian Group and the fate of the kidnappers. Ally and Simon exchanged a satisfied look when they heard how the kidnap attempt ended.

"It's not the end of the world Jonesy. Now I'll have more time with Simon. Maybe we could all stay at the cabin for a few days. We will pay our way Mr. MacKinnon."

"Suits me just dandy. Forget about paying. I'm told the ice fishing is great at the lake. I have the lumber to build a snug little fishing shack. Introduce you city folks to some of the joys of country living."

"As soon as you are discharged, we'll head for Levesque's and get supplies. You can tell us what we'll need Mr. MacKinnon. We'll fly out to the cabin in the chopper. Sound like a plan."

"Sounds good to me, but if we are to live together out at the cabin, drop the mister, call me Ally, Jonesy and Simon do."

"I'll do that, if you'll call me Michael."

The young doctor was surprised to see Simon and Ally fully dressed when he came into the room. "Where do you think you're going MacKinnon? I said Simon could go today, not you. That wound on your chest, I'd like to keep an eye on it for a little longer. You were lucky not to get yourself killed."

"C'mon doctor, I'll take care not to overdo things. It's not too serious, I've survived worse. I'll be OK. Sign the papers doctor."

Annoyed at the demanding tone the doctor said, "I insist you stay here for a few days. You can't leave now, I won't allow it." Questioning my judgement, who does he think he is? This backwoods know-it-all. One of two doctors at the hospital, he didn't enjoy been gainsaid by a patient. "You have to stay. The wound must be given time to heal. Damn it man, you could very easily rupture it and bleed to death out there in the bush."

"It's OK doctor, I'll take it easy. Hell this isn't the first time someone has tried to kill me. I'll take it easy out at the cabin."

Doctor David Zelliski, angry at this man's casual attitude to his diagnosis said "You will have to stay here for a few days, and that's final."

"Can I have my piece of paper? If not I'll sign myself out."

"Wait Ally, I have an idea. Doctor if I promise that he won't do any strenuous work out at the cabin and that he'll appear each morning at the hospital for his dressings to be changed, will you allow him to go home?"

Lowering his head for a moment in thought before looking directly at Michael he said, "OK, but no helping around the house. He must come into the hospital every day for a check-up, otherwise I won't allow it."

Grinning, Michael looked at Ally. "You heard the man, we can go. I'll see he drops in every day doctor. Do you think there's enough space in the parking lot for a chopper to land?"

Each morning for the next seven days, Ally walked from the chopper to the hospital, had his dressing changed, walked back to the chopper which lifted off as soon as he was aboard. In those seven days the cabin was scrubbed, the wall repaired, Jonesy flew out to Timmins and bought the material for Mrs. Green to make decorative window drapes. With the snow deep outside, the only way to get free of the cabin was to step into the snow shoes borrowed from Bill Levesque and Joe Green. Snowshoeing around the lake or ice fishing, coupled with the peace and quiet did wonders in healing the wounds of memory.

In the evenings after supper they settled themselves in front of the fire, at first the crackling logs and the hissing of the pressure lamps the only sound. Once the level of the generous pouring of amber liquid in their glasses was lowered a little, easy conversation followed. Malt whisky, sipped slowly while sitting around the fireplace became a nightly custom.

After days spent in setting the place in order there were still grim reminders of what had taken place in the cabin. No amount of soap and hot water and use of a heavy scrubbing brush could completely remove the spots on the floor.

Simon, curious about the ugly marks he had seen on Ally's legs while they were in hospital, quizzed Ally about them one evening.

Ally would only say, "I was in the wrong place at the wrong time. It happened a long time ago."

"Now I guess some of Simon's curiosity has rubbed off on me Ally. How did you get those scars on your legs?"

"If you must know Jonesy, I was wounded while serving with the French Foreign Legion, OK?"

Wide-eyed Simon asked, "How long were you in the Legion? Did you ever kill anyone?" He realized his faux pas. "Sorry."

" Don't get any fancy ideas about the Legion. The non-coms are tough, and were quick to give you a belt in the gut if you made a mistake."

"Simon, that's enough. Let it go."

"Aw c'mon Ally, you're kidding."

"You want to hear more? OK." Ally then went on to give a brief description of the tough grind that was the daily lot of a Legion recruit.

A slack-jawed Simon sat, eyes wide, as Ally talked. Jonesy and Michael too were paying close attention.

"Couldn't you complain to an officer?"

Ally smiled, "No Simon. It was part of a toughening process — mental as well as physical— that paid off down the road. I should say that while the NCOs were quick to punish, most of them were just as quick to praise when you did something right. For example, stripping your rifle and putting it back together in record time while blindfolded."

"Blindfolded, you're kidding Ally. That's impossible."

"It can be done Simon. Running around with two sandbags in your pack when you fail to get it right quickly sharpens your sense of touch."

"How could you put up with such treatment? Why did you?"

"You must remember Jonesy, I was young — not quite eighteen—and tough. I signed a five-year contract. I went in as a wet-behind-the-ears country lad and came out the other end a man. I'm proud to say that I served in the Legion. I served with some fine men, saw some of them die. But all in all it was a great adventure Jonesy."

"Did you see a lot of action; were you ever scared?"

"Scared, you bet I was scared Simon, often."

"After your contract, did you go back home and work on the farm?"

"No, there was nothing there for me, Jonesy. My best friend had immigrated to Australia. A local chap had taken my place on the farm. After a couple of weeks loafing at home I was bored out of my mind. A Canadian mining company's newspaper ad for men with mining experience grabbed my attention. I'd never been down a mine but I thought I'd fake it and have a go, so wrote away to an address in Glasgow. Six weeks later a gang of us were aboard a ship headed for Halifax, Canada."

"What was it like underground? You did go underground?

"Of course. After a short training period, I was teamed with a French-Canadian. We got along well the year and a half I worked at Gypsy Lode. In that time I never saw any gold."

"Not even a little nugget?" from a dismayed Simon.

"Not a glimmer. Anyway as soon as I had paid back my boat and train ticket I quit the mine."

"Any prospects? Were you planning to do move south and find a job?"

"I liked it in the North. I had no hankering to go down below, that is move South, Michael. I had a plan of sorts, of talking the publisher of the local paper into giving me a job. I was in the first group of Scots miners hired by Gypsy Lode. The company was banking that some of us would be shift boss and mine captain material.

"The local paper asked for a volunteer to write about our new life in Timmins. I volunteered. The editor told me after a couple of the pieces appeared in the paper, that if I ever decided to give up mining, he would give me a reporting job on the paper. I got the job, and when I left was city editor. I bought this place to have peace and quiet to try my hand at fiction.

"Quite a jump Ally, from miner to editor," Jonesy said.

"It didn't take long for me to get the hang of things. As a reporter, I met up with some of the local characters. They were a great group. I enjoyed their company. Some of them were prospectors. More than once, I grubstaked one of my pals. As a result of my friendship with these worthies I made some money in mining stocks and bought this place when the family of the former owner wanted to unload it."

"You've had quite an eventful life, Ally. I'm in the newspaper business too. Would you consider working for me?" He hurried on when he saw the look in Ally"s eyes. "Hear me out Ally. I'm buying a group of papers in the States. I had just begun talks with the Group's owner when I got news of the plane failing to show, I took off like a scalded cat for Ottawa. The rest you know. If you could see your way to nosing around the papers, do a backgrounder on the staff and the owners for me. They're in poor financial shape. Someone like you could mix with the reporters; get to know what's really going on. What do you say? It would be of great help to me in deciding whether to buy the Group, radio, TV stations and all, or bow out gracefully."

"That's quite a tall order Michael, it's a big respo...."

"You could do it Ally," an excited Simon declared.

"The question Simon, is do I want to do it? How long would it take to get the information you want Michael? Doing the cloak and dagger bit for a couple of weeks, might be fun."

"I hope that's all the time the job will take, but it could take longer."

"What the hell, I'll have a go,why not? A change of scenery will be as good as a holiday. I'll do it. When we get to Ottawa, I'll have to get some decent clothes to wear in the city. I'll have to look the part, right Simon?"

"Can I come along for the ride Dad, please?

"Sure, I think we all need a change of scene. We can spend a couple of days in Ottawa. There is a young lady down there I want to meet. Jonesy, I want you along too. That's it then; tomorrow we leave for home by way of Ottawa." Unaware of Robert's involvement in the kidnap plot, Michael continued, "After the funeral we head for Seattle."

EPILOGUE

After all those years, we meet again. I never twigged that it was the American branch of Fiona's family. It was brought home to me when I saw her picture in an annual report. Her husband died a while back. She has three kids. I wonder what would have happened had she said yes back then. I guess old Grant-James would have put his foot down and probably thrown Dad off the farm. At the time I would have done anything for her. She had me hook, line, and sinker. She was having a good time — a way to spend the holidays — and I thought it was the real thing. Mind you it was a great time. God we were a horny pair. Those were daft days. Now into the shower and then it's off to the 'big do'. You'll do, Ally me lad. Now it's down the hall to find out if Phyllis is ready for the fray.

It was quite a surprise, Michael inviting Phyllis to Seattle. I'm glad he did. She certainly is great company. I plan on getting to know her better. Could I convince her to stay in Seattle? Anyway, if not here, I can spend time in Ottawa to convince her to come up North.

Unknown to Ally, Jonesy was responsible for Phyllis's invitation. Her reason, she confided to Michael was the way Ally and Phyllis had clicked as soon as they met. "You know what I mean Michael."

"Hi, pleased to meet you Phyllis." Those eyes; so this is the woman who got things organized at the airport. Seems a friendly sort, but I suspect nobody's fool. She knows what's what.

"You're the one who went after the Russian; Michael told me." He could have been killed; it took guts. He has a nice smile. He doesn't look the tough guy.

A smiling Phyllis opened the door to Ally's knock. "Hi. Don't you look distinguished! I'll get my purse."

"Miss Cunningham, stunning is the word!"

"Well thank you, kind sir," followed by a mock curtsey.

In the cab Phyllis said, "This, the flight down here, meeting you and Mr. Braithwaite, and his wife being so nice, has a sort of dreamlike quality to it Alister. All I did was rent a helicopter."

"It's no dream. I'm alive, very much so when you're around." The brief silence was electric.

"Me too, but Ally we have only known each other for such a short time."

"Why don't you stay on here? The talks will take some time."

"But my job, I can't just take off and stay down here. I had to take unpaid leave for this trip."

"Couldn't you take annual leave? Say your granny's on her last legs."

"Now you're talking crazy. I'd love to stay, but I can't. You know that," as the taxi pulled into the driveway crowded with cars, Phyllis pecked him on the cheek and said, "Let's enjoy the party."

"OK. We'll talk about this again. Let's go."

\+ + +

I suppose it will be all over the business section this morning. Talks resume after a short delay. Local media group on the block, or some such headline. I was right, only it wasn't the business section there it was on the front page of the paper.

UK MEDIA GIANT TO TAKE OVER LOCAL MEDIA GROUP

There was a picture above the headline. God it can't be, no, no! It's impossible he was a farmer, what would he know about our business. It does look like him, though. The other man in the picture — Trevor Caldicott— is one of Braithwaite's people. My God it's him! It's Ally, standing next to Uncle Earl. He is Braithwaite's special assistant. When I left he was working with his father on one of our farms. God the things we did, we were shameless. Special assistant, what does that mean? He has certainly left the farmyard behind. A slight smile found her eyes as she remembered fumbling with buttons in the hay loft. We were mad; marriage would have been a disaster. Now the past is here and is now part of the present. Would he use his position to make things difficult? Maybe the smart thing would be to invite him over for dinner. Test the waters.

Fiona's thoughts were interrupted by the housekeeper refilling her coffee cup, "Thanks Raquel". Sipping her coffee, Fiona dreamily unlocked the door to memories, memories she had tucked away, supposedly for ever, and which were now bright in her mind's eye. He adored me and would have done anything for me. Would his memories be tainted by our final goodbye?

I'll phone Earl and get his read on having him over — better include Braithwaite and wife— to dinner. There was no way I would have married him. Dipping her toast into an egg yolk she mused further. He was only a farmer, a tenant farmer's son at that. It was after a football match, we were parked in the driveway to the house. He leaned over and kissed me. Then he had to go and spoil it all by proposing. I liked Ally, he was easy to get along with. And then there was the sex. My god, we were at it all the time. Once I remember in a horse stall with the horse chomping away at its oats. Finishing my coffee, I headed for the office.

On the drive to work, I remembered the wild times we had. Oh to have him again; it has been a long time. God the things we did — sneaking up the back stairs. Raquel would look after the kids. God he was wild. She shivered. I never thought I would miss him, but I did. We were great together. I wonder what would have happened had we married. He seems to have done well for himself. How would the family react? Ally was always easy going; of course he would fit in. Could it really happen again? I'm single — would the children put him off? He might want children of his own, now that might be a problem. Braithwaite would hesitate to fire the wife of his special assistant. Mrs. Ally MacKinnon, imagine! We'll see, I'll put my best face on.

At the office there was an appearance of normalcy, but layered just beneath the surface there was a tang of worry, of concern. Would the new guy bring in his own people? Everybody had read this morning's paper. I had no sooner settled at my desk and the phone went. It was Uncle Earl. "Hi Fiona, I guess you have seen the paper."

"Yes. How long are the talks likely to go on?"

"That's hard to say. The deal could be completed in a few days, or it could be months. Not to worry Fiona, I'm confident that Braithwaite will buy us out."

"And what happens then? He turns around and fires us all, as he did in Australia. Is that what happens?"

"I know, I have heard all the wild rumours too Fiona, but I don't think it was as bad as the stories would have us believe."

"This special assistant, you met with yesterday, are you sure he isn't— to put it bluntly — Braithwaite's terminator."

"I've heard that Braithwaite had problems with his last venture. I think Mr. MacKinnon is Braithwaite's way of ensuring that this time it is a right fit. If there are problems then he will deal with them."

Uncle Earl calling Ally, Mr. MacKinnon, sounded weird. Should I say anything about knowing Mr. MacKinnon.

"He is having a look at the newspapers today, tomorrow or the next day he will be visiting your shop."

"Good, I'll have everyone on their toes and ready to meet with

Braithwaite's bulldog."

"Hey Fiona, take it easy. MacKinnon is dropping in to have a look around, that's all. Nothing will happen for a bit, we have lots to discuss before any decision is made, either way."

"Yeah, I guess you're right." I couldn't dismiss from my mind the stories of Braithwaite's heavy hand when he bought a Group, similar to ours, in Australia. They kept niggling away at me. I enjoyed my job, and I wanted to keep it.

"You'll have the opportunity of looking the Braithwaite crew over on Saturday. Cecille has rented a tent. She is having one of her barbecue specials, late afternoon, see you then."

I guess that kills my idea of having him over for dinner. I am not sure I share Uncle Earl's confidence in "Mr. Midas" Braithwaite. What happened in Australia troubles me. There must be something to the stories; where there is smoke there is fire. Has Ally been hired to get rid of people? What does he know about this business? Not a bloody lot, I'd say.

Saturday afternoon, Fiona spent considerable time getting ready for the party. Parking at the rear of the house, she went in the back door and through the kitchen to the front of the house, where a maid took her coat. Her uncle Earl spotted her and motioned her to join him. "Mr. Braithwaite, I'd like to introduce Fiona Saunderson, Fiona took over the radio stations when her husband Lyall died. She's doing a great job."

A commotion at the front door caught everyone's attention. A man with his back to them was holding a laughing boy off the floor in a bear hug. Putting the boy down, the man turned to the smiling woman beside him; it was Ally. I saw that he was at ease in the packed room, he had changed. The boy must be Braithwaite's son. The woman wearing a fashionable black dress, with something silver at her left shoulder, attracted long looks from more than one man in the room. Her short reddish blonde hair framed a quiet face.

A grinning Braithwaite called, "Hello Alister. Poor Simon was worried, thought you were to miss the party." Ally put his arm around the boy's shoulders as they walked over to join them. Braithwaite said,. "Hi Phyllis, the word is spiffy."

"Thank you."

"Ally may I introduce Mrs. Saunderson, you have met the others. Oh excuse me Mrs. Grant-James, this man is my special assistant Mr. MacKinnon."

He was heavier, broader than the Ally I remembered. His dark hair cropped almost to the scalp had a touch of grey at the temples.

"How do you do Mrs. Grant-James?"

"Cecille, let's not be so formal."

"Cecille it is, and I'm Ally, OK? I'd like you to meet my friend Phyllis Cunningham." Turning he said, "Hello Fiona." She shivered slightly. "It's been a long time."

A quizzical look from Braithwaite and raised eyebrows from Earl brought a smile to Ally's face, "Fiona and I have met."

"Ally's dad was a farmer on the estate. His sister Morag was a friend." Flustered at the memories evoked by his nearness, she hurried on. "How is Morag? Is she married? When I left she and Dougie were the next thing to being engaged."

"We visited last time I went back to Bonnie for a holiday. She's doing very well. She's matron in a palliative care hospital in London."

"And Dougie?"

"You two have some catching up to do, we'll let you get on with it," Earl said as he, his wife and Phyllis moved away.

"He's in Australia, married with five kids. He took off shortly after I left. She was to have joined him when she completed her training."

"What happened? I always thought they would marry."

"I guess we all did, but it didn't happen. I found out when I went home for my father's funeral. We've kept in touch more since then."

"Oh, I'm sorry Ally. Your mother is she still at the farm? I remember her freshly baked scones, lots of farm butter and her homemade jam."

"She's in good health. Has a cottage in the village. Independent old dear, doesn't want or need us to butt into her life."

While carrying on their conversation, Fiona and Ally had moved aside and found themselves a small island of space away from the crowd. A woman joined them and said, "Excuse me is this a private conversation or can anyone join in?"

"Hello. Amanda I'd like you to meet Alister MacKinnon, Alister, Amanda Montgomery."

"How do you do Mrs. Montgomery. I take it you are a member of the clan?"

"Yes that's right. My husband is the firm's legal beagle. And you Mr. MacKinnon, what is your role in all this?"

"Keeping a friendly eye on what's going on here for Michael."

"Have you known the Braithwaites long?

"No, I met Simon and Michael when his plane landed on my doorstep."

"Braithwaite's son is a big fan of yours Alister. It seems that you and he had quite an adventure on your place in the Northern woods," Amanda continued.

"What were those great adventures Ally? Hunting bear and moose, tramping over the frozen tundra?"

"Fiona, contrary to what you may have heard, there is no tundra where I live. We were ice fishing." Ally said.

Fiona smiled. Where was Mrs. Midas? That must be her chatting with Ben. The pale yellow dress was expensive; she was slim. Her hair, was that black natural, framed an almond shaped face with a thin delicate nose, and firm chin.

"You have your own place Alister." Smiling she went on in an amused voice, "Sounds grand — retired and now a gentleman farmer. Isn't it too cold for farming way up there where you live?"

"It is on the cold side for farming, but the way you say, 'way up there' anyone would think it was just a step or two to the North Pole. I have five hundred acres, most of it trees, on a lake with a snug little cabin on the property. Michael has been trying to convince me that I should develop the property as a hunting and fishing camp."

"Will you? Lyall and his buddies would go off for a couple of weeks up in Canada at a fishing camp. Living rough, he said, recharged his batteries."

"The fishing camp idea is strictly Michael's. I bought the place, to get some peace and quiet, and get down to some serious writing."

"I hear that what Michael wants, Michael gets."

"You've heard the stories, I suppose. He's not like that. He's quite a guy, I like him. He's offered to upgrade the road into my place and install the hydro and telephone."

"Exactly, I rest my case. Just you wait, he'll buy you out and then dump you. It's what happens with everything he touches. It's what will happen here."

"You have it all wrong Fiona. He wants to do it as his way of saying thanks, for hauling Jonesy and Simon out of the plane."

Fiona allowed the acid of her dark thoughts to surface. She could see the life of ease that she enjoyed, the servants— the extended overseas vacations were already gone— all swept away by the newcomer's broom.

"We've all heard what happened in Australia. Braithwaite moves in and within six months the staff is fired because they wouldn't toe his line, right?"

"You have it all wrong. In Australia, two people were fired. The managing editor had his favourites which led to bad feelings in the newsroom. The guy was warned twice and still he persisted in playing favourites. The other firing was the sports editor. He had a drinking problem and refused an all-expenses-paid trip to a hospital. Y'know what, I think the problem is, people can't stomach his success."

"He certainly has won you over Alister. You haven't changed, still the naive country boy."

A grinning Alister said, "A lot of water has flown under the bridge since the days o' auld lang syne, the daft days, Fiona. Mind you, I never thought of myself as a country bumpkin — with straw in my hair. Quite the contrary with all that was going on."

At the oblique reference to what had been, Fiona looked at the others and in a lame attempt to lessen the effect of her harsh words said, "Sorry I didn't mean. ..." I hope my outburst hasn't ruined things. Fiona couldn't quite come to terms with Ally's metamorphosis from farmer to executive. Why couldn't I have smiled and set about charming him. She was saved further embarrassment by Phyllis joining them.

Phyllis nudged Ally and said, "Hi."

"Hi, you finally managed to break away from your discussion group."

"It was hot and heavy for a while."

After introductions were made, Phyllis remained close to Ally, listening to what was said, but not joining in.

Amanda spoke up, "I'm famished, let's eat." She continued her questioning while filling her plate, and afterwards at one of the tables set up in the tent. Talking around a mouthful of salad, she asked, "What exactly do you mean Alister when you say you will be keeping an eye on things."

"My job is to ensure that problems at whatever level are dealt with quickly."

"In other words, you will be looking over everyone's shoulder."

"No! Nothing like that Amanda. There will be changes, but none of them will see anyone lose his job."

Are you sure about that Ally?" Fiona questioned with a sceptical look.

"Maybe we should be calling you Mr. MacKinnon, Amanda quipped. "We don't want to get on the wrong side of you."

Amanda's husband Ben, tapped his wife on the shoulder, "Hello dear, what hobby horse are you riding tonight? Ben Montgomery, you'll have to excuse my wife. When she gets saddled up, there's no stopping her."

Alister, laughingly replied, "Amanda please, call me Ally. I have nothing to do with hiring or firing. All I do is write notes; what Michael chooses to do with them is up to him."

"Let us not be naive here. You have a direct line to the top man." Looking up at her husband she punched his arm and admonished him: "Watch your feet big boy; I'm wearing my favourite shoes;" and continued, "So in fact you have a lot of clout in the organization, right?"

"I suppose I do have some clout, but remember I'm only a minor player in a very large organization; one that managed very well without me."

Throughout the exchange Fiona remained silent, lost in thought. My God he could get me fired. He certainly has changed. Surely he wouldn't do it, after all we meant to each other. Her thoughts skipped sideways, are this Phyllis and Ally an item? If we had married and run away to America where would we be today?

We were from different worlds, she rationalized, choosing to ignore that the American branch of the family resulted from such a runaway marriage. Is there still a spark of feeling left — could we get back together again? When he visits the office I'll have him all to myself, maybe something will happen.

"Snap out of it Fiona. This is a party."

"Sorry, I was...."

"It's OK, no need to confess. We know you were drooling over what's on the dessert table."

Flustered, Fiona managed a thin smile. The others grinned. Fiona was grateful, good old Amanda.

Their host and his wife joined them in time to hear the quip about dessert, "In time I suppose we all get our just desserts. But here, only if you go to the buffet and pick it up," Earl said.

Ally with an arm around Phyllis said, "It's me for dessert. I'll have someone bring coffee."

"Here let me pour the coffee. I believe you and Fiona knew each other in Scotland," Ben said.

"I grew up on the Grant-James estate. I'd see her around the estate when she was home on holidays from school. Fiona and my sister were pals. Football was my main interest back then."

"That would be soccer, right?"

"That's right. Mmmhh, if this is our just dessert, let me say it tastes great. Try some Fiona?"

Fiona, shaped her mouth in a smile."

Jock Alexander was born, raised and educated in Scotland. After service overseas with the Parachute Regiment, he immigrated to Canada where he worked as a hard-rock miner, reporter on daily newspapers, press liaison officer with the British High Commission, Ottawa, Canada, and senior editor analyst with the Royal Canadian Mounted Police. Married, Jock and his wife Nancy have two children and a delightful grand-daughter.

Order this book online at www.trafford.com/07-0396
or email orders@trafford.com

Most Trafford titles are also available at major online book retailers.

Note for Librarians: A cataloguing record for this book is available from Library and Archives Canada at www.collectionscanada.ca/amicus/index-e.html

ISBN: 978-1-4251-1991-1

We at Trafford believe that it is the responsibility of us all, as both individuals and corporations, to make choices that are environmentally and socially sound. You, in turn, are supporting this responsible conduct each time you purchase a Trafford book, or make use of our publishing services. To find out how you are helping, please visit www.trafford.com/responsiblepublishing.html

Our mission is to efficiently provide the world's finest, most comprehensive book publishing service, enabling every author to experience success. To find out how to publish your book, your way, and have it available worldwide, visit us online at www.trafford.com/10510

www.trafford.com

North America & international
toll-free: 1 888 232 4444 (USA & Canada)
phone: 250 383 6864 ♦ fax: 250 383 6804 ♦ email: info@trafford.com

The United Kingdom & Europe
phone: +44 (0)1865 722 113 ♦ local rate: 0845 230 9601
facsimile: +44 (0)1865 722 868 ♦ email: info.uk@trafford.com

10 9 8 7 6 5 4 3 2

www.ingramcontent.com/pod-product-compliance
Ingram Content Group UK Ltd.
Pitfield, Milton Keynes, MK11 3LW, UK
UKHW020144250726
13967UKWH00002B/857

9 781425 119911